OF THE CURSE OR THE CROWN

V.B. LACEY

FICTION & FATE PRESS

THE VERIDIAN EMPIRE BOOK 2

OF THE CURSE OR THE CROWN

Exclusive Digitally Signed Edition

V. B. LACEY

AUTHOR'S NOTE

This book has scenes depicting anxiety and panic attacks, derealization, claustrophobia, brief animal cruelty, violence, on-screen death, traumatic flashbacks, mild strangulation, and unwanted physical touch.

Please be mindful of these and other possible triggers.

———

To the ones who were told to shrink, to soften, or to step aside—
Take my hand and pick up your crown.
It's your time to shine.

———

THE VERID
THE TEMPLE
CELESTRIA
ILUZE
CHAMPION'S RUN
LAKE LEZNEM
FEYWOOD FOREST
ARCANE APOTHECARY
FEYWOOD
LUNA PORT
AVONIGE OCEAN
MYSTHELM

...IAN EMPIRE
EMBERFELL
LIGHTSWORN ACADEMY
ELDERTIDE OCEAN
EMBERFELL PORT
GUARDIAN RANGE
SCARRE RIVER
VERIDIA CITY
DRAKORUM
GOVERNOR'S HOUSE
TENEBRA
MISTWOOD MOUNTAINS
TRAINING GROUNDS
SHADOWMERE WASTELANDS

MYSTHELM
AVONIGE OCEAN
PORT OF NORTH PINE
THE VERIDIAN EMPIRE
THE NORTH TERRITORY
REAUX MANSION
PALACE GRIMALDI
SILENUS MANOR
THE MID TERRITORY
THE ISLAND TERRITORY
PENWORTH ESTATES
THE BASE
THE SOUTH TERRITORY
AURELIA CLIFFS

Uneasy lies the head that wears a crown.
- William Shakespeare

In Case You Missed It...

This is book two in the Veridian Empire series. While it can be read as a standalone, I'm including this recap in case you need a refresher of what happened in book one, *In the Wake of the Wicked*. If you haven't read book one yet, you can either skip this (spoilers for book one!) or read at your own discretion.

In the Wake of the Wicked follows Rose Wolff, a twenty-five-year-old Alchemist and outcast in her province of Feywood. Six provinces exist in the Veridian Empire, each with their own unique strand of magic.

Feywood: home to Alchemists, people with the power to cast spells and enchantments using the nature around them.

Celestria: home to Striders, who can transport themselves from one place to another in the blink of an eye.

Iluze: home to Illusionists, who can create illusions in the minds of others.

Emberfell: home to Lightbenders, people who create and bend light to their will.

Drakorum: home to Shifters, who can shift into a given animal form.

Tenebra: home to Shadow Wielders, those who manipulate shadows.

Veridians came to possess this magic three hundred years ago when the Fates, the deities of this world, issued a prophecy to both the Veridian Empire and the Kingdom of Mysthelm. The prophecy stated that whoever could conquer the uninhabited island that held the magic of the Fates would be given their power.

The War of Beginnings ensued, and the Veridians won, causing a rift between them and Mysthelm. (*Remember this for book two.*) Veridians were granted magic, but it came with a catch: over time, its power wanes.

Rose's story picks up three hundred years later, right before the start of the thirty-second Decemvirate, a magical tournament held every ten years in order to replenish their fading magic. One challenger from each of the six provinces is chosen to compete in three dangerous trials. The winner's province is given the most magic, and so on, down to the sixth and last challenger, who receives barely a fraction of it.

Rose's uncle is this year's challenger for Feywood. As they travel to the capital, Veridia City, Rose's eyes are opened to the dangers of the empire.

Over the past two decades since the current emperor, Theodore Gayl, took power, Veridians have become divided. Those with the most magic and wealth are elevated above the weaker. Gayl made it illegal to travel between provinces except for some exceptions, so animosity among provinces is at an all-time high. People are scared to live in their own homes, but they can't afford to leave. Attacks and violence run rampant. The empire is crumbling.

On the way to the capital, Rose's family is attacked by a group of Shifters who are trying to sabotage Decemvirate challengers. Rose and her uncle defeat them, but another threat rises—Rose's uncle unexpectedly falls to the Somnivae curse. This sleeping curse has been ravaging the empire for twenty-seven years, ever since the former emperor Branock Aris's twin children were born. Everyone believes Branock and his cursed twins are the reason for the curse. Their hatred and fear drove him from his throne and allowed Theodore Gayl to swoop in and take over.

Now, Rose's uncle is frozen in a magical sleep, unable to participate in the Decemvirate and represent their province. Who could ever replace him?

Enter our brave heroine.

Rose is convinced to volunteer for the Decemvirate in her uncle's place by a new friend, the head architect of the tournament. Only, this architect isn't what she seems. Lark Everest is part of a secret rebellion set on bringing down Emperor Gayl, breaking the Somnivae curse, and restoring the empire to its former glory. She tells Rose her rebellion wants to use Rose as their undercover spy to dig up information on Theodore Gayl.

As Rose undergoes the deadly trials of the Decemvirate, she gets pulled into this rebellion and meets our found family of Sentinels: Clarissa Aris, leader and firstborn of the former Branock Aris (*hmm...could she be our new main character?*); her twin brother, Leo; the head architect, Lark; and two other rebels, Chaz and Horace, Rose's trusted guard.

Leo Aris is on a mission of personal revenge against Theodore Gayl. He wants retribution for what the man did to his father: chasing him from his throne and blaming him for the Somnivae curse. But Leo didn't expect a certain beautiful, stubborn, morally grey Alchemist to step into his life and distract him.

While Rose is committed to her new friends and the rebellion, she uncovers a life-changing secret from her past. Emperor Theodore Gayl is her uncle—her dead father's brother. The same man she's supposed to be working against.

But that's not all.

Gayl is an accomplished Alchemist—the most powerful the empire has ever seen. His secret? *Blood magic.* A type of dangerous Alchemy forbidden in Verldia because of how volatile and fatal it can be. But he convinces Rose of its uses and teaches her how to wield it. In time, she begins to believe he's not the evil, corrupt ruler everyone thinks he is.

Rose grapples with so many secrets and challenges thrown at her, all while keeping the truth of her blood magic from Leo and the other Sentinels. She's found the first group of people who have ever accepted her and is even falling in love—she doesn't want to risk losing it.

Eventually, the truth comes out, and she learns the danger of blood magic when its consequences continue to pile high, putting those she cares about in harm's way. She realizes Gayl is manipulating her and devises a plan to use Alchemy to try and incapacitate him, if she can get close enough.

Everything culminates in the final trial of the Decemvirate, where Gayl reveals that he's known about the secret rebellion all along and lays his final trap to kill them. He and Rose face off in an epic battle of wills and Alchemy. He confesses that he's the reason her father (his own brother) is dead, and that he's the one behind the Somnivae curse. Every time someone fell to the sleeping curse in the last twenty-seven years, *he* absorbed their power, turning him into the strongest Veridian to ever live.

At the last second, Rose performs a charm that siphons the magic from him and funnels into her, leaving him dead. In the aftermath, she discovers that she now holds the power to wake those who were under the Somnivae curse.

While she and Leo embark on a happily-ever-after adventure to rouse the sleeping victims across the entire empire, our new main character, Clarissa Aris, rises into her power as heir to the Veridian Empire. And so, her story begins...

PROLOGUE

"Tales have been spun of the legends of old, spanning centuries and centuries ago."

"Long before your kingdoms rose and fell,"

"And before your empires swelled."

"But it's time for us to weave our own,"

"For the end now readily awaits."

"I am the Creator."

"I am the Changer."

"And I am the Ender."

"Together, they call us the Fates."

"Now, come closer."

"Listen well."

"Let us tell you a story,"

"Of the king who thought he could trick the Fates,"

"And was cursed with his own crown of glory."

———

Nyses Grimaldi dismounted swiftly, taking in the blazing flames and scorched stone.

"My King!" a priest called as he approached with singed white robes trailing in the dirt. The elderly man's face was streaked with ash, his eyes full of distress.

"What is the meaning of this?" King Grimaldi boomed. His horse whinnied and pawed at the ground, wary of the burning temple before them.

"We do not know, sire," the priest rushed out. "The bells were rung by an apprentice not half an hour ago. I only arrived moments before you."

Nyses pulled on a pair of leather gloves and examined the destruction. Flames licked at the outer walls of the pristine temple, the scent of burnt wood enveloping him. Smoke rose against the night sky and smothered the stars looming above. A handful of priests scampered around them to avoid the inferno.

"Y-Your Majesty, please," the elderly priest begged. "Is there anything you can do? We have already lost three acolytes to the flames. The sacred texts, our artifacts, our life's work"—he paused and sucked in a breath, bringing a hand to his mouth as he gazed back at the temple—"*ruined*. There must be a way to stop it."

"And have you not petitioned your Fates?" Nyses asked, concealing the sneer in his tone.

"The Fates have—have not heard my pleas, Your Majesty." The priest lowered his eyes and twisted his hands in his robe.

"Hmm," Nyses responded, the sound rumbling through his chest. "Then perhaps they will answer your king."

He strode toward the fire roaring at the temple, his mahogany cloak swishing at his heels. "You," he caught an acolyte by the collar of his robes, hauling him backward, "show me where the altar is."

The boy's eyes widened and darted to the burning building. "In—in there, Your Majesty?"

"Yes," the king said, the word blending with the hissing of flames in the background.

The acolyte swallowed. "Won't we be harmed?"

Nyses rolled his eyes and pushed him toward the entrance. "If your Fates wish to keep their holy temple, they'll surely protect their faithful. Now, *show me.*"

With trembling legs, the boy stumbled closer to the fire, bringing his robe up to shield his face from the smoke. Heat licked at the king's skin as they burst through rubble that was once the grand oak doors. Wooden beams had fallen from the ceiling and lay scattered at the edges of the hall, weakened by the blaze. The stone columns still supported the tall arches, leaving a mostly clear path for the acolyte and king to tread. When they turned down another long hallway, a door to their right creaked and trembled with exertion as the heavy wood broke from its hinges and crashed to the ground mere inches from the boy's feet. He leaped back in alarm with a yelp.

"The altar," Nyses said curtly, hand still on his shoulder to lead him forward.

"B-But, Your Majesty—"

"*Now,*" the king ordered.

With a reluctant nod, the acolyte crept down the corridor until it opened into an enormous chamber. A high vaulted ceiling and marble columns lined the path to a raised dais. Timber fell forty feet from the roof, landing before them in a crash of burning embers and ash.

"You may go," Nyses said to the boy, who breathed out a sigh of relief. With one last look at his king, he pivoted on his heels and rushed back out of the crumbling temple.

Eyeing the stone altar before him, Nyses unclasped his robe from his neck and let it fall to the floor. He ascended the dais with steady steps. The sounds of the crackling flames and creaking wood faded into the background as he ran his hand along the flat, rough top of the altar, stained red by the blood from centuries of sacrifices.

The temple of the Fates was the oldest temple in all of Mysthelm, nestled in the center of the Mid Territory. It had withstood the test of time and carried the bulk of sacred texts, historical records, and a plethora of artifacts representing the kingdom of Mysthelm's faith in the Fates.

Nyses's jaw ticked. The almighty temple, brought to its knees by flames of men.

He reached into his pocket and felt the cool edges of gold coins against his fingers. Pulling out a handful, he dropped them atop the altar. "A sacrifice of great value, offered willingly to the divine Fates of legend," he said, his voice strong despite the sounds of beams crashing to the floor behind him. "I humbly beseech your presence to help your followers conquer this great evil against your sanctuary."

His eyes scanned the ceiling above him, waiting for some sign the three beings had heard his request. Surely, if they would answer for anything, it would be for the sake of their holy place.

He was met with silence.

Gritting his teeth, he yanked one glove off his hand and pulled his dagger from its sheath. He sliced a thin line down his palm, then brandished the wound over the altar and watched as red bubbled to the surface and spilled over, trickling onto the pile of gold.

A rush of wind broke through the heat radiating at his back.

"Put your flesh away, young king."

Chills spread across Nyses's skin at the feminine voice, a warning beating in his ears.

A second voice joined the first, this one higher and lighter. Ghostly fingers brushed his neck. **"Now, now, sister. I rather enjoy looking at his flesh. He is quite the handsome king, is he not?"**

"Handsome, perhaps, but what lurks beyond those dark eyes?"

There was a pause, and the air around Nyses swelled and pulsed, pushing at his skin. Clearing his throat, he said, "I have come to request the aid of the all-powerful Fates."

"We know why you're here, Your Greatness."

"Yes, Your Magnificence. We have seen your desires."

"Then why have you not stopped this fire? Don't you wish to save your temple?" Nyses pressed.

A high-pitched giggle echoed off the stone walls, and the second voice spoke again. **"Tell us, oh great Nyses Grimaldi,"**

"What would make the King of Mysthelm,"

"Burn his own temple to the ground?" a third finished the question, a deeper female voice than the others. Her words reverberated in his very bones.

"You have been a naughty king, Nyses Grimaldi."

He blinked. "I don't know what you speak of."

"Perhaps you should have removed the kindling from your boots—"

Something hit the top of his boots, making him look down to see twigs and leaves from the forest underbrush knocked to the floor.

"And cleaned the flint from your skin."

An invisible force gripped his wrist, holding it over the altar once more. Nyses bit back a grunt as the cut on his hand burned and more blood fell to the stone. Evidence of dark flint lingered on his bronze fingers. A moment later, his arm was released, causing him to stumble forward into the altar.

A snarl ripped unbidden from his throat. "If you believe I am the one responsible, why would you appear to me?"

"Because we are very curious beings."

"Very curious, indeed."

"Setting fire to your people? Letting them burn among the smoke and flames? You must be truly desperate to summon an audience with us."

A soft sensation fluttered at his ear as a voice purred, **"Yes, Nyses. So very desperate."** Tender fingers traced a path to his neck, raising the hair on his arms.

In an instant, the fingers hardened and gripped his throat.

"Well, Your Majesty?"

"What is it that you seek?"

"Magic," he spluttered, his fingers grasping at thin air around his neck.

The invisible hand vanished, replaced by a deep chuckle. The air buzzed with the pounding of blood rushing back to his head. Distantly, he heard more beams crashing to the ground as the fire continued to destroy the temple.

"That's what all of this was for?" the voice asked. "You desire magic?"

He massaged his sore throat. "Yes," he ground out. "Magic to rival that of the Veridian Empire. Magic *you* granted them."

"Magic they earned, Nyses."

"The Veridian Empire defeated your kingdom over a century ago."

"They conquered the power we offered to both of your lands."

"You asked what I sought," Nyses said. "That is my answer. Magic to rule over my people. Magic to conquer my foes. Magic greater than what you have given our enemies."

Smoke from the inferno billowed around the altar. When Nyses squinted, he thought he could see the form of three beings wavering in the haze, but they were gone when he blinked.

"We will grant your request, Your Majesty."

He could have sworn his heart stopped. "You will?"

That same giggle from earlier tickled his ears. **"You intrigue us, King Nyses. The handsome ruler who scoffs at our existence, yet sheds his blood on our altar."**

"But this will intrigue us even more."

"What will?" he asked warily.

"Not only will we give you this magic,"

"We will bestow it upon your entire bloodline as well."

"The great Grimaldis, gods among men."

His breath caught, hardly able to believe what he was hearing. They were going to grant his life's purpose. They were going to make him the most powerful king the world had ever known.

"But be careful what you wish for, oh great King,"

"For the time may come when you will see,"

"This magic is more than you thought it would be."

Their voices blended together, and a pressure built at the base of his spine, working its way up his back and into his chest. His pulse thrummed in every inch of his body. Anticipation, fear, and desire coiled in each breath that shuddered through his lungs.

Before he could blink, the fire raging in the temple flickered out.

He was left in silence and darkness, with the scent of burning wood and thick smoke choking him.

"*You want to be greater than the Veridian Empire?*"

"**To rival them in power and strength?**"

The pressure reached his skull. It wrapped around him, pushing from all sides until he clutched his head with a groan. "What are you doing to me?" he cried out.

A deep laugh echoed in the temple. "<u>Giving you what you asked for.</u>"

"*The power to rule your people,*"

"<u>To keep your kingdom safe,</u>"

"**To protect against your foes.**"

"*Greater than what your enemies possess.*"

Images flared through Nyses's mind. Slow and blurry at first, and then in rapid succession, the visions became clearer and clearer with each passing second.

His nightmares came to life.

Fields and homes razed to the ground. Unimaginable beasts prowled the earth, soldiers battled in pools of blood, spirits walked among the living. Crops and animals and land rotted before him. Screaming, mourning, pleading, crying.

Nyses gripped his hair and cried out in anguish. It burned the backs of his eyes, but no matter what he did, he couldn't get the visions to cease.

"What is this?" he roared as his knees buckled and hit the hard floor.

"*__The future,__*" all three Fates said at once.

"*We have given you everything you have ever wanted,*" one said.

"**The greatest gift you could dream of.**"

That same ominous laugh filled the room.

"<u>And the greatest burden you could bear.</u>"

Behind his closed eyelids, he saw himself, but many decades in the future. The same dark golden skin, wavy brown hair streaked with silver, a face sagging with wrinkles, and pain in his eyes. He watched his older self fall to the ground in an empty bedchamber, his body seizing and shaking until suddenly, he went still.

"Get up, King," one of the voices spat.

"*Did you think you could trick us?*"

"**Bargain with us?**"

"*Coerce us?*"

"**We are the Fates of this world,**" they responded together, the sound grating against his ears as they grew louder and louder.

"*You wished to be as powerful as us?*"

"**Then here you are.**"

"You shall see as we see."

"*Know as we know.*"

"**And when your descendants suffer in their reigns of renown,**" the voice began with a hiss, no longer playful and toying.

"*Do not forget, oh great and mighty King,*"

"That you are the one who cursed their crown."

I

CLARISSA
TWO HUNDRED YEARS LATER

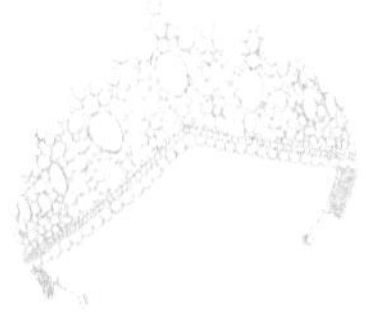

Aris,

Your presence is requested in the council room at precisely
eleven o'clock. I trust this gives you time to coordinate your extra-
neous activities so you will be prompt and prepared for our meeting.
Signed,
Everen Stryker

I narrowed my eyes at the message, sliding my tongue along my teeth as I crumpled it in my hand. Whirling to my desk in the far corner, I yanked out a fresh piece of parchment and pencil.

I spat the words aloud as I wrote them. "Thank—you—for—your—note—Lord—Stryker." I paused, the pencil biting into the paper. "Kindly—go—shove—your—foot—up—"

"Well, I certainly hope that message isn't for *me*."

Glancing up to the door, I saw the familiar blonde-and-gray hair wrapped in a low bun, kind hazel eyes, and wrinkled features of my mother, Evadine.

With a sigh, I set the pencil down. "Of course not, Mother. Just taking some frustration out."

"On your desk? Sweet girl, I don't think your father would approve of his antiques being treated as your battering ram."

"Well then, he shouldn't have left them here."

My mother's low hum was the only reaction to my comment. I closed my eyes and scratched at my brow. "I'm sorry. Lord Stryker and the rest of the council are getting to me."

She strode across the room and began straightening the haphazard pile of books, decrees, and letters on my desk. Ever the dutiful caretaker. Even more so since she recovered from a sickness that had her incapacitated in bed for over a decade.

Almost sixteen years. The same amount of time it had been since I lost my father.

"You don't have to be perfect all the time, Clarissa," she said quietly. "Even the great Empress of the Veridian Empire is allowed to have moments of weakness."

"*Future* empress, remember?" I scoffed. "There's still four months left of the provisional period." Even though my father had once been Veridia's emperor, when he abdicated the throne, he voluntarily gave up his line of succession. Emperor Theodore Gayl, the man who took his place, had to go through a similar provisional time over twenty years ago.

In the eyes of the law, it didn't matter who my father was. I had as much claim to the throne as anyone else.

Mother waved her hand in the air. "Technicalities. You've been running this empire for eight months now."

"Try telling that to Lord Stryker." I threw myself into the emerald cushioned chair behind my desk. "He's always there to remind me. To catch *every* imperfection. *Every* slip of the tongue. And constantly comparing me to Gayl, as if I could ever forget the man. 'Emperor Gayl wouldn't have allowed such frivolous travel among provinces,'" I mocked. "Well, my *beloved* predecessor also subjected thousands of people to a sleeping curse, so I'm not sure he's the best role model. Thanks, though."

My mother simply gave me her tight-lipped smile as I went on —her normal response when I went into my tirades. I had so few people I felt comfortable slipping out of my "official empress persona" around, and she was one of them.

I had stepped into this new position of power only eight months ago, after Theodore Gayl died. While some days it felt like I'd been preparing my whole life to take on this role, what with my father being emperor before the late Gayl, in the back of my mind, I never truly thought this time would come.

I'd spent *years* fighting against Gayl's rule from the shadows, forming a rebellion made up of those he'd wronged in his reign of all-consuming power. His entire purpose was to elevate the strongest of the land and crush the weaker beneath his boots. To create so much division and strife between his people that they resorted to fighting in the streets, forced to flee from their homes or hide away in seclusion. For so long, my sights had been set on the day we finally removed him from the throne and started to make things right.

But perhaps I hadn't fully prepared myself to move into the light. To trade my secrets, covert meetings, and network of spies for a title and a place on the world's stage.

"You're twenty-eight years old, Clarissa. The youngest ruler this land has ever seen." My mother rested her hands on the desk across from me. "You have caused a shockwave of change, my dear. If you believed the rebellion was difficult, leading these people may prove to be infinitely harder."

I pursed my lips. "Not exactly the encouragement I expected."

She dropped her chin and gave me a look. "Since when have you ever shied away from a challenge?"

Toying with my bottom lip, I ran a finger along the inside edge of my desk. It was my father's when he and Mother ruled this empire. I didn't have any memories of those days. My twin brother, Leo, and I were too young, barely toddlers when our father, Branock Aris, abdicated his throne and sequestered our family away to a lone cottage in the woods of Veridia City—the only home I'd ever known.

I knew next to nothing about what he was like as an emperor, besides what he and my mother used to talk about. Was he as firm and just of a ruler as he was a father? Did he love his people the way he'd loved Leo and me? Did he fight to protect them at every step, or did he let them make their own mistakes?

One thing I knew for certain was that he wouldn't have let his council walk all over him. Branock Aris had a steady hand. Brash at times, but unflinching. Unshakeable. Strong.

Strength came in many forms. If I had learned anything in the sixteen years since he died, it was that.

Mother crossed to my side, kneeling before me and taking my hands in hers. "You have done such wonderful things in such a short amount of time, Clarissa. Hold your chin high. Don't let the words of men who are threatened by the power of a woman make you think you are anything less than the rightful empress of this empire."

Swallowing, I nodded and squeezed her hands. Fates, I didn't know what I would've done without her by my side this whole time. I was thankful every single day she came out of her illness to be with us once more.

The Veridian Empire certainly looked different today than it did eight months ago when Theodore Gayl died. My predecessor spent his two decades on the throne bolstering those with a greater magic in the six provinces that made up our empire. He made everyone feel isolated by banning travel across each individual border, and he praised violence in his citizens. I'd never forget finding the families from Emberfell, the northernmost province, who moved to the capital of Veridia City to get away from dangers at their border.

They came here for safety and were met with brutality. The image of their ransacked cottage and blood-stained walls often appeared when I closed my eyes, and the smell of decay and fear still lingered in the air, more potent with my Shifter instincts.

I couldn't count the number of times I'd come across Gayl's Royal Guard in a back alleyway beating some poor Lightbender or Alchemist to a pulp. The attacks that my rebellion, the Sentinels, had stopped, the people they'd saved, the bones they'd broken in an effort to keep peace on the streets of Veridia City were an endless ledger.

But that was the past. We'd put those dark days behind us and forged a new path. One of hope and safety and *freedom*. One where my people didn't have to face fear when crossing their borders, one where they could openly explore this world and the rights they'd been given.

It seemed, however, this was not the future everyone envisioned. Those still loyal to Gayl, for example, thought my ideas were too weak. That I was carving the way for foreign threats to swoop in and stake their claim among a people too defenseless and unprotected.

They were idiots.

But they were idiots on *my* council, and I had to appease them to keep my life running somewhat smoothly. At least until my year-long provisional period was up in four months and I could kick them out of the palace for pissing me off.

A knock on the door made both of us look up. My mother used the edge of the desk to help herself stand, and when I offered my hand, she shooed me away.

"Come in," I called.

The heavy door swung open. On the other side was Larken Everest, my closest friend and advisor. Her dark features soured as she wheeled herself through in her wheelchair, scowling at me before I even had the chance to speak.

"I happened to notice there aren't any guards outside your door, Rissa," she said.

"Your powers of perception are amazing."

"It's not funny. Why do you keep sending them away? They're for your *protection*."

"I didn't need *protection* in the five years I was your Sentinel leader, and I don't plan to start needing it now."

Lark crossed her arms over her full chest and rested her elbows on the arms of the wheelchair. "That would be far more believable if you hadn't almost been assassinated two weeks ago."

I brushed off her words. "That was a misunderstanding."

"Yes, I'm sure I *misunderstood* the dagger in your pillow."

My mother let out a sigh as Lark continued to glare at me. "Clarissa, Lark is right," Mother said. "Times have changed. You have people whose responsibility is to protect and guard you. Let them do their job so *you* can do yours."

I knew this wasn't a fight I could win, not with the two of them teamed up against me. We'd been having the same argument for weeks, ever since the messenger from Drakorum found his way into my bedchambers and tried to put a knife through my skull. He left with a few less fingers.

There had been almost no complaints from any of the six provinces about my rise to power, *except* Drakorum. The mountainous province to the east was home to the Shifters—magic-wielders who could shift at will into their given animal form. They were the most volatile of the magic types, ruled by their temperamental emotions and primal instincts.

I should know. I was one of them.

My mother's ancestors lived in Drakorum until generations ago when they moved to the capital of Veridia City. That was where she met my father, the heir to the empire and an Alchemist with roots in the Feywood province. My brother inherited his Alchemist blood, whereas I took after my mother.

I'd never even *been* to Drakorum until five months ago. Emperor Gayl's laws had always forbidden traveling among the provinces. I felt no pull to the cold, rocky land, despite my heritage. There had never been this innate desire in me to connect to that part of my background.

And yet...they were *my* people. In more ways than one. They knew better than anyone what my life had been like, growing up as a Shifter, learning to deal with the unpredictable nature of our magic. Being so angry or scared or distraught that you were unable to control the shift. Forcing two vastly different sides of yourself into one body, one mind, one heart, and somehow having to decipher which was which.

The fact that it had been one of my own, a fellow Shifter, who'd tried to murder me in my sleep...

I didn't need to be accepted by everyone. That was what I told myself, anyway. But this constant strife with Drakorum pricked me on a deeper subconscious level than I'd expected.

"Fine," I said with a sigh. "I promise not to send the guards away again." My features softened as I took in Lark and my mother, two of the women who meant the most to me in this world. "Thank you for looking out for me. I know these last few months have been...*trying* for everyone, not just me."

My eyes lingered on Lark's wheelchair. Guilt bit at me every time I saw her. It may not have been my fault that she was in it, but I would never forget what we'd *both* suffered that day in those dark chambers. The day Gayl attacked and changed our lives forever. The day I tried so hard to not think about. Along with the fact that I still stood on two feet, while she would never be able to walk again.

Lark gave me a wry smile as she wheeled closer to my desk. "I know we'll have this same conversation again in a week, but I appreciate the sentiment."

I started to laugh—because we both knew she was right—when I noticed a pencil had fallen from my desk, landing in the path of one of her wheels.

The hard iron slowly crushed the small piece of wood.

Crack.

Something jolted through my body.

A fear, a *pain,* so visceral it echoed down my spine.

The sound of crunching bone filled my ears before the white-hot sting reverberated from my ankle. Looking down, I saw bone jutting from skin, the sharp edges of the break gleaming in the firelight.

Another crack.

Distantly, my mother and Lark's voices broke through the haze, but I barely registered the words coming from their mouths.

"Well, actually, Clarissa may not be here in a week for you to berate her again, Lark."

"Ah, yes, I almost forgot about the Mysthelm proposition," Lark said.

The room went out of focus, replaced with a vast chamber.

A scream ripped from my throat. I couldn't feel my shoulder, couldn't feel anything except for excruciating pain as a third snap vibrated through me.

And another.

And another.

His cold voice was all around me, filling me, breaking me. My skin and muscles sagged where bone had once been. I crumpled to the ground, already feeling the healing powers of my Shifter blood take effect, but it was too much. Too wrong. Too much pain.

"Clarissa, dear, are you feeling alright?" A soft, wrinkled hand rested on my upper arm. I flinched, my skin tingling as I took a deep breath and tried to pull myself from the memory.

"Yes—yes, I'm fine. Just...give me a moment. I need to get ready for the meeting," I said, offering Mother a placating smile. Without waiting to hear her response, I turned and threw open the door leading from my office to my bedchamber, shutting it with a *click*.

My breaths came out rapid and shallow as I leaned my head against the back of the door. I squeezed my eyes shut, willing the panic to pass, for the false pain to disappear. My Shifter half rose to the surface in my distress. I flattened my hands along the wall as my nails sharpened into claws. Sounds from outside the palace and the forest surrounding the perimeter reached my ears, which I could feel elongating, fur brushing against the skin at my neck.

Opening my eyes, I turned to face the mirror on the wall adjacent to me. Staring back were eyes tinged in yellow and soft, red ears coming to a point next to blonde hair, my features rippling back and forth.

Human and fox.

Focus. Steady. Don't lose control. Get it together, Rissa.

I didn't want the others to see me like this. What they thought was their strong, capable, competent leader, reduced to a trembling mess by a mere *sound*.

But there were times when I wasn't strong. Moments where I wasn't capable.

And when that memory swept in, when the hysteria took hold, I feared this nightmare would never go away.

2

CLARISSA

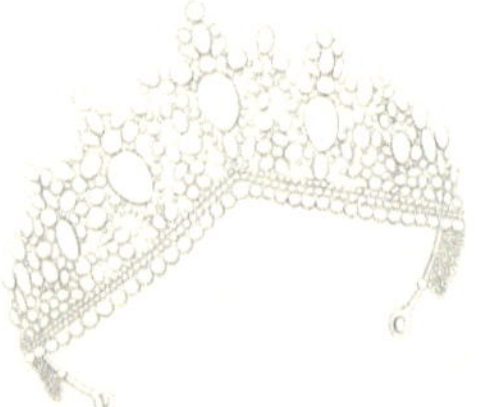

Lark, my mother, and I met Chaz, another one of my close advisors and former Sentinels, outside my chamber doors as we headed to the council meeting. Chaz greeted us with a dip of his chin and fell into line behind Lark, wheeling her chair down the long corridor.

"About time," he said in his deep voice. "I thought I was going to have to bang down the doors to get you to come out."

"We're not even late, Chaz." I smoothed down my blue pantsuit. "Stryker can wait five whole minutes for me to walk across the wing." We continued down the hall and descended a flight of stairs, striding along the deep green rugs that muffled the sound of our footsteps.

"It's not just him," Chaz said as we neared the council room. "They're all a bit antsy. What'd you do to them?"

I furrowed my brow. "Nothing. What are you talking about?"

Mother cleared her throat beside me. "That's what I wanted to tell you, dear. This meeting...well, I heard rumors from some of the wives. You know how we talk."

We came upon a pair of large wooden doors. Before I could question her further, two guards gripped the iron handles and pulled them open.

Something soured in my gut. I thought I knew what this meeting was about—the lords on my council had been trying to convince me for a while now to take a trip to Mysthelm, the kingdom to our south, to meet with their new king after the previous one died unexpectedly at the end of last year. Relations between the Veridian Empire and Mysthelm had been...well, nonexistent for the past three hundred years, ever since the great War of Beginnings made us enemies. It was a deadly, gruesome war between our two lands over the magic of the Fates, and when we won, nobody ever heard from our neighboring kingdom again.

Until last year.

I was on board with the idea of visiting Mysthelm. It would be a good way to usher in a new era of peace, not just within our borders, but across the world as well. I didn't want us to keep harboring such animosity over a war that happened centuries ago.

But the way my mother was talking...I got the feeling there was something I was missing.

I hated when that happened.

Chaz rolled Lark through the double doors, but my mother stopped me at the last moment with her hands on my shoulders. "Remember, if this isn't what you want, there's no shame in denying their request."

"Mother, what are you *talking* about? I've already said I'll go to Mysthelm."

She licked her lips worriedly. "Clarissa, it's not only that. The council has—"

"Ah, there you are, Aris," a slimy voice said from inside the council room. Everen Stryker. That man always made my hackles rise. "Considerate of you to join us."

The seven members of the all-male council reclined at a round table, several with glasses of water or pieces of parchment before them. I ignored the pale, sniveling face of Stryker directly to my right and nodded to the three oldest men sitting to the left of the entrance. Lords Leighton, Temvaren, and Cabot served at my father's side over twenty-eight years ago and still respected his reign. They were some of my strongest champions when I made a bid for the throne.

The other four were remnants of Theodore Gayl's time, including Everen Stryker. The four of them had given some push-back, but none more loudly than him. They all seemed to still be of the mindset that Gayl's idea of dominance over others by strength and magic were the best way to keep our empire protected. I thought a couple of them might be coming around to my way of thinking, but these past eight months had been like pulling teeth. Especially when arrogant scumbags like Stryker were in their ears every day, whispering of my fragile state, my "weakened, feminine mind," my vulnerability masked as compassion.

Unfortunately, I wasn't allowed to appoint new members or remove old ones until my year was up. I had to be content with dreaming of tossing them off the west tower.

I pasted on my respectful smile, falling easily into the demeanor I'd established as leader of the Sentinels. Calm, poised, collected. Ready to take anything the world had to offer. Holding back the tumultuous sea of emotions that was always at the surface of my Shifter half.

"Good afternoon, everyone," I said, taking a seat in the tall, wingback chair. "Are there any updates from the provinces to report?"

I always started with the same question. Gayl had evidently not been as concerned with the week-to-week operations of the six provinces, leaving many of them neglected and left to fend for themselves. No funding, no support, no aid when disaster struck.

That was one of the first things I changed. I appointed one council member to each province, plus one to the capital, with the responsibility of staying in communication with the governor of their assigned province. I wanted the provinces to feel important, that their grievances and triumphs alike were being heard and looked out for.

"Feywood has informed me that some of their greenhouses on

the border with Iluze have become spoiled in recent weeks." Lord Cabot stroked his dark, silver-flecked beard as he spoke, his umber forehead creasing. "They think foul play is involved, so I've advised them to set up a guard rotation to ensure nobody is sabotaging their crops."

Feywood and Iluze, two provinces to the west of Veridia City, had gone through periods of tension over the past decade. I hoped it wasn't a coordinated attack. We'd been working on improving relationships between all the provinces. The Alchemists of Feywood would be in an uproar if they believed someone was targeting their greenhouses, which grew all kinds of herbs and charms they needed for spellcrafting.

Lord Temvaren went next. "The drought in Celestria doesn't seem to be ending anytime soon. They've requested more aid. They've yielded a tenth of the crops since the beginning of summer, and they're growing desperate."

That was concerning. Agriculture was the main occupation in the usually temperate province of Celestria. "What can we spare to send?" I asked.

"Well, I suppose I could have a cargo ship stocked with at least two weeks' supply of food for now, and we can reevaluate as needed," Temvaren responded, his large red mustache bobbing as he scribbled notes on his paper.

A scoff came from my right, and I bit the inside of my cheek to hold back a snarl. Everen Stryker's voice rang out in the chamber. "Why should we send them food *our* people have toiled over? Don't they have fisheries? Animals? Surely, they can hunt enough to provide. You're coddling a lazy province, Aris, and they're going to grow dependent on our aid. Gayl would never have agreed to this."

Emperor's tits, if I heard that *one* more time...

I rested an elbow on the table and brushed a finger across my lower lip, suppressing the anger boiling inside me. I was used to dealing with conflict. Used to dealing with *people*. And I knew the difference between those who sparked conflict out of genuine concern and those who liked to hear themselves talk.

"You know, I bet they *are* lazy. I wonder, Lord Temvaren," I said without breaking eye contact with Stryker, "do you think the Celestrians are just sitting at home, watching their children wither away from starvation?"

Temvaren cleared his throat. "Err...no, Your Majesty."

"Then where *are* they?" I asked in mock concern. "I thought they were a lazy province."

Temvaren's lip twitched as he picked up on what I was playing at. "Reports say they've been working overtime at the docks and ranges, trying to make up for the loss. There aren't enough weapons for everyone who's come out to help."

"*Interesting.* What I'm hearing is that in the middle of an unprecedented drought, they're doing everything they can to feed an entire province without their main source of food. I believe we can spare two weeks of supplies, don't you?" I smiled at Stryker. "And, Lord Temvaren," I added, "send some more weapons and fishing gear. If *our* people want to work, they should have the resources to do so."

"It will be done."

"Good. Anything else?" I asked the table, ignoring Stryker's bloated, purple face as he glared at me. I didn't miss the shadows that leaked from his feet and hands beneath the table, slowly making their way to me. Lord Stryker's family hailed from Tenebra, the southern province of Shadow Wielders. His shadows always appeared when he was particularly perturbed.

Nodding to Lord Griffen, the horse Shifter who sat directly across from me in his purple suit, I asked, "Any news from Drakorum?"

His eyes slid around the table, then landed at his hands. His wild mane of hair wavered as he shook his head. "No, Your Majesty. Scarven still refuses to speak with me."

I expected as much. The Shifters and their governor, Kane Scarven, refused to have anything to do with me and my new way of running things. They preferred Gayl's way. Hands off the provinces, letting them do whatever they wanted, and keeping strong divisions between the weak and the powerful.

I wondered if Stryker and Kane Scarven traded notes on how to be the bigger pain in my neck.

"I appreciate you continuing to try," I encouraged Lord Griffen, giving him a soft smile. "They'll come around."

"Speaking of coming around," Lord Cabot interjected. "We wanted to discuss the idea of you traveling to Mysthelm." He exchanged a glance with Lord Leighton next to him, and for some reason, that look made my stomach twist into knots. "Mysthelm's correspondence team sent word on their recent trip here. There has been a...slight change of plans."

I took in the faces of the council, my heart sinking when I saw the smirk on Stryker's face. "What, exactly, has changed?"

"The new king has made an additional offer."

My eyebrows were so high up on my forehead, I feared I wouldn't be able to find them again. "Oh?"

"Of...marriage," Cabot said.

I blinked, and my mouth fell open. "*What?*"

On the other side of me, Stryker's smile widened. "King Galen Grimaldi has requested your hand in marriage upon arrival in Mysthelm in one week's time, and we have agreed."

White noise blanketed me. A wave of shock and anger slowly built in my core, then moved up my chest and neck, knocking any rational thought from my carefully curated mind.

"I'm sorry, you did *what?*" I spluttered, my eyes frantically searching their faces. "You want me to—to marry him? Shut *up*."

"E-Excuse me, Your Majesty?" Lord Cabot stammered.

Closing my eyes, I brought my trembling hands below the table and straightened my spine. *Firm but gentle. Strong but controlled. Pull it together, Rissa.*

When I opened my eyes again, I gave the men a tight smile and stood, the wooden legs of my chair screeching against the hard floor. "Give me just a moment."

I spun and headed to the door, catching my mother's eye in the back of the room. The unsurprised look on her face told me she knew about this. That was what she'd been trying to warn me of before.

She followed close on my heels as I exited the meeting room.

For the second time that day, my claws emerged from my fingertips as my heart rate picked up speed. I didn't often lose control like this, having learned from a young age how to subdue my emotions and keep my more animalistic instincts at bay. It was something all Shifters had to master, or else become a menace to society.

But these last few months had tested my patience.

"You knew they were planning this?" I hissed at my mother once the door shut behind her.

"I only just discovered it. I had breakfast this morning with Ladies Leighton and Cabot before I came to your office. They mentioned hearing their husbands discussing it two nights ago."

I threw my hands in the air. "For Fates' sake, how long has the council known? Why would they agree to this without asking me?"

"You don't have to do anything you don't want to, sweet girl." She took a step closer. "They cannot make this decision final without your consent."

"Yes, they can. I'm not the empress yet." Gritting my teeth, I took a deep breath. "Why does this Galen Grimaldi even *want* to marry me? He's never met me, never met *anyone* from this empire. We've been estranged for three centuries. Who *does* something like that? Marry a complete stranger?"

"Well, your father and I did," my mother said softly.

I blinked. "I—well, yes, I suppose you did."

I often forgot how my parents met. My father was in line for the throne, and *his* father had arranged a marriage for him to the daughter of a wealthy Shifter lord in the capital, a woman he'd barely known the name of. My mother, Evadine.

"But you two fell in love," I pointed out. "A once-in-a-lifetime kind of love. That's not something I can guarantee, Mother."

"No, it's not," she agreed. "But it's something you can *hope* for." She cupped my cheeks and forced me to meet her gaze, those hazel eyes as sharp as when I was a child. "I'm not going to lie to you and promise a fairytale future, my dear. You knew when you fought for this role that life was not going to look the way for you that it does for others. Your father and I had to make many sacrifices during our time in power. It doesn't make it easy. It doesn't make it fair. But it's always your *choice*. Don't let them take that away from you."

I was no stranger to sacrifices and difficult decisions. My twin brother and I grew up secluded from the world, isolated after my father abdicated the throne and was run out of the palace by people who believed he sparked the sleeping curse that once ravaged our empire. One Gayl was behind all along. My father died over a decade before we were able to clear his name. We'd lived in secrets and shadows, confined to our little cottage in the woods, recluses in our own home while the world spurned the Aris name.

We were hated. Spat upon. Ran from in anger and fear.

When he died and Mother fell sick, Leo and I went through adolescence and early adulthood with nothing but ourselves, our inadequately trained magic, and a couple of close friends. We made difficult decisions on a daily basis. And once we formed the rebellion, sacrifice became as easy as breathing. Time, energy, resources. Whatever I had went to our vision of a better future.

I would give *anything* for my family, my friends, and my Sentinels without a second thought.

I supposed a part of me...

A part of me believed one day I wouldn't have to. One day, the rest of my life would begin. One day, I'd be able to take something for myself simply because I wanted it.

Like love, for instance. Marriage. A family of my own.

But perhaps a life of responsibility, of *duty*, would always look the same. My people first. My empire first.

I closed my eyes. I could live with that. *If* it was truly for the good of them, I could live with it.

"Fine," I said. "Let's go back inside."

My mother furrowed her brow. "So you're agreeing to it? To this marriage?"

"Right now, I'm agreeing to hear them out." Reaching for the door handle, I added, "And they better have a good reason."

3

CLARISSA

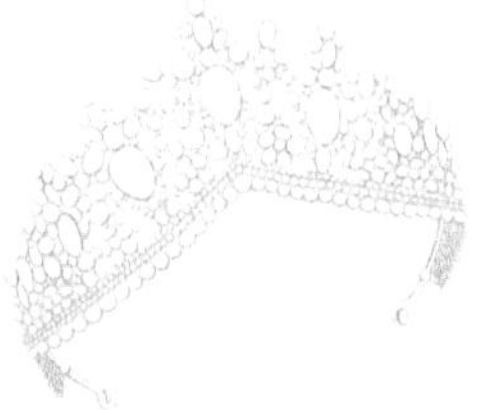

The murmurings of the council dimmed when I entered the chamber once more. As I took my seat, Lord Stryker opened his mouth, but I spoke over him. "Tell me the terms of King Grimaldi's request."

Again, Lord Cabot was the one who answered. "You're invited to Mysthelm in one week to tour their kingdom and meet the people in the hopes of improving relationships with them." Stryker grunted at that. "You'll be gone for approximately five weeks. King Grimaldi has told us he's already lined up celebrations in your honor in his four territories. But he—he believes a visit is simply not enough to strengthen our bond."

"What does he want then, a pair of handcuffs?" I muttered under my breath.

"What was that, Your Majesty?" Cabot raised an eyebrow.

"Nothing. Continue."

He cleared his throat. "Their king has proposed a marriage of alliance to unite the Veridian Empire and Mysthelm in a way our people haven't seen for centuries, if ever."

"I understand the idea of peace, but I won't abandon my empire to stand and play wife at his side," I said. "That's out of the question."

Lord Cabot nodded. "His terms don't request you relocate to Mysthelm permanently. Rather, he wishes for the marriage to be in name only. A symbol of the union. You will continue to rule the Veridian Empire while he reigns in Mysthelm, with the promise of aid if needed. Strength and solidarity from across the sea, so to speak."

I scratched the back of my ear, considering his words. "Has anything like this ever been done before?"

"Not that we know of," Cabot said. "There are many waters we'd need to navigate. Line of succession, for example. The possibility of heirs and what entity they would rule over once they come of age. These are things we can discuss with the Mysthelm council and come to an agreement on."

My heart stuttered at the thought of *heirs* with this stranger, and the implications it brought. The men must have noted my state of shock, for Lord Temvaren quickly interjected.

"If I may, Empress Aris," he said with a raised hand. His pale, freckled cheeks were flushed red, as if fearing my reaction. "I know it's sudden, and not all of the provinces will agree, but a marriage between the two of you would be most advantageous at this point in our rebuilding. It would secure good will, extinguishing any future possibility of war."

"Not to mention open up opportunities for trade with them," Lord Griffen added.

I rapped my fingers against the wooden tabletop as several of them nodded. Feet shuffled in the silence, with the occasional scratch of pencil on parchment as I took slow breaths.

They weren't wrong. There was a reason marriage alliances between families of power happened so often—my parents were proof of that. It strengthened ties and widened resources on both sides. If the Veridian Empire ever needed anything, Mysthelm would be obligated to provide what aid they could, and vice versa. And the king already insisted it would be a marriage on paper only. We could both continue ruling from our corners of the world. If the question of lineage came into play, perhaps our heirs could be born from consorts, if that was something we both agreed on and desired.

Honestly, it could work.

But it wasn't the proposal that grated on my nerves. It was the fact that I seemingly had no choice in the matter.

"And you've already told King Grimaldi that I've agreed to this?" I finally asked, meeting each of their eyes. A couple of them looked away.

It was Stryker who responded. "You seem to forget, Aris, that you have not yet been crowned, despite the titles others throw at you. We're well within our power to make this decision," he said, the hint of a sneer on his lips. "It is your *duty*, after all."

My congenial veneer began to slip again. It was so quiet in the chamber, I could hear each individual heartbeat with my Shifter senses. Slowly, I said, "What, exactly, do you mean by that, Lord Stryker?"

He shrugged. "You're young. Able-bodied." He tapped a pencil on the table as his gaze slipped below my neck with a smirk. "Women of your...affinity have a purpose, and it would be a waste not to fulfill that for your empire."

Rage, the kind I was usually able to bury and funnel into direction, blasted through me. My enhanced Shifter speed burst to the surface. Before anyone could blink, I was on my feet and at Stryker's side.

I ripped out one of the twin daggers I kept sheathed to my thigh and slammed it between his fingers, straight through the top of the table. The handle wobbled precariously back and forth. "For once in your life, Stryker, hold your tongue, or I will cut it from you and pin it to my wall."

To his credit, he held my gaze, but I didn't miss the way his shoulders shook as I pulled the blade out and backed away.

"I will marry their king," I said to the council, my voice unfamiliarly cold. "But if you *ever* make a decision regarding my life and my people without consulting me first, your days on this council will be over. Am I understood?"

A stilted chorus of agreement rang out in the hall. Flicking my hair over my shoulder, I turned to Lark. "Work out the plans for my departure. Lord Cabot will reside in my place while I'm gone, with you at his side. There will be no announcement of this engagement until I return."

Lark dipped her head at me. "Of course, Empress."

I glanced back at the council. "Gentlemen," I said, nodding stiffly. "We'll reconvene next week before I leave. Until then, all inquiries will go through Miss Everest."

Without waiting for a response, I strode to the door and pulled it open, heading straight for the north entrance of the palace. My fox half vibrated beneath my skin. I wouldn't be able to keep it at bay much longer.

I barged down the endless corridors until I reached the exit, throwing the doors wide and taking the steps two at a time as I passed the grand gardens arrayed in sunlight. The arid summer wind whipped at my cheeks, heat beating down on my exposed skin.

Reaching the thin forest surrounding the palace, I unlatched the door to my anger and frustration. It barreled into me, quick as lightning, and a growl erupted from my chest.

I broke into a run. Every cell, every muscle, every bone in my body began to shift, exploding inside me like a tidal wave. There was always a single, brief moment of pain as my body rewrote itself, but once the magic flooded me, it was euphoric. Like beams of gold lighting up my veins.

With a final burst of speed, I launched myself into the air, dried leaves and dirt spraying in my wake. Red fur ruptured across my skin. My legs and arms shortened and filled with muscle, my ears and nose lengthening as I shook my head back and forth. Claws split from my fingertips.

I landed on all fours in the middle of the forest. Paws pounding against hard grass, I sprinted into the afternoon, not once looking back.

4

THORNE

"You're rather dull tonight, my dear friend," Galen slurred from across his study as he threw his legs over the arm of the black velvet chair.

Scratching at my temple, I swirled the glass in my other hand. "Am I? Or are you perhaps drunker than usual, my dear king?" I mimicked his tone.

Galen laughed, the sound echoing off the light gray marble walls. Most definitely drunk. He tipped his glass to me. "Fair enough. I suppose the question is, why aren't you drunk as well?"

And I supposed the answer was *because someone needs to keep the king in line.*

Or my personal favorite, *because I'm not the one hiding from my responsibility in the bottom of every bottle in Mysthelm.*

"One of us has to be alert for the meeting in the morning, yes?" I said instead, giving him a smirk.

He rolled his eyes, and a lock of normally well-kept hair fell onto his golden-brown forehead. "Another meeting. Don't you ever get sick of all of them? One after another after another. They're so incredibly *boring.*"

Standing, I crossed to his chair and plucked the empty glass from his gloved hand. My boots padded against the thick black and gray rug. "Very. But considering you appointed me to be one of your advisors, I unfortunately still have to go. As do you."

"Says who? I'm the king. I can do whatever I want."

I bit down on my tongue. "Galen, I say this as your best friend. You're an insufferable drunk."

"And *you* used to be the fun one," he responded. "What happened to Thorne Reaux, the man whose idea of a casual night out was to drink me under the table, get kicked out of at least two bars, and take home any girl he wanted?"

He grew up, I thought, but couldn't help chuckling at the pout on Galen's face. "What happened is that your table is now plated in gold and says 'King of Mysthelm.' Our lives changed, Galen. In more ways than one."

He stared at me for a moment, then closed his eyes and leaned his head back. The glow from the fire crackling in the fireplace cast shadows over his dark features. "What I would give for just a moment of those old days again," he said, the slur now more pronounced.

My chest tightened. As much as he might irritate me at times, I knew these nights and this behavior came from a place of sorrow. Galen Grimaldi had the world thrust onto his shoulders seemingly overnight—and my best friend had never been one to carry weight well.

We sat in silence for a moment, with only the sound of flames snapping and popping in a hypnotic trance. Galen's study in the palace had become a safe haven of sorts. It wasn't so much a "study" as it was a place for us to go and drink and get away from the world. Two plush black velvet chairs sat opposite each other across the large rug, with the fireplace to our right and a towering bookshelf to our left. Behind Galen's chair stood his desk, which hadn't been used in Fates knew how long. A potted tree sat in the corner next to it. The space was dark but cozy, and not many people were allowed in.

"How's your mother doing?" I asked quietly.

He waved a hand in the air, eyes still closed. "Oh, you know.

Same as always. The nurses try to play me for an idiot, but I see the bloody cloths. I hear her coughing at night." He swallowed hard and kicked his feet against the side of the chair. "Sounds more and more like Father did."

Before the disease took him, I finished in my head. The former King of Mysthelm, Orion Grimaldi, had been dead for eight months now. Even if he barely talked about it, I knew it tore at Galen. I didn't want to imagine what he would turn into if his mother died of the same illness.

"I'm sure the healers will find a remedy soon," I said.

"Oh, yes," Galen burst out, jumping to his feet. He swayed for a moment, then righted himself. He began pacing the room on unsteady legs, almost stumbling over the low coffee table before the fireplace. "That's what everyone says. Talking down to me like I'm a child. They think telling me the same thing over and over will make me answer all their little *questions*," he drawled, then pitched his voice so it mocked those of his advisors.

"'The coffers are running low, Your Majesty.' And 'The Mid Territory is asking if you'll investigate the farmland fires.' And 'Please, King Grimaldi, we need you to sign off on the rehousing agreement from the floods.'" As he spoke, he took his frustration out on his gloves, tugging off the fingers one by one and throwing them on the ground to expose bare skin.

My spine stiffened when he paced closer to me, my eyes shifting to his hand. "Galen—"

"Honestly, I don't know how my father did it. But we always knew he was a better man than me. A better *king*." He drew nearer, holding out his ungloved hand to reach for the glass in mine.

"Galen, stop—"

"I just need a *moment* of peace, Thorne. Don't you understand? Is that too much to ask for?"

Heart hammering in my chest, I backed away and shouted, "Galen!"

He halted in his tracks. Cursing, he spun away, scrambling for the gloves discarded on the floor. "I'm sorry, Thorne. I wasn't thinking."

Squeezing my eyes shut, I blinked back the rush of adrenaline and let out a breath. "You've got to be more careful."

"Yes, I realize that," he snapped. "Why do you think I wear these"—he flapped the gloves angrily in the air—"day and night?"

Silence fell over us, thick and tense. He shoved the gloves back on.

I sighed. "Sober up, Galen. This meeting tomorrow is important."

"I know." He glanced at his feet, all signs of anger instantly gone. His face crumpled as he sank into his chair, rubbing a hand down his freshly shaven chin. "We *have* to get her here."

Her. The empress from across the sea.

When he'd found out a young, unmarried woman had taken over our neighbor to the north, hope had sparked inside him, turning him into an entirely new man. Galen had been pushing for her to come ever since he made contact with the Veridian Empire shortly after his father's passing. The meeting tomorrow was to finalize details for her arrival, as well as plans to announce their engagement.

For the life of me, I couldn't understand his sudden sense of urgency. All he would say was that he *needed* to marry this empress. Needed to unite our two lands. He would never give me a straight answer when I asked why he was so intent on this marriage, other than some vague soliloquy about wanting to right the wrongs of the Veridian Empire and Mysthelm.

"Not everyone will approve of her. You know that, don't you?" I warned him. "There will be unrest once you make this official."

"I know," he repeated.

"How do you plan to handle that?"

He threw his hands up. "How should I know, Thorne? I've never done this before. I'll do whatever the other regents and my council tell me to."

I turned my back on him in order to hide my clenched jaw. He'd been my best friend for as long as I could remember, but his indecisiveness and ignorance were more than I had the patience for sometimes. He didn't seem to care that I was trying to help him.

I *did* used to be the fun one. Now, I wasn't sure either of us were.

"And you still think bringing this empress over is a good idea?" I asked. Some of our people here in Mysthelm were vehemently opposed to a Veridian—someone with foreign, dangerous magic—entering our shores. Our *magic-less* shores. Even though the war between us had ended three hundred years ago, many still held grudges against them, so deeply entrenched in our history that it was difficult to shake.

I didn't know if Galen's tremulous hold on his citizens would last after this final straw. I'd already begun to hear disgruntled buzzing from the other territories, revealing their unhappiness since King Orion died. If Galen didn't get a handle on things, I feared tensions would only worsen.

"I'm not arguing with you about this again. I *have* to marry her, Thorne. End of discussion."

Facing him, I weighed the pros and cons of starting this debate once more before realizing a drunk Galen would get us nowhere. Nodding curtly, I said, "We'll have all the details worked out soon. Don't worry about getting her here—we'll make sure it happens, if that's truly what you want."

He cracked a smile, his eyes going in and out of focus. "I leave all the worrying for you now, don't I? I swear, you didn't have a wrinkle on that pretty face seven years ago." His brow furrowed. "Speaking of which, where's Marigold tonight?"

"With her grandmother."

"Ah, probably for the best. Wouldn't want her to see you having too much *fun*," he slurred. "Whaddya say, old friend? One more drink?"

I shook my head, but a laugh escaped me. "You're hopeless, and you're going to hate yourself in the morning."

"I didn't hear a no."

I grabbed a bottle, slipping back into the version of me he always tried to get me to become again. It felt like that man was harder and harder to find. "One more drink."

I raised a glass to my lips, but out of the corner of my eye, I spotted the once lush, tall tree by Galen's desk, now shriveled and black, shadows from the gnarled branches reaching toward us like claws.

5

CLARISSA

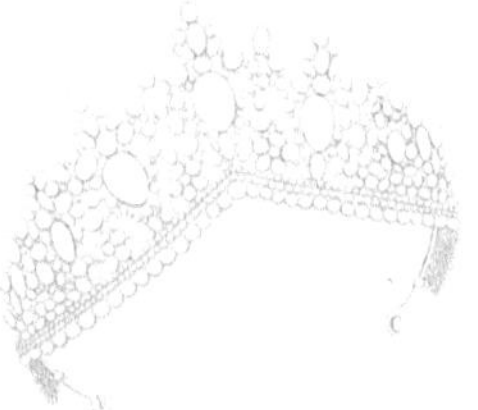

"I need to go soon!" I said with a laugh as Chaz slammed three small glasses on the table, courtesy of Dippy, our favorite bartender. "You know I have to be up early tomorrow."

"Yes, our big world traveler off on her epic adventure," Lark teased, holding up her drink.

"Something like that," I muttered.

"Then let me treat you to this last round, Your Majesty," Chaz said with a mocking bow, his nose almost hitting the top of the table.

"Her last round as a single woman," added Lark.

I rolled my eyes. "Fates, did you have to bring that up? I'm trying to enjoy the evening."

The familiar sights and sounds of the Drakin's Lair, our favorite bar in the south sector of the capital, washed over me and set my mind at ease. The carefree laughter, loud chattering, and the scent of stale peanuts and sweat. People from all walks of life filled the dusty old tavern to the brim. Cracked glass at the windows let in the dry summer air, a hint of moonlight sneaking in as insects buzzed in the background.

The Drakin's Lair had always been the meeting point for the

close members of the Sentinels, like Chaz, Lark, and my brother. Nobody asked questions. The south sector was often referred to as the underbelly of the capital, as people from various provinces who didn't have much power or money ended up finding their way here. They came to the safety of the bar to get away from their troubles, away from the Royal Guard or pompous Veridians who treated them like scum simply because of what they were born into.

It felt like home, in a way. A depiction of the true empire. A conglomerate of magic and people who just wanted somewhere to belong.

Thankfully, in the few months since I'd started pushing for changes, I could already see how much better off the citizens here were. Crime had gone down tremendously. There were hardly any attacks or thefts or vandalism like the kind we used to see when I had my Sentinels patrolling the streets. No more bodies found in alleyways, half beaten and left for dead. No more would-be arsonists attempting to set fire to storage facilities.

On days when it felt like I'd never live up to the expectations of my people or the legacy of my father's rule, I reminded myself of this. Of the people I'd helped. The lives I'd improved. It gave me the will to keep going.

"Promise me things won't change between us," I said to the two of them. "This marriage is in title only. Everything else will be exactly the same. I'll still be here with both of you, making sure you don't make fools of yourselves in front of half the sector."

Chaz snorted and scratched at the short-cropped black beard on his chin. "We're in the dirtiest tavern in the capital with the soon-to-be empress of the empire. I'd say not much has changed in the last year, Rissa. You taking some Mysthelm prick's last name isn't going to make a difference."

"Excuse me, I'm absolutely *not* taking his name."

"Good, because Clarissa Grimaldi is a bit too pretentious, even for my taste," Lark said, chuckling into her drink. She wore her dark curls in a thick braid wrapped around the crown of her head today, framing her deep brown features.

I was glad the three of us could get away for a night out before the trip. Our group had gotten smaller over the months, ever since Leo and our friend Rose had left on a mission across the provinces to help wake those who had fallen prey to the sleeping curse during Gayl's rule.

My eyes lingered briefly to the left of Chaz, where one last familiar face used to be. Horace, our dear friend and former Sentinel, had lost his life protecting Lark and me eight months ago. The same day Theodore Gayl died. The same day he—

A shudder swept over me, the ghostly pain of that day rippling through my bones once more. I shook off the sensation and gave them a tight smile across the table.

Lark set her drink down. "Seriously, Rissa, you don't have to go through with this if you don't want to. Nobody is forcing you to marry their king."

"Yeah, if you want a reason to get out of it, you can just marry me," Chaz said with a wink.

I laughed. "As romantic as that proposal is, I think I'm going to pass. Really, I'm alright. I've had some time to come to terms with it, and it's what's best for both our lands. You heard what the council said last week—this will open up trade agreements, give us more security against—"

Lark cut me off. "I wasn't asking Clarissa the Empress; I was asking *Rissa*. Our friend. This shouldn't just be some strategic political move. This is your *life*. You have a say in it."

I took a long sip of my drink. It was always irritating when others perceived me so well.

That was *my* job.

People were easy. Reading them, discovering what they wanted, working their motivations and desires in my favor—those were some of my strengths.

Being open with those closest to me was *not*, evidently.

"They're one and the same, Lark. My life is basically one large strategic move. You know that—it's been that way ever since we decided to start the Sentinels. And I'm fine with that, I *promise*," I said quickly as she opened her mouth to continue arguing. "I've never been some hopeless romantic. Love and marriage and all of that haven't even crossed my mind these last few years." I waved my hand in the air, trying to show my nonchalance.

It was only a partial lie. I *had* been far too busy with the Sentinels since my early twenties to even think of settling down. I'd had a few relationships over the years, but nothing serious. Nothing that outweighed my purpose.

But when Leo met Rose a little less than a year ago...

Watching my brother fall so deeply, so completely in love, pricked something in my heart. Not jealousy, per se—I wanted him to have all the happiness he deserved. And they truly were perfect for each other. It did, however, make me think about what I might be missing.

The way he lit up around her, the way she came alive with him, the way they were—sickeningly—all over each other...it was endearing. Beautiful.

Something I would never have. Not anymore.

And...that was alright. *I* was alright.

Lark leaned back in her wheelchair and crossed her arms. "I've always looked up to you, Rissa. You never fail to put the needs of others before your own."

I quirked an eyebrow. "Why do I get the feeling this is a reprimand and not a compliment?"

"Because she's great at those," Chaz interjected.

Shooting him a look, Lark continued, "Sometimes you need to be selfish, though. I'm worried you're going to look back on your life in thirty or forty years and realize you lived it for everyone but yourself."

Chaz added, "If she even makes it that long."

"Not helping."

"Just trying to bring some levity to the conversation."

I took another drink, listening to their banter as Lark's words sank into me. I lived for myself, didn't I? I'd done things for *me*, because I wanted to and for no other reason.

Hadn't I?

I let my gaze wander with my thoughts. At the window next to the corner table we occupied, a small sliver of light twisted through a crack in the glass. I leaned forward in my seat to get a better look. I thought it looked like Lightbender magic—thin, bright strands of light that could go through solid matter. Some drunk Lightbender must be showing off for their friends. I brought my hand up to the windowsill and smiled, letting the thin thread wrap around my fingers. It was so lightweight, I could hardly feel it, almost like a piece of hair tickling my skin.

Then an arrow whizzed through the hole in the window and embedded itself in my hand.

6

CLARISSA

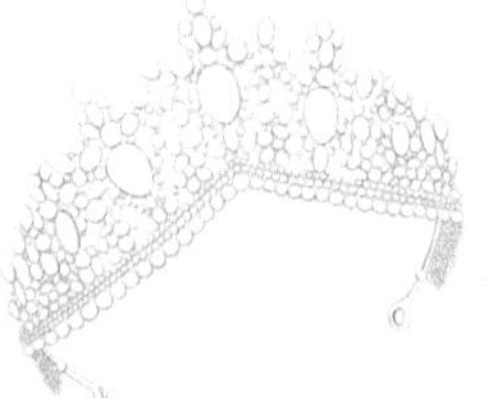

I cried out in alarm and staggered backward as pain radiated up my arm. Chaz was instantly on his feet, and Lark's shadows swirled at her hands beside him. Several patrons nearest our table had noticed the commotion. Drinks clattered and chairs screeched across the wooden floor, gasps filling the air.

Growling and biting back the sting, I ripped the arrow from my hand. My quick healing was already kicking in, thanks to my Shifter half. Blood trickled slowly from the closing wound as I held my hand as steady as I could, when something stuck at the base of the arrowhead caught my attention.

you can't run

A small note in a barely legible scrawl, its edges ripped and splattered in my blood.

"You need to get back, Rissa," Chaz ordered, pulling me away from the window.

I crumpled the note in my uninjured hand and shoved it in my pocket. "I'm fine; it's already starting to—"

I heard the soft *swoosh* of another arrow coming from outside the tavern and called on my Shifter instincts, spinning to catch it.

But before I could, a dark wall of shadows appeared before me, enveloping the oncoming arrow. Lark flicked her wrist, and it clattered to the ground.

Mumblings and quiet screams broke through the laughter and clinking of glasses as more patrons jumped to their feet.

"What was that?"

"Is someone shooting at us?"

"We're under attack!"

Their questions and exclamations rolled over one another, tension mounting. Chaz pulled me to stand behind a wooden pillar, then glanced back at the window. "I'm going to check the perimeter. I'll be back."

I didn't have time to protest before he vanished into thin air. "Striders," I muttered. He was from Celestria and had the ability to transport himself from one place to another faster than I could stop him. I hated when others were put in danger because of me. When *I* couldn't be the one to take action. If anything happened to my friends—

Lark wheeled herself to face me. "We need to get you out of here. Now. Those arrows were meant for *you*. I can't believe I let you talk me into coming out without more guards!"

I scanned the faces of the patrons scrambling in confusion, flexing my injured hand. I could feel the tissue repairing itself. "These people are frightened, Lark. I can't leave them when there could be danger nearby."

She threw her hands in the air. "You are their *empress*. Don't give me that provisional period nonsense. You *are*. If something happens to you, this entire empire devolves into chaos. We'll send a battalion out once we get back to the palace, and they can watch over the area."

My lips set into a thin line. "It's *because* I'm their empress that I have to stay. I have to keep them calm."

In the next second, Chaz reappeared at my side. "I couldn't find anyone. I think they left. There were fresh tracks about fifty yards into the woods." He pointed out the window toward the trees.

"Stride to the palace, Chaz," I instructed him. "Get a unit of the Royal Guard and have them sweep the sector. Make sure a couple of them are stationed here and other heavily populated areas in the village."

"What do you want us to do if we find the shooter?"

"Detain them. We can question them at the palace later."

He nodded and vanished once more. Turning to the rest of the bar, I cleared my voice and called for their attention. Slowly, the shouts died down, replaced with murmurings as I dropped my burgundy hood so they were able to see my face. A hush fell over the crowd. Many of them probably recognized me from my time with the Sentinels, before they knew me as Empress Aris. I'd worked hard to gain their trust. Their loyalty. We were one people, fighting for one cause, hoping for one future.

"I understand many of you are frightened," I started. "But the shooter is no longer a threat. One of my guards has ensured the immediate area is clear of any danger. We have more soldiers coming to watch over the sector tonight. If you will all please stay here until guards come to do a final search and help you get home safely, I'm sure our friends here will make you comfortable." I motioned to the pair of bartenders behind the bar. "Anything they want is on me. I'll cover all expenses and any trouble this may cause."

Dozens of eyes searched mine, and faces began to slacken in relief. I locked gazes with a young woman in front of me and gave her an encouraging smile. "Nobody has been harmed. I promise, we'll find whoever—"

Time stopped.

My nose twitched. I heard the faint rustle of dried grass, the quiet kiss of steel slicing through air. But I wasn't fast enough.

Another arrow came racing through the window.

The young woman before me furrowed her brow and turned her head.

The arrow planted itself in her throat.

"No!" I screamed, launching myself at her.

The entire bar erupted. Blood gurgled from her neck as her body convulsed and fell to the floor. I hastily scooped her into my arms. Her eyes flickered shut, and unintelligible garbles left her mouth.

My chest heaved. It was too late. I watched, helpless, as her chest rose once more and then sagged. Her eyelids fell shut. Blood trickled out of the corner of her mouth, mixing with what already coated her neck and chest.

That arrow was meant for *me*, and this innocent woman suffered the consequences. Sorrow and rage and regret ripped through me and crashed beneath my skin. She was one of *mine*. One of my people. I was supposed to keep her safe. I was supposed to provide a better life.

I didn't realize I was crying until a tear dropped onto her cheek. "I'm so sorry," I whispered, body shaking as I wiped a blood-soaked hand across my face.

I gently set her down and rose to my feet. My limbs continued to tremble, but not out of grief.

In that moment, I was pure vengeance.

Lark's features were ashen as she tried to grab my forearm. "Rissa, we *must* leave. It's too dangerous for—"

I tore from her grasp, a snarl building in my throat. My teeth sharpened, and my claws extended. "I'm going after them."

"*What?* Absolutely not. That is the worst possible—"

"Get out of my way, Lark," I said with a growl as I hurled myself toward the window and shifted, glass shattering beneath my paws.

I exploded into the night. Warm air whipped at my fur. Bolting into the thicket of trees outside the bar, I instantly smelled someone. Salty sweat mixed with a hint of steel and moss. But then, the scent changed. From human to...*other*.

A Shifter.

I let out a raspy bark as I followed the scent. They were moving quickly to the south. Grass and twigs crunched under my paws as I flexed my legs and put on a burst of speed. With the villages and nightlife fading behind me, the trees thickened, and the scent of the oncoming shoreline slammed into my senses. They were heading to the water.

I pushed myself faster, muscles straining and groaning with exertion. I was getting closer. I could *feel* it. Just a little farther—

There. I caught sight of a tan tail flailing through the underbrush, maybe thirty yards away. They must have sensed me gaining on them. When it turned its cat-like body, bright yellow eyes met mine for a breath before it launched himself up the closest tree.

A cougar Shifter. Male, by the looks of it, and not a particularly large one. No wonder Chaz found his tracks but wasn't able to see signs of him still at the bar—he'd probably climbed up a tree to hide.

Two could play that game.

My claws sank into the trunk. I propelled myself forward, dodging branches while keeping my eye on the cougar. He jumped onto a thick bough and slunk along the edge. Quicker than I thought possible, he sprang to the right and landed on the tree branch next to me. His lithe body was concealed by foliage, but my fox sight could make out his shape darting around the trunk.

I knew where he was going.

Eyeing the high branch of a tree directly across from him, I scrambled up and onto a bough facing it, my back legs vibrating with force as I sprinted down the narrow offshoot.

The cougar pushed off from his branch, aiming for the one before me.

My paws left the bark, and I soared through the air.

We collided with a crash, our snarls breaking the silence of the night. His back hit the hard ground first, and he let out a yowl as his back legs came up and pitched me off him. I skidded across dirt and leaves before catching my balance and hurling myself at him. He was bigger than me, but only just. I was an abnormally large fox —I took after my mother, who came from a long line of large canine Shifters.

And I'd fought worse than the likes of him.

I swiped at his nose, my claws connecting with skin and dragging until blood seeped beneath his eye. With a high-pitched scream, he reared up on his back legs and slammed a paw into my side, then lurched for my head with his jaw opened wide.

He was strong, but I was quicker. I slipped from his grasp, ignoring the pain shooting up my left side, and tore at his hind leg with my teeth. With an ironclad grip, I shook my head until he collapsed, his vicious shriek ringing in my ears. The salty tang of blood coated my tongue as I bit down harder. Then something sharp sliced through the back of my neck and down my shoulder.

I released him with a yelp and stumbled backward on all fours. That one felt deep. Breathing through the pain and flexing my right paw to make sure nothing was severely damaged, I barely had enough time to guard against his next attack.

He slammed into me and angled his teeth toward my neck. I knocked him back with another swipe to the eye. When he moved to go up on his hind legs again, I used his precarious balance to dive into his unprotected midsection and fling him to the ground.

All I could see was that young woman's face. All I could hear was her shallow breaths, her gurgled cries. The vision of that arrow flying and lodging into her throat replayed over and over in my mind.

My sharp claws dug into the cougar's flesh. I ripped skin and muscle from his shoulder, chunks of fur and blood blinding me in my rage.

It was sometimes easier, being in this animal form. Instinct took over, letting me follow my emotions instead of listening to the rational part of my brain. Hunt, protect, defend, kill. If someone hurt what I called mine, they paid the price in blood. That was how these primal urges worked.

And I could see it so clearly. My jaw wrapped around his neck, tearing his throat from his body, claiming my victory. My vengeance.

In the blink of an eye, the cougar shifted with a whimper.

My paws rested atop a pale man covered in dirt and blood, both mine and his. Light brown eyes filled with pain stared up at me, sharpening into resolve as he waited for me to take his life.

His human life.

I let out a growl as I forced my claws to retract and called back my human form. Delicate hands replaced red fur as I circled my fingers around his neck and kept his body pinned to the forest floor.

"*This* is mercy," I hissed, leaning down so my blonde hair fell over my shoulder and spilled onto his chest. "And it's the last time I'll give it to you."

Lifting the back of his head, I slammed it into the ground. His eyes fluttered shut as he passed out.

7

THORNE

Fading daylight darkened the grounds as I stared out the window of Reaux Mansion. In the distance, I could barely see the waves of the Avonige Ocean lapping against the shore and the towering palm trees that marked the edge of our property.

I'd lived here my whole life. Ran across those beaches a thousand times, often with Galen at my side. Took countless girls to gaze under those stars—*without* Galen, for once. All while being groomed to one day take over as Lord Reaux, Regent Lord of the North Territory of Mysthelm.

That title had become mine four years ago when I turned twenty-eight, after my father fled our home and was never heard from again.

The same year my wife left this world.

One by choice, one by force.

This mansion, this property, this entire *territory* was under my charge...and yet, I'd never felt further from home. That was what happened when a worthless father abandoned his family and duty without a backward glance.

"Daddy? Will you read me a story?"

I uncrossed my arms and turned to face the sweet voice, those big brown eyes looking up at me with a plea.

How a father could leave something like this, I would never understand.

Kneeling to her eye level, I brushed a strand of dark bronze hair behind her little ear. "Of course. But then it's bedtime, yes? I've already kept you up too late." I softly tapped her nose, which crinkled with a smile, a gap between her two front teeth peeking out.

"Okay. Come on, I've picked it out," Marigold said, grabbing my pinky and leading me to her bed across the room. For her seventh birthday a few weeks ago, my mother had her entire bedchamber redecorated however Marigold desired—which meant pink, purple, and white covered every inch of the space. An artist painted a mural of a whimsical garden on the wall facing her door, and carpenters built a new bed frame and canopy with pink translucent curtains that flowed over her bed like a veil. Portraits of castles and Marigold's favorite animals dotted the walls, and more toys than I could count were nestled in various corners.

I told my mother she was spoiling her rotten. I was fairly confident this bedroom was the most valuable chamber in the mansion.

But the look on Marigold's freckled face when she saw it for the first time...

I would give her a *thousand* rooms to see that smile.

"This one." She plopped onto her bed and held out a thin, leather-bound book.

I raised an eyebrow. "Again?"

"You know it's my favorite, Daddy."

"I think you could recite it to me by memory at this point," I said with a chuckle, tying back my long hair with a strap of leather before climbing onto the bed with her. *The Lost Princess*. She'd been obsessed with this book since Galen gave it to her last year.

"Alright. *The Lost Princess*," I began, opening the book to the title page with artwork depicting a young girl and a crown at her feet. Marigold slipped under the covers and nudged my elbow with her head so she could nestle into my side. Her fingers came up to feel the wrinkled pages, as she always loved to do. Kissing the top of her head, I rested the book between us.

"Once upon a time, there was a little princess who lived in a beautiful castle. She had a mother and father who loved her very much. They would let her play in the meadows and ride her pony in the fields, and tucked her into bed every night with a kiss.

"One night, there was a loud, scary storm. Thunder boomed and lightning cracked outside the little princess's window, and she became scared. But right before she was about to hide under her covers, a soft, pretty lullaby began playing. The music became louder as a figure appeared from the shadows of her room. It was a beautiful woman, with hair like gold and eyes as bright and purple as the princess's favorite flower, a violet."

"Daddy, violets are *my* favorite flower too!" Marigold exclaimed.

I chuckled. "I know, sweetheart." Last year it was a rose, and the year before that, a daisy.

"Keep going," she insisted.

"You're the boss." I cleared my throat. "The strange woman smiled at the princess and asked, 'Are you afraid of the storm, little one?'"

"Do the *voices*, Daddy," Marigold interrupted.

"Alright, alright, if you insist." I pitched my voice higher as I continued, "'I can take you somewhere safe,' the woman said, holding out her hand. 'Somewhere the monsters and storms can't reach you.'

"When another blast of thunder shook the room, the princess jumped up and took the woman's hand. In the blink of an eye, she was transported to a wonderful garden, full of friendly animals and flowers and blue skies."

"How did she get there?" Marigold asked. This was part of our nightly routine—no matter how many times we read the same book, she would always ask questions, always wanting to know more.

"Magic, I suppose."

"Is magic *real?*"

I hesitated. There was so much about this world she didn't understand yet. To her, magic was some fanciful, sparkly idea that granted wishes and made life better.

She didn't know how magic could be a curse.

"Some magic is real," I answered truthfully. "I think there's magic in the way your grandmother and I love you. There's magic in the world around us—the pretty flowers outside your door, how the sky lights up pink and gold when the sun goes down."

"And my mommy?" she asked. "You say Mommy looks down on us from the stars. Is that magic too?"

I swallowed the lump in my throat and smoothed out her hair. "Yes, sweetheart. That's magic. And your mother loves you very much, even if she's not here anymore."

We sat in silence for a moment. I thought she'd fallen asleep when she quietly whispered, "Will you keep reading?"

Pulling her closer into my side, I continued, "At first, the little princess loved the enchanted garden. She ran through the tall grass as birds and butterflies swooped at her side. But soon, she got lonely. She missed her friends, her bed, and her mother and father. Spinning around, she called for the woman who had brought her there.

"'I want to go home,' she said when the woman with golden hair appeared. She smiled at the princess, her teeth perfectly white and her skin glowing like the sun. 'This *is* your home now, little one. I brought you here to protect you from the storms. You can have everything you ever wanted,' the woman said.

"The little girl began to cry. 'All I want is my mommy!' she pleaded. 'She must be looking for me. I've been gone for so long.'

"The beautiful woman's face suddenly fell. The sky around them darkened, and shadows swirled at the grass beneath their feet. Her eyes burned red as her face twisted into an ugly snarl. 'Ungrateful child! You belong to *me* now. And you will never see your mother and father again.'

"With that, she vanished, leaving the princess all alone. She didn't know what to do. She was hungry and scared, and didn't want to be trapped there anymore. Looking beyond the field of flowers, she saw a scary forest. She wanted to run away from it but remembered how frightened she'd been of the storm. If she had only faced her fear, maybe she wouldn't have been taken away. Wiping the tears from her cheeks, she ran toward the dark forest, telling herself to be brave.

"When she reached the first tree, a large yellow pear fell to the ground. She picked it up, so thankful to have found food, but a strange noise made her stop. From the thick bushes beside her staggered an old crone. She hunched over a wooden cane as strands of gray hair fell from her wrinkled scalp. The old woman grimaced at the princess, showing off jagged black-and-yellow teeth.

"'Would you mind sparing me some food?' the crone asked, her voice wobbly.

"The princess gripped the pear tighter and swallowed down her fear. Holding the fruit out, she said, 'Here. We can share.'

"The stranger raised her eyebrows. 'You would be kind to me, someone you have never even met?'

"The girl took a step closer, urging the woman to take the pear. 'My mommy and daddy always taught me to give to those who have less than me.'

"With a smile, the crone took the pear. 'Because of your kindness, little princess, I will help you get home.' Starlight gathered at the woman's hands, surrounding the princess in magic. Before she disappeared, the woman said, 'Remember that goodness is not found in beauty, child, but in the heart.'

"Waving her hand, the woman sent the princess back to her room. She landed in her soft bed with the thunder and lightning still raging outside, but it didn't scare her this time. The little princess was home, and she would never wish to leave again."

I gently closed the book and looked down to see my daughter's chest rising and falling evenly, little puffs of breath against my hand indicating she'd fallen asleep.

I always wondered why she loved that story so much. Perhaps it was the idea of a little girl wanting to get back to her mother and father that resonated with her. Marigold had never truly known her mother. My Iris died of a heart disease when Marigold was barely three years old. Sometimes, I thought she remembered the *idea* of her mother, but she was far too young to recall the moments they spent together.

Easing my arm out from beneath her, I slowly lifted off the bed and placed the book on her bookshelf. Something about the story stuck in my mind tonight more than it did the other nights: how eager we could often be to trust anything that promised to bring us out of our fears.

It made me think of myself.

I used to throw myself at all this kingdom had to offer in an attempt to get out of my own head. Lesson after lesson my father would force me through in the hopes that one day I'd serve in his place. Lord Thorne Reaux. I saw my future as clear as day: in a love-less marriage, raising children the way one raises cattle, spending my days in meetings listening to others complain, and drowning my nights in a bottle. The spitting image of my father. A man who abandoned his family just to escape the life he'd created.

And that scared me more than anything.

So Galen and I found freedom and comfort in things that made us *feel*. Taverns, women, drinking, gambling, jumping off cliffs into the Avonige Ocean. He had his responsibilities as a prince— granted, on a much greater scale than mine—and we'd bonded from a young age over trying to avoid the inevitable emptiness of our future by filling our present with *life*.

Now we had both stepped into those futures, earlier than either of us expected. But I had been given a gift. A beautiful, bronze-haired, brown-eyed gift that filled me with joy and completeness every single day. Even when her mother was taken from me, when the world turned into shades of gray and the light was sucked from my spirit, Marigold kept me whole.

Galen...he didn't have that.

Galen had a cursed crown on his head and a legacy of pain in his heart, still searching for something beautiful to take it all away. He held this unwavering, inexplicable faith that this woman, this empress from the Veridian Empire, was the answer to his problems.

If that was the case, I only hoped she could save him before it was too late.

8

CLARISSA

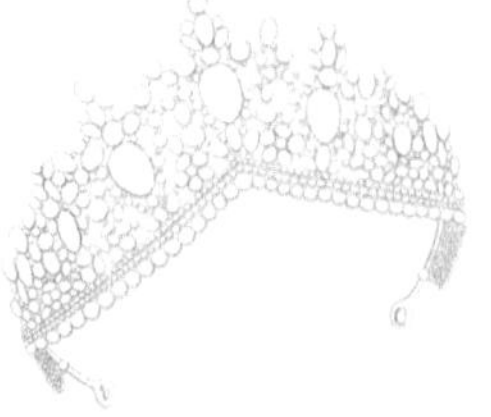

I paced back and forth in front of the cell, clenching and unclenching my fists as Chaz questioned the cougar Shifter behind bars. My friend's broad shoulders cast a menacing shadow over the small cell with barely any moonlight streaming in through the circular, barred window. His teeth gleamed against dark skin as he snarled at the man slumped on an overturned bucket.

"Who sent you tonight?" Chaz's deep voice boomed in the quiet, dank space. "Who's targeting Empress Aris?"

The man chuckled and shook his head, shaggy brown hair falling over his face. His shoulders moved up and down while his hands stayed tied with rope behind his back. "You think I'm afraid of you?" he muttered hoarsely. "A handful of amateurs trying to run an empire?"

"Amateur or not, I've got all night to make you purr, kitten," Chaz crooned, ice coating his words. A dagger appeared in his hand. I held in a sigh—I knew some things had to come by force, but I tried to save violence as a last resort.

Well, in my human half. My fox half sometimes got away from me.

"Do your worst," the cougar Shifter said simply. Then his tone darkened. "Trust me, I've seen it all."

He jerked his neck to move hair out of his eyes, and when he did, my attention snagged on a long white scar stretching from below his ear to across his throat.

"Where's that scar from?" I asked from the other side of the bars. Shifters didn't *have* scars. Our healing abilities left nothing behind when we were injured.

The prisoner met my eyes from across the cell. "Like I said, I'm not afraid of you," he rasped.

Fates, what was Drakorum *doing* to these people? I had a friend, a dragon Shifter who grew up there, who recently told us how brutal Kane Scarven, the Drakorum governor, and those who served him could be. He'd been vague about it, but I got the gist. Holding people captive—especially *powerful* people—and using them as weapons or spies, conducting experiments on them, keeping them from their families. And with the way this cougar Shifter was acting, I bet they had some *creative* ways of keeping their subjects from betraying them.

That was the kind of man I was facing. Scarven had made it abundantly clear he didn't want me in power. He didn't approve of my regime, of my changes, of my way of ruling. And he was willing to take action to have me removed.

I held the Shifter's stare for another second, then flicked my gaze to Chaz. "He's not going to talk. Let him go."

Chaz did a double take back at me. "Let him—*what?* He just tried to kill you. And he *did* kill that woman."

To my surprise, the prisoner flinched. "That was an accident," he growled.

My hand balled into a fist at my side at the mention of the innocent woman. Part of me screamed that she deserved retribution. That her killer should pay the price in blood.

But I didn't become the leader of the Sentinels by following a streak of vengeance. And I wasn't going to become empress by putting down everyone who defied me.

"We will let him go." I forced steadiness into my voice. "He'll go back to Drakorum with his tail between his legs and tell Scarven to stop sending his boys to do his dirty work. It's *weak*," I spat, reaching out and gripping the cell bars. "And I don't fear weakness, Shifter. Your governor can come after me himself."

I threw the wadded, bloody note from the arrow on the ground at his feet, then spun on my heels and left.

———

THE GILDED EDGES of the mirror in my vanity gleamed back at me as I ran a brush through my hair. Everything about this room screamed of wealth and indulgence. The porcelain basin in my wash room, the cotton towels that felt like clouds, the thin gold threads in my emerald comforter. Eight months, and I still wasn't used to it.

I often missed our little cottage in the woods. When my father had given up his throne, we made a home for ourselves outside the hustle and bustle of the capital. It was hard, yes, and more nights full of weariness and anxiety than comfort and contentment. But it was the only home I'd ever known. It was where Leo and I grew up, where we'd learned our magic—him with his Alchemy, his potions and spells, and me with my uncontrollable fox half.

It was where we mourned our father and watched our mother grow sick. It was where we spent days without eating or sleeping, where the cold and hunger of the winter crept in on two unsuspecting teenagers. It was where I dragged myself back, beaten and bruised by those who hated the Aris family and feared a young Shifter who couldn't get a handle on her magic.

It was where we learned to fight.

It was where we started the Sentinels. It was where we took back our power.

It was funny how here, at the highest possible position, with more resources and people and praise at my disposal than I'd ever had before, was when I sometimes felt the smallest.

I set my brush down and stared into the onyx eyes shining at me from the mirror, thoughts swirling behind them. Mysthelm and this trip, the engagement, the council, Scarven's continued attacks. The woman who died in my arms. How I hadn't been able to stop it.

Pressing my forehead to the cool marble of the vanity, I took a deep breath. Was I cut out for this? For all the good I'd hoped to do in this empire, people were still getting hurt. People were still angry and restless. Perhaps this was the fate of every ruler. You could never make everyone happy, could never force everyone to fall in line—not without becoming someone like Gayl.

My critics thought I was too passive. Too swayed by my feminine whims. Too placating and peaceful. I'd let the assassin go tonight—something no other ruler would have done. Maybe I'd come to regret that decision. Maybe I'd wake up in the middle of the night with a dagger in my chest. But giving that Shifter a taste of mercy would have more of an impact than punishment. If mercy made me *passive* or *weak*, then so be it.

Clarissa Aris, the weakest empress of the Veridian Empire.

I let out a half chuckle, half groan as I lifted my head from the vanity. A knock on my chamber door made me straighten, followed by a soft, "Are you awake, dear?"

I crossed over the cream rug in front of the fireplace and reached for the door. "It's late, Mother. What are you still doing up?" I asked when her petite frame appeared in the doorway.

Her fingers rubbed anxiously back and forth on the candleholder in her grasp. "I wanted to see how you were doing. I heard about what happened tonight."

I sighed. I tried to keep her away from as much of this as possible—it only made her worry more. "Of course you did. Who told you?"

"The maids know everything."

My mother would hear gossip from the birds if they could talk. She made friends everywhere she went. Or, rather, *connections*. Evadine Aris may have been a sweet, doting mother, but she was also a former empress. Cunning and sly and resourceful. Her little brunches with the wives of the council members weren't because she loved scones so much. She often came back with more secrets than even *I'd* known.

"I'm fine, Mother." I stepped to the side to let her in. She set her candle down on a nearby pedestal and enveloped me in a tight hug. "He missed his mark. Again. These assassins they keep sending are lousy," I mumbled into her shoulder.

She swatted me on the back. "This isn't funny, Clarissa."

"Well, if I don't find some sort of morbid humor in the situation, it's going to make me stick my head in the fireplace."

Mother *tsk*ed and pulled away. "I'm sorry you've been dealing with so much, sweet girl. But you're handling it beautifully. Your father would be so proud."

I quickly swallowed the lump that formed in my throat. "A woman died tonight. She was hit by an arrow meant for me. I...I couldn't do anything to help her."

"Oh, Clarissa," she said softly. Her lips curved downward, and a crease appeared at her brow. Taking my hand, she led me to the cushioned bench at the foot of my bed.

"You're not going to be able to help everyone. You don't have the power to stop all bad things from happening, as much as you wish you could. Branock was the same. His heart was so big, his desire to do right by his people so great, that he was often too hard on himself when things didn't go how he wanted. There will be bad days, bad weeks, bad *years*. But it's not your fault. That poor woman's death was *not* your fault."

I stared straight ahead into the fire, its embers beginning to fade. "She would still be alive if I hadn't been in that tavern tonight. The assassin was targeting *me*. I guess we were lucky there was only one casualty. That entire bar was full of innocent people, and I put them all at risk."

With a groan, I leaned forward and held my head in my hands. "Lark's going to be up to her ears in damage control. People were in such a panic, and it's only going to get worse once stories spread.

The assassin even left me a note. It said, 'You can't run.' How can I leave in the morning when this is such a mess?" I asked, glancing over at Mother.

"Maybe it's for the best that you're going," she said. "It could be a good thing. You could make a statement first thing in the morning about the attack to show how this hasn't shaken you. That the empire stands firm. Taking some time away from the situation might be good for you too. And it will allow your opposition to calm down and see things more rationally."

I scoffed. "It's Scarven, Mother. I don't think that Drakorum tyrant know the meaning of the word 'rational.'"

"He simply wants to get under your skin. He obviously heard you're planning to secure ties with Mysthelm and is trying to prevent that from happening. You know how elitist they get about anything outside of Veridia." She shook her head. "No, I think scaring you into canceling your trip is *exactly* what he wants. It would show he has power over you. His note says as much—he's trying to scare you."

My jaw clenched. "Wouldn't he love that."

"Then *show him*. You're not afraid of his savagery. Go strengthen this alliance and show the empire you're bringing us into a new age, one where we won't be beaten down by threats."

I hadn't thought about it that way. Perhaps she was right. As much as I hated the idea of leaving my people after tonight, I trusted Lark and my council—for the most part—to contain the hysteria. I trusted my guards to keep those I cared about safe. I just had to trust myself.

"Will you come with me?" I asked without thinking, taking her hand in mine. "I know we hadn't planned on it, and I know it's short notice, but..." *Sometimes a girl needs her mother.* "I could really use your help over there."

She smiled at me, eyes twinkling in the firelight. "Of course, Clarissa. I already have my bags packed."

I laughed. "That was presumptuous of you."

"Missing my daughter's engagement? I was ready to throw

myself onto that boat if you didn't ask me. Who else is going to put the fear of the Fates into that king?"

With a chuckle, I leaned over and rested my head against her shoulder. Her arm came behind my back and stroked my hair. Closing my eyes, I let my muscles relax. I hadn't realized how long it had been since I allowed myself to breathe. To take just one moment of peace with—

A log shifted in the fireplace, breaking in half with a resounding *snap*.

My chest tightened as I jolted, every nerve ending in my body going into high alert.

Panic gripped me. The phantom memory of bones crunching and poking through my skin made bile crawl up my throat. I turned away from my mother to hide my sudden shortness of breath, squeezing my eyes shut while I tried to calm my Shifter half.

A steady hand rubbed my back as her other hand held my upper arm. "Is it still happening?" she whispered.

I swallowed hard. My muscles shook from how tightly I'd clenched them. "Sometimes," I said on an exhale. "It's the sound. It —" I cut myself off, the words catching in my throat.

She moved her hand in circles across my back. "It's alright, sweet girl. You're safe. You have nothing to fear." Smoothing hair away from the nape of my neck, she gently coaxed me to face her again.

My mother knew about that night. She'd witnessed a couple of my panic attacks at the beginning and had always done her best to listen or give me space.

Eight months ago, the former emperor Theodore Gayl tried to kill me.

He knew I was his predecessor's daughter and the rightful heir to the throne. He knew I'd been working for *years* to bring him down. And he'd wanted to teach us a lesson.

It felt like a veil had been thrown over my mind every time I thought back to that night in those darkened chambers. How my friends Horace and Lark had tried to fight him after finding out he was the one to cast the sleeping curse that ravaged our empire. How he'd been siphoning magic from *thousands* of Veridians who had fallen into the frozen sleep, using their power to bolster his own.

We'd attacked him in a moment of distraction.

Horace died. Protecting *me*.

Lark and I were clueless to the extent of Gayl's power. He was so much stronger than we'd ever anticipated. We were idiots to think we could go up against him with the force of all those people's stored magic behind him.

He'd retaliated without a second thought.

I still heard the first crack ringing through my ears in my dreams.

Bones breaking. One by one. With a flick of his hand, he snapped the bones in mine and Lark's bodies, over and over. She, thankfully, passed out after the first few, and he ceased punishing her. She didn't remember the agonizing pain. She didn't remember listening to the sound of our bodies crumbling.

But my Shifter half was strong. My healing abilities didn't allow me the blessed reprieve of unconsciousness. And Gayl had a personal vendetta. I remembered every single one of the ninety-eight bones he broke. I could feel each snap, each rupture, each stab of pain. I heard Lark's initial cries and the terror that swept through me when she went silent.

It was the only time in my life I'd cursed my magic and how quickly it healed me. The bones repaired themselves *too* fast—they hadn't set right, and the healers had to go in and break them again to set them before my powers came into effect.

I remembered wishing for death. I remembered the pain being so blinding, but my mind wouldn't go black. It made me watch and feel and hear every excruciating moment. And when that ended, I remembered the guilt. Guilt that my best friend had been so close to never waking again, all because of her proximity to me. Lark's life forever changed that day. Now she was confined to a wheelchair, her body unable to function the way it once could.

"I just want it to go away," I said to my mother. "I keep thinking time will pass, and it won't be as bad. But I—I'm afraid it'll never stop. I'll never be able to get away from it."

She wrapped her arms around me and pulled me into her, like she would when I was a child. I missed the days when my world was so small that her embrace would make all the bad things in life go away.

"It takes time to heal," she murmured. "Maybe not physically, but in here"—she touched my temple—"and in here." Her hand that reached around my midsection landed on my heart, patting it softly. "You don't have to hide these moments from me. Do you want to talk about—"

"No," I said quickly, clearing my throat and pulling away. "I'm fine. It always fades. I just—I just need some quiet." When her shoulders sagged at my rushed tone, I offered her a small smile. "We have a long few days of travel coming, Mother. I don't want us to be too tired."

And the Fates only knew I didn't need to dwell on that night any longer. I couldn't give voice to this weakness, to the deep, unending fear and guilt. To how powerless I was against it. If I wasn't even strong enough to push past this, how could I be expected to lead an entire people through hardships? How could I ask them to put their faith in me as their empress when I was a prisoner to my own past?

My mother's gaze searched mine for a moment, but she didn't push. With a nod, she rose from the cushioned bench and kissed the top of my head. "Get some rest, dear," she said as she leaned away and walked to the chamber door.

"I love you," I called after her retreating figure. I'd learned long ago to take every opportunity to tell those closest to you how much you cared about them.

You never knew when it would be the last.

9

CLARISSA

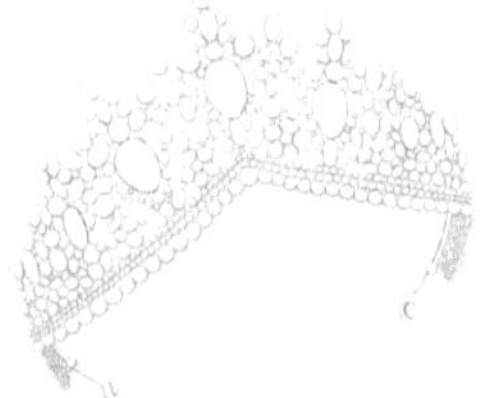

I gazed over the waters of the Avonige Ocean from the stern of the ship. We'd left my empire behind six days ago to set sail for Mysthelm, and watching the retreating shores of the only land I'd ever known was like saying goodbye to a part of me, especially since I had no clue what to expect in the new kingdom.

I'd felt it the moment we crossed out of Veridia's borders. Magic only existed within the empire, and once you left the boundaries, it disappeared. It was as if my magic was suffocated and buried deep in a locked box inside me, where I could never access it again. My fox half wouldn't so much as stir. It was the most helpless, most vulnerable sensation I'd ever felt. Like someone had shoved an arm through my spirit and clamped a hand around it, stifling its wild nature. Silencing my magic. Losing a piece of myself made me jittery and anxious, defenseless against anything that might seek me harm.

It affected everyone around me. The small Veridian crew, my guards, and my mother could all feel it. The hole where our powers once rested, the quiet that used to be thriving magic. A sensation you couldn't quite place that made you think something vital was *missing*.

Even now, six days later, it was like I couldn't draw a full breath. I didn't know how I was going to make it four more *weeks* like this.

Suffice it to say, we were a fun group to be around right now.

I held up a hand to block the sun as it came from behind a cloud, its rays sparkling across the blue waters. Not many people in the last three hundred years since the War of Beginnings had traveled this far—or left Veridian borders at all. Before the war, relations between Mysthelm and the Veridian Empire were fairly amicable, but as it so often does, the idea of power corrupted everything it touched.

The Fates—the closest thing we had to deities—had long ago imbued the small, uninhabited island in the center of our empire with their power. Power that later translated into the six kinds of magic gifted to Veridians: spell casting, light bending, shadow wielding, illusions of the mind, traveling between space, and shifting into an animal form.

The three Fates issued a prophecy to us and to Mysthelm: whoever could conquer this land would be given its magic.

And so, the War of Beginnings was born. A brutal war that spanned across both our lands and affected hundreds of thousands of people. All because everyone wanted what the Fates had to offer: a magic our kind hadn't seen or heard of in our entire existence.

The Veridian Empire won, leading to our provinces each receiving a portion of the magic, giving us our unique magical abilities. We closed ourselves off from the rest of the world and, as far as I knew, had no contact with Mysthelm in centuries.

We hadn't exactly parted on friendly terms. I wanted to change that. Apparently King Galen Grimaldi did too. Although he sailed way past *friends* and straight to *wife*.

"How are you doing?" my mother asked from behind me. She approached in her light blue cotton dress that fluttered in the breeze. Her gray-and-blonde hair was in a bun at the top of her head, a pair of bifocals resting on the bridge of her nose.

"Fine," I said absently. "Ready to be on solid ground again."

She brushed my hair back. "You should wear a hat. Something

to cover your skin before it burns. I can already feel this heat getting to me."

She wasn't wrong. As we'd traveled farther south, the air had grown denser, and sweat stuck to the back of my neck even in my sleep. Our summers in the capital were hot, but it was a dry heat—not this wet, heavy warmth that made every breath feel like drowning.

"Excuse me, Your Grace," a crew member said as he dipped his head toward my mother, then me. "Your Majesty, look out the front of the ship."

He beckoned us forward, and I exchanged a look with Mother before shrugging and following him across the wooden planks, around the captain's quarters in the center of the quarter deck, and to the bow.

"Welcome to Mysthelm," he said, eyes fixed to a spot beyond the waters. Sure enough, looming ahead was a massive stretch of tan land.

We had made it.

I could barely make out tiny groupings of tall, skinny trees with what looked like drooping leaves dotting the landscape. They reminded me of palm trees I'd seen in drawings of the beaches in Iluze. When I squinted, I saw—

Something slammed into the bottom of the ship, making it rock precariously. I grabbed on to Mother with one hand and the railing with my other. Around us, the crew jerked to attention.

"What was that?" I asked the nearest man.

"We're not sure, Your Majesty. The lookout hasn't reported any obstructions in our path."

Another thud echoed around us, coming from beneath this time. The waves surrounding the ship were no longer rippling and peaceful but choppy and wild. The vessel rocked hard enough that Mother and I had to grip the railing with both hands to avoid toppling over.

Crewmembers shouted behind us as they tried to locate the

source of the attack. Barks of commands and creaking of wood beneath feet met my ears, but my focus was on something else.

I leaned forward over the rail, my lips parting at what I saw on the surface. "Are those...are those *fish*?"

Hundreds of little bubbles appeared in the water, followed by multicolored, scaly bodies. Some as small as my little finger, others as big as my arm, spread out around the front of the boat and beyond.

All of them, dead.

Sucking in a breath, I raced over to the left side of the ship. I was met with the same sight: dozens and *dozens* of sea creatures had floated to the surface, unmoving, save for the swaying of the water that carried them along. As the ship moved forward, I heard something clunk against wood. A few seconds later, a massive splash came from the back of the ship.

My mother and I both scurried toward the sound and found the body of an enormous beast bobbing above the waves. Mother gasped. I stepped closer, taking in its length, easily sixty feet long. Its underbelly was dark gray, rough, and thick, with grooves running along the side. It remained motionless, even as the bodies of other sea creatures bumped into its protruding fins.

A *whale*.

I'd never seen one in person before—besides the time Leo and I had raced to the southern coast of Veridia City as teenagers, and I thought I'd glimpsed one from a distance jumping out of the water. What could have possibly killed one of these magnificent beasts? And was it after us next?

"We have to get to shore. *Now*," I commanded, spinning on my heels to find the captain. Before I could take another step, something large and white landed at my feet with a resounding crash. Feathers flew into the air, and it took all of my willpower to not let out a screech.

Another one fell into the ocean behind me, sending up a spray of salt water.

I cursed. What was *happening*?

Shadows spilled over the deck, and I frantically looked to the sky, expecting to see a torrent of dead birds preparing to drop on our heads.

No birds. But what greeted me still sent chills down my spine. I grabbed my mother, pushing her toward the steps that would take her below deck.

"You have to get under cover before this storm hits," I said when she tried to protest.

In what seemed like a single second, the sky had gone from bright blue and sunny to an angry sea of dark clouds. The waves picked up speed, rolling and crashing into the side of the ship, dousing us with drops of water. Seaweed and rocks had broken off from beneath the surface and now swirled with the dead creatures, their movements morbidly graceful as they danced and weaved in the storm.

Booms of thunder rang out. The ship jostled unsteadily, and men scrambled above the deck to man their stations. The captain ran forward when he saw me. "Your Majesty, you need to move below before you get—"

Another peal of thunder sounded, and the skies opened, sending blankets of cold rain over us.

"—wet," he finished with a splutter.

I gritted my teeth. "Just get us to shore!" I shouted over the cacophony of noise. "Preferably *not* dead."

I was already soaked to the bone, my clothes clinging to me and my hair tangled around my neck. My shoes squelched as I plodded over the wood planks.

What had we gotten ourselves into?

Anxiety and irritation swelled in my gut as I glanced at the enigma out in the waters. All those dead creatures, this sudden storm, right as we reached the kingdom...something wasn't right.

I *hated* not having answers. I hated not knowing what awaited us on those distant shores.

And I hated being wet.

Welcome to Mysthelm, indeed.

IO

THORNE

Leaning against my carriage, I crossed one ankle over the other and watched the oncoming vessel as it pulled into the dock. Green and gold sails billowed from the mast, with holes poking through the fabric. It wasn't a surprise to see they were battered, considering the size of the storm that had blown through the shores of the North Territory.

Such a strong tempest was unusual for the heart of summer. We'd seen it forming out on the horizon, and before we knew it, it gained in speed and ferocity and practically tore the Port of North Pine apart. Now we had to welcome the empress and her crew with barely enough space to bring their ship in.

I'd gathered as many workers as I could to clear the path and get the worst of the wreckage out of the way in the hours since, but, of course, Galen was nowhere to be found.

This storm *shouldn't* have left the port in shambles. Our structures should've been sound enough to survive. The fishermen and dock workers here had been begging the crown for support to rebuild the old foundations, and now I saw why.

Galen had been putting off responding to their requests, either because he hadn't even *seen* them or had let them get lost in his stacks of reports. My hands clenched involuntarily at my sides.

74

How long would these people have to spend repairing the docks, something that should have been fixed long ago?

Shaking off my mounting annoyance with a sigh, I uncrossed my legs and stood straighter. Now that the Veridian ship was closer, I could see the hull was worse for wear. Barnacles and seaweed were plastered to the front, but considering they'd been on a multi-day journey, some weathering and damage were bound to happen on the open sea.

That wasn't what caught my eye.

Streaks of dark red painted the wood, as if blood had been smeared across its length.

I snapped to attention and strode from the carriage to the steps of the dock, where crewmembers were guiding the ship in. Galen was going to be *furious* if something happened to his would-be fiancée.

I was so focused on reaching the Veridian ship that I didn't see a small group of servants crossing my path. I bumped into one of the maids before coming to my senses.

"Oh! I'm so sorry, Your Grace, I didn't see—"

"No, no, it's completely my fault," I said to the young woman, gripping her hands to steady her. "Did I hurt you?"

A blush crept up her cheeks as her eyelashes fluttered under my gaze. She *was* rather attractive. The kind of woman I would have been drawn to in the old days with Galen. Shoulder-length brown hair tied into a loose braid, a long, slender neck, light eyes hidden behind thick lashes. I flashed her a smile, and the blush deepened.

"Of course not, Your Grace. I'm perfectly fine." She slipped into a curtsy and gave me a coy grin as I removed my hands. Once upon a time, I would have forsaken my responsibilities and followed her back to whatever household she served. I would have snuck her away for the night to go dancing in the taverns. I would have forgotten her name by the morning as my father berated me over my raging hangover.

But those days were behind me.

I raised her hand and placed a chaste kiss on her knuckles. "Have a good day," I said, allowing her and the others to pass. My eyes lingered on her curves before making my way to the ship once more.

Stepping onto the raised platform, I saw deckhands lowering the gangway, followed by several figures descending from the main deck of the ship. First came two Veridian guards wearing silver uniforms with swords strapped to their waists. Then an elderly female with graying hair held together in a bun. She looked tired but smiled at a deckhand as he helped her down the gangway.

I heard the next person before I saw her.

"Emperor's tits, I don't need your help, Captain—I got wet, not stabbed. Thank you, though," the voice said right as a mass of drenched blonde hair appeared from the deck. The sound would have been melodic, if it wasn't laced with irritation.

She turned her head forward, her eyes drinking in the sight like a predator assessing its surroundings. Cunning, wary, powerful.

And very pissed-off.

She stormed down the path, water dripping from her with every step. Against my better judgment, my lips twitched into a grin.

That was my first mistake.

Those dark eyes didn't miss a beat. They landed on me with precision, and she stalked across the dock toward me.

"Is something funny?" she asked, eyebrow raised.

I cleared my throat. "Not at all, ma'am. Just wondering why you chose to take a swim before arriving."

And *that* was my second.

Her mouth shut with a snap, and I could've sworn her eyes changed color with the way they heated in anger at my words.

I wasn't sure what made me say it. Even as wet as a feral cat, this woman was beautiful. Beautiful things often had a way of taking control of my lips before my mind could catch up. Most women found it charming. Obviously not this one.

"You'll have to understand, sir, if I'm not in a particularly humorous mood at the moment." She took another step toward me, her voice cold and sharp like a knife. "Perhaps you wouldn't be, either, if you'd been caught in some freak thunderstorm and almost decapitated by fowl."

I blinked. "A foul...what?"

"Not foul, *fowl*. Literal birds. Falling from the sky."

My mouth opened and closed. "I'm still not following."

A growl rumbled from her throat as she swung her hair over her shoulder, exposing how wet the thin fabric at her chest was. My stomach tightened as I tore my gaze back to her face.

"Never mind. I'm looking for Lord Thorne Reaux. The correspondence team said he'd be escorting me to the palace on King Grimaldi's behalf."

This was Clarissa Aris, Empress of the Veridian Empire? My best friend's future wife? The woman I'd insulted the *second* she stepped onto Mysthelm soil?

"Well," I said, giving her a wry smile. "You're in luck, Empress."

Her stare raked over me, and I felt that same clenching in my gut. "Of *course*, you're him."

"At your service."

Straightening, she shook out her shoulders, sending water splattering to the ground. How she still managed to look dignified while her blonde hair sopped down her back and her wet clothes smelled like salt, I would never understand.

"Clarissa, let's get you a towel before you catch a cold," said the older woman I'd seen walking off the boat. She approached and placed a hand on Clarissa's elbow. I could tell the resemblance immediately—the same mouth, same nose, same freckles on the cheeks.

"Catch a cold? Mother, it's boiling out here." The empress ran a hand down her wet arms with a grimace. "I'm not sure if most of this is water or sweat at this point."

I pinched my lips together to hide a smirk. She was a firecracker. A bright, golden firecracker. "Hello, Your Grace," I said to her mother, giving a polite bow. "I hope you had a pleasant journey?"

"Quite the gentleman now, I see. She gets a bow, and I got a joke. And not a particularly funny one," Clarissa snapped at me before her mother could reply.

"Would you like me to bow for you, Empress?" The words left my mouth unbidden. I waited for her sneer of dismissal, but evidently, my question was a challenge. Heat burrowed under my skin as she stared me down and uttered a single word.

"Yes."

I licked my lips and shot her mother a wink, whose head cocked in curiosity. Placing one hand behind my back, I bent low, my eyes skating over Clarissa's tight pants that hugged the curves of her legs. I reached out my other hand to grab hers and skimmed my lips across her knuckles.

"Is this acceptable, Your Majesty?" I murmured, my heart already thudding at the anger rolling from her in waves.

This was far too much fun.

And she's your best friend's fiancée.

I swallowed and released her hand, spine stiffening and pulling back into an upright position.

Her mother's lips twitched. "Why, this one is charming," she said with a laugh.

"Don't encourage him."

"What's your name, young man?" her mother asked.

"Lord Thorne Reaux. I'm in charge of bringing Her Majesty and those accompanying her to King Grimaldi's palace."

"It's a pleasure to meet you, Lord Reaux." She held out a hand for me to shake. "My name is Evadine Aris, but you may call me Eva."

I took her hand. "The pleasure is all mine, ma'am."

When I glanced at Clarissa, she pursed her lips. "And you may call *me* Empress Aris."

I stifled a chuckle. Galen was going to have his hands full. "Can I ask what happened on the boat? Why your mother remains dry, but you seem to have..." I trailed off, smart enough not to insult her again. Jokingly or not.

"Because I made her go below deck when the storm hit."

"Why didn't you go?"

"I wasn't going to leave the others in the middle of danger."

My smile faltered. "You—you stayed with them?"

"Of course. They're my men."

This empress was not what I expected. The leader of an entire empire, who probably had servants who would throw themselves on top of her to keep her covered if she commanded, yet she stood before me without a single inch of dry space on her body.

"I'm sorry you had such bad weather," I said.

Evadine began wringing out Clarissa's clothes, much to the empress's chagrin. "Yes, well, I'm more concerned about the spontaneous burst of dead sea life we had to wade through," Clarissa muttered.

I froze. "What did you just say?"

She noticed my change in demeanor. Her eyes locked on my hands, which had formed into balls at my sides. I unclenched them and tried to ease my tense posture, but she was quick and observant, nothing escaping her gaze. "Hordes of fish and other creatures showed up dead all around our ship, just beyond *your* borders. There was no other threat we could see. Have you ever seen anything like that?"

Not again.

I let out a noncommittal hum. "How strange. No, can't say that I have."

She took a step closer. "Do you know how it could have happened?"

I chose my words carefully. "I have no idea, but again, I'm sorry you had to go through that."

Her eyes narrowed. "Don't you think someone should look into it? Make sure it can't happen again? Or worse, make it to land and harm people?"

She'd been here all of five minutes, and she was already taking charge. The worst part was, she was right. But what she didn't know was there was nothing either of us could do about it.

I nodded. "Of course. I'll bring it up to His Majesty at once." Clarissa opened her mouth to speak again, but I swiftly looped her mother's arm through mine and changed the subject. "Why don't I help you two to my carriage and have your things delivered to the palace? I'm sure you'd like to rest."

"What I'd *like* is for someone to answer my questions," Clarissa countered.

Good luck being married to Galen, then.

"My dear, the young man has already told us he doesn't have your answers," Evadine said, patting my hand. "You've had a rough few hours—let's get you some dry clothes and a bath, yes?"

"A wise woman," I agreed.

To my surprise, Clarissa scoffed. "Careful, *Lord* Reaux. My bark may be bad, but her bite is worse."

And with that, she strode ahead of me toward my carriage, her shoulders straight and head high.

Evadine Aris shot me a smile. "This is going to be fun."

II

CLARISSA

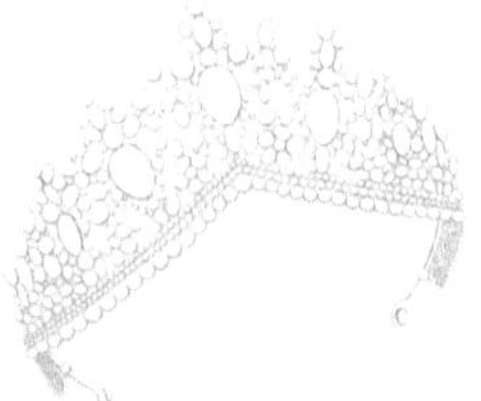

The bumpy carriage ride was made even more intolerable by the fact that my clothes were still soaked, and the water had combined with sweat to create a layer of brine on my skin. The roads nearest the port were the worst. The storm had blown tree limbs and other debris onto the path.

Every jostle, dip, and turn made my knees bump against Lord Reaux's across from me in the enclosed space of the carriage. I tried angling my body to stay out of his personal bubble—the *polite* thing to do—but he simply sat there, his long, solid legs stretched wide and proud. How very *masculine*. Not even bothering to give me more room. Every time I caught his eyes and narrowed mine, he seemed to be on the verge of smirking.

My mother was none the wiser to this silent war between him and myself. Her elbow was propped delicately on the carriage window as she gazed outside.

I took a deep breath and glanced out the other window to my left, willing myself to let go of the foul mood the trip had put me in. For now, I wanted to take in these first moments in the new land.

Evidence of the storm faded as we traveled farther inland. Unlike the forests of Veridia City, with their massive trunks and broad-leaved trees that spread out above you and blocked out the sun, the trees here were much thinner. Palm trees, I knew they were called. Similar to ones I'd seen in portraits of Iluze, the most tropical province of the empire. Tall and gangly, with bright green leaves that fanned from the top of the trunks and blew in the breeze.

The road we were on was elevated, and as the carriage continued rolling along, I looked out the window behind us to see the shoreline growing more and more distant. Blue and white waves lapped against the tan sand near the port, and seagulls' calls echoed through the carriage doors. On the ground near the path were patches of blooming flowers—it was difficult to focus on them at our swift pace, but I caught glimpses of tall blue larkspur mixed with vibrant violets and golden daffodils.

This place was undeniably beautiful. And *hot*. I supposed that explained Lord Reaux's attire. I was used to guards and court members in the capital wearing their usual heavy silver uniforms or stuffy cloaks that spoke of wealth and grandeur. But Thorne Reaux was casually dressed in loose brown pants rolled once at the ankles and a thin white shirt with the first couple of buttons undone at the top, exposing tan skin and a smattering of dark hair at his chest that matched the brown locks flowing to his shoulders.

I had to admit, the long hair suited him.

My eyes moved down and rested on a gold chain hanging around his neck, bearing what looked like some kind of flower dangling at the end.

You're staring at his chest.

Emperor's tits. I ripped my gaze from him and back to the window, but not before I caught his lips twitching upward.

"How much longer till we reach the palace?" I asked, a bit sharper than I intended.

"Eager to meet your future husband?" Lord Reaux responded lightheartedly. Fates, this man either had no sense of self-preservation or was entirely too confident. I'd wager the latter, given how

I'd seen his hands all over that maid at the port before I stepped off the ship. It shouldn't surprise me that he'd started openly flirting with me not five seconds later.

"As enjoyable as your company has been, Lord Reaux, I find I'm ready for a change of scenery," I said.

He chuckled, which grated on my nerves even more. "Lord Reaux was my father. Just call me Thorne."

"Appropriate." I shot him a saccharine smile. *Since you seem intent on being one in my side.*

"We're nearly there," Thorne answered. "I'm not sure how much the two of you know of our kingdom, but we're split into four territories. The one we're in now is the northern, then farther south is the Mid Territory, and below that is the southern one. To our east is the Island Territory, the only part not connected to the mainland. We sometimes refer to the territories by the name of the current regent family in each one."

"Regent family?" I asked.

"Families in charge of a specific territory. A couple of ranks below the king but still incredibly powerful. Regents have to answer to the crown, although they can also make decisions for their territory if the king is found unfit. There's Zeloria out on the island, Penworth to the far south, and Silenus right below us."

"And what about this territory?" I asked, although I had a feeling I knew the answer. "Who's the regent family here?"

He smiled, and the twisting in my stomach at those ridiculously perfect teeth made me want to punch something. "Mine is."

The carriage came to a halt. A few seconds later, there was a tap at the door before it opened. Thorne descended first, then helped my mother climb down the steps. I paused when my eyes hit the bright sunlight to take in the sight.

I hadn't known what to expect when coming to this new kingdom. My only frame of reference was the palace in Veridia City, with its multiple tall, gilded spires raised like a beacon. Our dark stone walls and rich rugs and tapestries lining the corridors came with an air of formality I'd never thought twice about—not until seeing the Mysthelm palace.

I couldn't explain it, but it had the same *feeling* as Thorne. Casual and sun-kissed but majestic at the same time.

The carriage stopped at the end of a road opening to an enormous lawn of swaying green grass and tall palm trees. On the opposite end of the lawn stood the palace on a raised incline. It was made of granite, a stunning shade of cream that almost glowed in the sun. Two sets of stairs extended from either side of the entrance, leading to matching granite columns that formed an open-aired walkway to the front doors.

From the distance, I could see men and women traipsing around the lawn and giant stairs, none of whom wore the gaudy gowns and robes I was used to seeing at our palace. The men were dressed in a similar fashion to Thorne, and many of the women wore shirts that reached their midriff and linen pants or skirts that billowed loosely in the humid, tropical air. Bands and bands of bracelets and other jewelry lined their arms, ankles, and necks, glinting like freshly shined metal.

"This way, Empress," Thorne said, his deep voice rolling over me and breaking me from my observations.

He held out his hand, and I only hesitated for a split second before I took it. His rough, callused skin pressed into mine, his thumb briefly skating across my knuckles as he helped me down. When he released his grip, I felt the lingering ghost of his skin against mine. I squeezed my hand shut to banish the feeling and followed him as he and a couple of guards escorted Mother and me over the sandy pathway and up the granite staircase.

On instinct, I reached out to take my mother's arm as the steps grew steeper, and to my surprise, Thorne did the same.

"By the Fates, I'm not *dead,* you two," Mother said, her words trailing into a laugh. "I can walk up a set of stairs."

She hated it when I coddled her. But after watching her waste away for almost sixteen years in a bed, it was hard not to feel an innate sense of protection around her.

Thorne chuckled but still kept my mother's arm tucked into his. "Then humor me, for if *my* mother caught wind of my terrible manners, she'd—"

"What would I do?" a new, clipped voice said from around the corner at the top of the stairs.

As I took the last couple of steps, I saw a woman who appeared to be in her late sixties waiting for us, her lips quirked into a smile. The sight was at odds with her stern features, her sharp jaw, arched eyebrows, and dark brown hair streaked with gray coiled into a tight bun atop her head. Her green dress reminded me of the clothing the wealthy councilmember's wives back in Veridia City would wear.

Thorne straightened at her voice, then smiled back at her. "I didn't expect to see you here, Mother." Gesturing to the woman, he said, "This is Lady Azura Reaux. My mother."

"His Majesty invited me to come welcome our new guests. I couldn't very well miss this momentous day," the woman, Azura, said. Her eyes shifted to me, and I could see the similarity to Thorne—they had the same clear, light blue gaze. She tilted her head, that tight smile still plastered across her lips.

Something about it made my hackles rise.

But I couldn't dwell on the feeling long before footsteps reached my ears, coming from behind Thorne's mother.

The most beautiful man I'd ever seen stepped into view.

Bright hazel eyes scanned the scene, a dimple appearing on golden-brown skin when he smiled at us. He ran his gloved fingers through short, wavy brown hair, stretching the sleeves of his gray button-down shirt. With his high cheekbones, perfectly shaven face, and chiseled features, he may as well have been carved from stone.

"You must be Empress Aris," he said, his voice smooth as he held a gloved hand out to me.

I looked up at the stranger and smiled politely. "Clarissa is fine. And you are...?"

His grin widened. "Oh, forgive me. My name is Galen. Galen Grimaldi."

I schooled my face to mask my sudden surprise. This was the *king*? He was...not what I expected. Emperor Gayl had always paraded around in his royal apparel, his thick, dark cloak making him seem all the more ominous. Not to mention the guards and advisors who flocked at his heels.

This man...he looked rather like Thorne, actually. Carefree and casual, with his linen pants and loose shirt. And not a guard in sight.

My mother glanced at me and raised an eyebrow. So, this was my future husband.

Not bad.

For an arranged marriage, at least.

12

CLARISSA

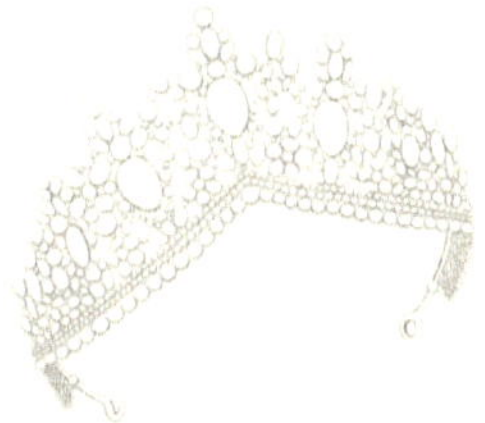

"I had no idea we'd be meeting you so soon, Your Majesty. I haven't had a chance to recover from the journey," I said quickly, my appalling scent of salt and sweat hitting me in full force.

"Nonsense, you look beautiful. And please, none of that 'Your Majesty' here. I'm just Galen." He turned to my side. "And this must be your mother?"

Mother offered him her hand. "Evadine Aris."

"I heard you would be joining us. I'm so glad you both could make it." Galen held out his arm for me to take. I felt Thorne's icy blue stare on us. For some reason, his body tensed when I wrapped my hand around the sleeve of Galen's forearm before relaxing once more.

"I'll show you to your rooms, and we can meet again for dinner tonight to go over details of the tour. How does that sound?" Galen asked, breaking my stare from Thorne.

"Wonderful. Thank you, Galen," I said as we made our way through the entrance, unable to stop myself from gazing at the high granite columns that lined the walkway. "Your home is beautiful. I've never seen anything like it."

A pair of guards held open the grand double doors for us. A

sweet floral scent wafted over me as we strolled beneath the archway adorned with white wisteria. The beautiful vines cascaded over the frame and swung in the summer breeze.

I was taken aback by how *bright* everything here was—this wing of the palace was three or four stories tall, with a ceiling made entirely of glass above us. Natural sunlight shone down on the corridors, a refreshing change from the darkness of my own palace.

"I'm glad you like it. Many generations of Grimalidis have ruled here," he said, his tone conversational. As if we were old friends and not two strangers who just met a few seconds ago. We passed a ballroom, a library, and several other chambers while he rattled off various facts about the different wings.

"And this," he remarked as we came upon a set of winding stairs, "leads to the Orion Observatory. Named after my father. Perhaps we can go view it sometime."

"I was sorry to learn about him," I cut in. "Your father, I mean. From what I understand, his death was unexpected."

He raised a dark eyebrow at me. "Is that what they've told you?"

I faltered. Come to think of it, nobody on the council had actually said *how* the late King Orion Grimaldi passed at the end of the previous year, just that Mysthelm had reached out about urgent matters.

"I assumed, since your initial contact with us was so... unprecedented."

For some reason, my words made him uneasy. He rubbed at the back of his neck with his other gloved hand as we proceeded down another hallway.

"Ah, well...his death changed things. But, no, it wasn't unexpected. My father had been sick for some time with a lung disease he couldn't seem to shake. It finally claimed his life last fall."

"I'm so sorry," I said again. "I know that isn't easy. I lost my father at a young age." I stole a glance back at my mother, who was conversing with Thorne behind us. "Is your moth—"

"Here we are," he said abruptly, slathering on a dazzling smile as he brandished an arm toward a pair of large wooden doors at the end of the corridor. "Your chambers. You and your mother have separate suites, but they're adjoined in the center. Your bags have already been brought in, and your lady's maids will help you prepare for dinner this evening."

He'd barely gotten the words out before he was already retreating down the hall. My brow furrowed from the whiplash of the last few moments, but I shook it off. "Thank you," I called out, catching Galen's friendly wave, Lady Reaux's cold smile, and Thorne's lingering gaze.

When they were out of earshot, I leaned toward Mother and murmured, "Do they seem...*off* to you?"

"I wouldn't trust these people further than I can throw them," she said, turning the gold handle to her door and pushing it open. "But they certainly know how to impress."

My mouth fell open. The room was like something out of a fairytale. Floor-to-ceiling windows took up the entire wall across from us and faced the open gardens, giving us a breathtaking view of the sloping fields of flowers and fountains. Ornate portraits of landscapes hung from the cream walls, and lush, multi-colored rugs lined the floor. Against the wall to the right rested a bed that could fit five people. A huge wooden canopy towered above it, with sheer curtains of sky blue twisted around the four-poster frame.

I couldn't stop myself from skipping over to the adjoining door like a giddy schoolgirl. Pulling it open, I was met with an almost identical room, with undertones of blush instead of blue. And by the door to what I assumed was a bathing chamber stood a wide rack *full* of gowns.

I may have been the leader of a treasonous rebellion who grew up on scraps and daggers and secrets, but, Fates, did I love pretty things.

Rushing to the opposite side, I ran my fingers along the myriad of fabrics. Sheer tulle, rough beads, smooth silk, and soft velvet. So many colors and patterns, from a low-cut, jeweled dress as dark as midnight, to a floor-length ball gown of gold and white.

"Are these mine?" I asked out loud, taking in the rack with awe.

"Yes, Your Majesty," a voice responded. "For the tour."

I jumped backward and clutched my chest. "And who are you?" I asked the two women who had appeared soundlessly at the adjoining door behind me.

"Sorry to frighten you, ma'am," the dark-haired one on the left said. "We're your lady's maids. I'm Katrine." She curtsied, holding out her white skirt. When she rose again, kind brown eyes looked back at me, a hesitant smile on her umber features. She looked rather young, maybe eighteen or nineteen years old, with a sort of vibrant innocence that made my chest constrict. I had the sudden urge to tuck this young woman under my wing and shield her from the terrors of this world.

"And I'm Devora," the other woman said. She inclined her head in respect, red waves like a sunrise cascading down her broad shoulder and swishing above her wide hips. Bright blue-green eyes met mine. She was closer to my age, perhaps her mid-twenties, if I had to guess. Her stare was sharp and knowing behind black-rimmed glasses, one side of her thick, red lips quirking up at the end.

"We're here for anything you may need, anything at all," Katrine rushed out. "And we'll be accompanying you on your tour of the kingdom to make sure your journey goes smoothly. You won't need to so much as lift a *finger*, Your Majesty."

I shared a glance with my mother over their shoulders. Her hand was at her mouth to hide a chuckle.

"That's...great," I said to the two women, forcing a smile. "You're very kind. But I promise, I don't need—"

"Oh, it's not a problem, Your Majesty." Katrine beamed. "It's an honor to serve you. I've been looking forward to this for *weeks*. The Empress of the Veridian Empire, right here in our palace!" The words were a squeal, and my smile slipped into a wince. She flew forward and began scrolling through the racks of dresses. "You can wear any of these you'd like to dinner with the king tonight. He had a selection picked for you—I even chose some of them myself."

Out of the corner of my eye, I saw Devora, the other maid, flash me a quick smirk before saying, "Katrine, let her settle into the room first, yes?"

Katrine's cheeks darkened. "Yes, yes, you're right—I apologize, Your Majesty. We'll be back soon to help you get ready for dinner. If you need anything, please—"

"I'll let you know, I promise," I assured her. "And please, girls, call me Rissa."

When Katrine turned to exit, I mouthed *"Thank you,"* to Devora, who merely tipped her head in response and shot me a quick wink.

The door shut with a click. Mother chuckled. "Well, they are going to be a handful, aren't they?"

I let out a sigh and faced her, walking to where she stood at the door frame separating our rooms. "We'll deal with that later. First thing's first," I started, kissing her once on the cheek before reaching to shut the door between us. "We're both in *desperate* need of baths."

13

CLARISSA

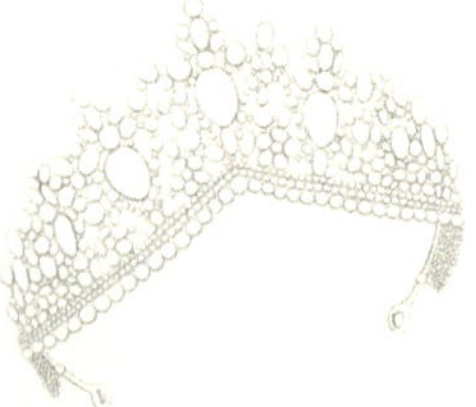

Two guards followed Mother and me as we entered the dining hall on the first floor, facing the ocean to the north. Instead of an outer wall, there was a set of open rolling doors, exposing an outdoor patio and letting in the humid night air. From the palace's elevated position, I could nearly make out the Avonige Ocean a few miles north beneath the clear, bright moon that set the land aglow.

Long banquet tables stood inside the room, as well as one on the attached patio. Galen and Thorne were already seated outside, engaged in a whispered but heated conversation.

I exchanged a look with Mother as we silently made our way over. I hadn't been able to get a good read on the two of them yet. One moment they were easy-going; the next they were elusive and intense. Thorne's back was to me, but I could see him clutching his glass of water, his forearms tight and knuckles white.

"...understand why you refuse to tell her," I caught him saying once we were within earshot.

Galen's light brown eyes immediately found mine behind Thorne. The crease in his brow disappeared as he swallowed, replaced with that cheery smile from before. One I was beginning to think wasn't as sincere as he wanted us to believe.

All three of them—him, Lady Reaux, and Galen—had given me a strange feeling, like something nagging in the back of my mind. But I couldn't pinpoint *why*. I'd spent mere *minutes* with these people—I had no reason to be suspicious of them, no reason to assume the worst. That was always Leo's first inclination, but I tried to enter scenarios and relationships with an open mind. Cautious yet optimistic.

I was probably just uneasy because I no longer had my magic. That pit in my stomach, that clenching sensation like a fist squeezing my gut, hadn't gone away since the moment we left Veridian borders. I'd never realized how much I relied on my fox half.

"Clarissa, Evadine, you both look lovely!" Galen stood and extended a gloved hand to the chair beside him. We took our seats right as two new men emerged from the side door, both dressed in formal pants and button-down shirts.

Galen greeted them. "Ah, yes. May I introduce you to Lord Sadim and Lord Davies, two members of my council." The two newcomers bowed, then pulled out their chairs at the other end of the table. "And, of course, you already know Lord Reaux."

Thorne's stare landed on me, still heated from whatever his conversation with Galen was about. He ran his fingers through his long hair and took a breath, nodding to me.

"I've had the kitchen prepare an assortment of traditional Mysthelm dishes for your first evening here." Galen waved a hand in the air to signal to the servants in the interior of the dining hall.

They rushed out tray after tray of silver plates, with more food than six people could possibly eat. A tiered platter bearing several different kinds of fish was set in the center. Small jars of honey and pears were scattered across the table. Bowls and bowls of rice, little cylinders that appeared to be some kind of noodle, and spiced potatoes followed. The briny scent of salt and fish mixed with the sweet, fruity one of the pear preserves, creating an enticing combination as it wafted over me.

"We have salmon, trout, and cod," Galen explained, gesturing to each of the fish layered decoratively across their platter. "With a salted pear and honey preserve. Pears are our specialty," he added.

"This looks wonderful," Mother said.

"It smells delicious," I agreed as I spooned several of the side dishes onto my plate, then glanced at the platter of salmon. I could've sworn the fish was staring at me, its little eye wide and fixed on my forehead. Flashes of the great mass of dead fish floating on the surface of the water raced across my mind.

"I take it the fish industry is quite large here, being so close to the coast?" I asked Galen.

"The largest one in the North Territory, yes," he responded. "We have fisheries up and down the coast, catching and harvesting all year round."

I hummed. "So you'd know if they were experiencing any issues lately?"

Across the table, Thorne shot me an exasperated look, his lips thinning into a grim line. His eyes said "let it go." I merely tilted my head to the side and swirled my glass.

Galen hesitated. "I suppose so. What types of issues do you mean?"

"Oh, I don't know. Some sort of disease, perhaps? Or an infestation? A predator that might be wiping out large amounts of sea life?"

Thorne cleared his throat, and Galen looked between the two of us, confusion written on his features. "Not that I'm aware of. Why do you ask?"

I glared at Thorne. So much for *"I'll bring it up to His Majesty at once."* He hadn't even bothered.

"Well, as I'm sure you were made aware of"—my gaze sliced to Thorne's and then back— "we had quite an experience on our trip here. Just a little ways off your shores, right before the storm hit, there was some sort of...attack. All the animals fell dead around us, and —"

"Ah, yes, there you are! You, pour some more wine for our guests," Galen interrupted to call out to a passing servant, averting his eyes from mine. I bit down on my lip to hide the surge of frustration.

"Thank you, but I don't need any." I put a hand over my glass, bumping into the servant's arm. A gasp slipped out when the cool red liquid spilled across myself and the table. Jumping to my feet, I grabbed a napkin and began dabbing at the small pool of wine.

"I'm so sorry; I didn't see you," I said to the young girl.

"Don't bother, Clarissa. That's their job." Galen waved a hand to usher me away from the mess.

Annoyance flared inside me again. I shouldn't have expected anything different—a king born into luxury with servants waiting on him hand and foot from the moment he drew breath. I probably would've been the same way, had my father remained the emperor, and I'd grown up in the silver spoon-fed environment of the palace.

But I hadn't. And I wasn't in the habit of justifying poor behavior in those who treated others as less than.

"It's not a problem. It was my fault, anyway. Here, let me help," I said to the servant girl. Taking the clean cloth from her hand, I dried my arm and sopped up the remaining liquid, which had stained the rose-gold satin fabric of my gown. I ignored the pointed stares of the lords, but I could feel one in particular—a guarded icy blue pair of eyes that hadn't left my skin since I first arrived.

The servant bowed to me before she scampered off to get more wine. Another pair of footsteps echoed from the interior dining hall, causing me to peer over Thorne's head to find his mother striding toward us. She wore a blood-red gown that trailed behind her, with sheer sleeves that fell past her wrists. Her brown-and-gray hair was no longer in a bun but hung loose down her back, the top half slicked back and collected in a clip.

"I apologize, Marigold's nanny was late," she said in her clipped tone as she came to a stop at Thorne's side and leaned over, brushing her cheek briefly against his. "I assume I haven't missed anything important."

"We were just about to discuss details of the tour, Azura," Galen said smoothly.

I blinked. No, that *wasn't* what we'd been discussing, but one stern look from my mother told me this wasn't a hill I wanted to die on.

"Yes, the *tour*," Azura Reaux repeated, her eyes shifting to mine before taking a seat next to Thorne and across from my mother. "We will have our hands full keeping these two boys in line for the next few weeks, won't we?" she said to Mother and me, pasting on that same tight smile from earlier.

I looked between her, Thorne, and Galen, finally resting on her son. "You're coming with us?"

"Surprised, Empress?" Thorne responded as he brought his glass of water to his lips. I tried not to notice the way his throat bobbed as he swallowed, or how that curious necklace he still wore swayed and brushed against a hint of dark hair at his chest. Something hot fell from my cheeks to my stomach, pooling there as a reminder of my irritation.

Ignoring him and his cocky tone, I turned to Galen. "When will we be leaving?"

"In the morning. We have a rather full itinerary. Lord Davies, can you fill Her Majesty in on the festivities?" Galen nodded to the white-mustached man at the other end of the table.

Lord Davies rifled through a handful of parchment. "Yes, Your Majesty. You will depart early tomorrow morning for the Mid Territory and arrive by the evening, where you'll dine with the Silenus regent family and stay with them for several days. They have plans to take you through their planting district and host the annual Harvest Tournament and Festival at the end of your stay. You'll then journey to the Penworth Estates in the South Territory."

"Both Silenus and Penworth will be tricky," the other man, Lord Sadim, interjected. He stroked his thick chin and leaned forward on the table. "Dion has been difficult to work with, even with Vespera attempting to calm him. And Rhys Penworth's territory has been divided ever since the announcement was made."

I furrowed my brow at the onslaught of new names and places I didn't recognize, trying to pick out the important pieces. "What does that mean? What announcement?" I asked, turning to Galen.

He licked his lips. "We sent a formal proclamation to the territories to inform them of your impending arrival. Not every regent has been...ah, fully accepting of me bringing someone of your... descendancy to our shores. Dion Silenus and Rhys Penworth, regents of the Mid and South Territories, have been loudest. But you shouldn't worry," he rushed out. "That's what this tour is for. To show our people they have nothing to fear in welcoming you to our kingdom."

My eyes swept the table. Lady Reaux hummed softly into her glass of wine, meeting my gaze with an unreadable expression. I caught Thorne staring at Galen with a furrowed brow. His strong jaw tightened, as if gritting his teeth to refrain from saying something.

I couldn't figure these people out, and it was like an itch under my skin.

After spending most of my formative years and all of adulthood learning how to read people, how to find out what made them tick, how to keep their loyalty and ward off the untrustworthy, I'd grown adept at seeing beneath the surface. The twitches, the eye shifts, the forced smiles. The hidden meaning behind words. The kind tones laced with venom. Desire, anger, envy, truth.

Something was wrong. Something I couldn't put my finger on.

My mind swam with what the two lords and Galen had said. I'd been so focused on *getting* here, on the idea of leaving my home and traveling somewhere new, I hadn't given much thought to what would happen after the fact. These regent families I'd be staying with, the people I'd meet, this new place with their customs and celebrations and expectations hanging over my head...what if they didn't even *want* to ally with Veridia? What if they were like Drakorum, with their ideals of a land closed off from others? What if they refused to put the past behind us?

Lord Davies continued, oblivious to my mounting inner

turmoil. "Arrangements have been made to tour the jewel mines in the South Territory and visit the coast before a celebratory ball in your honor."

"The ball will be very important," Lord Sadim interrupted again, pointing his finger in the air. "The last opportunity to gain the favor of Lord Penworth and those loyal to him."

A weight sank in my chest, pressure rising.

"After that," Lord Davies said, "the trip to Zeloria's territory on the island will take about a day by boat."

Galen chimed in with a soft snort. "I'll be interested to see what the islanders have planned for us."

"Interested indeed," Lady Reaux added, rapping her nails on the tabletop.

"Well, they're certainly excited to meet their future queen," Lord Sadim said.

Future queen.

The words took me off guard. They pounded through my skull, making my hands clammy with sweat. Of course, I knew what I'd agreed to with this proposal—but hearing him say it was something else entirely. Calling me *their* queen. I imagined meeting this kingdom and feeling responsible for yet *another* land full of people —ones who evidently weren't sure if they were going to hate me or not.

It all slammed into me at once. This wasn't a vacation. This wasn't a task to check off a list. Once I married Galen, these would be *my* people too, even if from afar. My life. My purpose. I didn't know how I ever thought I'd be able to come here and then go back to my old life without bringing a piece of this with me. Without letting it change me.

I wasn't even sure I could lead my *own* empire. And on top of that, I was about to add this kingdom to the list.

I squeezed my eyes shut and took a deep breath. When I opened them again, Thorne was staring at me from across the table. His eyes flicked to Galen, who seemed to notice my silence and the food barely touched on my plate.

"I think that's enough business talk for now," Galen said, his hand coming up to rest on mine. I fought the urge to flinch at the supple leather of his gloves. "Would you like to take a walk with me through the gardens?" he offered.

I cleared my throat and nodded. The night had always been my solace, and I needed a moment away from the planning and scrutiny. Everything was happening so quickly. Without my fox half to put my mind at ease, the world was spinning faster than I could keep up.

I took his hand and let him lead me across the patio, down several granite steps to two lion statues that marked rows of beautiful flowers. Swinging lanterns were lit every few feet, allowing enough light for us to see over the stretch of land. The same wisteria that lined the entrance door to the palace climbed down the lantern posts, with a backdrop of violets, daffodils, larkspur, and roses blooming in the moonlight.

We walked in silence for a moment, and my heart slowly went back to normal, no longer thumping through my ears. I took three deep breaths, letting them slide from me and carry the lingering anxiety away.

"I apologize for Lord Sadim's comment," Galen finally said. "The 'future queen' bit. I know we haven't had much time to discuss that particular part of the agreement." I glanced over to see his gloved hand rubbing the back of his neck. "I fear this dinner moved a little too fast. I'm sorry I didn't give you more time to adjust."

Maybe it was because we were away from the others, but the king seemed...softer than before. More genuine. A little unsure, which I found rather endearing compared to the lazy smiles and forced charm.

"I should've expected it," I admitted. "I know what I agreed to by coming here. It's just a lot to take in all at once."

He nodded. "You were appointed empress at the end of last year, correct?"

"Yes. Well, technically I haven't been sworn in yet. I'm in what our law calls a 'provisional period' for a year, since I'm not a direct descendant of the last emperor, and my father before him abdicated the throne. Nobody's managed to take it from me yet, though," I said with a soft snort. "Not for lack of trying."

He chuckled. "It's nice to hear I'm not the only one facing challenges. Let me guess—poison in your wine?"

"Dagger to the pillow. And arrow to the hand." I held out the hand that was shot the night before we left Veridia City.

"Impressive," he said with a low whistle. "I suppose it's a rite of passage. You're not doing your job if someone hasn't tried to kill you."

"Well, let's hope your people don't feel that way while we're on this tour."

"Oh, don't worry about what Lord Sadim said. He's always a pessimist," Galen said, waving a hand in the air. "Mysthelm is going to adore you. How could they not?" He paused, and I came to a stop beside him as he turned to face me, taking my hand again. "A beautiful, brave woman who took down a power-hungry tyrant and his wicked curse, leading her people out from under his hold."

His gloved thumb rubbed against my wrist. I swallowed, forcing myself to look into his hazel eyes, to feel *some* sort of...of warmth or magic in the moment, with the moonlight shining down on us, the soft hum of insects in the garden, the gentle curve of his lips as he smiled at me.

This was how the fairytales went. A young, handsome king sweeps the princess off her feet with his sweet words and dazzling eyes. He makes her his queen and whisks her away to his grand palace, where they live happily ever after.

But I wasn't a princess. This wasn't a fairytale. And I felt nothing. No warmth, no flicker of attraction, no butterflies.

Nothing except duty to my people and an obligation to follow through on my word.

"You make it sound larger than life." I slipped my hand from his, and we resumed our stroll down the grassy path. "I can tell you've done your research, Your Majesty."

"I admit, I had my advisors make some inquiries with your council over the last few months," he said. "My correspondence team managed to find out quite a bit."

"It seems I'm at a disadvantage, then, since I don't know much about you beyond your father passing away late last year and you taking the throne in his place. Is your mother still with us?"

He rolled his lips, taking his time responding. "She's alive. She lives here in the palace, but her health has been declining. She finds social gatherings to be a bit taxing. But she's very much looking forward to meeting you."

"I'm sorry to hear about her health. I know what that's like. I'm not sure how much my council told you, but my father died sixteen years ago, and it set Mother on a downward spiral." I cleared my throat as memories of the last decade came back to light. "She became unresponsive after a while, barely managing to eat and drink enough to keep her alive. My twin brother and I had all but given up hope of her mind ever returning to her."

Galen gave me an incredulous look. "Your mother? The same woman I met today?" He motioned back to the dining patio we'd long left behind.

I laughed. "I know it's hard to believe. Leo and I hardly believed it ourselves, at first. You know my parents ruled the empire before Emperor Gayl, right?" He nodded. "There was...bad blood between them. Gayl is actually the reason my family went into hiding. It's a long story, but we think Gayl had some sort of magical hold over Mother. When he died, his magic broke, and it released something in her. Almost like an...unlocking, of sorts. Over the last few months, she's returned completely to normal."

"That's incredible," he said, eyes wide. We walked a few more yards and came upon a wooden gazebo with a swinging bench. Dark vines clung to the railings, with lanterns and fireflies emitting small bursts of light every other second.

"Can you tell me about it?" he asked as he took a seat on the bench. "The magic in your home?"

"Well, there are six different types," I responded, sitting next to him. We slowly kicked our feet, and the bench swung back and forth, the breeze tickling my neck. "My mother and I are Shifters, which means we can turn into our given animal forms at will. My brother is an Alchemist—someone who casts spells and enchantments. There are Shadow Wielders who can manipulate shadows and Lightbenders who create light magic. Then there are Striders, which is what we call people who can transport themselves from one spot to another in the blink of an eye. And then Illusionists, who cast illusions into your mind, making you see something that isn't really there."

"I can't even imagine." He breathed out as he ran his fingers through his hair. "And you get to see this magic all the time? What's it like?"

"I've never really thought about it," I said with a shrug. "It's just always been there. You go to the nearest market and watch people wield shadows or light, see Shifters walking around as animals or Striders vanishing into thin air... You get used to it, I suppose. It's a part of us." I hesitated before admitting, "Coming here has actually been more difficult than I thought."

"Why is that?"

"Because magic doesn't exist beyond the Veridian Empire. Once we left the borders, our powers stopped working. It's like a piece of me has disappeared." I glanced down at my hands.

"And you're *sure* you don't feel it here? Any magic at all?" he asked, his forehead creasing.

"No," I said. "How could I?" There wasn't such a thing as magic in Mysthelm. Or anywhere except our empire.

Unless...

I abruptly shifted the conversation back to what had been nagging me all day. "Galen, do you know what happened on our ship? The dead fish and birds, the wild storm coming out of nowhere. Nobody will give me answers, but I *know* that wasn't natural. I just want to know if something is going on here. Maybe it's something I can help with, if you'll explain it to me."

His tongue flicked against his bottom lip. "Storms happen, Clarissa. I'm not sure what else you want me to say."

I kept my voice calm, my tone mild, although it felt like the ghost of my fox half was trying to growl its way up my chest. "You know that's not my point, Your Majesty. You and Lord Reaux have both been avoiding my questions. *Multiple* times." My head cocked to the side. "It makes me wonder what you have to hide."

He stood quickly, causing the bench to sway forward. I held out my arms to keep from ramming into his side.

"Don't—don't touch me!" he bit out, lurching away from me. I dug my heels into the ground to slow the momentum of the bench, my heart jumping to my throat at his aggressive outburst.

"I have nothing to hide," he ground out, but his eyes flashed a warning. "There are certain things about this kingdom I can't explain. That I can't make you understand yet."

I pushed to my feet, adrenaline racing. It felt like we were teetering on an important precipice, if only I could figure out what was going on. "Try me."

He sucked in a sharp breath, but before he could respond, his gaze flew to something over my shoulder.

"Your Majesty, I apologize for the intrusion," a gruff male voice said behind me. "Your mother requires your assistance."

I whirled around to face the unfamiliar guard, thinking for a split second he was speaking to me, but Galen passed me in a hurry.

"Lord Reaux will answer any questions you may have about the tour. I'll see you tomorrow, Clarissa," he said hastily, then disappeared down the dark path.

Frustration roared back in full force. What was he keeping from me? What was so terrible, so secretive, that he couldn't explain? I was once again left with more questions than answers, more thoughts to send me spinning.

My eyes caught on a strand of vine that had fallen from the top of the gazebo. I knelt to the wooden floor and examined the dead greenery, its stem now blackened and crumbling between the small slits in the wood.

Every kingdom had their secrets. Their skeletons in the closet, their unspoken truths. This king wanted to keep them buried. To distract me with pretty words and fancy dinners and innocent strolls in the garden.

But I was used to dealing with what waited beneath the surface. And I was going to dig these bones up, piece by brittle piece.

14

THORNE

Reaux Mansion was a short carriage ride north from the palace. Mother and I arrived to a dark and quiet house. Marigold was fast asleep at this hour, with her nanny keeping careful watch over her on nights like this when Mother and I had obligations elsewhere. The urge to go check on her was always poking at the back of my mind, but I didn't want to disturb her. She needed her rest before the trip tomorrow.

Bringing Marigold along on the tour wasn't my first choice, but neither was leaving her for four weeks. I had never been away from her for that long. Galen suggested she accompany us, and she begged me for days to let her come on an "adventure." When she roped my mother into agreeing with it, it was suddenly three against one.

She was so excited, it was hard not to give in. She'd been planning her outfits with her nanny's help, picking which stuffed animals to bring along, painting pictures of what she hoped to see. With Mother and her nanny coming to watch her when I couldn't, I was confident the trip would go smoothly.

I truly didn't know what I would've done these past four years without Iris had I not had my own mother and the staff here to help take care of Marigold. And even in the short time before that, when Iris's heart disease worsened and my attention was torn between tending to her, raising our daughter, and learning how to carry on the title of Regent Lord of the North Territory in my father's sudden absence.

My mother could be...standoffish, but she loved that little girl more than life. And I owed her a debt I could never repay for the way she stepped in during a time when I was broken beyond repair.

Nobody was equipped to deal with losing the love of their life. Nobody was prepared to watch them suffer day after day, to see the fatigue and weakness and surrender grow painfully evident in their eyes. To know there was no hope.

To wake up and realize *you* had to be the one to move on. *You* had to be the strong one for those left behind.

In those days, I didn't know if I would ever be strong again. Sometimes I still didn't know if I could be. I had lost a vital piece of myself. The world had lost its color, its light and hope, leaving everything in shadows. But watching Mother pick herself back up when my father abandoned her after *decades* of a life together gave me the fortitude to keep going—if not for myself, then for my daughter. For the people in this territory who relied on me.

Now, the three of us were all each other had. Mother and I didn't always see eye to eye on everything, but we'd been through too much for small disagreements to make me turn my back on her the way my father had four years ago.

"Galen doesn't have a clue what he's doing with that girl, does he?" Mother asked with a derisive laugh as she swept across the entrance hall.

Even when she made it particularly difficult to get along with her.

"She's more than 'that girl,' Mother," I drawled, hiding my frustration. "Don't underestimate her. There's a reason she's their empress." Multiple reasons, from what today showed me of the feisty, enigmatic woman.

Mother unclasped the large ruby necklace at the back of her

neck. "Yes, yes. Be that as it may, she certainly won't be *our* queen, if we have anything to do with it. But with the way things are going, Silenus and Penworth may take care of that for us. And Galen isn't doing a *thing* about it."

My hands clenched at my sides. Of course he wasn't. He'd known some of his people were unhappy about Clarissa's arrival and the engagement, and he'd done *nothing*. Simply brushed it off as a problem that would eventually work itself out, as he always did. It was like he didn't even *care* what his kingdom wanted or needed, didn't care about the whispers of rebellion that reached our ears. I knew it wasn't from a place of malice, but apathy could sometimes be worse.

My mother, however, was practically giddy over his indolence.

"Please, Mother, do try and hide your excitement," I said dryly.

She tilted her head and looked at me, arching an eyebrow. "Oh, come now, Thorne. I know he's your best friend. And you know I love him dearly." She walked toward me and took my hands, soothing out my tight grip. "I would never want anything bad to happen to him. But do you truly think he's the best leader for this kingdom?"

I looked away, unable to meet her blue eyes. It didn't matter—she knew my answer anyway.

He *was* my best friend. My closest companion, the man I'd walked with through youth and into adulthood and its weighted expectations. He was funny and impulsive and generous with those he loved. The way my daughter's eyes lit up whenever she saw her "Uncle Galen" always made me smile.

But those qualities did not make him a good king.

He was lazy. He was overwhelmed. He was a young man whose spirit was meant for another life and was instead forced into being the heir of Mysthelm. And no matter what guidance I tried to provide, no matter what counsel his other advisors gave him, nothing got through to him.

Our people suffered for it—that much was evident just this morning with the unexpected storm. The northern port and surrounding communities *should* have had the infrastructure to withstand it, if they'd received the funding from their many, many requests to the crown.

The South and Island Territories had both undergone severe floods and fires recently, and had been left to their own devices to recover. The Mid Territory had been fighting a deadly blight for months. Even now, with two of the regent families baring their teeth at the idea of Clarissa Aris invading their home, Galen did nothing to appease them. Nothing to *acknowledge* them.

Sometimes that was all people needed. To simply be heard. When their king couldn't even manage that, I wasn't sure what kind of future our kingdom faced.

Mother's hands came up to my face, pinching my cheeks the way she used to get my attention. "Think of how much better off our people would be with someone *else* on the throne."

"What, someone like you? Like *me*?" I asked, but my tone held no bite. I knew where this conversation was going. We'd had it many times before, always leading to the same place.

She shrugged and dropped her hands. "The Reaux family is as good an option as any. We are a strong bloodline, and we've served the crown well throughout the generations."

"I've never wanted to be a king, Mother. You know that," I said with a sigh as I turned away from her.

"You don't know *what* you want," she responded dismissively. "You haven't been given the chance, what with your father grooming you all those years, and then Iris coming along and..." She trailed off when I shot her a dark look. Taking a deep breath, she said, "Your life has never quite been your own. I know I'm partially to blame for that, but you know all I want is what's best for you, Marigold, and our people." She placed a hand on my upper arm and squeezed, offering a smile.

I rubbed a hand along my beard, the roughness against my fingertips helping to ground me. "I don't want to hurt him, Mother. We're some of the only people he has left."

"I know, dear," she crooned. "We won't. Leave everything to

me. You simply focus on ensuring he doesn't marry that empress, yes?"

This had become Mother's plan when Galen announced he was bringing Clarissa overseas. Galen was convinced an alliance would ultimately make him stronger. And that was something my mother didn't want. Once he had the might of the Veridian Empire at his back, it would be infinitely more difficult to get him to step down.

Mother's goal was simple: keep Galen weak by forcing all his allies, including the empress, away. Make him see that the best option would be to release his crown—a title he hadn't wanted to begin with.

Only eight months into his reign and he'd already proven to be an ineffective ruler. It wouldn't take much to push him over the edge into abdication—or worse, for the people to take matters into their own hands. The faintest rumors of an uprising had begun to circulate, and that was the last thing I wanted. That was why a peaceful removal was our best hope.

But if the anomaly Clarissa and her crew discovered this morning was any indication...I feared our problems were becoming worse than we'd thought.

I didn't know what the right thing was anymore. Were we doing the kingdom a favor by getting Galen off the throne? I'd always urged him to put the people first, and he continued to refuse. Mother was right—we couldn't hope to survive with the Grimaldis still in control, as much as I loved my friend.

Maybe this empress wasn't the answer, as Galen was so convinced. Maybe...maybe *this* was the answer. Maybe his removal would finally stop the disasters plaguing this land and give us a chance to start fresh.

As long as he would be safe. That mattered to me as much as the future of Mysthelm. He would learn to forgive me with time.

"Yes, Mother." I pulled myself from her grasp and turned toward mine and Marigold's wing of the mansion. "I'll do what you need me to do."

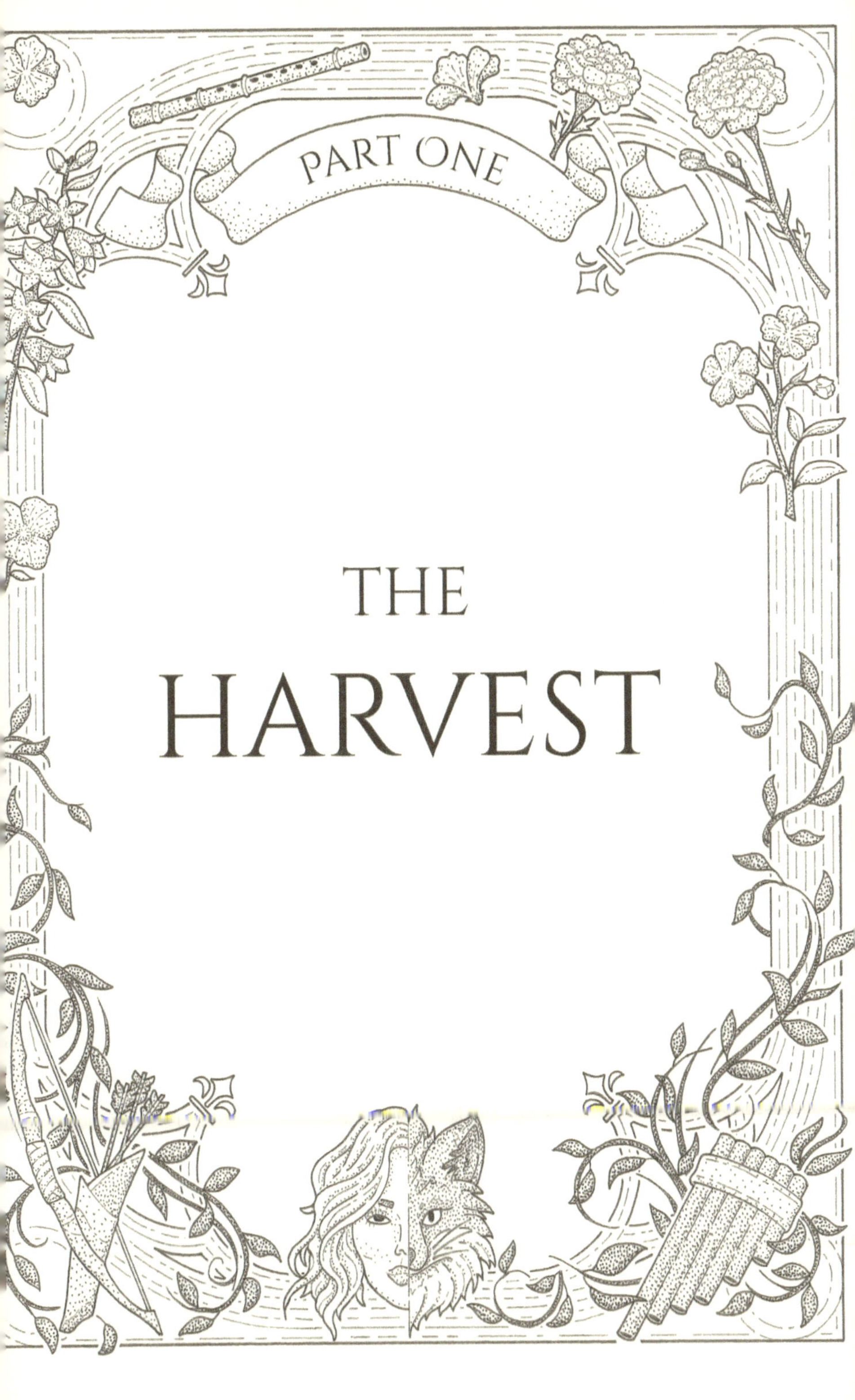
PART ONE
THE
HARVEST

15

CLARISSA

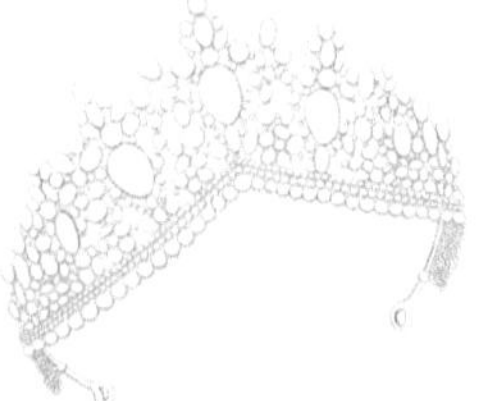

"Did you hear His Majesty, Clarissa?" my mother asked, followed by a gentle nudge of her elbow.

My head jerked forward to face Galen. "I'm sorry, what did you say?"

"I said, I trust you had a good night's sleep?"

I blinked away the fog in my head. Truthfully, I hadn't—my first night in the new kingdom left me restless, tossing and turning all throughout the night. We'd woken at the crack of dawn to load our trunks into the caravan of carriages and left the palace while the sun's rays were barely cresting over the horizon. I hadn't even gotten to enjoy my beautiful room for more than a handful of hours.

"As good as it could be," I responded, assessing his demeanor. Galen didn't look like he'd slept well either. Dark circles hung beneath his eyes, his normal golden-brown complexion slightly ashen. He'd been avoiding my gaze all morning, ever since he left so abruptly during our conversation in the gardens. "How's your mother?" I asked.

He swallowed and stared out the carriage window, his gloved fingers tapping on his thigh. "She'll be fine. Had some difficulty breathing last night but seems to have recovered this morning."

"That's good." I rolled my lips at the sudden awkward silence. I wondered if Mother noticed the tension between the king and me.

The three of us sat in the quiet space, the rocking and steady swaying of the carriage along the gravel path lulling me into a tentative sense of ease. The sun climbed higher as we rode. I propped my elbow on the window to my left and stared out onto the changing landscape, drinking in the new scenery.

We'd left behind the coastal terrain of the palace. Open fields replaced the flowing palm trees, with small, rolling hills dotting the view. Instead of the closely packed villages and stone homes of the North Territory, the communities as we traveled farther to the Mid Territory were more spread out. A handful of brick and wood farmhouses popped up here and there, with plenty of land and grazing animals in between.

I didn't know anything about the Mid Territory beyond the glimpses they'd revealed at dinner last night. Namely, the regent family's opposition to me. Lord Davies mentioned they had planting districts, and it was obvious this area was predominantly used for growing crops.

When we passed through a busier marketplace, I noticed the men and women dressed in sturdier clothing, as opposed to the lightweight linen of the North Territory. They wore overalls and long pants or skirts, with pieces of cloth tied at their heads or around their necks to protect against the sun.

A couple of times, I could have sworn I saw patches of blackened, dead grass amidst the lush greenery of the fields. Or a trail of rotted trees with gnarled branches and overturned roots leading to the bright, vibrant forest beyond.

But in the blink of an eye, it was gone—somewhere behind us as the carriage raced down the road. I would shake my head to clear away the mirage. A trick of the glaring sunlight on my eyes, perhaps.

Anytime I tried to engage Galen in polite conversation, he offered grunts or single-word responses. I had to walk on eggshells around this man and his mood swings. I'd been packed in this tight carriage with him and my mother for hours, letting my questions and irritations fester in the sun, and I was sick of being ignored.

I folded my arms across my chest and broke the silence. "So, Galen, tell me—how do you think the Silenus family plans to murder me? In my sleep, perhaps?"

His eyes shot to mine. "*What?*"

"Just making sure you could hear me." I smiled pleasantly and crossed my legs. "What are these people like?"

A crease appeared on his forehead. "Well, they're not going to assassinate you, if that's what you're asking. Nobody would dare lay a finger on any of us."

I've been told that *before*. "Good to know. Tell me more about them. Who will I be meeting? How can I make sure they're comfortable with me? Your advisors last night didn't exactly inspire confidence that this tour would go over well." I scratched at the inside of my arm, some of my insecurities shining through without meaning to. "I just...want to be ready. I want to make a good impression."

He rubbed the back of his ear and sighed. "We'll be meeting the Regent Lord Dion Silenus and his wife, Vespera. The main occupation here is farming, as you've probably seen, and the people are very...attuned to the land."

"What does that mean?" my mother interjected.

"They're a spiritually-minded group. Constantly praying and sacrificing to the Fates for a good harvest and good weather, that sort of thing. There are several rituals they follow at every season of the year. Even the Harvest Festival we'll be going to at the end of our stay is deeply rooted in their history."

"And Dion Silenus?" I prompted. "Wasn't he one of the regents opposed to my coming here?"

He shrugged, and his nonchalance grated at my nerves. "My advisors say Lord Silenus has been...less than enthusiastic. I can never tell what Dion approves of these days. He's very difficult to read. You'll be better off trying to appeal to his wife."

Alright, now we were getting somewhere. There was always a

way in with people, always a way to crack open even the toughest of exteriors. You just had to know where to poke. "And why is that?"

"Dion's first wife died about a decade ago without bearing him an heir, and he remarried shortly after. Vespera is half his age and the crown jewel of the Mid Territory," Galen said with a slight snort. "Everybody loves her; they merely tolerate him. They have a son now. He's..." Galen's nose wrinkled in thought. "Actually, I'm not sure how old he is. He was an answer to many prayers and is doted on like a little prince. If there's a way into their good graces, it's through Vespera and her son."

I smiled, feeling the ghost of my fangs press into my lower lip. "Perfect. That's all I needed to know."

He glanced at me with a small grin. The strain in the carriage had lightened throughout our exchange. "I have a feeling you're going to be just fine here, Clarissa Aris."

"She usually is," Mother said with a chuckle. "She's like her father in that regard. There's not much she can't do."

The look Galen gave me sent a shiver of trepidation down my spine. It was fleeting, but I saw it all the same—one of desperation and longing, but for *what*, I wasn't sure.

"I'm counting on it," he said quietly.

The carriage gave a sudden lurch to the side, sending the three of us slamming into the left wall. The sound of scraping metal coming from outside made my skin crawl.

Rubbing my head where a welt was already starting to form, I glanced out the window and cursed. We were riding at a dangerous speed over a bridge, with a river raging beneath us. But the carriage...the carriage was veering to the left.

Toward the low wooden parapet.

"Stop the carriage!" Galen shouted, thumping on the wall separating us from the driver's box. The horses' hooves pounded on the bridge as we careened farther left. My heart flew into my throat when the side of it grated against the railing. Several planks came loose, and I held my breath as I watched them splinter off and fall into the churning waters below.

The left side tilted even farther. The bottom of the carriage ground on the bridge as we spun, the back-end colliding with the railing and jolting us forward. Mother let out a sharp gasp, and I clutched her tightly, prepared to shield her body if we were thrown out of the carriage.

We came to an abrupt stop.

The three of us stared at each other with wide eyes, scared to so much as breathe.

The carriage door flew open. Our driver, a tall man with sweat dripping down his pale features, brandished a dagger.

He lunged at me.

The force sent the carriage rocking. I instinctively kicked the man's chest before he got too close, throwing out an arm to block his wrist. Galen shouted and tried to grab his arm. The driver moved as swift as lightning as he dodged Galen, turned on his heel, and shoved the king right out the carriage door.

"Who are you?" I shouted, keeping my mother at my back. "What do you want?"

"It's just business," he said. "Nothing personal." He flipped the blade in his hand, then charged at me again.

"Sure feels personal," I muttered. I jumped out of his reach, but there was hardly any space left in the small carriage. He swiped at my stomach, and I knocked his hand to the side with my elbow. The blade missed my midsection but nicked the top of my arm. I hissed at the sharp sting, baring my teeth against the pain.

"I don't want to hurt you," I snarled.

He gave me a smirk that raised my hackles. "I don't think that'll be a problem, Your Majesty."

This time when he attacked, I grabbed the bar at the top of the carriage with both hands and kicked my legs, connecting with his chest and sending him flying out the door, where Galen still lay crumpled on the ground. I let go and used my momentum to carry myself forward through the door and landed with a crouch on the bridge.

I almost lost my focus when I saw where we were.

The back third of the carriage was tipping precariously over the edge of the broken parapet. Just a few more feet, and the entire thing would have toppled into the river. The member of the King's Guard who had been riding in the box with the driver lay dead several yards away.

"Clarissa!" Galen yelled.

I barely had time to grab one of the daggers sheathed to my thigh as the driver barreled into my side. We both fell to the ground and rolled for a few feet before he pinned me down, his blade at my throat and my body caged between his legs. I swung my own dagger in an arc above my face, but he lifted both hands and easily blocked it, sending the knife flying from my grip.

"Stop fighting, and I'll make this easy," he hissed, bringing his blade back to my neck.

"How considerate of you," I rasped. "Too bad I can't promise the same."

I took the second dagger I'd grabbed when he'd released his hold on me a second ago and drove it into his wrist. With a cry, he dropped his knife and clutched at his hand. I used his distraction to shove his body off me and roll to the side, then stood and grabbed his shirt. Slamming his back into the ground, I wedged my knee into his neck.

"Who sent you?" I shouted.

"It doesn't matter," he said between gasps. "Just kill me. If you don't, they will."

"Who is 'they?'" Galen snarled as he approached from behind me.

"I'm sorry, Your Majesty," the driver wheezed out. With one final burst of strength, he used his good hand to throw my leg off his throat, grab the discarded dagger, and tried to plunge it into my chest.

My blade found him first.

With a sickening squelch, it drove through his stomach. His eyes went wide as he looked down at the knife protruding from him. I yanked it out, and he staggered backward.

"Wait!" I cried out, but it was too late. His imbalance carried him over the broken railing and straight to the roaring river below. Galen and I scrambled to the edge, watching his body land with a splash.

My chest heaved as I tried to catch my breath. "What was that about"—I sucked in another lungful of air—"nobody laying a finger on us?"

Galen gave me a grim look. "I suppose we better start walking."

———

Two of the other carriages in our caravan caught up to us quickly, and we were able to ride with them the rest of the way to Silenus Manor. Galen joined Thorne and his mother in theirs, while Mother and I rode with our lady's maids and a couple of guards.

I tried to wipe away the driver's blood from my hands, but some of it dried and crusted into my skin in a layer of red and brown. I hated that I was used to this, that fighting strangers in the streets had become part of a daily routine in my time as the Sentinels' leader. I was desensitized to the constant threats and daggers at my throat.

I'd been in this kingdom for twenty-four hours, and someone had already tried to kill me. That had to be some kind of record.

Katrine, the younger maid, was practically hyperventilating with worry the rest of the way, but the red-headed Devora kept her calm, seeming to know I needed to collect myself. She bandaged my injured arm deftly and quietly while Mother stuck close to my side. The three of them let me mull over my thoughts as I stared out the window at the slowly approaching sunset.

I was back in my Sentinels days. Analyzing the attack from

every position, scrolling through my interactions in the last twenty-four hours, trying to put together pieces that didn't exist.

I didn't even *know* these people. I had done nothing to warrant their hatred, except for simply existing. Were they so blinded by centuries of animosity toward Veridians, so opposed to me being here, that someone had resorted to murder?

I was sure Galen would be launching a full investigation, but with our main lead now at the bottom of the river, I doubted he'd find anything useful.

The strategic part of my brain began to overlap with nerves as Silenus Manor loomed large against the setting summer sun. The light red brick house stood three stories tall, with lanterns lighting the windows and entryway like a beacon. What looked like two separate wings had matching pointed roofs that reached into the darkening sky. When we drew nearer and I could see nearly a dozen figures waiting along the path leading to the entrance door, my palms began to sweat.

I sighed. Sure, a fight to the death on a broken bridge didn't bother me, but thinking about what other people thought of me was apparently too much.

I wasn't even sure why I was anxious. That these people wouldn't like me? I snorted. Too late for that. It was trivial, considering how long I'd been scrutinized by people who feared and disapproved of me in equal measure. It shouldn't matter if people *liked* you as long as they could respect you. And that was something I could earn—I'd done it before. You just had to find what motivated them.

They're certainly excited to meet their future queen.

Lord Sadim's words trickled through my mind. Ruling my own empire was still daunting, and being partially responsible for a land I didn't know—even if it was in name only—felt like a heavier burden than I'd expected to bear. I knew myself. I knew if I spent time with these strangers, if I saw how they lived, how they worked and dreamed and loved...I would get attached. I would want to do my best to care for them. How could I do that when I had thousands upon thousands of Veridians to consider as well?

Or I could simply be nervous that someone was going to try and gut me in my sleep.

No matter what it was, something twisted in my stomach as our carriage came to a stop. The driver appeared in the doorway to help the maids and my mother down the steps.

I paused at the little door, heart pounding in my chest. Perhaps the events of the day were catching up to me. The sound of footsteps crunching across the white gravel was magnified, almost reminding me of white bones gleaming and crunching and—

Closing my eyes, I took a deep breath, willing away the familiar sensation of panic. Phantom pain began to creep up my leg.

Please, not now, I begged whatever Fates were listening. I had to keep control for these first few moments. Get past the introductions, the niceties, a quick dinner, then—

"Breathe, Empress," a voice murmured at the door of the carriage.

I opened my eyes to find long brown hair, a full beard, and blue eyes staring back at me. Thorne leaned in through the opening, barely a foot away. His steady breaths fanned across the small space and instantly banished the chill that had set into my bones.

"Heard you had a rough day," he said, his voice slipping over me like warm honey.

That brought a scoff to my lips. "You could say that."

He glanced over his shoulder at the line of strangers waiting to meet me. "They're just people, like you or me. Don't let them scare you."

"I'm not scared of them," I whispered, letting the panic flow out of me on an exhale.

He gave a small smirk and held out his hand. "Good."

My eyes flitted from his face down to his outstretched arm, something buzzing along my fingertips as I let him take my hand. His skin burned hot against mine, and as the evening breeze hit me at the same time, a flush crept over my body.

The tip of my foot caught on the last step. My half-stumble caused our hands to press into his chest as his other hand came out to grip my arm. I sucked in a gasp and pulled away as pain radiated from the knife wound the assassin had dealt. Devora had bandaged it as best she could, but without my Shifter powers, I was left to heal the old-fashioned way.

"He hurt you," Thorne said, a dip appearing in the space between his eyes. It wasn't a question.

"I hurt him worse," I replied.

His eyes searched mine for a moment before he took a step back, throat bobbing as he left me and made his way to the carriage behind us to help his mother and a young girl I didn't recognize.

I went to stand next to Mother and tried to catch my breath. I searched for Galen, only to see him in a whispered conversation with two of the men waiting to greet us. All three of them bore expressions of frustration: clenched jaws, downturned lips, creased brows. The two strangers saw me looking and schooled their features into ones of neutrality. But not before I saw the narrowed eyes and brief sneers as they scanned both my mother and me.

Galen made his way to me, looking as tired as I felt. "Come, Clarissa—let's meet the regent family." He held out an arm for me to take, and I wrapped my hand around the smooth fabric of his tunic, squeezing my mother's hand before she fell into place behind us.

With each step, I took a breath. I steeled myself and found the polished part of me that always lurked at the surface. My spine straightened and my shoulders loosened as we strode, my chin rising to meet the eyes of the Silenus family and staff

What if they were the ones who ordered your death?

I shook away the paranoid thought. I couldn't go into every interaction assuming they were all assassins. That was no way to build trust or an alliance. I had to be smart—win them over while still watching my own back. Vigilant, not cynical.

I was greeted with curt smiles and stiff bows, the guarded looks of people wary of an intruder in their home. I could understand that, and I didn't fault them for it.

But I would prove I was worthy of more.

At the end of the row of men and women in servant uniforms stood a man in his seventies, with a significantly younger woman at his side. She held the hand of a young boy, maybe four or five years old, whose golden eyes gazed at us in curiosity. I gave him a small smile, which he returned shyly, full lips against dark skin curving up at me.

Galen released me. "Dion. It's good to see you," he said, tired but cheerful. He grasped the older man's hand in his own.

So this was Lord Dion Silenus. He was about the same height as his wife, his back slightly more hunched in his age, with gray hair adorning the sides of his pale head.

I stood back as Galen shook hands with both Dion and his wife, Vespera, even getting on his knees to look their son in the eye. Air brushed against my back and a sickly-sweet floral perfume hit my senses. Azura and Thorne came to stand beside me. Thorne turned to speak with one of the guards along the path, leaving his mother and me in an awkward space of quiet.

Azura Reaux's clipped tone sounded low in my ear. "I'm so glad you and your mother weren't injured in the accident, dear. What an awful thing," she said, clicking her tongue. I looked over to see her frowning in concern. "Is there anything you need? It must have been so frightening."

"No, we're fine," I said. "Just thankful we all made it out safely."

"Yes, of course. We are as well." She put a hand on my shoulder. "But a word of advice, if I may."

I tilted my head, my eyes flicking over her carefully fixed features.

"I fear carriages are not the only place you need to watch where you tread. Be careful in this kingdom, young Empress. Not everyone here can be won over as easily as our king."

I remained motionless as she smiled and patted my cheek. She turned to Thorne and jumped seamlessly into his conversation as if nothing had happened.

Well. *That* sounded like a challenge.

Perhaps I wasn't the only fox lying in wait.

16

CLARISSA

"We had a bit of a setback on the way here," Galen started, "but we've made it. I'm delighted to introduce you to Her Majesty Clarissa Aris, future Empress of the Veridian Empire." He brandished an arm toward me.

Stepping forward, I inclined my head to Lord and Lady Silenus, racking my memory for the few pieces of information Galen gave about the regent family before the incident.

I kept eye contact with Dion as I said, "It's wonderful to meet you. Your territory is beautiful—you're truly blessed by the Fates." Bringing my attention to Vespera, I offered a smile. "I look forward to getting to know you better in the coming days."

She exchanged a swift glance with her husband, causing her long, thick black locks to swish along the front of her navy dress. When her dark eyes met mine again, they were hesitant but not unkind.

"We're so sorry to hear about what happened but are happy to have you in our home, Your Majesties." She curtsied to both Galen and me, but Lord Silenus remained unmoving, assessing us with an impassive expression on his pale, wrinkled face.

"Maurice," Vespera said gently, looking down at the little boy at her side and urging him forward. He peeked up at us as he stuck his thumb in his mouth and bowed, the movement causing him to stumble.

I grinned and knelt into a crouch, discreetly pulling a gold coin from the pocket in my pants. "And who might you be?"

He took his thumb out of his mouth long enough to say, "My name is Mo."

"He can't say 'Maurice' yet," his mother explained.

My smile widened. "Well, I think Mo is a great name. And look what I found." I gave an exaggerated gasp and reached out to "pluck" the gold coin from behind his ear.

His eyes flashed, and he slowly lowered his thumb, staring at the coin in awe. "Is that *mine*?"

I chuckled. "It can be. If your parents say yes, of course," I said, deferring to Vespera. She tilted her head as her lips curved into a small smile and nodded once. Maurice took the coin from my fingers and marveled at the gilded edges.

"Thank you, miss," he said, the last word coming out as a whistle.

Shooting him a wink, I said, "You can call me Rissa."

"If you will follow me, Your Majesties, I can show you around the property," Vespera said, her smile now more relaxed. "We weren't sure what time you would arrive, so we don't have our formal dining room in order, but we've had the kitchen prepare a small dinner in the drawing room."

"Will you and Lord Silenus be eating with us?" I asked as we stepped over the threshold and into their home.

Dion was already several paces ahead and didn't look back when his name was mentioned. The side of Vespera's jaw twitched. "The lord has some affairs to attend to. But I'll accompany you, if that's alright."

"Of course," I said. "Please, you and Maurice should both join."

Maurice tugged on his mother's hand. "Can I, Mama? Please?"

Without breaking her stride, she scooped him into her arms. "Now, you know it's far past your bedtime, young man. I already let you stay up late to greet our guests."

His lips turned down into a pout, and the sight was so adorable, I couldn't help but smile. Vespera bade her son goodnight and passed him off to a nearby maid. He waved to me as she carried him away, and the rest of us continued our trek through the manor. It was simple but beautiful, with a sort of rustic edge. Cozy rust-colored rugs ran along the dark, hardwood floor, and a handful of portraits of the Silenus trio decorated the wooden walls.

"You've already made a good impression on one Silenus, at least," Galen whispered next to me. "You're wonderful with children."

I shrugged. "They're just like anyone else—they want to be noticed and appreciated. Everyone should be made to feel special every once in a while." *And I highly doubt his father does that*, I thought to myself.

We were ushered down another corridor and into an open chamber, lit with a roaring fire on the back wall and several iron lanterns surrounding three couches and a grand piano. On a table in the center rested a pitcher of water and plates of sandwiches, fruits, vegetables, and a selection of cheeses.

Vespera, Galen, Mother, and I sat on the velvet cushions. While Vespera questioned Mother about the incident on the road, I saw a maid stop Thorne at the door and whisper something in his ear. He abruptly nodded and turned on his heel, following her down the hall and out of sight. My eyes tracked his movements until I felt Azura Reaux's cold gaze lingering on me before she went after her son.

I turned my attention back to the food. The others engaged in polite conversation while I sat back and observed. Vespera had been withdrawn at first but was now a lively and animated host, constantly refreshing our glasses and filling any uncomfortable silence with talk of her son, our journey, and what we'd be doing over the next few days. I had an inkling her change in demeanor was due to her stiff-necked husband no longer at her side.

"We'll spend the next four days introducing you to the

community. Farm tours, visits to the marketplace, that sort of thing. Oh, I can't wait to show you some of my favorite food vendors," Vespera said, taking a bite of her sandwich. "After that, the fifth day is when we'll hold a tournament in preparation for the Harvest Festival. People bring their crops and livestock to be judged and are awarded prizes that evening at the festival, where we offer the best of the harvest as sacrifices to the Fates."

"It sounds like you have many traditions here," Mother commented.

Vespera nodded. "We're very close people. It's hard not to be when you spend so much of your time working with each other, relying on the land itself and the Fates to provide what we need. That's all we can really depend on, in the end. People fall short, but not the Fates. Not after everything they've given us."

I could see what Galen meant about the Mid Territory being so spiritual. They really put their faith in the Fates. There were some devout followers back in Veridia City, but it was becoming more and more rare. In the empire, the Fates had faded into more of a myth—beings to place blame on when things didn't go your way, but never really carrying much weight.

I supposed, over the course of time, we'd begun putting our faith in our magic. Veridians were so reliant on the power that ran through our blood, there wasn't much room for the three divine beings in our lives. But Mysthelm...they didn't have that magic. The Fates were their sole source of power, however absent they may be.

Something else pricked in the back of my mind from our carriage ride down here. "Lady Silenus, I noticed some of the fields in the area seem to be..." I searched for the right word for what I'd seen. "Well, it almost looked like they were rotting. Have you had droughts or anything this summer?"

Her sunny disposition immediately shifted, her smile fading and eyes falling to the plate in her hands. She took her time before responding, "Not droughts, but there is a strange blight occurring in a number of the farms, yes. We don't know what the cause is, but we've been told it's being investigated." Her eyes shot to Galen and back down again, the motion so quick I almost missed it.

"Yes, that's most peculiar." He took one more drink of water before standing. "Not to worry—I've had the best of my academics researching the problem. I'm confident we'll have a solution for you soon."

Vespera stood as he crossed the room to her, dipping her head in respect. "I'm going to turn in for the evening. Your hospitality is much appreciated, Lady Silenus," Galen said.

Next to me, my mother stifled a yawn, and I put a hand on her shoulder. "We had a long day, Mother. You should go get some rest."

"I should be saying the same to you. Are you sure you're alright?"

"I'm fine, Mother. I promise. I'll follow you soon," I said.

"Let me accompany you to your room, Evadine," Galen said, holding out his arm for her. A chorus of "good nights" followed them as Galen and my mother made their way out of the drawing room, leaving me alone with Vespera.

I smoothed my hands along my pants. "I'm sorry to hear about the blight," I started. "Is it hurting your people? Your crops and animals?"

She licked her lips and kept her hands busy by rearranging the empty trays of food on the table. "You're kind to ask, but it's really nothing you need to worry about. King Grimaldi said it's being taken care of. I know that's not why you're here, anyway."

Leaning over, I placed my hands on top of hers to stop her fidgeting. "I *want* to know. It doesn't matter if that's not the reason for our trip. If there's anything that can be done for your territory, I want to help."

Her light brown eyes, almost as gold as her son's in the firelight, searched mine. "Why would you care about us, Your Majesty?" It wasn't a judgmental question, merely curious. As if she truly couldn't understand why I'd show such concern for a land that wasn't mine. For a land we'd had a centuries-old grudge against out of no fault of our own.

My brow furrowed. "Because if people are suffering, and nothing is being done to end it, it becomes the responsibility of those with power—those with a *voice*—to do something about it. It doesn't matter if that voice is Veridian or Mysthelm."

She let out a breath as her eyes softened. "You aren't what we expected, Your Majesty."

"I'll take that as a compliment," I said, letting go of her hands. "And you can call me Rissa."

With a grin, she stood and walked to a metal liquor cart behind the couch. "I think we need something a little stronger, don't you?"

I smirked. "I knew I liked you for a reason."

As she poured us both a drink, she said, "The blight started about five months ago. That's just what we call it—we don't know exactly *what* it is. One day, farmers started noticing patches of farmland dying with no warning. Green and thriving one moment, black and dead the next. It was small areas at first, not enough to cause much panic. But then...it spread. Trees in the forests beyond the fields rotted and died. Farmers would dig up root vegetables and find them completely destroyed.

"We never know when it's going to strike. It's so sporadic, without any type of pattern. And it's happening all over, so we know it's not based on location." Vespera paused to press a finger to her temple. "We're still producing enough food for now, but if we can't put an end to it soon..." She trailed off, her worries evident on her features.

This had been happening for five months? Had Galen known about it this whole time? Frustration boiled inside me at the way he'd brushed it off before he left. What was he doing to help them? To ease their fears and find a long-term solution if the blight kept getting worse?

Was he even doing *anything*?

"I want to see it," I blurted out.

Her lips parted. "The blight?"

"Yes," I said firmly. "Tomorrow when we explore the farms, I want to see it." Maybe there was something people were missing. I knew next to nothing about crops, but I would never know if I didn't look for myself.

"Vespera," said a gruff voice from the entrance to the drawing room. Dion Silenus stood there, arms crossed over his chest. "It's late."

She lowered her gaze and nodded, giving me a wistful smile. "I hope you have a pleasant night, Your Majesty," she said as she stood to follow her husband. "Please let the staff know if you need anything."

And just like that, they were gone.

17

CLARISSA

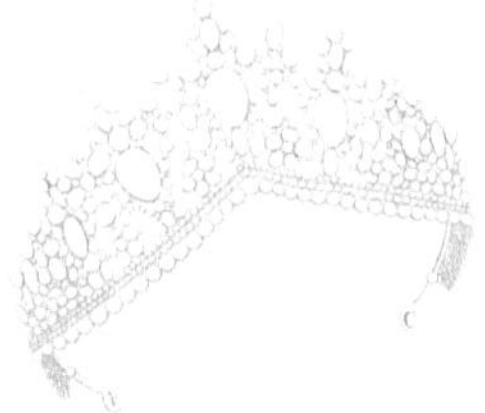

I was woken the next morning by the bright morning sun. Katrine and Devora threw the thick curtains aside to let in the blinding light.

"It's time to get ready for your first day, Your Majesty," Katrine said in her lively voice.

My mother peeked her head around the corner of the large two-bedroom suite the Silenuses had given us. "I thought I heard you awake in there," she said, sipping from a steaming mug. "You slept in late, dear."

I rubbed my eyes and only managed a grunt of acknowledgment before tossing the covers off my legs. I carefully stretched out my injured arm, working out the stiffness and wincing slightly at the jab of pain. Sleep hadn't found me easily last night. I kept dozing off, only to be jolted awake by the faint memory of the driver lunging with his dagger.

Devora led me to the vanity by my bed and had me sit while she dabbed a cream beneath my eyes. "Trouble sleeping, my lady?"

I gave a tired smile. "Is it that obvious?"

"Do you want my honest answer?" she asked, her blue-green

131

eyes sparkling behind her thick glasses with a sort of mischief that made me think of my friend Rose.

"That depends."

She tapped a spot above my cheek. "These circles under your eyes could rival a full moon."

I barked out a laugh. She definitely reminded me of Rose. "Alright, maybe we tone down the honesty just a bit."

"Noted." She gave me a quick wink before rustling in her bag for more cosmetics.

I stifled a yawn. "So, how long have you been working in His Majesty's palace?"

"About two years." She applied a light pink color to my lips. "He hired me from another family. Before that, I was lucky to find work in a tavern or inn in the North Territory."

"What about your family? What do they do?"

Her hands stiffened, then went back to searching the bag. "I don't know, Your Majesty. I've never met them."

I opened and closed my mouth quickly. My eyes found my mother, who was chatting with Katrine across our shared suite as the maid helped button her dress. I couldn't imagine not knowing my parents. Even though my father died when I was twelve, I still remembered what it was like to grow up with both of them at my side. To feel their unconditional love, their firm hand, their pride and wisdom.

"I'm sorry to hear that," I murmured.

"Don't be, my lady. I didn't tell you to earn your pity," she said with a shrug, although her eyes stayed averted from mine. "I've made a life for myself on my own terms."

My lips twitched up. She was rather growing on me. "How did you end up at the palace?"

She paused before finally saying, "How much did you want me to tone down the honesty, Your Majesty?"

I searched her features, surprised by her cryptic answer. "Whatever you feel comfortable with."

Licking her lips, she said, "Before he became king, His Majesty would often spend his evenings at taverns in the villages. I had the occasional evening off work, and I...caught his attention one night. He brought me back to the palace and requested I be hired on as a maid. He paid far better than my previous employer, so it wasn't a difficult decision. He's been known to do that with those he wishes to...keep."

Her bright eyes stayed on mine, and I could read between the lines. I had no misconceptions about what this marriage was going to look like. No ideas of a faithful husband and dutiful wife...not while we were an entire ocean apart. It would be in name only—a way to keep peace between our kingdoms. He was free to do whatever he wished, as much as the idea of collecting people like one collects seashells made my lip curl.

She finished with my makeup, and I rose from the seat. "Thank you, Devora." I squeezed her shoulder gently.

She rolled her lips, hesitancy crossing over her features. "I don't keep his attention anymore, Your Majesty. I just thought you should know that."

I gave her a close-lipped smile and nodded. Before I could respond, Katrine let out a groan from the room next to us. Devora and I rounded the corner to find the maid with her sleeve stuck to the back of my mother's dress.

"I'm sorry, Your Grace. I think I've gotten myself stuck," Katrine said to Mother.

I chuckled. "It's alright; we just need to unhook—"

"I've got it," Devora said, striding past me. In a flash, she lifted her skirt, pulled a small blade from a sheath at her thigh, and cut through the strand of fabric tethering Katrine to the dress.

I blinked in surprise.

Devora shrugged. "Always be prepared. Now, let's get you both to breakfast."

———

WE ATE a quick breakfast of oatmeal and berries while Vespera ran us through our day. The Silenuses were going to accompany Galen and me through a couple of the nearby farms while we met the citizens and learned about their work. Thorne and my mother chose to come, but Azura stayed back. I couldn't say I was disappointed. After my conversation with the older woman yesterday evening and her stiff, cold smiles, something about her set me on edge.

As Mother and I made our way to the carriages, Galen appeared with a grim look on his face.

"Clarissa, I won't be joining you," he said. "Dion and I need to discuss the attack yesterday. There are a couple of leads he wants to follow, and I want to make sure we have safety measures in place for you going forward."

"Then should I stay back too? If you don't think it'll be safe?"

"No, no, you go ahead. This tour was for you. I've doubled the number of guards with you, and Thorne will be there to keep an eye out." Without waiting for me to respond, he tipped his head to someone behind me.

I twisted my neck to find Thorne's gaze on me. I quickly turned back to Galen and forced my features to stay impassive.

"Fine. I'll see you this evening, then," I responded smoothly. He lifted two fingers in a brief wave before following Dion back into the manor. Vespera replaced him seconds later, looping her arm through mine and steering me toward the carriage.

"It's for the best," she leaned in and whispered. "The men make it so unbearably dull."

"I heard that," Thorne said.

The driver stepped down from the box. I instinctively narrowed my eyes at him, trying to see if I could spot any concealed weapons. Perhaps a sharp chip on his shoulder. Or the words "assassin" written on his forehead.

He held out his hand to assist my mother and Vespera into the carriage, and Thorne stopped at my side. "Don't worry, Empress. He's been investigated. He's clear."

"Oh—thank you," I said, surprised he'd noticed my fixation. "Good to know."

We all settled into the small space. The wheels of the carriage rolled over gravel, jostling us as we crossed onto the main road. Thorne's knee grazed mine when he adjusted his position, his leg brushing against the thin fabric of my pants. Warmth seeped through the material. My eyes briefly locked onto his, and I shifted my leg out of the way.

Vespera spent the short ride asking questions about the provinces in the Veridian Empire, and Mother and I took turns answering. We talked about the forests of Feywood, the cliffs of Drakorum, the haunted Shadowmere Wastelands of Tenebra. She was especially interested in the magic. It seemed Mysthelm didn't have a very thorough knowledge of how the magic the Fates had given our empire worked, and she was wide-eyed throughout our entire description of the six types.

"What about you, Rissa?" she asked me. I'd finally gotten her to stop referring to me by my title. "What magic do you have?"

"My mother and I are both Shifters."

She exhaled, a look of awe on her dark features. "What kind of animal? No—wait, let me guess. Something graceful. And regal. A deer, maybe?"

"She's some sort of predator," Thorne said. It was the first time he'd spoken. His eyes scanned me. "Something proud but quiet. An animal you wouldn't see coming."

My smile faltered. He was...alarmingly perceptive. "What makes you say that, Lord Reaux?"

The corner of his mouth lifted. "Just a hunch."

"Like a hawk? Or a large cat of some kind?" Vespera offered.

Thorne leaned back against the thin cushion. I fought the urge to wiggle in my seat under his scrutiny. I simply held his gaze, wishing for the thousandth time that I could still feel my fox half. The missing magic weighed on me every minute of the day.

"Close." I broke our staring contest and looked back at Vespera. "My Shifter half is a fox. And my mother's is a wolf."

Intrigue flared in Thorne's eyes. Vespera sighed and said, "It must be wonderful, having all of that power. Seeing magic everywhere you go. Like something out of a fairytale."

I swallowed and stared out the window to my left, taking in the rolling green hills. "Magic has its troubles too."

The carriage came to a stop in front of a charming little market. A dozen or so tables were set up, with canvas coverings lifted high above each to block the sunlight. I stepped out of the carriage and saw that each table was occupied by men, women, and some children, all selling or trading different wares. Many had booths full of colorful produce. Red tomatoes, enormous carrots and other root vegetables, buckets of bright fruit. Others sold knives and tools. Behind them stretched a massive piece of land that went as far as I could see, with countless straw-hatted workers roaming among the rows of crops.

"This is Gold Row," Vespera said next to me. "A community sector of farmland managed by several of the families around here. It provides jobs for a third of the Mid Territory's citizens and is the kingdom's largest agricultural producer. They have wagons going weekly to all the other territories, dropping off orders of produce and other things like eggs or milk." She raised a hand to shield her eyes and looked off into the distant fields, a smile forming on her face. She looked so *proud* of her territory. It sparked something warm in my chest.

"Come on," she said brightly, grabbing my hand and motioning to my mother. "Let's go see what booths are up today."

We ventured to the little market, where every single person waved and smiled fondly at Vespera as she passed. When their attention fell to me, however, their faces turned into hesitation. Confusion. And for some, recognition. They pursed their lips and cast their gazes downward.

"Hello there, Aiman. How are things going today?" Vespera asked a tall man behind a table of potatoes.

His light eyes flitted from me and back to Vespera. "Going well, my lady. We've had lots of customers so far."

"You know, the empress here was *just* telling me how she was craving some of our leek and potato soup tonight, weren't you, Your Majesty?" Vespera turned to me, raising an eyebrow.

"Oh, yes," I said, catching on. "And these potatoes look wonderful. Do you grow them yourself?"

Biting his bottom lip, the farmer paused before saying, "Well, my partner and son do a lot of the work too. It's a family effort, you know."

"You're very kind to share all of this with us. I'd love to try some with dinner tonight. I'll purchase a bag," I said, pointing to the nearest sack of potatoes.

His mouth fell open. "A-A whole bag?"

I smiled. "We have many mouths to feed." I wasn't sure if that was true, but this man looked like I'd made his entire week. I'd eat potatoes for breakfast, lunch, and dinner if I had to.

"Of course, Your Majesty." His lips split into a grin as he hauled the bag off the table and I counted out my payment.

"Oh, Lord Reaux can take care of that," I said when he held the bag out to me. I caught Thorne lingering with my plethora of guards a few feet behind us and gave him a grin. He shook his head, but the corner of his lips tugged upward.

"Thank you, Your Majesty. Come back anytime," the farmer said, taking my coins. He was no longer cautious, but sunny and welcoming.

From then on, the vendors were much less guarded. They greeted Vespera and me as we came around, and I had to admit that Lady Silenus was an absolute master at making others feel comfortable.

I found myself intrigued by the lives and stories of the people, and we spent hours—and far too much money—with them. One woman selling eggs had a chicken pecking around her tent that she swore once laid a golden egg that she sold to buy her patch of farmland farther south. Another man and his son sold beautiful handmade jewelry made of dried flowers pressed between pieces of glass. Each one was engraved on the back with the initials of the man's wife, who had passed away three years previously.

With every smile, every tale, my heart opened to this kingdom. And I could see their wariness leaving them as well. Whatever misconceptions they had about the Veridian Empire didn't seem to matter as much when one could see that we were all just *people*.

We approached a booth with a mother and two little girls, who both stood at opposite ends of the table. A huge carton of berries sat between them: strawberries, blueberries, raspberries, and several I didn't recognize. The girl on the right held the biggest strawberry I'd ever seen in my life—it was half the size of her head, at least.

I laughed and said, "My, I'm surprised you can lift that!"

Their mother smiled and wiped her hands on her apron. "It's her prized possession. She hasn't let go of it since we picked it. Won't stop calling it 'His Majesty.'"

"Because its spots look just like a big letter 'G!'" the girl called out, shoving the berry in my face. "For King Grimaldi!"

The spots didn't take any particular shape that I could make out, but I smiled along with her. "I'm sure His Majesty would be thrilled to see that."

"I wanted to show him today," she pouted. "He's never come here before."

Taken aback, I blinked and looked over at Vespera, whose lips fell into a thin line. I faced the little girl again. "Well, I'll tell him all about it. He'll be honored."

He hadn't been here before? Did Galen never visit his territories? I didn't see how one could hope to rule well if they didn't take the time to get to know their own people. That was one of the first things I'd done when I became interim empress—traveled across all six provinces, even the ones who hated me. I would never claim to know everything about being a good leader, but having some sort of relationship with those who followed you was high on my list.

Vespera must have seen the irritation on my face as we turned away from the booth, for she rushed out, "His Majesty is a very busy man. He must not—"

She was cut off by the sight of a man hurtling toward the potato booth, sweat rolling from his stricken face. He exchanged a few words with the other farmer, and they both began frantically packing up their produce.

Vespera and I made our way to them. "What's going on, Aiman?" she asked.

"It—it's the blight," he responded, voice shaking. He wiped dirt from his forehead. "Our field's been hit."

The blight. The one Vespera told me of last night. "Where is it?" I asked without thinking. "Your field."

"Just over there, Your Majesty. On the northern end of Gold Row." He pointed north as his partner began hauling sacks of potatoes away.

"I want to see it," I said to Vespera. "We'll go with you."

Her forehead wrinkled. "Your Majesty, it might not be safe."

At that moment, Thorne chose to reappear at my side. "Lady Silenus is right. Galen wouldn't want you putting yourself in danger."

I rounded on him. "If I'm meant to marry into this kingdom, Lord Reaux, then I want to know *exactly* what I'm getting myself into. If you won't take me to the fields, I'll go myself."

He stared back at me, a silent battle taking place between us. Each second under the hot sun sent another bead of sweat rolling along the column of my throat. His eyes dragged down my neck, watching the droplet glide over my skin and out of sight. When they met mine once more, his jaw tightened.

"Fine," he finally said, running a hand over his dark beard. "Let's go."

———

Thorne and I rode in the back of Aiman's wagon with several guards to his fields on the north end, while Vespera and my mother stayed behind to calm the nerves of the other vendors. Anticipation built inside me during the short trip. I didn't know what to expect. The way Vespera had described it was like a plague eating the land. I wondered how far it had spread or if anyone had been hurt.

The look on the farmers' faces was so permanent. Devastated. Hopeless. As if once the blight hit, there was no return. And this was their *livelihood* at stake. If they could no longer grow crops or breed livestock, if their *only* method of providing for their families was wiped away...I could see why the thought caused such panic.

My heart raced as we drew nearer to the site and the wagon slowed.

I saw it the moment I stepped down.

It was like an invisible line had been drawn in the ground. On one side was vibrant greenery, rows and rows of golden wheat stalks and green foliage of potato plants shining under the sun. And on the other side was darkness.

Death stretched back beyond the field and into the surrounding forest. Every single leaf, stem, and flower was rotted and crumbled, some of it blowing away in the wind. What were once rows of strong stalks were now lines of wilted, black thickets with torn roots breaking through the soil like claws rising to strangle anything in its path. Even the dirt looked sunken and starved.

Words failed me. I ran my fingers through my tangled hair, letting it blow to the side in the soft summer breeze as I thought about what these farmers might be feeling. What words of comfort I could offer, what empty promises I could make. A small crowd had gathered around us, what I assumed were Aiman's employees and neighbors muttering with arms crossed over their chests and fear in their downcast eyes.

When I stepped toward the blackened land, a callused hand grabbed mine. "You can't, Clarissa," Thorne said in his low voice. "It will kill you."

I looked back at him. A warning shone in his eyes—not to control me, but out of genuine fear. Protection.

As if this had happened to others.

"How do you know? It's just a blight. It only affects the land." I moved closer, my forehead creasing. "Right?"

His jaw clenched, but he didn't answer. His throat bobbed as he swallowed. "There's nothing you can do. What's done is done. We need to get back to the manor."

I looked back at the rotted field. "More secrets," I murmured. This kingdom was full of them. First the dead sea life, now this. Lord Reaux knew more than he was letting on.

"Clarissa, look—"

"Don't worry, Lord Reaux," I said, removing my hand from his. "I'll find them out eventually."

18

CLARISSA

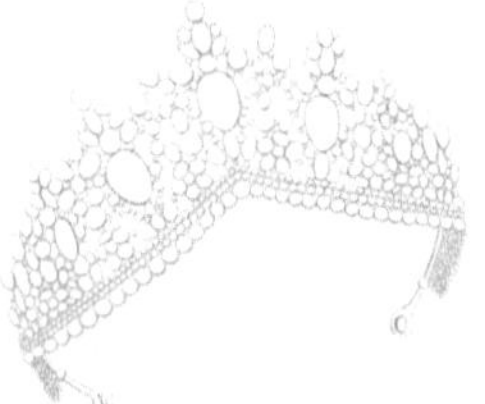

When we returned to Silenus Manor, Thorne immediately disappeared to Fates knew wherever Galen and Dion Silenus were. They all resurfaced briefly for dinner. Galen's features were strained and pale, his behavior jumpier than normal. I was sure Thorne's report of the blight hitting the field today put him and Dion both under immense pressure.

I couldn't take my mind off it. How *dead* everything was. Like something had sucked the life right out of every cell, every inch. I'd seen dead crops before, and they didn't look anything like that. I imagined it spreading, hurting more and more farms, killing every-thing in its path. Thorne said there was nothing they could do, but were they even *trying*?

I spent hours pacing in mine and my mother's shared suite, fixating and rearranging all my luggage, then the decorations in the room. Mother's soft snores eventually dragged me out of the suite so I'd avoid waking her.

The corridors were empty, without so much as a guard or maid in sight this late. A clock on the wall of the drawing room read eleven o'clock. I'd never been able to go to sleep at a decent hour. Mother always said it was the fox in me. Always alert late into the night, my mind unable to rest, my senses coming alive when the sun went down.

I ventured down several hallways until I found a door leading outside. It opened to the back of the manor, which had a stone path curving into a hedge maze. The bushes were neatly trimmed and dark green in the light of the moon, towering high over my head. Taking a deep breath to loosen my muscles, I headed into the maze, needing something to do while my thoughts kept wandering.

The solitude didn't last for long, though.

"Can't sleep?" a deep voice said behind me.

I turned to find Thorne leaning against a hedge at the starting point, one ankle crossed over the other.

Of course he was here.

"It's not that I can't, just that I haven't tried. If you'll excuse me, Lord Reaux." I faced forward and continued my exploration, once again missing my fox half. The moon and stars barely provided enough light to see my way around the winding hedges. My Shifter eyesight would've allowed me much more visibility.

"Do you often take walks in places you've never been after nearly being killed?"

I pursed my lips and held out a hand to feel around the next bend. "Do you often follow women down dark paths when they're alone?"

"No. They're usually the ones following me."

I let out a scoff and picked up speed. I heard his footfalls on the grass behind me. Emperor's tits, this lord couldn't take a hint.

His low chuckle reached my ears, caressing my neck. "Oh, come on. It was a *joke*. Are you always so tightly wound?"

I stopped in my tracks. *Tightly wound?* I didn't think anyone had ever called me that in my life. *Leo* was tightly wound. I was the fun, adventurous twin.

Spinning on my heels, I pointed my finger. "And are *you* always so—" I halted when my finger met his solid chest. He was closer than I'd thought. His steady heart beat against the tip, rumbling into my hand and down my arm.

I snatched my hand away and took a step backward. My spine met the sharp leaves of the hedge. Thorne smirked and moved forward, bringing an arm to rest above my head and caging me in.

"Always so what, Empress?" A scent I'd never noticed before, like the light, sweet smell of grass mixed with heavy leather, washed over me, and I involuntarily sucked in a breath.

"Arrogant," I gritted out.

His smirk widened. "You don't even know me."

My fingers sank into the shrubs behind me as if my claws were trying to emerge. He was too close. His broad shoulders covered my line of sight, and he was all I could see.

I swallowed hard. "Yes, well," I started, sliding out from beneath his raised arm to put some distance between us. "I know men *like* you."

"And what's that supposed to mean?" He fell into step beside me when I whipped around another corner. His tone was light and humorous, as if taking pleasure in my irritation.

"Men who think they own every room they walk into. Who hide behind lies and are used to charming their way into anything they want with a nice smile and pretty words."

"You think I have a nice smile?"

A quiet growl escaped me as I pinched the bridge of my nose between my fingers. He quickened his pace and got in front of me, only to spin on his heel to face me. He walked backward as he laughed. "I mean you no harm, Empress. It's just too easy to get under your skin."

I sighed. "You're going to run into something."

"I'll take my chances. This is a better view, anyway." When I glowered at him, his eyes crinkled into a smile. "See? Far too easy."

My nose twitched, and I cursed my traitorous lips for trying to smile.

"What did you mean earlier, about men who hide behind lies?" he asked, his grin fading.

I stopped walking. "You said you would talk to Galen about all the dead sea creatures, but that didn't happen."

"Oh. That again."

"Yes, *that again.* And today with the blight, you obviously weren't being truthful. There's *something* going on."

"You just don't let things go, do you?"

"Says the man following me even when I've asked him to leave."

He scratched his beard. "Technically, you haven't asked me to leave, Empress."

I sucked on my teeth, assessing him with another sigh before continuing my walk through the maze. "Why *are* you following me, anyway?"

"I was out here first. I saw you head into the hedges and got curious." He shrugged. "Wanted to be sure you were okay after what happened today and yesterday."

"I wish everyone would stop asking me that."

He made an exasperated sound in the back of his throat. "Is it such a burden to know people care about you? You were *attacked.* You almost died, and you killed someone in the process."

I swallowed. "Wouldn't be the first time."

"Cryptic, I see."

I stopped walking again and crossed my arms over my chest. "*I'm* cryptic?" I shook my head, causing my hair to brush against my arms. "You know what? Never mind. It's been a long few days, and I was trying to clear my head out here. If you're not going to start telling me the truth, then please, just leave me alone."

He closed his eyes. "Clarissa, there's so much that—"

I didn't let him finish his sentence, for something behind him caught my eye and made my stomach drop.

"Thorne," I gasped out, instinctively reaching for him. At the sound of his name, his eyes flew open, and he grasped my arm, pulling me to his side.

"What is it?" he asked quickly.

"It—it's the hedge. Look." I pointed behind him, where an

entire section of the well-trimmed bushes was now black and gnarled. Dead leaves fell from the hedge like dark rainfall, collecting on the ground in a heap. "Did that just happen?"

His eyes widened, and his face fell. Licking his lips, he tried to regain his casual composure, but I'd already seen the slip. "I'm sure it's nothing," he said. "Perhaps the servants forgot to water this area."

Oh, absolutely not. I was *done* with these people and their attempts to cover the truth. Anger flooded me, almost strong enough to fill the hollow pit where my magic used to be.

I yanked my arm from his hold. "Alright, that's it. I've had it with all of these poor excuses. *Something* is going on in this kingdom. The dead sea creatures? The blight in the farms? You and Galen have been ignoring me, acting like everything I'm seeing is a figment of my imagination."

I prowled closer to him, my nostrils flaring. "This is supposed to be an *alliance*. Fates, I'm supposed to *marry* him. I deserve to know what I'm getting myself and my empire into. I will not willingly join forces with a kingdom that's hiding information from me. If you and your king want this union to work, if you want peace with Veridians, someone needs to start being honest with me."

I was close enough now that, even in the darkness, I could see every inch of his face. His blue eyes were tight and guarded as they shifted between mine. A breeze came through and rustled our hair, my blonde locks mixing with his dark brown. My chest heaved from my outburst, and his lips parted as I glared up at him.

Just when I thought he wasn't going to give in, he let out a sigh and took a step back.

"There's something you should know, Empress."

19

THORNE

Galen was going to kill me.

But he'd had the chance to tell her. *Multiple* chances. Yet he still refused. Even after I tried to convince him that she needed to know the truth, especially after she saw it first-hand today.

My mother would agree. She would think knowing the full story would convince Clarissa to not go through with this marriage.

Perhaps that was true, but that wasn't why I was telling her. Nobody deserved to be in the dark when making decisions that would impact the rest of their life. Nobody deserved to have the truth concealed from them, as Clarissa pointed out. And it was becoming more and more difficult to respect Galen's wishes to keep this from her.

If discovering the truth caused her to leave, then so be it.

Maybe then Galen would see the wisdom in stepping down, and we could do as my mother desired: put someone on the throne who would do right by the people.

Clarissa's breath caught at my words, eyes blinking in triumph as she straightened her spine. "Tell me."

There was no turning back now.

"You're right," I said slowly. "Everything you've seen is connected. The dead animals, the rotted fields, this hedge, all of it. But it goes back further than that." I paused and scrubbed a hand down my face. "Do you know anything about the Grimaldi line?"

Clarissa shook her head. "Galen is the first king we've had contact with since the war ended, that I'm aware of. I'm not familiar with any of his ancestors."

I anticipated as much. The Grimaldis kept this particular piece of their history private from most people, even in their own kingdom. "Two hundred years ago, Nyses Grimaldi and his entire bloodline were cursed by the Fates after he propositioned them into granting him magic."

Her mouth gaped open. "*What?*"

I nodded grimly. "He wanted magic like what the Veridians received after the war, so he thought he could bargain with the Fates. They agreed to meet with him and even granted his wish—but not in the way he was expecting. They gave him a curse instead. One that changed and grew with every Grimaldi heir.

"Nyses was given the ability to see the future. A powerful gift, but it overwhelmed him. It warped him, making him rash, paranoid, and near-delusional. His son was cursed with a different type of magic, and so on. The details of each of their powers are somewhat murky, but Galen says they ranged from seeing spirits to inflicting pain. His own father was cursed with being forced to change into a wild beast every night. Each generation gets a little more volatile, a little more...erratic."

And it was getting worse, if Galen's curse was even reaching the Avonige Ocean now.

Clarissa swallowed. "All this time...there's been *magic* in Mysthelm?"

"Only in the crown. The Grimaldi heir is the only one who inherits it, and it doesn't happen until they take the throne." Mother had a theory that if Galen was removed from power, if the Grimaldis were no longer in line for the throne, then the curse would break. It was another reason why she was so insistent on her plan.

"I'm guessing your people don't have any idea what's going on?" Clarissa asked.

I shook my head. "Most don't know the truth. Just those of us closest to him. Any incident over the centuries has always been twisted into some believable accident."

"And Galen? What's his curse?" she asked quietly.

I was waiting for that.

"Everything he touches..." I bit down on my bottom lip. "Everything he touches dies."

The air was silent. I could see her making connections and fitting pieces together behind those dark eyes. How Galen always wore gloves, how he never let anyone touch his skin. How things around him suddenly rotted and died.

She slumped against a non-cursed hedge as she exhaled loudly. "I don't know what I was expecting, but it wasn't all of that."

"Yes, well, it's not exactly something he takes pride in. He's been scared to tell you. This has haunted his legacy for centuries."

Her eyes flashed. "He still should've told me."

"I know, you're right. There's no excuse," I said with a wince. Defending Galen was as natural as breathing at this point.

"That doesn't explain why the sea creatures were struck dead on our trip, though," she said. "Or that farm we saw today. He hasn't been going around touching all of those fields. And he wasn't here tonight, when this happened." She extended a hand to the rotted hedge.

"It's become a bit more complicated. Like I said, every generation's curse seems to grow more and more volatile. And they never know what their power will be until they become king. At first, it was just touch. Galen would accidentally skim a tree and it would die, things like that." My heart pounded as I thought back to those months at the end of last year when he first realized what he'd been burdened with. Death and rot everywhere.

The trees, the fields, the animals.

The bodies.

"But within the last few months, it's...expanded. We started hearing reports of livestock, crops, and sea life winding up dead out of nowhere. We had no explanation for it except that his curse was spreading. Affecting areas even when he hadn't been near them."

"It's killing your entire kingdom," Clarissa murmured.

I closed my eyes. "That's what it seems like, yes."

"And Galen is doing nothing to stop it."

It wasn't a question, but still, I refused to answer. He was my best friend and my king. Accusing him of negligence was akin to treason.

It didn't matter; she knew.

"Thorne..." The soft way she said my name made my entire body hinge on the words coming from her lips. "Has he killed anyone?"

I swallowed hard and turned away from her. "That's not a question for me to answer, Empress."

Her softness immediately solidified into steel. "Then tell me where he is."

"What?"

She began walking back the way we came. "Galen. Show me what room he's in. This conversation is overdue, anyway."

I blinked back my surprise, nearly stumbling as I tried to follow her. "Clarissa, you can't go barging into his room in the dead of night. He's the King of Mysthelm."

She whirled on me. Her dark eyes burned gold, a snarl ripping from her. "And I'm the Empress of the Veridian Empire. I'm done waiting for answers."

20

CLARISSA

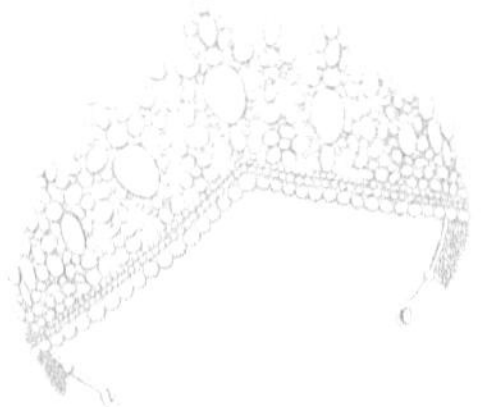

I stormed through the winding maze and back up the path to Silenus Manor. Thorne's heavy footsteps sounded behind me, but he didn't make any effort to stop me.

My mind reeled with everything I'd learned. The fact that Mysthelm had magic in any form was something I hadn't expected in my wildest dreams, much less this vengeful curse the Fates had placed on the Grimaldis.

It made sense, though. The way Galen was so careful not to touch me with his bare skin, how his hands and arms were covered at all times. That one moment in the garden when I reached out to touch him and he got so angry.

What would happen if I *did* touch him?

How many people had discovered the hard way?

And what Thorne said about it becoming uncontrollable and spreading to the rest of the kingdom... If nobody could figure out a way to stop his curse, how much longer would his people withstand it? How much longer until his subjects began to fall prey to this deadly rot too? Till their crops and livestock died off, and they were left with nothing?

This was more than I'd been prepared to handle. And they'd played me for a fool.

I gritted my teeth. I should have been *told*. I shouldn't be having to force secrets from the king's advisor and charge into Galen's bedchamber like a raging lion.

But here I was.

I stopped at the intersection of two corridors, glancing down each one. Thorne chose that moment to finally speak. "Clarissa, think about—"

"Where is he?" I hissed.

Pursing his lips, the muscles at his jaw clenched as he pointed a resigned finger to the left. I marched down the hall until I came across a pair of wide double doors with two guards stationed in front.

"Let me in," I ordered.

The guards exchanged a wary glance with each other. "Your Majesty, it's the middle of the night."

"I'm aware, thank you. I need to see King Grimaldi."

One of them eyed Thorne, who simply looked at me as if to say, *you got yourself into this.*

I sighed. "I just need to speak with him for a moment. If you could please tell him that—"

The door opened, and Galen's head peeked out, his brown hair mussed from sleep. "What's going on?" His eyes sharpened when he spotted Thorne and me. "Clarissa? What's the matter?"

I leveled him with a stare. "We need to talk."

His face paled. He searched Thorne's features for a moment before his shoulders fell and he opened the door wider. "Come in."

The door shut behind us, and Galen moved to light a lamp at his bedside table, casting the space in a soft golden glow. Dark red curtains were drawn back from the window. Moonlight illuminated the wide bed with its oak headboard and a myriad of white and gray throw pillows. A gray rug sat on the floor in the center of the room beneath a small table and two burgundy wingback chairs. Galen's trunks rested in a corner, with several cloaks and tunics hanging inside an open armoire.

He turned to face me, weariness heavy in his eyes. "Clarissa, could this have waited until—"

"Why didn't you tell me?" I snapped. "This power. This curse. Did you not think I had the right to know?"

Instead of answering me, he glared at Thorne. "You told her?"

"Don't blame him. *You're* the one who asked to ally with my empire, Galen. You asked to *marry* me. Don't you think this was information I should've had before I agreed to any of it?"

"Would it have changed your mind?" he countered.

I threw my hands in the air. "I don't know! But I wanted the *choice*. It's become more than just about me, though. This land is suffering, and your people don't even know why." I let out a disbelieving breath as something occurred to me. "Was that your plan? Get me to come here and agree to be your queen so I could help you solve your problems? So you could exploit me and use Veridia's magic?"

"No—no, Clarissa, that wasn't it. I swear," Galen said, taking a step toward me.

I backed up. My hand accidentally brushed against Thorne's and sent a flare up my arm before I pulled away.

"I wasn't trying to trick you," Galen continued. "I just...this was the only thing I knew to do. There's more to the story—please, let me explain."

My anger turned to hesitancy, and I glanced up at Thorne. His gaze was fixed on Galen, the crease at his forehead deepening. "What are you talking about, Galen?"

So Thorne didn't know everything, either.

More secrets.

"What else is there?" I asked.

Galen ran his gloved fingers through his hair. A dark brown lock fell over his eyebrow. "It's the real reason I reached out to your council. The reason I asked you to come here. It—it wasn't just for an alliance." A pause. "*You're* the only way to break this curse, Clarissa."

A ringing formed low in my ears. "I—I don't understand."

"Thorne told you about my ancestor Nyses, yes?" Galen asked, and I nodded. "His son gained an audience with the Fates several decades after Nyses died. He was penitent and tried to get them to grant him and his descendants mercy, saying they shouldn't inherit the sins of one man. The Fates made a deal with him: since the curse was born out of greed and envy toward the Veridian Empire, the only way to end it would be to join the two lands. Unite Mysthelm and Veridia under a bond of marriage, and the curse would break."

"*What?*" Thorne snapped.

Chills spread across my skin. I started pacing the floor, unable to look at either of them as I processed this.

A bond of marriage. That was why he was so urgent. Why he reached out to us so quickly after his father's death, why he pushed for this engagement as opposed to a simple alliance. If he wanted to break this curse, he had to marry *me.*

"How has nobody tried to do this before now?" I asked.

"Some of my ancestors have tried to contact your empire, but nobody ever responded. Either they never received our attempts, or they ignored us. But not all Grimaldis have wanted to bridge the gap—their pride was strong, their hatred for the Veridian Empire too consuming to ask for their help. You're the first one who's shown any interest in peace."

I scoffed at that. "And look how that turned out for me."

Galen pressed on. "I know it was under somewhat false pretenses, but do you honestly think you'd be here if I had led with the entire truth?"

I chewed on my bottom lip. "I don't know." Crossing to one of the chairs, I sank into the cushion, resting my elbow on the armrest.

There were so many conflicting emotions warring inside me. Anger, of course, although that was swiftly morphing to hurt. Betrayal, even. Which was ridiculous, considering I barely knew these people. Why should I feel betrayed by two men who'd been complete strangers—bordering on my *enemies,* if you took into account the feud over the last three centuries—until three days ago?

Part of me felt used. Disposable, like I was some pawn they could move around and twist into doing their bidding to get what they wanted. The vulnerable, volatile woman Lord Stryker always painted me as.

My thoughts screamed, begging for an outlet. Even without my Shifter half, I was still just as emotional, just as easily riled. But it had nowhere to go. No magic to consume my emotions and turn them into power. It was like when I was a child and couldn't let my feelings out, couldn't control the rage and hurt and confusion that swirled in me like a storm.

I took a deep breath and did what my mother taught me to do as a young Shifter.

Focus on three things I could see.

The silver moonlight coming in from the window, casting the floor in shadows. The broad leaves of a potted plant by the armoire. The dwindling embers in the fireplace a few feet from my chair. I let my breaths even out to their yellow and orange glow.

Two things I could feel.

The velvet of the armrest coated in burgundy fabric, soft and fuzzy beneath my fingers. The weight of my hair resting against my chest and lightly brushing my exposed arm when I turned my head.

One thing I could smell.

Leather and sweet grass.

My eyes locked with Thorne's. His gaze bore into mine, and the tidal wave subsided.

"I understand if you want to leave, Clarissa," Galen said, causing both Thorne and me to turn back to him. "I would never try to hold you here against your will. The choice is yours, as it should've been all along." He chewed on his bottom lip before adding, "But...I hope you'll consider it. What this would mean, not just for me, but my entire kingdom."

I nodded and rose to my feet, my normal composure washing

over me. "I need to think. It's not a no, Galen," I said when his face fell. "Give me a little bit of time. You owe me that much."

A muscle in his neck twitched, but he gave a curt nod. When I opened and shut the door to his chambers behind me, I leaned my head against the hard wood for a moment before heading in the direction I'd come from, desperate to feel the night's wind on my skin before I suffocated.

21

THORNE

"You had no right to tell her," Galen barked at me.

My mouth fell open. "You can't be serious."

He stalked toward me, his forlorn expression from earlier with Clarissa now shifting to indignation. "It is *my* curse to bear, and *my* call to make. We've spoken about this, and you knew I wasn't ready. You went behind my back and—"

"That's the problem, Galen," I interrupted, trying to keep my voice even. "*You* should have told her already. All of this could have been avoided if you'd been honest with her. It took her stumbling upon a cursed piece of the hedge maze tonight for her to finally snap and break through the lies. I don't know if it's because of your pride or your fear, but either way, it might have cost you greatly."

His chest swelled with anger. "How *dare* you speak to me that way? I am your *king*, Thorne. You forget your place."

"You mean, your place as a royal advisor? Or as a friend? Why didn't you tell me about the Fates and their deal?" All of my irritation with him burst to the surface, like fire racing through my veins. With it came a sting of betrayal. After all we'd been through, after the way I'd stood by him, he'd still kept such an enormous part of the curse from me.

This changed *everything*.

Mother thought Galen's removal would break the curse. She thought putting someone else in his place was the best hope for a better future. But now? Now that I knew this marriage to Clarissa would take away the curse? It was the cause of so much pain, so much death, so many fears. It made sense why Galen was insistent on bringing Clarissa over. She *was* his hope. She was his answer.

But he isn't our *answer,* a voice that sounded like my mother's whispered in the back of my mind. *He can't rule our people.*

Perhaps he wasn't what was best for Mysthelm, but that didn't mean I wanted to see him hurt. That didn't mean I wanted him to endure this curse until it got too late. After seeing with my own eyes how widespread his powers were reaching, I was beginning to fear my mother's theory wouldn't work. That *nothing* could stop it.

Nothing except...Clarissa.

What if she left, Galen stepped down, and the curse persisted? Still continued to kill our land? Our *people*? What if *she* was our only chance?

Doubts crept in my mind. In the span of mere minutes, I'd learned the empress might be our greatest hope for survival, then watched her walk straight out the doors. It sent a wave of helplessness skittering across my skin.

He needed her. *We* needed her. Even if it went against my mother's plan.

"I'm going to go find her," I said, spinning on my heel and ignoring Galen's flared nostrils and the bulging vein in his neck. "Imprison me for disobedience if you want, Galen, but someone has to fix this."

If he responded, I didn't hear it. I was already out of the room and striding down the hall. If I had to guess, I didn't think Clarissa would go to bed. I imagined she'd be...

Her blonde waves were the first thing I saw when I opened the doors leading to the grounds at the back of the manor. She was pacing furiously back and forth in front of the entrance to the hedge maze. A gentle breeze lifted the bottom of her short-sleeved green jumpsuit, and I absentmindedly wondered if she might be cold.

From the door, I could vaguely see her expression in the moonlight and a couple of swinging lanterns staked into the ground. Her pinched brow, the pink blush of vexation on her cheeks, the way her lips fluttered silently as if having a conversation with herself.

This empress became more and more intriguing every time I was with her. Back in Galen's chambers, I had *seen* her change. It was a visible transformation, the way she went from intoxicating rage to calm and collected in mere seconds. I could tell she felt her emotions so deeply. From her annoyance the day I met her at the ship, to how poised she was when meeting Galen and the Silenus regent family, to anger and betrayal when we were in the hedge maze. But she was able to turn it off like flicking out a candle. At the drop of a hat, she could stand regal. Strong.

As I stared at the ends of her hair swirling in the breeze, her hands clenching and unclenching at her sides, her jaw shifting and eyes burning...I realized I wanted to know this empress. The *true* Clarissa Aris. The way she was when she thought nobody was around.

Unfiltered. Raw. Honest.

I wanted to see her undone.

That fleeting thought scared me more than any curse or crown.

I stepped out of the shadows and onto the path leading to where she paced. As I approached, a twig snapped loudly under my foot, alerting her of my presence.

Her entire body reacted to the noise. Her shoulders sank, and her neck twisted to find the source as she staggered backward. A hand flew to her heart, and her chest rose and fell with deep, ragged breaths.

My brow furrowed. Was she that surprised by me?

She drew in another gasping breath and kept stumbling, her hand reaching to find purchase on something solid.

"Clarissa, what's wrong?" I asked quickly once I got to her side. I grabbed her outstretched hand to steady her, but she yanked it back with a half-sob. Fear gripped me until I saw her eyes darting around, wide and scared, with the pupils blown out.

She was having some sort of panic attack.

"Breathe, Empress," I said. "Here—come sit down." She let me put a hand on her shoulder and guide her to a nearby bench, her body trembling the whole way. When she sat, I knelt at her feet. "Can you hear me?"

After a moment, she nodded. Her breaths were still uneven and shaky.

"Good. You're safe, Clarissa. Nothing is going to hurt you." I swallowed. "Can I touch you?"

For the first time, her eyes locked onto mine. They still looked distant, as if she was somewhere else and not truly focused on me, but again, she nodded. I leaned forward to put my hands on either side of her neck. Her pulse raced, erratic and strong.

"Just breathe. Listen to the sound of my voice. Do you feel the ground at your feet?" I waited, and she let out a breath before nodding. "Focus on that. It's tethering you here, to me. Not wherever your mind took you. Are you in pain?" She closed her eyes and flinched, and I instinctively rubbed my thumb along the pulse point at her neck. Her warm skin was soft and smooth where the rough pad of my thumb grazed.

"Do you feel my fingers, Clarissa?" A nod. "Does it hurt?"

With another inhale, her pulse began to slowly even out, and her breaths along with it. She swallowed, her neck contracting beneath my touch, then she quietly replied, "No. That doesn't hurt."

"Then focus on that. The bench, the ground, my hands. Nothing else is touching you. Nothing else can hurt you. This is what's real—what's right in front of you."

Her eyes opened. Dark jewels shone back at me, wary and hesitant but clear.

"Are you alright?" I began to move my hands away. She quickly raised her arms and grasped my wrists, keeping them in place for a split second before lowering them and shifting farther onto the bench.

"Yes," she said. "I'm fine. I—I'm sorry."

I shook my head. "You have nothing to be sorry for."

"How—how did you know what to do?" she asked, her voice still quiet.

"My daughter suffers from panic attacks as well," I explained.

They had started after her mother died four years ago, and it didn't take long for me to see what she was going through. It wasn't until Marigold was old enough to put her feelings into words that I learned how to talk her down from these episodes. I wasn't sure Marigold even knew what triggered them. She could barely remember Iris or how she died. But she seemed to have a subconscious fear around any of those she loved getting hurt or being taken from her, and I often had to reassure her that I was safe. It was another reason why I didn't want to leave her to go on this tour. I didn't know how she would handle the separation, with nothing to calm her anxiety about my absence.

Clarissa blinked at me. "I didn't know you had a daughter."

A smile formed on my lips. "Marigold. She's seven years old. She's here with us, actually. On the tour."

"Oh," Clarissa said softly. "I must not have met her yet. Or her mother."

My eyes fell to the ground as I stood and dusted off my knees. "Her mother is no longer with us."

There was a small intake of breath. "I'm so sorry."

"Thank you," I said. "It was a long time ago. But Marigold has similar episodes." I gestured to Clarissa. "Did something happen to cause it? Was it everything with Galen?"

"No, no, it wasn't that. I   " She cut herself off. It looked like she wanted to say more, but she simply shook her head. "It doesn't matter. Thank you, Thorne," she added, her lips curving slightly around my name. Perhaps the first time she'd said it without a scoff or sneer.

Two nights ago, I was plotting with my mother about how to

get her to leave. Now, I found myself wondering how I could get that smile to stay.

She has to marry your best friend.

I blinked the thought away. "Listen, I'm sorry I didn't tell you about the curse before. It's not that I thought you didn't have the right to know. It's just...it's bigger than me. And apparently, bigger than Galen and the Grimaldis."

"I take it you didn't know about the marriage bit, either."

I pursed my lips and shook my head. "How are you doing with all of that?"

She resumed her pacing. "How do you think? I was tricked into coming here by a king who couldn't be bothered to tell me the truth. He just wants to use me to break this curse. And the thing is, I *get* it. It's bad. Especially after seeing what's been happening in just this territory alone. Nobody should be forced to suffer because of some power-hungry king who lived two hundred years ago." She paused, biting her bottom lip in thought.

"I would have said yes," she said, quieter this time. "If he'd told me from the beginning, I would've said yes. How could I not, if saying no would mean letting this kingdom get destroyed?"

"That's not your responsibility," I countered.

She let out a humorless laugh. "What, don't you want me to stay and marry him? Save Mysthelm and all of that?"

I swallowed, too many voices and opinions of others whispering in my ear. "Of course I want to help my people. But it should be *your* choice. I may not know you very well, Empress, but you seem like the kind of person who would do anything if it meant helping others. Even if it wasn't in your own best interests."

Her brow pinched. "Is that such a bad thing?"

"No," I said, stepping closer to her. "As long as it's what you want. You have your own life, your own empire, to consider. Don't do this just for him or out of some sense of guilt."

Clarissa searched my features for a moment, underscored by the buzzing insects and whistling of wind through the hedges. Then she sat back down and rolled her neck to gaze up at the stars.

She was lost in thought, those dark eyes expressing so much in their silence.

She, like Galen, held the weight of her people on her shoulders. But unlike Galen, she bore hers with strength instead of letting it drown her.

"We would be lucky to have you as our queen, Clarissa," I said softly, unsure what urged me to speak it, other than it was the truth. Even if I hadn't uncovered the deepest secret of the curse tonight, I would've believed in those words.

She gave me another one of those tentative, wistful, crooked smiles. "You don't even know me."

"I don't have to," I said simply.

"This suits you, you know," she said, tilting her head. "It's genuine. Better than the cocky act."

Something constricted in my chest. I so rarely let the mask fall, I hadn't even realized she'd sent it crashing down. "Who said it was an act?"

She let out a small chuckle that turned into a sigh. Then she asked, "Is he worth it, Thorne? Will he do right by his people? If I do this, will he do right by *me*?"

"Galen has a good heart," I said, almost without thinking. They were words I'd thought to myself so many times over the last few months. "He's just...lost. Misguided."

"Why do you keep defending him? What has he done to earn such loyalty from you?"

An uncomfortable knot settled in my gut. "He's my best friend. He's been through some terrible times, but I..." I exhaled and closed my eyes, then dropped to the bench beside her. "You want genuine? The answer is I don't know, Empress. But this *kingdom* is worth it."

"I think so too." Her words were quiet but not weak. She rested a hand on my shoulder as she stood. "Thanks for following me tonight," she said. "I'll see you around, Lord Reaux."

Her smile, the first true, uninhibited one she'd given me,

slammed through my chest. Her handprint was like a brand on my shoulder when she moved back toward the manor.

I knew at that moment that she was going to do it. She was going to be our queen, end this curse, and save our kingdom.

She was going to marry Galen.

That thought should have filled me with relief. Many of our problems would soon be solved, and we'd no longer have to worry about the rotting or dying or what curse would be passed on for the next generation. It may not be exactly how my mother wanted it to happen, but I realized now what mattered most was stopping this curse. This death.

And I *was* relieved. But that didn't explain the heavy weight that sank in my stomach as I watched her walk away from me and toward her future with the king.

22

CLARISSA

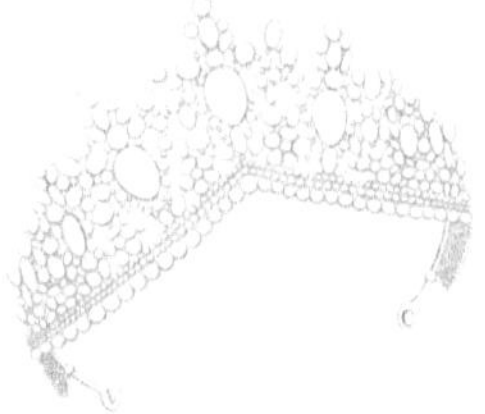

Morning hit me like a tree branch to the snout. I didn't even know what time I made it to the suite last night. Past two in the morning, at least.

We faced another day of exploring the farms of the Mid Territory. Galen had left a note saying *once again*, he was going to be absent. I could sense a pattern in his habit of hiding from difficult things.

I was still reeling from the night before. Still angry with his decision to keep such important details from me. If I was being honest, I didn't want to see him. He hadn't done much to prove to me that I could trust him. Even his best friend was reluctant to put too much confidence in him.

My thoughts lingered on Thorne as I changed into the loose cotton dress Katrine had laid out for me. I had no idea he had a daughter. I vaguely remembered seeing a young girl step out of the carriage with Azura Reaux when we arrived in the territory, but the fact that she was *his* daughter hadn't even crossed my mind.

I wondered what happened to her mother. Thorne might try and hide behind his flirtations, but I saw the pain when he spoke of her last night. It was one of the more genuine moments he had. Maybe I'd judged him too quickly. We all had darkness staining our lives—shadows and pockets of grief we wanted to tuck away. How we chose to mask them was up to us.

It was always difficult for me to sleep after I had one of my panic attacks, when the sound of snapping bones and the feel of tearing skin lingered fresh in my mind. But last night was different. That memory was clouded by another one, one of a warm thumb brushing against my pulse.

Goosebumps trailed up my arm as I stared in the mirror of the vanity, trying to put away the ghost of his skin on mine. I couldn't believe he'd seen me like that. I hadn't let anyone besides my mother, brother, and occasionally Lark witness those episodes. And yet I wasn't able to hide it from a man I'd barely spoken to, who'd spent most of the time we'd known each other keeping things from me.

I didn't want him or others to think any less of me. To think I was weak, the way my mind convinced me in those moments that I was.

The plan today was to head farther west to a fishing village along the coast. Like yesterday, Vespera was in charge of showing Mother and me around, while Thorne was our ever-faithful watchdog in Galen's place.

He was more animated today. More involved in the conversation, instead of lounging in silence. It was different, seeing him like this. The same way he was last night after my panic attack. A...*good* different.

He and Vespera talked about their territories, the stubborn citizens they had to deal with, and the most far-fetched requests they'd heard. Like someone in the North Territory submitting a marriage license to marry a ghost, or the time Vespera was asked to formally knight a cat because the owner said it saved their life.

Eventually, the two of them and my mother began swapping stories about their children. I promptly removed myself from the conversation the moment Mother mentioned me running naked through the forest outside our cottage.

I stared out the window of the carriage as we drove over the hills. The occasional farm would pass by, with livestock grazing in fields and wagons traveling on roads in the distance. I was about to knock on the console separating us and the driver to ask how much farther, when something strange on an upcoming hill caught my attention.

I leaned forward, putting my nose as close to the window as I could.

It was something…dark. Blackened. Like rot.

"Thorne." I put a hand on his knee across from me. He went rigid beneath my touch, and I quickly pulled away. "Look."

He glanced out the window and paled. "That's…a lot," he breathed.

It was. It looked as if it had spread out across the entire side of the hill, overtaking everything that had once been lush and green. But as we stared at it, my hands went cold.

"Is it *moving*?"

It was hard to tell with the speed of the carriage, but I could have sworn the death curse was inching farther and farther down the hill, toward the little village waiting below.

"It's never done that before," he whispered.

Our quiet voices had caught Vespera and Mother's attention. "What's going on over there?" my mother asked.

Vespera peered around our shoulders and let out a gasp. "We have to turn around. We have to go tell Dion and His Majesty."

"What are they going to do? We're already three hours out. We should go help the village," I countered.

"Clarissa's right," Thorne said. "Evadine, Vespera, we can have the two of you dropped off somewhere safe nearby, but—"

"These are my people, Reaux. If they're in trouble, I want to help," Vespera said, her dark eyes determined.

Mother nodded firmly. "Let's go. Don't look at me like that—I'll be alright, Clarissa."

I sighed and twisted my lips to the side, but relented. Reaching across the carriage, I slid open the console between us and the driver and directed him toward the hill.

"*Quickly,*" I added, and he snapped the reins.

We flew down the path, the rotted land drawing nearer with every passing minute. It slowly descended down the hill like blackened fingers crawling over rocks and trees, unspooling onto the unsuspecting town. When we took a sharp right turn, it disappeared onto the other side of the carriage, and I had to crane my neck up as it loomed larger.

Commotion from the village reached our ears the closer we got. They had definitely noticed the blight. It was a small community, maybe a couple dozen houses closer to the bottom of the hill and a large town square near the main path. Families were scrambling around, trying to wrangle their possessions into wagons and carts, hurried voices and shouts filling the air as the blight edged closer.

I flung open the carriage door and rushed forward, Thorne close on my heels. "Why is this happening?" I hissed. "I know Galen doesn't have control over it, but something has to be able to stop it!"

"I don't know. Sometimes I think it's triggered by an emotional reaction," he confessed as we ran. "He's...in distress. Worried about what happened yesterday and how bad it's gotten. Maybe that's why this one is so much bigger."

We came upon a man giving orders to a group, and I slowed to a stop. "We're here from Silenus Manor," I said. "Tell us how we can help."

"The border of the village," the man replied without question, barely looking at me as he ran his fingers over his balding head. "We don't know who's left over there. I don't have eyes on it, and we need to evacuate."

"Got it." I turned on my heel, heading to the base of the hill, when Thorne grabbed my hand. I swung to face him. "If you tell me not to go, I swear—"

"Be careful," he said. "Be smart. This magic is potent. Don't get too close to it, alright?"

I blinked in surprise and slowly nodded. "I'll be careful."

His thumb grazed the sensitive skin at my palm before he released his grip. "Then let's go."

We raced toward the hill. The sky darkened as its large shadow fell over us, replacing the sun with the rotted hillside. The edge of the curse crept ever nearer, now reaching the bottom of the slope. It was as if a blanket had been thrown over the entire land, twisting every tree into a gnarled stump, eating away at the grass and turning rocks to dust.

Barely a quarter mile from the incline stood the first row of houses. The occupants were running around their yards, gathering children and supplies into wagons, some even attempting to herd horses and cattle.

Thorne and I threw ourselves into action. We helped tie down covers and secure supplies, making sure all the children were accounted for and reining in as many of the animals as we could.

"We're out of time!" I shouted as the curse crested the first stretch of farmland. "We have to move!"

It was a mad dash out of there. Family after family rushed away in their wagons or on horseback, fleeing the scene as quickly as they could. A group of them stayed behind with Thorne and me as we knocked down the doors of each house to make sure no one was left behind.

The curse reached the closest house to the hill.

"Come on," Thorne said. "We've done what we can. We need to go."

We headed back to the main path when one of the men behind us called out, "Help me! It's stuck!"

I turned to find him pulling at the enclosure to a paddock near the edge, where a dozen horses and a handful of cows pawed anxiously at the ground. The animals converged on the entrance, their senses heightened by the nearby threat. The rot was swiftly closing in on the opposite end of the pasture.

Thorne sprinted back to the man, and I sucked in a breath. "Thorne, wait—"

"I'll be fine, Empress. Stay there!" he called. "Make sure the others don't need anything."

I watched from across the road as the two of them struggled with the latch, which had something wedged in it, keeping it from opening.

Still, the curse snaked closer. Inching its way across the paddock, the edge of it trailed along the grass toward the animals, making them go wild with fear. The horses snorted, tossing their manes back and rearing up on their hind legs to kick the paddock enclosure.

Crack.

My body doubled over at the sound, as if it had come from my own spine. I gasped against the wave of panic that made my vision waver. *Fight it, fight it, fight it—*

The tall fence had snapped. Voices of the other men rang around me in alarm. Animal after animal bolted out of the pasture, trampling everything in sight. Including—

"Thorne!" I wheezed, my mind clearing away the memories of bones fracturing, only to be replaced with a new terror.

The other man had moved out of the way in time, but Thorne had been thrown onto his back. He tried to pull himself up using the fence, his legs dragging and his face contorted in pain. The broken fence buckled beneath his weight, and he went crashing back to the ground.

I shouted his name again and ran forward. The curse had almost made its way across the entire pasture. Its edges curled mere yards from him, getting closer with every second. Heavy anticipation pounded through me as a boulder sank in my chest.

I reached my hand out to him. "Come on!"

He saw the look on my face. "I'll only slow you down, Clarissa. Please, go—"

"I'm not leaving you," I snapped. "Now *take my hand.*"

Gripping my arm, he hauled himself forward, wincing when he put weight on his left foot. He leaned on my shoulder as I dragged him away, glancing over my shoulder at the curse.

We only had seconds left.

It was so close, I could smell it—sour and musty, like decaying leaves mixed with stale dust. It clung to my nostrils and wrapped around me, making my head swim.

But there was something else.

At first it was a soft buzz. Hardly noticeable, like an insect flying around my ears. It crept along my skin, raising the hair at the back of my neck and thrumming to the beat of my pulse.

It felt like...*magic.*

"Clarissa, we're not going to make—"

On instinct, I put both of my hands on his shoulders and shoved with every ounce of strength I could muster. He went sprawling forward with a strangled yell.

The curse crashed into me.

23
CLARISSA

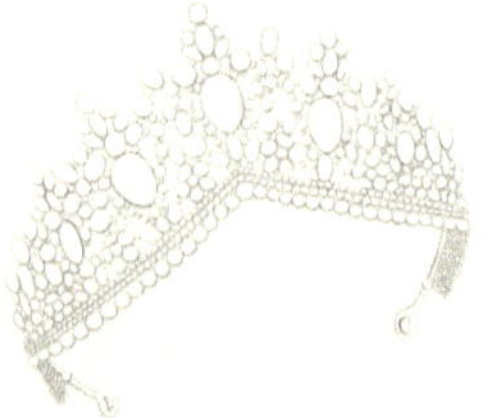

Magic jolted through my body, like molten gold lighting every cell on fire. I stretched my arms out wide as the wind whipped at my hair, sending it whirling around my face.

My fox half slammed back to life. It was like...like coming home after a lifetime away. Like having a veil lifted from your eyes and finally seeing the sun once more. It was beautiful. *Freeing.*

And the curse...it had stopped moving.

Sparks burst behind my eyes. I barely contained a groan as the familiar magic soared in my bones, my veins, my heart. That empty well inside me filled to the brim with warm, glowing power, as if a dam had been released.

But...

The magic kept coming.

It poured from me like a torrent of water. When I tried to grasp it in my hands, it slipped right through my fingers, flooding me. Panic bubbled up inside my chest, colliding into me, spilling over.

It was too much.

I couldn't control it.

Magic exploded from my feet all the way to the tips of my ears. I staggered to my feet and met Thorne's eyes for a split second before my fox half burst from beneath my skin with a snarl that echoed across the village. My red fur rippled in the breeze, my claws sinking into the crumbled soil as my muscles and joints screamed for release.

Every sensation barreled into me. Every sound, smell, taste. Along with all the heightened emotions I'd been suppressing these past few days. The fear, the anger, the adrenaline and irritation were all sharp claws scraping at my mind.

It was an onslaught. My limbs vibrated with the force of it. It clouded my vision, making everything hazy, and when a shadowed form stumbled closer, I let out a growl. My ears stood so straight, an ache formed from the strain.

I flinched when a muffled voice called out to me. Other sounds filled the air, more unfamiliar forms closing in.

A hand reached out, and I snapped.

I swiped my paw through the air, connecting with something solid. My claws embedded themselves into soft flesh.

"Clarissa," the voice said with a grunt of pain. I retracted my claws, and the fog in my mind lifted. A man fell to his knees at my feet, clutching his chest.

Thorne.

Four jagged claw marks striped the front of his linen shirt, with a line of blood trailing from each. When I caught the eyes of the remaining men around us, I whined and started to take a step forward. The scent of dirt and sweat and something else emanated from them in waves. Something sharp and metallic. Biting.

Fear.

Their eyes went wide as they took me in. Shouts filled the air, some scrambling backward while others grabbed forgotten rakes and shovels from the ground, pointing the sharp ends toward me.

My heart plummeted. Memories from my childhood slammed into me, those dark days of sneers and taunts echoing in my ears. Fists against my skin, shears plunging into fur, black and blue blooming on tender flesh.

Those people from my past had feared me. Even as a child, they were scared of my lack of control. Of the volatility of a young Shifter, of the daughter of the despised emperor Branock Aris. They made me hate my own power. They made me unable to sleep at night for fear of waking up the next morning and enduring it all over again. The shame, the pain, the mockery.

Another whine escaped me as I padded backward, tail burrowed between my back legs. One man leaped forward with his rake aimed at me, and I saw that same fear from almost two decades ago. History repeating itself.

They still hated me.

With a groan, Thorne lurched to his feet to stand in front of me. He threw out a hand at the advancing farmer and commanded him to stop. When Thorne turned to face me again, his features softened, his breaths still ragged.

He took a cautious step forward. Tension hung thick in the air, coiling in the waves of summer heat like a snake ready to strike. My ears flattened against the side of my head as my eyes flitted across all the strangers, taking in their curled lips, their pinched brows, their taut muscles. They landed once again on Thorne, and all I could see was blood and scars.

My fault.

Thorne extended a hand, and I flinched.

"I'm not going to hurt you, Clarissa," he murmured.

I let out a quiet whine as I pawed the ground.

"*You* hurt *her*? She almost killed you!" a gruff voice called. The man with the rake pointed the end at me. "She's a monster. A *beast*. Her kind are dangerous," he spat.

Others raised their voices in concern, their words pounding down my spine like battle drums. I shook my head, limbs quivering as I took another step back.

"Clarissa, wait—" Thorne called, but it was too late.

I turned and darted toward the hill.

24

CLARISSA

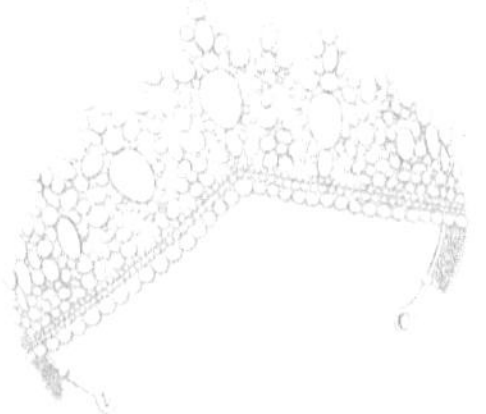

A hand gripped my blonde hair and yanked hard enough to tear strands from my scalp, making me cry out with a high-pitched bark. The teenage boy sneered at me, "What's wrong with your face, you freak?"

I tried to rub away the tears in my eyes, only to remember that my hand had accidentally shifted into a paw at the wrist. One of my claws snagged on the tip of my snout where my fox nose met human cheeks.

"Half fox, half girl," he said with a scoff. "Like a filthy half-breed."

"Look what she did to me!" another girl screeched. Her eyes spat fire at me as she held her wounded arm. Four shallow claw marks marred her forearm, already welling with blood. "Mother always said the Shifters are beasts. She belongs in the woods with the rest of the animals."

She gave a swift kick to my knee, and I went crashing to the ground. The older boy stomped on my exposed claws. I let out a yelp as I cradled the injured hand against my chest, my knees buried in the hard dirt of the forest floor.

A shadow appeared against the leaves.

"Don't you dare touch her again," a familiar voice said, menacing even in his youth.

I craned my neck to see my twin hovering over me, blocking out the *sun like a fierce cloud. His dark hair, the opposite of mine, matched our near-black eyes as he scowled at the other two. A bundle of herbs was clutched in his hand. Only twelve years old and he still managed to look intimidating.*

"What are you gonna do about it, Alchemist?" the older boy taunted. Shadows billowed at his feet and wrapped around his legs and arms, but they were weak. Light and airy, instead of the dark smoke I'd seen around the strongest Shadow Wielders in Veridia City.

Leo didn't even give him time to attack first. He brought his herbs to his lips and said, "Incendar."

Flames erupted at the two teenagers' feet, forcing them away from us. An errant spark flicked onto the boy's boot and traveled up his pants, his cruel features instantly turning to horror. He and the girl batted at their clothing, flailing around like chickens as they tried to stop the magical fire.

Leo looked down at me cowering on the ground. "What did they do to you, Rissa?"

"It was my fault," I choked out. "I—I couldn't control it. I hurt her first. It was an accident. It was—it was my fault."

I soared along the bottom of the hill, needing to get as far away from the village as possible. I had to rely on my senses to navigate back to the main roads before I lost myself in this territory.

The euphoria of having my magic back was overshadowed by shame. I'd *just* started to earn the trust of these people, to prove that Veridians were like them, that we were kind and compassionate and *normal*...only to once again be unable to control my magic.

Monster. Beast. Freak.

Those people would never be comfortable around me now. I'd spent the last decade and a half learning to rein in this other half of me that constantly lived beneath my skin, struggling to tame the wildness into what others wanted to see. To be disciplined. Able to manage my emotions instead of letting them overtake me.

I never wanted to hurt anyone the way I'd clawed that girl so long ago, and others like her. But I'd hurt him.

I'd hurt Thorne.

I shouldn't have slipped. It was my fault.

I slowed to a walk when the main road we'd been traveling on earlier came into view. Staying out of sight in the line of trees, I tugged on that well of magic inside me to shift back into my human form. I needed to find my mother and make sure she was alright, then get to Silenus Manor before I made things worse.

But nothing happened. My human half wouldn't emerge.

I couldn't shift back.

It was normally as natural as breathing, but something…something was blocking it. I could still *sense* my magic; it just wouldn't answer me.

A fresh wave of panic rose. Questions spun around me, a frenzy building along my spine. What if I couldn't shift at all? Was I stuck like this? Was there something wrong with the magic of the curse? What would they do to my mother if they thought we were a threat to them?

I didn't know what to do. Where to go. How to *fix this*. I could charm and negotiate my way into and out of most problems in my life, but I was completely helpless here. Weak and out of control.

Thoughts jumbled in my head as I made my way on four unsteady legs to lean against the trunk of a large tree. I tried to shift again, but my panic was too strong. I couldn't focus; every snapped twig, crinkle of grass, and rush of wind through the trees had my neck jerking and tail tucking. What if someone came after me? Or Mother? What if—

I smelled him before I heard him. Sweet grass and leather. A bit of that same stench of death from the field mingled with a thin layer of sweat and blood. There was another animal with him too. A horse. I could hear its hooves crunching against leaves.

"Clarissa?" he called hesitantly, his dark boots appearing in my line of sight as they bounced against the side of his horse. My gaze traveled upward over his wrinkled pants and light blue shirt streaked with blood.

My fault.

The wound had stopped bleeding, but those marks...those four claw marks glared back at me, shining and jagged in his skin.

His eyes found me, and the deep crease in his forehead disappeared. "It's just me." He kept his voice even as he dismounted and slowly approached me with a limp. "You're safe. Look, I'm alright too. I'm alive. I'm not angry with you—you were scared, but it's okay now."

How was any of this *okay*? I'd hurt him. I'd terrorized a dozen farmers and was almost skewered with a rake. This whole territory was going to hate me.

"Clarissa, what you did...it was *incredible*."

That made me rear back. I cocked my head to the side, one ear perked while the other flopped down.

He continued, "You ran away too quickly to see. But the rot... after you touched it, it—it disappeared. I've never seen anything like it. Everything went back to normal. The entire cursed side of the hill literally *regrew*. As if nothing had happened." He moved another inch closer, and I didn't flinch. "You must have done something." Extending an arm, his hand hovered near my face.

"Don't be afraid of me. You're safe," he repeated, slowly lowering his fingers to the fur beneath my ear.

His warm hand touched me, and I closed my eyes, my nose involuntarily turning and nuzzling into his palm.

Magic tugged at my chest, and this time when I pulled on it, it responded. It ripped through me like a storm, chaotic and uncontrolled.

In the blink of an eye, I shifted back to my human form, with Thorne's hand still cupping my cheek. I sucked in a shaky breath at the sudden change, and his other arm came up to the side of my neck to steady me. We were both on our knees in the grass and dirt, my hands clinging to his elbows as if he was the only thing keeping me from collapsing.

His gaze flicked down my body and then shot back up to meet my eyes, his lips parting on an exhale. Slowly, without tearing his eyes from mine, he began unbuttoning his shirt, deft fingers moving over the fabric. When he shrugged it off his massive shoulders, my eyes widened.

"What are you—"

"Here," he said, handing me the blood-stained shirt.

I glanced down and gasped. I'd torn through my cotton dress, leaving it in tatters draped over my shoulders and around my hips. From a young age, Shifters must figure out how to control the shift, along with our clothing. We're taught how to anchor it to our magic so it can also shift at our will. It's one of the first things we learn—otherwise you wind up naked in the middle of the marketplace. But this shift...it wasn't controlled. It wasn't planned. My body and my magic were at odds, creating an imbalance that shredded through me.

I bit down on my bottom lip and took the shirt, hastily shoving my arms into the holes and struggling to do the buttons. I made it halfway before my fingers shook too fiercely, the aftermath of my shock making it hard to focus.

Strong hands replaced mine. "May I?" he asked, eyes still on mine.

I swallowed and gave a small nod.

Warmth emanated from him, seeping into my skin. The occasional graze of his fingertip against the top of my chest sent little fissures of lightning up my neck. His fingers made quick work of the rest of the buttons, lingering for a moment on my collarbone before he pulled away. The end of the blue shirt swayed against my knees. I looked back up at him, my eyes raking over the hard planes of his stomach to the dark hair curling around the claw marks in his skin, now on full display across his solid, bare chest.

My stomach tightened. "Thorne, I—I'm so sorry. I didn't mean to hurt you," I croaked.

"I know. I don't blame you. You were just scared," he repeated. "Are *you* alright?"

Shame from earlier crept back in. I wished he didn't keep seeing me like this. These moments of weakness. How my confidence was a cover for the fear that lived in every inch of me.

I cleared my throat and got to my feet, sweeping past him as I brushed out my hair. "I'm fine. We should get back to the others."

He didn't move. "You saved me."

"You'd do the same for me. Or anyone else who needed help."

"When I saw the curse touch you..." He shook his head and got to his feet. "How did you know it wouldn't hurt you?"

I shrugged. "I didn't, for sure. It was this...feeling. I could feel its magic calling to me. And I figured it was the fastest way to get you out of its path."

"Thank you." His eyes held mine. "I owe you my life. As do the rest of them." At that, I scoffed, and he frowned. "Why did you run, Clarissa?"

My brow furrowed. "Didn't you see the way those people reacted? They didn't think I *saved* anything. They were angry and afraid. I was only making it worse by staying. I—I had to get out of there."

She's a monster. A beast. Her kind are dangerous.

Tears stung the backs of my eyes. I reached instinctively for my fox half—ironic that the thing that comforted me most in my distress was what caused my volatile nature to begin with. But it was a part of me. It *was* me. Just...the half of me people hated. That they feared.

I let out a shuddering gasp as my hand flew to my chest.

My magic—it was fading again. Barely a sliver of it was left. I stretched out my other arm and rested it against a tree trunk, squeezing my eyes shut to fight back the dismay crashing around me. It was just like when we crossed the Veridian Empire borders —suffocating, empty, hollow. As if I was being sucked dry and left to rot.

And then...it was gone. Again.

A hand wrapped around my upper arm. "What's wrong?" Thorne asked.

I jerked away from him. Tears welled in my eyes, and I angrily brushed them away. "I need to be alone for—for five minutes. Please. Go find the others. I—I'll—" My voice cracked, and I swallowed hard, turning away from him again. It all swirled behind my eyelids like a raging tempest. The curse, my magic, hurting him, the sneers of the people, those memories...

Leaves crinkled under his steps as he moved closer. "Empress, I—"

"Why is it always *you*?" I gritted out, whirling on him. "Why can't you leave me *alone*?"

He winced slightly. "What are you talking about?"

"I don't need anyone to see me like this, Thorne. Just—please, get out. I'll be *fine*." My hand trembled as I pointed toward the main road, willing myself to stay in control. To not snap and crumble until I was alone again.

That was what it felt like without my magic. My other half.

Alone.

And I didn't let anyone see this side of me.

"See you like what?" He was refusing to do as I asked. "Hurt? Scared? We *all* feel those things." He shook his head in disbelief. "Is that what you think? That something is wrong with you?"

I didn't respond. I simply glared at him, biting back the words I couldn't say.

Strong emotions like this made me unstable. They made me dangerous. And when I couldn't control them, they became my weakness. My magic may have healed my injuries over the years, but the bruises and scars still lined my body beneath the surface. The sting of rejection still pierced my skin.

And the proof of that was forever branded on *his* skin now too.

He ran his tongue along his lower lip before straightening his shoulders. "I'll leave you alone, if that's what you want. But there's nothing wrong with whatever it is you're feeling, Clarissa. Everyone has moments that are hard to face, even the strongest of us." He brandished a hand toward me at the last part.

I let out a scoff. "None of this would be happening if I was *strong* enough."

"You can't honestly believe that." When I stayed silent, he raised his voice in irritation. "I don't know what's happened to you to make you think you're not 'enough' of anything. I barely know you, and I can already see how you've given *all* of yourself, not only to your own people, but to a kingdom you've spent barely a few days in. A lesser person wouldn't even *consider* doing what you're doing. You're strong for everybody else in your life, Clarissa Aris." He was only a foot away from me, his jaw tight as a tendril of dark hair escaped from its strap and drifted down the side of his face. His breath was hot on my nose and cheeks, but his next words left me cold.

"Who is strong for *you*?"

I blinked up at him, my shoulders sagging as he took a step back. Then he pivoted on his heel and walked toward his horse, a slight limp still in his gait.

My eyes closed. I told myself I'd gotten what I wanted. To be left alone in the aftermath of this horrid day.

I wouldn't let myself be weak. I wouldn't let myself be helpless. Not in front of the rest of them, anyway. But right now...right now, I could let myself feel.

I sank to the ground and let the tears come.

25

CLARISSA

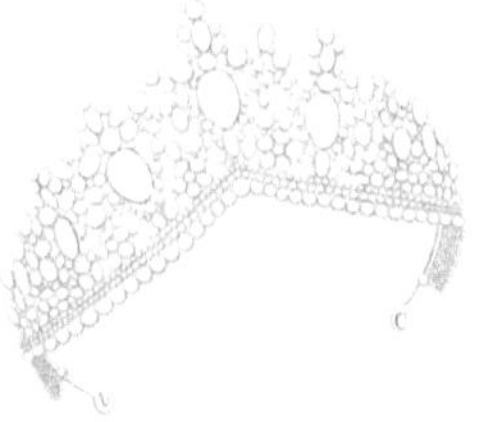

"Alright, now tell me what *actually* happened to you," my mother said the second the door to our suite in Silenus Manor shut.

I sighed and dropped into a cushioned chair. When I finally left the solace of the trees, I found her, Vespera, and Thorne in the village, working on damage control and getting the citizens settled again. I borrowed a cloak from a kind farmer and fed them some story about tracking down the starting point of the blight and getting caught in a bramblebush, then stayed silent the entire ride home.

She gestured to my torn dress and Thorne's bloodied shirt. "You're a mess, sweetheart—"

"Gee, thanks, Mother."

"—and the rumors from the farmers...is it true?" She scanned me from head to toe, coming closer to put a hand on my shoulder. "Did you shift?"

I paused, then nodded.

Her slight intake of breath was the only sign of surprise. "How?"

"Thorne and I got stuck near the edge of the blight." I pinched the bridge of my nose. Fates, I forgot she didn't know about the curse. I hadn't had time to tell her everything I'd learned the night before. I didn't even know where to start.

I leaned back in the chair. "You may want to sit down. This could take a while."

I spent the next quarter of an hour telling her of my conversation with Thorne last night, how we'd stumbled on the hedge in the back gardens that had rotted, and I pressed him for the truth. How I'd confronted Galen and learned the Fates had cursed his ancestors, and a marriage alliance with the Veridian Empire was the only way to break it. How his curse had grown and was affecting the entire kingdom.

"There's been magic in Mysthelm all this time," I said. "It's just been confined to the Grimaldi line. And when the rot touched me, the magic of the curse sort of...funneled into me, I guess. I got my magic back, stronger than ever before. Thorne said the field and hill came back to life, too, like me siphoning up that power cured the rot. It—it took away the curse."

"And your magic is truly back?"

I forced my features not to fall. "Not anymore. I don't think it's permanent."

She stood and paced in front of my chair, pushing her graying hair behind her ears. "Still, this is...unexpected, of course, but fascinating. Imagine if we could visit all the affected areas and take the rot away. I wonder how the Fates made this curse work? If it's of the same basic magic rooted in our empire? It's—" She caught my eye and halted. "What's wrong, Clarissa?"

"You're right. It could be good. I—I hadn't thought about it that way. But, Mother, these people...you didn't see them when I shifted. They didn't think this was a *good* thing. They were so scared of me, so *angry*, it was like..." I trailed off, but she knew what I was thinking.

My mother had been there during the early days, before our father died and she slowly faded into her mind. She'd done her best to help me navigate life as a young Shifter, how to shift at will and learn when to contain it. She was the only person in our family who understood what it was like, having two halves constantly yearning to be free.

Her gaze softened as she took my hand. "I'm sure if you simply give them time, they will come to see there is nothing to fear. If anything, they should be *grateful*. People are always frightened of what they don't understand, but you just have to show them we're on the same side." She squeezed my hand and let me go. "You should speak with the regent family at dinner tonight and see if they can—"

I stood. "No, I can't go to dinner." I made my way through the open door into my personal room and pulled one of my travel bags onto the bed. One by one, I began taking out articles of clothing, needing to keep my hands occupied. "I'll talk to Galen and let things settle down. Word must have spread by now. He's probably got a lot to handle, and my showing up won't help things."

"Clarissa—Clarissa!" my mother said firmly over my rambling, and I stopped to look at her. "If this were your council in the capital, you would never back down from them. You have been dealing with difficult people your entire life. Why do a handful of strangers have you hiding?"

I set down the nightgown I'd been folding. She was right.

I hated how a single moment of vulnerability had brought my insecurities from almost two decades ago rearing to the surface and undoing all the work I'd done on myself. All the lessons in finding strength. All the hours I spent learning to love both halves of me.

"This day has just...messed with my head," I said with a long sigh.

"And perhaps last night did as well." Mother gave me a look.

"What do you mean?" I asked abruptly. A vision of Thorne on his knees before me at the bench swept through my mind.

"I *mean*, are you certain you still want to go through with this marriage? After everything that's happened?"

"I don't think that's the question that matters anymore, Mother," I said, holding up a deep green gown from the bottom of my bag. A silver belt layered with jewels sparkled back at me. "It's whether or not this kingdom wants *me*."

Because she was right, as always. I couldn't hide from them anymore.

———

Devora guided Mother and me to the formal dining hall. Every step down the dark, rustic hallway had nerves coiling in my stomach before I squashed them.

You are a leader. You are an empress. And soon, you will be their queen.

I let my years of training bolster me, felt my spine straighten and shoulders relax as we strode to the double doors. The clinking of glasses, chattering of voices, and scraping of metal on plates reached my ears. Dinner had evidently already begun. I held my breath when a pair of guards grabbed the bronze door handles and pulled them open.

We were met with the scent of smoked meats and fresh vegetables, and the sight of a long, deep cherry-tinted wood table and matching benches occupied by several familiar faces and many I didn't know. Devora had told me there were other members of nobility in attendance tonight, with this being the first opportunity for many of them to meet me. Dion and Vespera Silenus sat at the head, and Galen to their right. Thorne and his mother were across from him. The rest of the guests bore equal expressions of trepidation and contempt when their heads swiveled to the entrance.

All conversation stopped.

The quiet popping of flames in the iron candelabras hanging above us was the only sound. A couple of the strangers looked back at Dion and Galen, as if seeking answers for my appearance.

This was already going well.

Devora leaned into my ear from behind me, her voice so low I could barely hear it. "You are the predator, Your Majesty. Don't let them forget that." I turned my neck slightly to give an appreciative glance, and her bright eyes gleamed under her black glasses. "And if they do, there are plenty of knives at that table."

I held back a smile as she tapped her nose, then retreated to the wall with a line of other servants.

The whisperings began.

"Did you hear what happened today?"

"Can we even *trust* her?"

"Sawyer said he's never seen anything like it."

"What if there are more of them? More like *her*?"

From across the room, I found Thorne sitting with his hand gripped around his glass, knuckles white and jaw clenched. Vespera stood and rushed around the table toward me as the ruffled ends of her lavender gown trailed behind her. Her dark eyes pinched together in concern.

"Clarissa, I was so worried. They've been saying the strangest things. Are you alright?"

"Vespera, step away from her," her husband's voice croaked from the head of the table. Dion Silenus stood, his pale, wrinkled features hard under the light of the candles. A long purple robe was fastened at his neck. "Her kind cannot be trusted. Get back here at once."

My hackles rose. Not for my sake, but at the way he spoke to his own *wife*. I took a step forward, my nostrils flaring when she flinched at his words. This man was just like Lord Stryker and many men before him. Eager to assert their idea of dominance by trampling strong women beneath their feet.

"My kind? And what exactly is that, Lord Silenus?" I tilted my head. "An empress? A woman? Both exceed you in ability, don't they?"

His jaw ticked. "A Veridian. An *animal*."

My eyes skated over to Galen, whose gloved hands were wrapped tightly around a flute of wine. I briefly wondered if he'd stand up for me. If he'd defend the woman he'd begged to marry him. He met my gaze and swallowed, then looked away.

I guessed that was my answer.

It didn't matter. I didn't need him.

My voice was cool and calm. "Yes, I'm Veridian. I assumed when you allowed us to stay in your territory that you knew where I came from, Lord Silenus, but perhaps I need to get you a map?" A chorus of gasps and a few snickers rose from the table. "Nothing has changed since I arrived. I am who I've always been."

Red splotches appeared at Dion's neck. "What are you playing at? We were told your"—his voice lowered— "*magic* would not work here. That we would be safe. Is this part of a—a plan to invade our borders?" He spun to Galen, throwing a hand out in frustration. "My King, how could you let her come here?"

Vespera hurried back to her husband, features strained as she pushed her dark locks behind her ears. "Dion, please, let's sit down and—"

He swiped a hand in the air in front of her face. She instantly went silent. Anger unfurled in my gut like sharp claws, but I remained steady.

"Are any of your people hurt, Lord Silenus?" I asked. I willed myself not to look at Thorne, to not think about the gash lining his chest. "What have I done to endanger your lives? If I have, I will *gladly* pay the price. I would never do anything to cause your people harm. What happened today was just as unexpected for me as it was for you. I did *not* cause this; you must see that."

"And we're supposed to take your word for it?" he shot back. "Hundreds of years of silence from your empire, and all of a sudden, you're so eager to sink your teeth into our kingdom. Did you not take enough from us during the war?"

Even from across the long table, I could see the shift in him. The way his lips twitched and his hands shook. The way his eyes flitted away from me when I spoke. This wasn't just anger—this was fear. That, I could understand. Fear always made people lash out. If I wanted to calm them, I had to show them they could trust me.

Again, I looked at Galen. He watched Dion as his finger tapped anxiously on his wine glass. I saw that same fear reflected on his face, and suddenly, it became clear. Galen may be King of Mysthelm, but he was also *afraid*. It wasn't that he didn't care about his people. It was that this curse he'd lived with, that he'd watched grow and ravage his kingdom, froze him. He was stagnant, unable to move, unable to *act* when it mattered most.

Thorne had told me last night that most of the people didn't know the truth. If they did, how would they react? If they were this up in arms about me and my single instance of magic, how would they feel about their *king* being the one to cause it all?

My heart softened to him, but only slightly. I didn't think Galen was a bad man.

But leaders couldn't let fear control them.

To my surprise, Thorne's voice filled the room. "With all due respect, Lord Silenus," he began, without a single drop of respect in his tone, "I was there during the incident today. I saw what happened. And I watched as the rotted hill and fields were completely healed. Every drop of the blight disappeared. How is that a bad thing? She did this." Thorne's eyes fixed on me. I couldn't seem to look away. "She was incredible. You should be singing her praises, not condemning her for starting an act of war."

"Is this true?" an older woman I'd never met before asked from the opposite end of the table.

"He's right. I heard the same thing from Tycus," said a balding man next to Thorne with a handkerchief clutched in his fingers. Several of the others exchanged murmurs, the narrative quickly shifting from suspicion to curiosity.

"Could it be possible?"

"What does this mean?"

"Can she stop the blight?"

Voices rose, blending together in a sea of questions. Benches scratched against the floor as some stood to argue, Dion's words the loudest of all. Eyes sought me out among the growing frenzy, but mine were locked on icy blue.

Once again, he was there. Always there.

Galen cleared his throat, and every head turned to him. His features were smoothed into the picturesque, handsome king with everything under control. It struck me that we were similar in that way—both able to turn our masks on and off when we knew eyes were on us.

He made his way toward me, extending an arm as he asked, "Will you show me?"

I blinked. "Show you...my magic?"

"Thorne mentioned an area of the hedge maze that's been hit by the blight. Take us there and show us what you can do."

"My King, are you sure this is a good idea?" Dion interjected.

"Do not question me, Dion," Galen responded, not bothering to look back at the regent lord.

Show us what you can do. He wanted me to touch it. To take the blight away, as I'd done today in the village. But what if I lost control again? What if there was something in this curse, this magic, that made things worse?

My eyes strayed to Thorne and the bloody scars I knew were on his chest. He tipped his chin up at me and held my stare, as if in a silent challenge.

"Okay." I finally nodded. "Let's go."

Galen, Dion and his wife, and several others followed Thorne and me through the manor and out the back entrance to the hedge maze. My heart picked up speed as we neared the tall, dark walls of greenery. I was prepared this time, wasn't I? I knew what to expect. I wouldn't let the magic overtake me and hurt someone again.

"Breathe, Empress," Thorne murmured at my side, right as we turned a corner and the blackened section of the maze came into view.

I licked my lips but stayed silent. Galen stepped ahead of us and examined the dead greenery, his features unreadable. Then he turned and held out his hand to me.

Firm but gentle. Strong but controlled. I repeated my mantra as I took it, soft leather against smooth skin.

It was as if the entire garden held its breath while we

approached. Galen's stare pierced me, his anticipation and hope vibrating through those hazel eyes. Taking one final, deep breath, I held out my hand to the shriveled hedge.

The moment my fingers touched it, my body came alive.

That same beautiful, warm, golden magic shot into me, filling me. But this time it wasn't as powerful. Not nearly as potent. It felt like a drop of water instead of an entire ocean pouring into me. I slowed my breaths and imagined the magic as golden ribbons twisting and twining with my fox half, and I easily brought it under my control.

It must be the size of the affected area. That was the only explanation. Before, it had been an enormous hill—now, it was the size of a large bush. The bigger the space, the more magic it contained.

"Clarissa, *look*," Galen murmured, and I glanced up.

Thorne was right. I hadn't focused on it the first time, but now...

Before our eyes, life seeped back into the base of the hedge. The jagged stems straightened and regrew, sturdier and more elegant than before. Bright green leaves formed and flourished with each passing second. Even the soil on the ground around it went from black and charred to a rich, healthy brown.

I backed away, and Galen squeezed my hand. His lips parted, his eyes wide and roving over me as if he were a blind man seeing for the first time.

Starved. Desperate. Joyful. Like he'd been saved.

"It's you," he breathed out. "You're really the answer."

I swallowed hard and broke his stare.

I hadn't shifted. I stayed in control. Relief swept through me, but with it came a sense of determination. As much as the uncertainty and contempt of those around me tried to take it away, I was *proud* of who I was. What I could do. And I didn't want to hide it from these people.

I slipped out of Galen's grasp and cleared my throat. The handful of guests who were with us went quiet.

"I didn't come to your kingdom to harm you," I started. "I didn't come here under false pretenses, or to bring the magic of my empire to your borders. I came here to bring *peace*. I came to start mending paths between our two lands, not tear them down. And if my magic will help you"—I waved an arm behind me to the hedge—"then I'll do everything in my power to aid King Grimaldi. You don't deserve to suffer. I want to help you. Please, *let* me help you," I directed the final part to Dion Silenus.

"But you have to know who I am," I continued. "Because it's my *magic* that can stop this blight, and I don't want you to fear me or what I can do." With a deep breath, I tugged on that familiar power, that small pocket of magic that I could feel fading by the second. I shifted my right hand into one of my fox paws, relishing the way my claws extended, sharp and glinting. The soft red fur swayed where it met human skin halfway up my forearm.

Fates, I missed this.

The night was filled with soft intakes of breath, but nobody cried out in alarm. Nobody snarled at me. Nobody pulled away. They stared at me in fascination. Curious and hopeful.

The magic was waning. That hedge didn't hold enough of the curse to give me my powers back for long. Without having to use any effort, my paw slowly shrank back to a human hand, the fur retracting into my skin as the black pads became delicate calluses once more. In a heartbeat, the kernel of magic was gone.

Nobody moved. The air was silent as Dion Silenus slowly approached. His wrinkled face was an unreadable mask. Lifting a shaking arm, he pointed a hand at me, tilting his head to the right. I sucked in a breath and prepared for the worst.

"I—I was wrong," he said quietly. "The Fates...they have answered our prayers. They have *delivered* us. You are not an animal, Your Majesty." The moonlight caught the rings on his fingers, making them shine like coals in a flame. The eyes of everyone there rested on me, heavy and waiting.

"You are our savior."

26

THORNE

"We missed you today, Daddy," Marigold said, holding her stuffed doll by the hand as she trod to the bed in the guest suite of Silenus Manor. She and I were given a room next door to Galen's, with my mother right across the hall.

"I know, sweetheart. I missed you too." I lifted the edge of the comforter to let her crawl under the sheets, pulling her doll in safely at her side. "Did you have fun with your grandmother?"

She nodded. "We walked in the gardens and had tiny little sandwiches for lunch, and Grandma even let me drink out of the fancy glasses, and then we found Mo and some of the other babies in the palace and played with them." She took a deep breath, and I smiled. She often got like this when we hadn't seen each other all day—her words fell from her like a river, and I loved listening to her replay her memories for me.

"The nanny and Grandma took us all to the flower market, and I got to pick a bunch of flowers! I saved some for you." She reached over to her nightstand where a small handful of purple violets rested on top. She crooked her little finger at me, and I chuckled at the mischievous smile on her tan, freckled face. She looked more and more like her mother every day. A little dimple had even started appearing on the left side when she smiled in the last few months, just like Iris had.

With a giggle, she put one of the stems behind my ear, tucking it in so it stayed in place. "You look so pretty, Daddy."

"Thank you, sweetheart." I leaned in and kissed her forehead. "Did you play nice with the other children?" I never had to worry about Marigold getting along with others—if anything, she was *too* outgoing. I'd nearly lost my mind several times when I took her into the busy villages and would lose sight of her, only to find her behind some stranger's booth, already fast friends with everyone in earshot.

"Yes, and I even got to help take care of them. I was the oldest one, but it was still fun. I like watching the babies. Daddy, will you ever have another baby?"

The question took me so off guard, my knee bumped into the side of her bed as I straightened. Wincing, I rubbed the tender spot and said, "I don't know. I suppose anything is possible."

Marigold mused over my words as she spun her doll around on top of her chest. "Where do babies come from, anyway?"

Oh, Fates. "Babies...well, they come from love." I took one of the flowers still in her hand and placed it behind her ear, mirroring mine. "Your mother and I loved each other very much, and when the time was right, we were given you. And we immediately loved you more than anything else in the world."

That was a sentiment I always made sure our daughter knew. She may never fully remember her mother, but I made every effort to ensure she didn't forget how deeply Iris and I adored her.

The last thing on our minds when we first met eight and a half years ago was children. We were still so young—I was twenty-four, and Iris was only a year younger. I was focused on outrunning my legacy with Galen at my side, spending our nights knee-deep in whatever trouble found us.

Until *she* found *me*.

I still remembered the first moment I saw her. She was a recent hire at a pub Galen and I often frequented, but that night, I'd been alone. I'd had an enormous fight with my father over how I'd never amount to the man I was expected to be. I'd tucked myself away in a dark booth, too ashamed to drown in a bottle and too hurt to face the light.

Iris had found me in my hiding space nursing a bruised jaw and ego. Bronze curls were pulled into a braid down her back, and big brown eyes took in my purple mark, my dirty cloak, my slumped shoulders. She shifted a tray with empty glasses onto her hip.

"My name is Iris. If there's anything you need, don't hesitate to call for me, alright?" A small crease appeared at her tan brow as she assessed my sorry state once more before walking off to another customer. I must have looked pitiful. A pampered son of a lord in my pretentious silver-lined cloak, brooding and pouting in a corner.

I didn't call for her. But she came anyway.

An hour later, a cold rag slapped against the table, making me jump. "For your jaw," she said, pointing to my now swollen cheek. "You should get that looked at, you know."

"Trust me, nobody wants to look at this," I muttered and grabbed the rag. "Thank you." I placed it gingerly against the bruise. After sucking in a breath, I relaxed into the cushioned booth, the pulse in my cheek pumping with the shock of cold.

"Who'd you piss off?" she asked, wiping down the table with another rag.

"My future, evidently," was all I said.

She raised an eyebrow but didn't ask questions. "Well, your future has a mean right hook. I don't think I want to meet it."

We'd spent the rest of the night in a steady flow of banter. Iris was the sharpest woman I'd ever met—constantly surprising me with little quips and comments, keeping me on my toes and distracting me from what awaited me when I went back home. She told me how her father had recently fallen ill to a heart condition and was no longer able to work, so she'd taken on a second job at the pub to help provide for her parents and three younger siblings.

We talked about our families, our pet peeves and guilty pleasures and crazy dreams. I learned her youngest sister was eleven and was more like a daughter to her than a sibling. I learned she dreamed of going to an academy to become a nurse but felt bound to taking care of her sick father. When she finally forced a meal in front of my face, I begged her to eat it with me. I learned she hated for her food to be touching. I learned she rolled her eyes when she was embarrassed, she had a birthmark in the shape of a heart on the side of her neck, and she was deathly afraid of open water.

I'd known from the instant we spoke that she wasn't like any of the other girls I'd usually take home after these nights out. The thought of her as another one of my flings hadn't even crossed my mind. One hour turned into six, until the bartender threatened to kick us out if we didn't leave.

I saw her every night after that.

She had joked that she didn't want to meet my future, yet she became the most important part of it.

I bought a ring two weeks later but didn't ask her to marry me for five months. I couldn't work up the nerve. She'd found the ring tucked into one of my shoes when she used it to kill a particularly large spider in my room. The diamond had fallen onto her toe, and she'd shrieked, thinking it was another bug and immediately began beating at it.

She'd said yes in a heartbeat.

My parents were *furious*. I'd ruined their plans, they said. I was supposed to marry a nice, respectable daughter of nobility, someone to oversee the North Territory with me once I became regent lord and bear me plenty of suitable heirs. They thought this was one of my "rebellious phases" and that I'd grow out of it eventually.

They never understood. Father came from a family bred to do as he was told, to marry well while holding duty over love. They hadn't known what it felt like to have your entire soul, your entire being, wrapped around a single person. Iris was that person. Iris *was* my future, my duty and my love.

Until she wasn't. Until the same heart disease that took her father shortly after we were married claimed her life too.

The feel of our daughter's hand pulling mine into the bed beside her dragged me from my memories. "Read me a story, please?" she asked, those sweet brown eyes staring up at me.

I cleared my throat. "What would you like me to read?"

"That one." She pointed to a small book on her nightstand.

Leaning across to pick up the new book, I read the title on the cover aloud. "*Frostine the Fairy and Her Tower in the Sky*. This one looks new."

"Mo's nanny let me borrow it!" Marigold said enthusiastically. "She told me I look like the fairy."

She was right. Frostine the Fairy was front and center on the cover, with her brown, wavy hair spilling onto bright blue wings as she stared out the window of a tall tower. I opened to the first page and began to read, with Marigold's fingers sweeping over the pages, as was our nightly tradition.

"Frostine the Fairy was born in Fairyland, a magical forest full of all sorts of creatures. She lived with her mother and father and baby fairy brother, until one day, a wicked witch took her from her home and flew her to the highest tower in the kingdom of the giants."

The rest of the story went on to describe the friends Frostine made in her tower, from the birds who would fly by to the flowers on the vine outside the window that sang songs with her. They tried to help her escape, but Frostine's fairy wings weren't strong enough to get her down from the tower.

The wicked witch told Frostine the only way she would be able to leave was if she found her one true love. Frostine spent year after year locked in her tower until one day, a friendly, handsome giant heard her beautiful singing from all the way on the ground. The birds and butterflies who loved Frostine so much told the giant to climb the tower to rescue her.

"The giant used the vine to climb up to her window, and when he saw her, he thought she was the most beautiful, kindest creature he'd ever seen. They fell in love at first sight and, true to her word, the wicked witch gave magic to Frostine's wings that let her finally leave her tower. Frostine and the giant celebrated with her new friends, and they lived happily ever after."

I looked down at Marigold, whose soft snores filled the room as her head drooped over my arm. I smiled and lightly kissed the top of her head before extricating myself from the sheets. When I stood and faced the open door, I saw my mother leaning against the frame, a glass of red wine swirling in her grip.

"That's an interesting story to be telling her," she said as we backed into the hall and I shut the door with a *snick*.

"Let me guess: you don't approve."

"It's just these stories of finding your one true love and love at first sight," she waved her wine glass in the air with a heavy sigh, "it puts all these fanciful thoughts in her head."

"And you don't believe in those things, Mother?"

"They're pretty to think about, but that's not life. Love won't rescue you. Only you can do that for yourself." Padding across the hall to her guest room, she added, "I remember what this idea of love did to you, Thorne. I remember how it broke you. And I would never wish the kind of pain we've had on that little girl."

"I think both can be true," I said quietly. "I wouldn't trade away what I had. The good or the bad."

Iris had rescued me. She'd saved me from a future caught under my parents' thumbs, from a downward spiral of regrets and shallow pleasures that would have never fulfilled me. And, in the end, her love was what helped me rescue myself. What gave me the strength to overcome her loss and be the father Marigold needed me to be.

"Then you're a fool," Mother said simply, settling into an armchair in front of the fire in her suite. Her navy gown trailed at her feet, the dark blue jewels around her neck catching the light of the glowing embers.

I rolled my eyes but didn't argue, knowing full well how she was when she got in these moods. Azura Reaux wasn't a dreamer.

She was ambitious and pragmatic, doing what needed to be done to reach a desired goal. Principled and realistic. I believed she loved my father, in her own way—out of a sense of responsibility and loyalty. Because that was what she was supposed to do. And when he left her four years ago, I'm not sure it broke her heart so much as it broke an intrinsic part of her that trusted him to fulfill his duty. She was betrayed and left to pick up the pieces of a life they'd made for themselves. It had turned her even colder and more calculated, and part of me couldn't blame her.

Her next words were so soft and unexpected, they startled me.

"I do know what it's like, you know." She stared into the crackling fire. "I was in love once. Long ago."

I sank into the chair across from her. "I'm guessing this isn't about Father."

"Your father was...well, he was good at what he did." She shrugged, her gaze still on the fire. "Managing the territory. Keeping the people in line. Answering to the king. Everything we were supposed to be. But...he was not the man I'd intended to marry."

She'd never spoken of this before. I didn't know much about her youth, besides the fact that she and her parents hadn't gotten along. I'd never met my grandparents because of their estranged relationship.

"We grew up together," she continued, the firelight dancing in her eyes. "He was...everything to me. A best friend, a confidant, one who could always make me smile. You know, I saw a bit of myself in you that first time you brought Iris home to us. That same epic love." She smiled wistfully at me, and warmth settled around us. "I know I was hard on you about her. I supposed I just knew the kind of heartache that could come from a love like that, and I feared for you. I never wanted any pain to come to you."

I cleared my throat and looked away. "What happened to him? The other man?"

The brief hint of nostalgia I'd seen in her hardened once more. "I said I was in love. I never said *he* was."

I shifted in my seat. "I'm sorry, Mother. I didn't know."

"It doesn't matter." She took a long sip of her wine. "That's when I learned to put duty over love." Pausing, she studied me with a tilt of her head. "Oh, don't pity me, dear. I don't regret it for a moment, for then I wouldn't have you." Her lips rose into a tight smile, the closest to comforting that she could get. "Warm" was not a word one would use to describe my mother, but that was simply who she was. Perhaps when she was younger, things were different…but this world and a marriage to a hard man who put his title over his family had chipped away at her edges.

That momentary softness never lasted long. But I always held on to it when it came.

"And what about you, Thorne?" she asked, eyes piercing. "Are you going to put duty over *your* emotions?"

I licked my lips. "What are you talking about?"

She set her glass on the coffee table, and the clang echoed in the quiet room. "It appears Clarissa is still going to marry him. Not only that, but the territory has now fallen in love with her. *You* made them fall in love with her. What happened to our plan?"

I scowled. "You mean *your* plan, Mother. I went along with it when I thought it was what was best for the people."

"What's best for our people is to not have some lazy, ill-suited *boy* for a king. Tonight was the perfect opportunity for these people to see her as a monster and drive her away for good. To set in motion the wheels of Galen's removal. Yet you practically pushed her into their arms, painting her as this hero we've needed. A *savior*," she huffed. "As if someone from her empire would ever use their magic to save us."

"What do you have against Veridians?"

"They slaughtered our people, Thorne," she said in disgust. "They're power-hungry and only care about themselves. They did *anything* to get their precious magic, so don't think for a single moment that they wouldn't do anything to keep it. To keep us inferior to them and their empire."

"It was a *war*, Mother. Their people died too. And it was over three hundred years ago. You don't know anything about them and what they want. Didn't you see what Clarissa *did*?" I asked. "She can take away this blight! We need her, Mother. And she *wants* to help us. She's not who you think she is."

Mother scanned me again, slowly leaning back into her chair. "I see," she said, drawing the word out. "You're falling for this girl."

"*What?*" My features screwed in disbelief. "That's ridiculous. I'm not—I don't have feelings for her. She has to marry Galen. I never understood why he was so adamant about bringing her here, but now I do. It's more than just her magic being able to cure the blight. Their marriage will end this curse. For *good*."

To my surprise, Mother stood in alarm. "What did you just say?" she breathed out.

"The entire Grimaldi line kept it a secret, but Galen told me last night," I explained. "The Fates made a deal with Nyses Grimaldi's son. If someone in his bloodline marries someone from the Veridian Empire, the curse will break. I know how important you think it is to remove the Grimaldis from the throne altogether, but isn't this *more* important? To have the curse completely lifted?"

I stood and took a step toward her around the coffee table. "Clarissa would be good for this kingdom. I've seen it. She might even be able to help Galen pull himself together. Be the king we need him to be."

Mother spun on her heel and paced in front of the fireplace, rubbing a wrinkled hand along the back of her neck. "This...this changes things."

"I know. Will you stop your scheming now?" I asked. "This marriage...it's a good thing, Mother." I knew the words were true, but they tasted sour on my tongue. "You just have to give them a chance."

She met my eyes, her expression as stony and unreadable as ever. I saw something ripple across her face, and her cheek twitched before she smoothed it over. Then she gave me a reassuring smile.

"Perhaps you're right."

My shoulders sagged in relief. "So, we're in agreement. No more plans to stop their engagement or convince him to abdicate. The curse will finally be broken. That's what we've wanted all along, isn't it?"

She took a few steps to me and put a hand on my cheek. "Of course, Thorne. You're a good boy. Galen is lucky to have you." Her smile tightened, becoming more of a grimace. "You know everything I do is for you, don't you? You and Marigold?"

My brow furrowed. "I know, Mother."

"Good." She patted my cheek once. "Don't ever forget that. Good night, dear."

27

CLARISSA

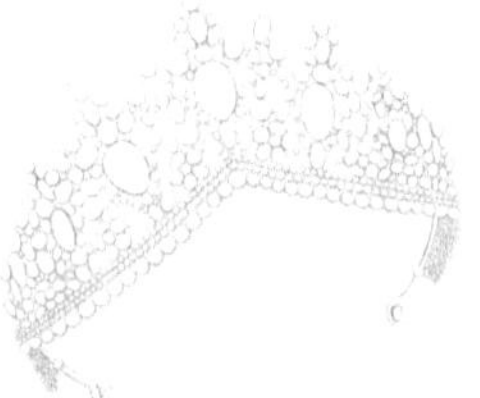

The next two days in the Mid Territory passed in a whirlwind. Word spread like wildfire that I could heal land cursed by the blight, and Mother and I woke to *dozens* of families at the door of Silenus Manor begging for us to come help them.

We went without a second thought.

There was no better feeling than knowing I was doing good with my magic. That the people no longer feared me, despite the less-than-warm welcome I'd initially received. I might have been too forgiving of the way they'd treated me, but I understood where it came from.

Mother and I spent the entire day traveling from farm to farm, field to field, market to market, banishing the rot and bringing new life. Katrine and Devora accompanied us to help us make a good impression, given the fact that some still didn't trust us Veridians. And, of course, I couldn't go anywhere without the guards Galen sent to make sure I was protected.

In just two short days, we reached as many people in the Mid Territory as possible. It was exhausting, but it was also *inspiring*. I'd grown up in the confines of a small cottage—the farthest, most adventurous place I'd ever traveled before last year was a handful of miles to the southern beach of the capital.

But here...there was so much to see. We rode up the side of rolling hills, looking down on the markets and streets below and taking in the sun steadily rising over the valleys. We ventured along winding rivers and cooled off at the streams, dipping our bare feet into the water. We talked with hundreds of strangers, learning about their farms and lives.

I'd always loved connecting with people, once I'd learned to control my Shifter half and wasn't worried about what they would think of me anymore. It was one of the reasons I'd formed the Sentinels years ago—because I'd gotten close enough with others to see how bad things were for them, even in our small corner of the empire. And I wanted to make a *difference.*

That was exactly what we were doing now.

Today was our fifth and final day in the Mid Territory. Our last day here to show a strong, united front between Mysthelm and Veridia at the annual Harvest Tournament and Festival. And it was certainly shaping up to be an interesting day.

"This one has a nice backside, don't you think?"

I craned my neck at Galen's words to get a better view. "Yes, hers is definitely larger. I'm not quite sure what we're supposed to be looking for, but it's very..." I shaped my hands in the air to mimic grabbing the pair of curves. "Round."

He let out an unkingly snort. The owner of the pig before us, a stout man with a red mustache, bowed low to the ground when we nodded at him in dismissal. He led his pig out of the square paddock as the next farmer took his place to showcase his hog.

In the short period of down-time between contestants, Galen said, "I hope you've been enjoying the Tournament."

I *had* enjoyed the morning so far. We'd spent the early hours in the fields of Gold Row, which had been turned into a temporary event space. Half a dozen large paddocks like the one we occupied now were scattered around the market, along with vendors selling smoked meats on a stick, cups of cold apple mead, and fruits dipped in chocolate. When I'd stepped out of the carriage at eight in the morning, the fields and streets had already been filled with excited citizens purchasing food or getting ready for the competitions.

Galen and I had been asked to judge the events and were given seats of honor at each one. The judges' tables sat atop a high platform right outside the paddocks, with a clear view of the contestants and their various livestock and produce. So far, we'd watched horses race, weighed squirming chickens with our bare hands, and seen more tomatoes and cucumbers than I'd ever counted in my life—some that were as large as my head. A hen laid an egg in my lap, and the potato farmer from the other day, Aiman, brought me a whole new bag of golden potatoes. I was pretty sure I had straw in my undergarments and horse manure on my shoes.

And it was the most fun I'd had in as long as I could remember.

The people were ecstatic to finally be meeting their king, and it clenched something in my heart when they looked at me with recognition and kindness instead of hostility. In just a few days, I'd really begun to *know* them. I recognized faces and remembered that Loretta from the south had a daughter living in the North Territory, and Cillian who worked on the farm next to Aiman's just found a puppy on the side of the road that he decided to keep, and young Marcus the stablehand couldn't keep his eyes off the carpenter's daughter.

"It's been a good day," I said to Galen with a smile. "I'm glad you came."

I'd tried to put the animosity I felt toward him behind me. If I would be tied to him for the rest of my life, it may as well be with a cord of mutual respect and understanding instead of distrust. I didn't need to love my husband to want what was best for him.

Love.

The thought made a frozen pit open in my stomach as he smiled back at me, the sun highlighting notes of dark gold in his brown hair. The leather of his gloves pressed into my lower back as we walked down the steps of the judges' table. Spectators grinned and waved when we passed, with guards both in front and behind us to keep bodies from getting too close. Galen's hand stiffened every time an arm or leg strayed near him, even though the only exposed area of his skin was his face.

There were a couple of women who caught my eye as their envious gazes rested on Galen's hand at my back, and I couldn't help but think how many of them would rather be in my shoes. Preparing to marry the handsome king, blushing when he grazed a hand over their cheeks or whispered promises of passion in their ears.

The image of long hair and strong hands appeared in my mind. Of fingers brushing my neck and a broad chest hovering in front of me, veined forearms flexing above my head under the stars. Of what those arms would feel like wrapped around me, that rough beard skimming my sensitive skin.

Flames erupted on my cheeks and rippled down my back until they met a gloved hand.

My body went cold.

Well, *that* was new. I definitely shouldn't be thinking about *him* right now.

Spine straightening, I pasted on a smile as we made our way through the crowds to our next assigned spot. Vespera thought it would be a good idea to allow a couple of hours for people to approach Galen and me individually, the way his father Orion used to grant an audience to citizens in his palace.

The guards led us to a makeshift dais with two large chairs in the middle of a clearing of wildflowers, still within earshot of the noise and laughter of the tournament. I looked over my shoulder to watch their revelry when my eyes latched onto someone else.

Thorne stood at the edge of Gold Row in fitted brown pants and a loose tan tunic that exposed a bit of dark hair at the top of his chest, along with a hint of white bandages that made guilt squirm through my stomach.

But the brightest grin I'd ever seen was stretched across his face. And on top of his shoulders rested a young girl with hands clenched around his neck. Her eyes beamed with laughter as she leaned back and squealed, his hands coming up to keep her steady. Long, dark bronze waves tangled together in the breeze. He tickled her side, and she squealed again, loud enough that I could hear it halfway across the clearing. In one smooth motion, he lifted her off his shoulders and set her on the ground, enveloping her in more tickles while she cackled and gasped for breath. He finally stopped and wrapped his arms around her little body.

A smile tugged at the corner of my lips. She was beautiful. *He* was beautiful. Carefree and joyful and adoring.

When he swung her in the air and pressed a kiss to her temple, his eyes locked on mine.

I didn't look away.

Not until a different hand pulled at my fingers, and a different voice asked, "Are you ready, Clarissa?"

I blinked and turned to face Galen. "Of course."

He led me up the steps and to our seats, and within minutes, people gathered among the rows of flowers after being searched by guards. Their curious faces wiped the image of Thorne and his daughter from my mind. Several of the guards positioned themselves at our backs and along the outside of the clearing as a line formed. The first ones to step forward were a mother and daughter who introduced themselves as Ronnie and Meredith.

"It's so wonderful for you to come visit, Your Majesty," the mother, Ronnie, said. "We've been looking forward to this day for quite a while."

"I'm so glad to hear it," Galen responded. "What's that you have here?" He gestured to the large basket hanging from her arm. The lid jostled as if something were moving beneath it.

"Oh! Yes," she cried. She set the basket down and carefully removed the lid, and the gasp that left my lips was nothing short of embarrassing.

"Our shepherding dog gave birth recently, and we wanted to bring you a gift for your fields," Ronnie explained. "She's the largest and strongest of the litter. She comes from good stock." She lifted the wiggling puppy from the basket with a look of pride. When the guards gave her permission to approach, she climbed up the steps and held the precious creature out to us.

Big black eyes inlaid in brown fur stared back at Galen and me, tan paws swiping playfully at her own nose. A strap of leather circled her throat, with a thin rope tied to it that trailed on the ground.

My chest swelled. I'd always wanted a dog.

I instinctively reached to take her from the woman, cradling the ball of fur to my chest. "Galen, this is the most adorable thing I've ever—" I glanced up and cut myself off when I saw the wistful, aching smile on his features as he looked back at me.

Turning to Ronnie and her daughter, he said, "You are far too kind. Thank you for this gift. We'll give her a good home."

They left the basket with us and retreated down the steps. Galen and I took our seats again, my new friend already thoroughly licking every inch of skin at my neck and cheeks.

"I had a dog once," he said, voice soft as he watched the little pup squirm in my arms. "He was a good dog. A hunting dog. He died when I was young. I wanted another one, but when I—when I inherited the curse..." He trailed off and looked away. "You may keep her, if you wish. She's already taken a liking to you. And I can't... It's too dangerous. For her and me."

A lump formed in my throat, and I swallowed hard to force it down. I hadn't even thought about that. About how he couldn't so much as pet this sweet animal without his gloves. How he hadn't felt the true warmth of a touch, whether it be skin or fur, since ascending the throne and bearing this curse.

"You'll be able to again soon, Galen," I said firmly. "I promise."

His sad gaze lingered on me. "I know."

The next few interactions passed uneventfully. People gifted us baskets and baskets of fresh produce, bread, and other trinkets. A little boy ran up to hand me a small bouquet of sunflowers and weeds, which Mia—what I'd chosen to call the pup—promptly tried to make her lunch. I tied her rope to the leg of my chair so she could roam a few feet into the clearing without getting lost, and she was having a grand time lunging at butterflies and pouncing at flowers.

She was precious. I loved her. She made my dormant fox half ache with joy as I snuck glimpses of her frolicking in her little patch of grass.

"Can I pet her?" a sweet voice asked, drawing my attention back to the line of people. I sucked in a quiet breath when I came face-to-face with Thorne and his daughter. Galen was talking to another family, but these two had snuck out of place to say hello.

From this close, I could see how much she resembled him. While his eyes were light blue like a calm sea and hers were deep brown, they both crinkled at the corner when they smiled. She had his tan skin, the same straight nose and long, dark hair with hints of bronze.

"Why, sure you can," I said with a smile, bending low to scoop Mia into my arms. She licked my neck as her tail beat against my chest.

"New friend, Empress?" Thorne asked with a smirk, his hand on his daughter's back.

"*Best* friend. Aren't you, Mia?" I cooed, nuzzling into her soft fur before coaxing the little girl closer. "Here, she's very friendly."

"Go on, Marigold," Thorne said. She looked up at him with a grin, an adorable dimple appearing on her cheek. Reaching out a hand, she scratched behind Mia's ears, giggling when she instantly jumped free from my grip and crouched at Marigold's feet. Her tail brushed excitedly across the stone of the dais.

"Marigold. That's a beautiful name," I commented.

Thorne only had eyes for his daughter as she snuggled her face into Mia's neck. "There was a bouquet of yellow marigolds on the bed next to my wife when she gave birth. She labored for twenty-seven hours, and at one point she grabbed the vase and threw it across the room." He chuckled and scratched his beard. "When her contraction passed, she looked at the broken glass and flower petals and said, 'Marigold would be a good name for a girl.'"

"She sounds spirited," I said with a laugh.

"She was." His lip twitched upward as he gazed at Marigold and Mia, who were both now rolling in the grass to the side of the dais. "And I fear I have my hands full with this one."

"Well, with parents like you and Iris, what can you expect?" Galen said, finishing his conversation with the family and clapping his friend on the back. "You should have *seen* Thorne back in the day. 'Wild' was his middle name until Iris made an honest man out of him."

I smirked at the way Thorne's lips pursed. "I can only imagine. Chase many women through dark gardens, Lord Reaux?" I asked, my eyebrow quirking in a silent challenge.

Thorne gave a lazy, innocent grin. "Only when they don't ask me to leave."

Galen looked between us and cleared his throat. "Yes, well, have you and Marigold had a good time at your first Harvest Tournament?"

"The *best*, Uncle Galen!" Marigold squealed from the ground to my left. When she met her father's stern look, she leaped to her feet and brushed the blades of grass from her dress. "I mean...*Your Majesty*," she corrected as she scampered up the dais and curtsied to Galen.

"Oh, don't listen to your father. I'm always Uncle Galen to you," the king said, crouching low and gently flicking the tip of her nose. I noticed he was still careful to keep his distance—small touches with others here and there, but nothing too close to his skin. Nothing too dangerous.

While Marigold jabbered on to him about her day, I snuck a glance at Thorne. "She's beautiful," I said.

A soft smile spread over his face as he crossed his arms. "She's everything."

We stood in silence for a moment before I finally asked, "How's your injury?" I gestured toward his chest, and my fingers accidentally grazed the fabric. A hint of hard muscle met my fingertips. I jerked my hand away.

"It's healing. It'll leave a nasty scar, but I hear women like that sort of thing."

A laugh escaped me. "You can tell them it was a great big bear you fought off. Something more exciting," I suggested.

"I don't know. The true story is rather remarkable." His eyes flicked over me, and I bit down on my bottom lip.

"I really am sorry, you know," I said quietly. "And I...I never got to thank you the other night. For defending me at dinner."

He raised an eyebrow. "No scolding for trying to help you this time?"

"I'm sorry about that too," I admitted. "I guess that's something I'm not very good at." I ran my thumb along my index finger and felt the bite of my nail against the pad, imagining sharp claws unfurling like they did in moments of vulnerability. "Letting others help."

"An apology *and* a confession," he said, eyes sparkling with humor. "From a monarch, no less."

I held his gaze. "I'm not like any monarch you've met before, Lord Reaux."

"Oh, I know, Empress," he murmured, reaching for his daughter. When he crossed me, his fingers grazed the side of my hand.

It was quick. Probably unintentional. Barely a breath of skin against mine. But it sent a jolt of lightning up my arm, through my shoulder and into my chest.

"Let's go, sweetheart," he said to Marigold. "We shouldn't take up more of their time."

"Goodbye, Empress Aris!" Marigold sang, holding out her hand to me. "I really like your puppy!"

I chuckled and bent low. "You're welcome to play with her anytime. And call me Rissa, yes? Emperor Aris was my father." I winked up at Thorne, remembering him saying similar words to me the day I met him.

Had that really only been a week ago? I could've sworn I'd been in this kingdom longer than that. I missed Veridia City and my people—the magic, the energy, the dry air that didn't make it feel like I was wearing a second skin of sweat. I missed Lark and Chaz. I missed my fox half with a desperation that never faded.

But a soft spot had grown in my heart for Mysthelm, even though I'd barely seen any of it yet. I loved the exploration and challenges that came with learning new people. I loved the vibrant colors and unusual clothes and the *food*. Fates, the food was good. I loved the smells, how the breeze carried with it notes of salt and sun from the shores not too far away on all sides. And the scent of sweet grass and leather…

I cleared my throat and stood, watching as Thorne and Marigold walked off and the next citizen in line approached cautiously.

"Your Majesty," the middle-aged man said, bowing low and exposing a balding spot at the top of his head surrounded by wiry light blond hair. He wiped the sweat from his forehead with a stained handkerchief. The poor man looked like he was melting in his heavy brown cloak—an interesting choice in this heat.

"Hello, good sir," Galen said, sitting back down in his tall chair. "And what is your name?"

The man's tongue flitted against his lips as his cheeks twitched into an awkward smile. "Tovar, Your Majesty." He bowed again, his feet shuffling forward another step with the movement.

The hair on the back of my neck stood.

"Have you met Empress Clarissa Aris yet?" Galen swept a hand toward me, and I dipped my head in greeting.

"Haven't had the pleasure, Your Majesty," Tovar responded, eyes flitting briefly to me and then over my shoulder to the guard standing at attention. The glance was so brief, I almost missed it.

He's just nervous, I chided myself. Meeting their king for the first time would make anyone a little anxious. Mia's nose nudged against my calf, and I leaned forward to scratch her ears, keeping my eyes trained on Galen and the stranger.

Galen tilted his head at the uncomfortable silence that filled the space, examining the man with that same charming smile still on his face. "Well, what can we help you with, Tovar?" he prompted.

"Oh, yes," Tovar said, jerking forward. "I—I have something for you, King Grimaldi. A gift. You see, I'm a cobbler, and my daughter and I, we—we make shoes. Well, *I* do. She used to, until..." He shook his head, licking his lips again as he took another step. "Anyway, she always made the most beautiful suede shoes, and this was the last pair she ever..." He trailed off once more, his speech becoming more hurried as he went on.

My heart beat a little faster as he reached into the lining of his cloak. I watched the slight tremble in his hands, the way his nose twitched when his tongue flicked out over his lips, how his eyes shifted back and forth over Galen's body.

Something was wrong.

"Here, Your Majesty." Tovar's arm moved, and I clung to the edge of my seat, muscles clenched with a warning I couldn't place. "For you." He pulled out a pair of beautiful black suede shoes, with golden buckles shining brightly in the sunlight.

When he handed them to the king, something else glinted.

Steel.

Everything happened so fast.

Tovar's jaw tightened as Galen reached out to take the shoes. In the blink of an eye, the man plunged his hand into the opening of the right shoe and snatched the handle of the blade.

I lunged from my chair and threw myself into action, kicking the toe of my boot into the back of his knee. He staggered to the side and whirled to face me, sharp knife in hand. His features were crazed, his pupils blown out, splotches of red on his pale cheeks. Mia's high-pitched barks sounded behind us as he hurled himself toward me.

Tovar was sloppy and inexperienced, operating on emotions instead of skill. I'd fought my fair share of enraged fanatics in my time with the Sentinels—people who acted out of anger, not careful calculation. And this man...he was wild with anger.

Anger made people stupid. It made them careless. But it also made them dangerous.

With a growl, he swiped at my neck with his blade. I reared back and brought my hand down on his wrist to block his attack. The knife clattered to the ground as I drove my other fist into his stomach, making him double over with a groan. The guards behind our chairs rushed forward, yanked Tovar to his feet, and pulled his arms behind his back so quickly, I heard his shoulder pop out of place.

The sound...

I gritted my teeth against my blurring vision, focusing on my racing adrenaline and the danger of the moment to keep me grounded. Present. I could feel soft fur rubbing against exposed skin at my ankle, Mia's body trembling while her yaps filled the air.

Tovar's eyes locked on mine before they pulled him away. With a sound that bordered on a whimper, he whispered hoarsely, "Do you know what he's done? The man you stand beside?"

Galen shot to his feet, brows creased in fury. "I have done *nothing* to you. But you will suffer the consequences for this attack." He flicked a hand at the guards, wrath radiating in waves from his tall frame.

Tovar's eyes flashed. A ripple of emotion crossed his features. Determination, vengeance, longing, misery. He struggled against the guards' hold on him before spitting at Galen's feet.

"My name is Tovar Printh. And *you* murdered my daughter."

28

CLARISSA

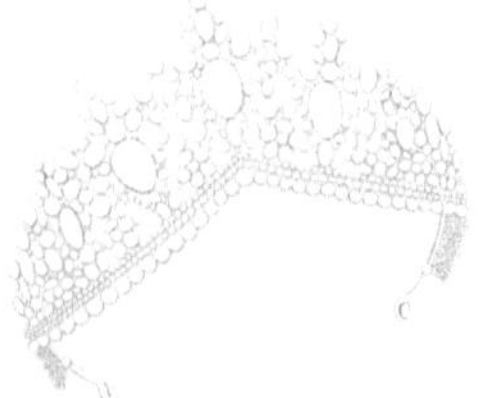

Galen's face went ashen.

"How did he get through with *this*?" he hissed at the nearest guard, pointing to the weapon. "Guests were supposed to be searched!"

"We'll find out, Your Majesty," the guard grunted. Several of them dragged Tovar away, down the aisle of waiting citizens and toward a sleek black carriage with bars on the window. Gasps of confusion echoed, some people rushing out of the way while others converged on us to get a better look.

"Galen, what did that man mean?" I asked, watching the uneasy crowd. "Why did he say you murdered his daughter?"

He faced me, hazel eyes distant. "Because I did."

My heart dropped to my feet as he turned, straightened his shoulders, and put on a smile. "Not to worry, everyone. Just a small misunderstanding, but it's been taken care of. We must leave to prepare for the Harvest Festival tonight. I hope to see you all this evening," he finished, nodding to those nearest us.

Whispers spread when more of the King's Guard walked up the center of the clearing to escort us out. One took Galen's arm while another reached for my shoulder. I batted him away and grabbed Galen's free hand to get his attention. "We need to talk," I said through my teeth, trying to keep a relaxed posture to avoid upsetting the crowd.

He flinched and tugged his arm away. "Not now, Clarissa." He kept his eyes straight ahead. The guards motioned for us to follow, and I untied Mia's leash from my chair and tucked her under my arm. She wiggled and turned her body until her front paws rested on my shoulder so she could see what was going on behind us. Her soft ear brushed my cheek every time she moved, her keen senses on high alert after the attack.

The guards ushered us down the steps of the dais. I took a deep breath and tried to block out the sounds of my own hammering heart and people's murmurs of concern. It seemed Galen's short speech had mollified them enough to keep pandemonium from breaking out, but it felt like it was hanging by a thread.

We made it to the edge of the clearing where a royal carriage waited, with more armed men planted firmly in place.

"Where's my mother?" I whispered, peering over the guards' heads and behind us, desperate to catch a glimpse of her. The crowd began to move away from the clearing and back to the other activities. A handful of lingering, frightened eyes glanced back at us, but soon, conversations started up again.

"She'll be escorted to Silenus Manor, Your Majesty," one of the guards answered. "Our priority is to retrieve you and His Majesty. We must get you to safety."

He tried to grasp me again, but I ripped out of his hold. Mia let out a soft growl. "It was an isolated attack, not a revolution," I said. "You've already apprehended the one responsible. Please, I need to find my mother."

"His Majesty's orders. Get in the carriage, Empress Aris." His tone held no room for argument, but still, I craned my neck to see around him and Mia's ears. While I didn't think any other assassination attempts would be made, people acted rashly when emotions were high, and Mother and I were easy targets among those in fear. All it took was one person emboldened by the chaos and holding a grudge against Veridians to act out.

I scanned the scene, looking for my mother's familiar blonde-and-gray bun among the tan, linen, and leather.

Instead, my gaze snagged on someone else. "Thorne!" I said on an exhale, pushing against the guard who tried to shove me into the carriage.

Thorne instantly found me and covered the space between us in three quick strides. Mia's tail thumped against my back. When Thorne saw the guard yank my arm, his light blue eyes darkened to stormy ice.

"Take your hands off her," he said, his voice so low, it was almost a growl. The sound sent a shiver down my spine. The guard released me but kept an arm across my stomach, urging me toward the carriage.

"Thorne—find my mother," I insisted. "Make sure she's safe." I kept my tone as calm as I could, aware of how every action could send others into a frenzy, but I instinctively reached my free hand toward him as my feet were forced farther away. My fingers brushed the tips of his.

"Of course, Empress. I'll find her," he promised.

My shoulders fell in relief. Thorne would help her. He would make sure she was safe. I didn't have to worry.

I didn't know when I had begun to trust him...but I did.

Leather skimmed my waist as Galen's strong grip pulled me inside the carriage. Thorne's fingers fell away, his eyes flicking to Galen's gloved hand resting on my hip before he nodded to me and disappeared into the crowd.

The door to the carriage shut, and the only sound filling the space was Mia's heavy pants. I set her on the bench beside me and let her wander across the small area, making sure to keep her leash short enough that she couldn't cross to Galen.

"What just happened?" I gritted out.

He leaned forward and held his head in his hands as the carriage rocked beneath us, fingers clawing at his tousled brown hair. "I didn't recognize him at first. I—I didn't know him. But

217

when he said his last name…" He looked up at me, face ashen and eyes bloodshot. "I never forget a name."

I fell back onto the bench across from him, my breath leaving me in a *whoosh* as I took in his words. Mia's tail brushed my side while she sniffed around the seat.

"You have to understand—this curse, it…it took over my life, Clarissa. It *controlled* me. I woke up as a king the day my father died, with this Grimaldi curse passed onto my head. Nobody knew what it would be. Nobody knew what—what power I'd inherit.

"Myths from my lineage say the magic stems from our greatest flaws. The idols that plague our minds, the one thing we can't live without. My ancestor Nyses was obsessed with seeking power and control to create a legacy far into the future. So his curse was to *see* that future. To watch it unfold…horrific or not.

"And my grandfather was a—a harsh man. Even before he was king, he enjoyed inflicting pain on others. Watching them suffer." A shudder went through Galen. "When he became cursed, he was forced to endure the same pain he administered. Every punishment, every whipping, he experienced it too."

My brows pinched closer and closer together as he explained how the Fates had designed this curse. It was so deliberate. So *personal.* It sounded as if some of his ancestors may have deserved their fate, but Galen? He wasn't cruel. He may have been misguided, but he was trying to make things right.

He paused, and I waited quietly, giving him space to work through his thoughts. My fingers found Mia and scratched her back to give my hands something to do.

He turned to look out the window. "You know my curse. How my touch will rot. I've always been so…dependent on physical contact. My parents were good, fair rulers, but they left little time for me as a boy. I craved my mother's affection, which was only given after I'd done something for her. 'Be a good little boy at the ceremony today.' 'Do as Mommy says, and you can have dinner with us tonight.'"

His voice broke, and he cleared his throat. "I came to associate her attention, her touch, with validation. And as I got older, it became far too easy to transfer that to every facet of my life. Men, women, everything you could possibly want could be won with careful devotion. With *touch*. I found confidence in the way I could get approval and compassion with my body. The nights out with Thorne, the years spent in another's company, a different partner in my bed. It was what I thought I had to do. It's the only thing I *could* do.

"And when that was taken away from me...when I could no longer so much as *feel* another person's skin against my own... You don't know what that's like. How difficult it was to accept." He took a deep breath. "Even when I began killing people."

A chill filled the carriage. "What happened?" I whispered.

He scrubbed a hand over his cleanshaven face. "The first one was my maid, Lydia. She brought breakfast to my bed the morning after my father died, when I'd been unofficially crowned king. The heir to the throne and the family curse. My fingers...they barely skimmed hers. And it was so slow, I didn't believe *I* had done it at first. She made it all the way out the chamber doors before I heard her fall. It looked as if the life had been drained from her." He pressed his thumbs into his eyes. "She was dead. Nobody could explain it, and it wasn't until strange things kept happening to me that I wondered if it had been *me*."

I could almost hear my heart beating in the silence. My shoulders were tight with tension, my breath shaking as I waited for him to continue.

"I tripped against a root on my way to the stables and caught myself on a tree trunk, and it withered. That was when I became truly scared. I touched every piece of shrubbery I could find, *praying* it was a mistake, but each one rotted and died. Shriveled before my very eyes. I knew it was the Grimaldi curse; I knew I couldn't escape it.

"I tore back through the palace, avoiding everyone who came in my path, and holed myself in my chambers for a week. My mother needed me. My *people* needed me. I was supposed to be crowned their king, and I wouldn't even show my face. They—they thought I was drunk or ignoring my responsibilities, and perhaps I was. I should have been there for them. But I didn't know what to do. I *still* don't know what to do most of the time.

"There was a—a girl." He swallowed. "From this territory. A... servant I'd hired several months before. She frequented my bedroom often." He glanced up at me, but I didn't react. "She knew of a secret door behind a tapestry in my room. She took it upon herself to persuade me to crawl out of my hiding spot. I'd forgotten to block that door and wasn't expecting anyone to come through it. She came in the middle of the night. Crawled into my bed and tried to wake me. I found her dead the next morning, her decayed arm thrown over my naked chest." He paused. "Her name was Vivian Printh."

I grimaced as bile crept up my throat. Mia padded over to my lap and curled into a ball, resting her chin on my chest and looking up at me with her big eyes.

"So, yes, Clarissa," he said, voice tired. His eyes were both hollow and full of anguish at the same time. "I *did* kill that man's daughter. And she's not the only one."

I didn't know what to say.

He was right—I couldn't possibly understand. He had no choice in this legacy, no choice in the nightmare his life had become. All he could choose was how he reacted. How he pushed forward.

I'd felt many emotions toward this man since I met him. Intrigue, frustration, confusion, anger. But now...now I felt pity. Now I understood what rested beneath his layers. After seeing what was taken from him, something that represented so much more than mere touch.

He just wanted to be loved.

And I couldn't even give that to him.

"Does Tovar Printh know how it happened?" I asked quietly.

Galen shook his head. "Thorne and my mother helped me cover it up. Thorne was heavily opposed to the idea, but I think that man would do almost anything to protect those he loves. We said Vivian fell ill, and there was nothing we could do. But the servants spoke, and rumors spread in the wake of my absence. Printh wrote many letters. My guards told me he'd even tried to storm the palace after he didn't hear from his daughter in several months, demanding to see her body, but I...we..."

He shook his head and slumped back in his seat. "We'd burned it. There couldn't be any proof of what I'd done. I sent a courier to pay him and his family handsomely, ensuring they'd be set for life. Of course, that didn't make up for any of it. I'm not surprised he tried to kill me today." Leaning forward, he held his head in his hands once more, his shoulders deflating as he let out a long breath.

"You must think I'm a monster," he said, so softly I barely heard him.

I bit down on my bottom lip. "I don't think you're a monster. You didn't do this to them on purpose. You didn't *want* this curse. But Galen...your people needed you. All these months you've been hiding away at your palace, these families have been fighting a blight threatening to wipe out everything they've worked for."

"What good would it have done?" he asked. "I can't take the rot away. I can't stop the curse. If anything, being near them would have put them in *more* danger. Can't you see that?"

"Being their king doesn't mean you're going to solve all their problems with a wave of your hand. Sometimes it simply means *being there*. Listening. Acknowledging them and giving them hope. Making them feel heard, not abandoned."

I expected him to get defensive, to snap back and remind me of my place in this kingdom. Instead, he lowered his head. "I do care for these people, Clarissa. I do. But I don't know how to lead them. I don't know how to help them when I'm the one causing their pain. I don't—I don't know what to do anymore."

This man was trapped. Immobilized by his own mind, his own fears. Too frightened and ashamed to take any steps forward, even if that meant he was leaving them in the dark.

I put a hand on his knee. "I see your fear, Galen. I have since that first night in your palace. But what I haven't been able to figure out is if you're afraid of the curse," I cocked my head to the side, "or the crown?"

He let out a breath. "They're the same thing, aren't they? I can't have one without the other. Until you came."

"*You* are their king, Galen. Not me. I can't solve your problems for you."

"But you could help me." He grasped my hands. I jolted at the contact of leather on my skin. "Have you made your decision yet? Will you still agree to marry me?"

If I was being honest, I never needed time. There wasn't a doubt in my mind about what I had to do.

I'd already accepted his proposal once, albeit via correspondence with his council, but for some reason...this felt different.

Because I didn't feel anything at all.

"Of course, Galen."

His hands instantly squeezed mine as a breath of relief left his lips. He reached into the pocket of his jacket, fishing for something until he pulled out a small box.

"I've been carrying this on me, waiting for this conversation. I wanted to make sure it was your choice." He looked around the tiny space of the carriage. "There isn't really a proper way to do this in here, but..." He opened the box to reveal a ring with a large diamond in the center. Smaller gemstones dotted the silver band. Tiny rubies, emeralds, and sapphires, all shining back at me.

"Clarissa Aris, will you marry me?"

I wanted to feel something. *Anything*. Besides this churning in my gut and a sinking weight in my heart.

I nodded. "Yes. I will."

He gave me a forlorn smile and slid the ring onto my left hand. It was a perfect fit, but it felt out of place. Heavy.

I knew this was how it would be. This was an obligation, even more so now than it had been a week ago. It was never going to be a love match. I was never going to have the fairytale ending my brother had with Rose.

But that was okay, because I'd be doing so much *good*.

"I may not know you very well, Empress, but you seem like the kind of person who would do anything if it meant helping others. Even if it wasn't in your own best interests."

Thorne's deep voice caressed the back of my mind, and I shoved it away. He was an idealist. A dreamer. When the future of thousands of people lay in the palm of your hand, you couldn't think of your own best interests or desires.

This looming marriage felt like both a salvation and a noose at the same time.

I squeezed my hand shut, running my thumb along the sharp edges of the center diamond. "Why are we bothering to go through with the rest of this tour? Why not get married as soon as tonight, with as bad as the curse is getting?"

He sighed. "Trust me, I wish it were as simple as that. But I need to be sure the regents will approve."

"But you're their king." I squinted at him in confusion. "Since when do you need permission on who and when to marry?"

"It's not their permission, necessarily. The regents are powerful families. While I may sit on the throne, they have nearly as much sway over their territories as I do. I'd rather know I have their backing before charging headfirst into an alliance with an empire we've spent the last three centuries despising. No offense," he added hastily. "But can you imagine the uproar we'd cause if we got married in secret, without at least attempting to get them on our side? I don't need a rebellion on my hands. Not on top of every-thing else."

"Then...why don't you tell the regents the urgency of breaking the curse? Surely, they'd understand."

"Clarissa, they can *never* know of this curse," he said. "Thorne and Azura only know because of their proximity to my family. If anyone else found out who I am, *what* I am...if they knew *I* was the one causing the blight..." He shook his head. "They would bust down the palace walls and have my head before I could blink. And I would deserve it."

We fell into a strained silence, and he slowly sat upright, looking outside the window as Silenus Manor drew nearer. Wheels crunched over gravel and hooves clattered against rock, while the sun shone through the glass and highlighted his sharp, anxious features.

"It will all be over soon," I whispered, partially to myself, and partially to ease the distress this day had brought to him.

"No, Clarissa." His chest deflated on a sigh. "The curse may break, but what I've done...that will stay with me as long as I live."

29

CLARISSA

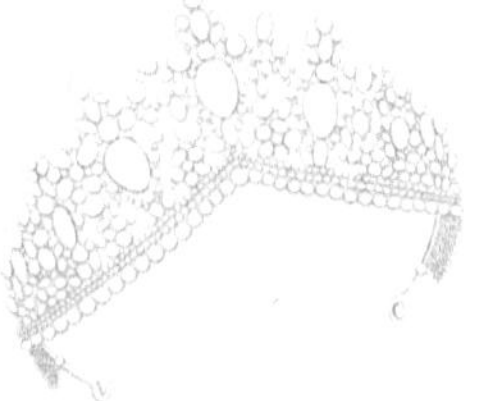

Everyone arrived back at the manor shortly after Galen and I did. I recounted what Galen had told me to my mother before Devora and Katrine appeared. The latter frantically forced us into our respective baths to wash up from the fields. Mia was enjoying her new domain and had sniffed every single item she could reach, then collapsed on the rug in the center of my room and napped peacefully. I sent Devora out to find some food and toys for her while Katrine begged me to get ready for the Harvest Festival. I couldn't believe they were still continuing with the event, but Galen insisted on things happening as planned.

I felt...disconnected. Unfocused. Like my body was trying to put on a show, smiling and prancing around these events as if nothing was wrong. But my mind was spiraling through the secrets of this kingdom and this curse, everything I'd seen and heard in the last week.

And lately, those spiraling sessions included light blue eyes, a smirk that wasn't afraid to call me out when I was in my own head, and warm hands that kept me grounded.

A knock sounded on the door to our suite. Mia instantly bolted awake and let out a high bark, rushing to the sound with Devora on her heels. My maid answered it with a sweet, "Why, hello there!"

I turned away from the mirror where Katrine was buttoning up my dress to find Marigold in the doorway, with Mia up on her hind legs and yapping away excitedly. Marigold giggled as the dog licked her arms. She was precious in her pink and purple tulle skirt and flower crown.

"You look like a fairy queen!" she exclaimed, pointing at my dress while petting Mia with her other hand.

Katrine was incredibly talented—she had outdone herself with this one. The bottom layer of my lightweight gown was a soft cream color that flowed from my waist and trailed behind me, with a high slit in the front coming up to my thigh. A thin outer layer of shimmering gold fabric covered the entire dress. Green threads that looked like vines with multi-colored flowers snaked their way down the tight corset and over the waistline, spreading out among the gold and cream.

"Well, thank you," I said with a laugh. "And you look like a little princess." My grin faltered when Thorne's large body came into view, his hand on her back as he glanced around the room sheepishly.

"I'm sorry to bother you, but she kept asking if she could play with the pup again..." He trailed off as his eyes found me. The way they slowly drifted up from the slit at my legs to my neck made heat pulse against my skin.

"You look beautiful, Empress," he said, voice rough.

"Look, Daddy, we match!" Marigold cried, drawing my attention back to her. She motioned to the flower crown on top of her head. I smiled and touched the one I wore, which Devora had made out of green vines, pearls, and wisteria.

"Hello, Lord Reaux," my mother called from her room, poking her head out and raising an eyebrow at me before smiling at Thorne. "I thought I heard you."

He nodded to her. "Evadine, sorry to intrude."

"Oh, nonsense. And who is this precious little girl?" my mother asked.

Thorne shuffled Marigold farther into the suite. "This is my daughter, Marigold. Marigold, say hello to Ms. Aris."

Marigold waved shyly at my mother, rocking back and forth on her heels. "Are you Rissa's mommy?"

"Why yes, I am."

"She looks like you. She's very pretty," Marigold said earnestly.

"Yes, she is," Thorne remarked, so quietly I thought I misheard. My grin faded as I looked at him in surprise. He cleared his throat. "They both are, of course."

An awkward silence filled the room. I could feel my mother's knowing gaze digging into my back.

"Well, I'll be in here if anyone needs me," Mother said, retreating back to her room. "The rest of you, have fun at the festival."

"Daddy said I can't go tonight," Marigold said, gazing longingly at my dress.

He sighed. "It'll be past your bedtime. And you, little girl, need your sleep after the exciting day you had."

I chuckled at the way she tilted her head up to look at him with those big brown eyes, a tactic I'm sure worked like a charm for her. Pair that with the puppy nudging sweetly at Thorne's ankle, and I could see his resolve crumbling bit by bit.

I crossed the room and knelt before Marigold, taking both her hands in mine. "How about you watch Mia for me tonight while I'm gone?" Her neck snapped back to me. "Would you like that?"

She nodded and grinned, showing off her dimple and the small gap between her teeth.

"Now, taking care of a dog is a big responsibility," I said in a mockingly stern voice. "You have to make sure she has enough food and water, and take her outside on her leash every couple of hours so she doesn't have an accident inside your room."

Marigold nodded again, this time at Mia, an adorable crease appearing at her brow as she concentrated hard on my words.

"And she needs *lots* of playtime to get all her energy out. Do you think you can do that?"

"I'll take such good care of her, I promise," she said, then craned her neck to look at her father again. "Can I, Daddy? Please?"

I gave him a slight smirk as I cocked my head. "Can she, Lord Reaux? Please?"

His answering glare sent a thrill through me. "You two will be the death of me."

"Then what a way to go," I responded.

His jaw shifted and he took a deep, exaggerated breath. "Just *one* night."

Marigold squealed before he even got the full sentence out, then wrapped her arms around my neck. "Thank you, Rissa!" she said into my hair. I returned the hug, glancing up to catch Thorne's eyes fixed on us, the column of his throat moving as he swallowed. The look he was giving us made my toes curl and my heart constrict, an unfamiliar emotion flooding my chest.

I smoothed out Marigold's hair and tapped her nose. "You two have fun tonight, yes?"

She beamed and nodded vigorously, brown hair swaying. "I think you're my new favorite. I'm so glad you're marrying Uncle Galen!"

And just like that, the warm feeling was gone. I plastered a smile on my face and said, "Thank you, sweet girl," before standing to gather the few possessions we had for Mia.

When the three of them left, my mother padded from her room and into mine, her perceptive eyes resting on my face.

"Don't give me that look."

She raised an eyebrow. "And what look might that be?"

"Why aren't you getting ready, anyway?" I asked, ignoring her question. She was still in her robe and holding a book with a letter sticking out between the pages. When she caught me glancing at it, she shoved the piece of paper out of sight.

"Oh, I think I'll stay in tonight. Let you younger ones have fun. Today was an adventure enough for me."

I frowned and crossed over to her. She *did* look tired. I often forgot how much she'd aged in those years wasting away in our cottage, before her mind returned to her. I still remembered the version of my mother that was constantly on the move when Leo and I were children.

I squeezed her hand. "I'm sorry, Mother. I feel like we've barely seen each other on this trip."

She scoffed. "Clarissa, after missing nearly sixteen years of your life, any moment I have with you is a blessing. Do *not* be sorry. I'm perfectly content being your shadow and watching you take this kingdom by storm." Patting my cheek as she always did, she smiled softly. "I just hope you're being careful."

"Of course," I said. "I always am."

"And I don't simply mean with politics and court intrigue." She tilted her head. "I mean with your *heart*."

"My heart has nothing to do with this, Mother. Will you hand me those shoes?" I asked quickly, pointing to the gold sandals by the armoire.

She let out one of her long I'm-not-happy-with-you sighs just as Devora and Katrine appeared by the suite door. "If you no longer need us, we'll head to our dinner now," Katrine said, giving us a curtsy.

"Actually, there is something I need." I walked over to grab the two of them by the hand and pull them back, an idea forming in my mind. I flashed a smile. "You're coming with me. You two deserve a night of fun."

Katrine's eyes widened in excitement, but Devora's lips turned down for a fraction of a second before she schooled her features.

"Your Majesty, it's probably best that we—" she started, but Katrine cut her off.

"But what will we wear?" Katrine asked breathlessly.

I gave them a wink. "I'm sure we'll find something."

———

THE FIELDS of Gold Row had been transformed from the tournament to the Harvest Festival, and the sight of it as our carriage pulled off the gravel road took my breath away.

Small lanterns hung from strands of rope tied to steel posts in the ground, creating an enormous circle that spanned several fields. The outskirts of the wide area were occupied by tents and booths of more vendors—people selling food and drinks and little trinkets like corn dolls and prayer talismans. Vespera had told me how traditional this festival was, with their rituals and sacrifices to the Fates. What she didn't mention was that it was basically a glorified outdoor ball.

Within the large border of the festival was a handful of bonfires spread out across the fields, with people already dancing and drinking around them like they'd been there for hours. Even though the sun had set, the light from the hanging lanterns and blazing fires was enough to illuminate their bright eyes. Several musicians with stringed instruments were playing fast-tempo songs with catchy beats that already had my feet tapping along.

The scent of sweet wine and smoked meats wafted closer, drawing me in as Galen, Thorne, Devora, Katrine, and I made our way to the entrance, with a throng of guards, Lady Reaux, and the Silenus family trailing us closely.

"Well, they know how to put on a show," Galen said appreciatively, eyebrows rising as he took in the scene. He wore a light-weight brown jacket and pants over a white button-down. A thin golden band rested on top of his head as a crown. It had hints of the same wisteria as mine wrapped around it.

"It's absolutely amazing," Katrine replied with wondrous eyes.

"It's...a lot of people," Devora muttered under her breath. I chuckled and linked my arm through hers, earning me a sharp glance of surprise. She had forgone her black glasses tonight and let me braid her thick red hair into a crown around her head.

Katrine had found the pair of them a couple of floral knee-length dresses from some of the maids at Silenus Manor. The younger maid was coming alive under the orange haze of the flames, her umber features blossoming like the flowers she'd stuck in her hair. But Devora was still a bit hesitant. A shadow crossed her face as she gnawed on her bottom lip, so very different from the fierce girl who whipped knives out of her thigh sheath like it was second nature.

"Just ignore them," I said, leaning in and nudging her shoulder with mine. "Have fun. Enjoy your night out with no expectations."

She gave me a small smile. "Is that what you plan to do?"

"If only," I said. "I, unfortunately, always have expectations to meet. But *you*"—I whirled in front of her and grabbed both of her hands, dragging her after Katrine and Galen—"can let loose. When will you ever see these people again? Do whatever you want. *Be* whoever you want." I gave her a little twirl with one hand and smiled when her eyes sparkled back at me.

"Wouldn't that be something," she said, so quietly I hardly heard her over the music.

"Ready to make the rounds, Clarissa?" Galen asked a few steps ahead of me, holding out his arm.

I nodded. "I'll see you two later," I said to Katrine and Devora, grinning at the reluctant expression on Devora's face as Katrine hauled her to the nearest vendor.

Galen and I spent nearly an hour visiting each booth, making polite conversation with the citizens and eating our weight in the food they shoved in our hands. Little cucumber and spicy pepper sandwiches dipped in a honey sauce, chocolate-covered coffee beans, and dried pieces of bacon topped with some gray, gelatinous mush that I didn't care to question.

It was difficult not to notice that double the usual number of guards followed closely on our heels, earning the occasional wary glance from passersby. But for the most part, it felt like a normal night. *Fun*, even. I could almost forget that the man beside me was nearly assassinated nine hours ago for accidentally murdering an innocent man's daughter.

Almost.

People greeted us with excitement, bowing low and shaking

our hands as we moved from group to group. They were delighted to have their king in their presence, but to my surprise, more of them focused on *me*.

"It's so good to see you again, Empress Aris."

"Our fields have never been better ever since you cleared the blight away!"

"How can we thank you for what you've done?"

The comments, kind words, and gratitude were endless. It filled my heart to see them no longer have to worry about the blight, and by the end of our first trip around the large circle, my cheeks hurt from smiling so much.

"They love you," Galen said when we took a break to watch the dancing. "You must be adored by your people back home."

I let out a short laugh. "I'm getting there."

If only he knew.

Dion Silenus approached, his pale cheeks pink from exertion, a thin smile on his normally scowling face. The faint scent of alcohol lingered around him. "Your Majesty, Your Majesty," he said, bowing to each of us in turn. I raised an eyebrow, still not used to his change in demeanor.

"I'm sorry to take you away so soon, but would it be alright if I borrowed Galen for just a few moments? I'll bring him back to you before the sacrifices begin," Dion assured me.

"Of course," I said. "I wanted to try a drink, anyway." I waved them off as they walked toward the entrance, then searched for a vendor selling some of the delicious drink I'd smelled earlier.

A few minutes later, I had a cup in hand and found a less busy side of one of the bonfires to plant myself, taking some time away from the crowds to watch them dance and sing and mingle. I didn't have many moments like this anymore, where I could blend into the background and hear myself think, without the pressure of a meeting or someone needing me.

I swayed to the lively band, my eyes tracing the path of flames and smoke curling against the starry sky. Sweet flavors of cherry and spice burst on my tongue when I took a sip, and I hummed as it coated my throat.

"Careful," a deep voice said behind me, making me jump. "That wine is strong."

I turned, and a slow thrill dripped through my body. "Good evening, Lord Reaux."

He smirked back at me. "Evening, Empress."

30

THORNE

I was an idiot.

I shouldn't have walked over to her. I wasn't even sure why I did. Clarissa appeared so calm, so unrestrained, so *free*. I was like a moth drawn to her fire, that blazing spirit I could never quite predict but that entranced me all the same.

And when she looked the way she did tonight...

I was helpless.

Her dress pooled around her feet, with gold threads like sunlight flowing over the fabric and making her shine as brilliantly as her smile. A flower crown was nestled in her blonde waves, and that slit at her leg exposed fair skin that begged to have my handprint on it.

I mentally slammed a wall on that sudden image.

Fates, where did that come from? It was as if the old Thorne were knocking at the door, bringing back a side of me I hadn't seen in years. Nobody since Iris had caught my attention like this. Nobody since Iris made heat spark in my blood.

Nobody since Iris stopped my heart when holding my daughter.

"How are you doing after today?" I asked. I'd been just outside the clearing with Marigold when we heard the gasps from the crowd, but I couldn't get close enough to get a good look. It wasn't until I passed Marigold off to my mother that I saw the guards barreling the would-be assassin toward a prisoner's carriage, followed closely by Clarissa and Galen.

She looked every bit the strong empress she was as she tried to hold herself together, but I saw the fear in her dark eyes. The confusion. And when I watched that guard grab her by the arm...it was like some beast roared inside of me, the need to protect her so strong, I wanted to rip his arm out of his socket. How dare he touch her like that? An empress and his soon-to-be queen?

That wasn't *me*. I wasn't easily angered. I didn't have emotions that surged through me like this, white-hot and branding. I was casual, laid-back, sometimes irritable, often worried, but never consumed.

Until this empress.

This strong-willed, sharp-tongued, secretly vulnerable woman whose heart was twice the size of anyone I'd ever met.

I'd known she was beautiful since the moment I saw her. I wasn't a stranger to beautiful women, and I didn't go throwing myself at the feet of every one I came across. But something about *her* had me on my knees twice now without even thinking.

I kept telling myself she and Galen would be married soon, and then she'd go back to her empire, living her life away from us. The diamond on her finger that kept catching the light of the fire and glittering back at me was proof enough of that.

This was a momentary attraction. It would pass. And everything would go back to the way it was supposed to be.

She sighed. "I'm fine, but I don't really want to talk about it. I just want to forget all of it for a few hours." She lifted the cup to her lips once more, and I forced myself not to watch the slender column of her throat move up and down as she drank.

"You know, I wasn't kidding about the wine."

"Please. You should see the stuff we have back in Veridia City." She took another sip and met my stare. Everything was a challenge to this woman.

It made heat burst through me.

She's marrying your best friend.

"There's a green wine called Luxe, which is stronger than any normal wine," she went on. "Lowers your inhibitions faster than you can blink. And a gray one, Grimlock, makes you incapable of lying."

"Well, I'm glad we don't have that here."

Cocking her head at me with that devilish look I'd seen several times, she asked, "And what truths do you have to hide, Lord Reaux?"

She was definitely flirting with me.

I met her stare for a beat before turning back to the fire. "Wouldn't you like to know?"

And perhaps I was flirting back.

We stared at the flickering flames in silence until she said, "You know, you're not who I thought you were."

That took me by surprise. I let out a soft snort. "Yes, I seem to remember you calling me a—what was it? A man who's used to charming his way into anything he wants with a nice smile and pretty words," I said, recalling her accusation from the night in the Silenus gardens. I was teasing, but truthfully, her words stung more painfully than I'd expected.

Probably because, once upon a time, they were true.

She winced as she swirled her cup. "It sounds so much worse when you say it like that."

"Well, it didn't exactly sound *nice* the first time, either." I smirked at her. I didn't blame her. I knew she'd had a difficult few days when she'd said those things, and I certainly hadn't made her time any easier. I loved getting under her skin too much. And I knew what kind of front I put on. It was all too easy to pretend to slip back into the man I used to be, especially when it kept things light.

"You're none of those things, Thorne. And I'm sorry I judged you so harshly." She sighed and took another long sip, then stepped closer to me. Close enough that I could smell her, sweet like lemons and crisp like pine needles on a forest floor, with a hint of the strong wine I was sure she'd had too much of.

"You're a good friend to Galen," she continued. "Even when he doesn't always deserve it. And...you're a good friend to me."

"Ah, so we're friends now, Empress?" I replied. She was too close, my heart too open, the foot of space between us too charged. It made me retreat into my mask of charm and quick wit, afraid of what would happen if I let myself be as vulnerable as her.

"Don't interrupt," she snapped playfully. "This is probably the nicest I'll ever be to you." A hint of her crooked smile glowed up at me. I chuckled until her next words made the grin fade from my face.

"You're a good father, Thorne. I can't imagine how difficult it's been to raise Marigold on your own, but she seems so *happy*. So protected and loved. She's beautiful and full of life, and I know we haven't known each other very long, but I think...I think that comes from you."

I didn't know how to respond. I hadn't expected her to say anything like that, and it clenched around my heart like a vise.

"Thank you," I said after a moment. "That's all I want for her, you know. To be kind and happy. To know how loved she is." I wasn't sure what made the words spill out of me, but now that they started, I couldn't stop them. "We've been fortunate to have so many people support us and dote on her since her mother died, but a part of me feels compelled to love her enough for *both* of us. That me by myself wouldn't be enough, and she'd always be missing something if I didn't fill that hole. Nothing can truly fill it, of course, but it doesn't stop me from trying. And often failing."

Clarissa's brow furrowed, the flower crown resting on her head casting shadows onto her cheeks and the tip of her nose. "The only way you could ever fail her is by not being there. I was watching you today at the tournament—that little girl looks at you like you're her entire world. I don't think you have to make up for anything. She just needs *you*." She tucked a loose strand of hair behind her ear. "Trust me, as someone who lost her father sixteen years ago, she's lucky to have you in her life the way that you are."

"I'm sorry about your father," I said. "If I may ask...what happened to him?"

She took another sip. "He died of a heart attack when my twin brother and I were twelve. Well...that's what the healers said, anyway. My brother believes it was his own fault. He thinks it was the consequence of dark Alchemist magic he used as a boy. I don't know if we'll ever know the truth, but it doesn't change what happened."

I'd never get used to the way she spoke of magic so casually, as if it were something they all possessed and could turn on and off at will. Normal and expected. Not this poisonous, evil magic that only Galen and his ancestors had, that slowly ate away at their family and our entire kingdom. I briefly wondered what it would be like to see a magic that didn't always bring hardships.

But then I realized...I *had* seen it. Watching Clarissa transform into her fox half after touching the blight was remarkable. Natural and powerful, like that was how it should be.

Everything about her was remarkable.

"Was that when the next emperor took his place? Emperor Gayl?" I recalled the name from a letter with her council. I knew Clarissa's father was Emperor of the Veridian Empire at some point, but something had happened to make the new man, Theodore Gayl, take over.

She shook her head and downed more of her drink. "No, my father hadn't been emperor for years. He abdicated his throne when I was practically a baby and moved our family to a cottage in the woods."

I let out a disbelieving laugh. "What could possibly make an emperor give up that life?"

"You didn't think your kingdom was the only one burdened with a terrible curse, did you?" she asked, quirking an eyebrow. Her cheeks were flushed from the bonfire and the cup of wine she'd almost finished.

"There were...complications when my brother and I were born. Leo and my mother almost didn't survive." She shifted on her feet. "Emperor Gayl was a powerful Alchemist, and he saved their lives —but it was all just a ruse. What he actually did was use that moment of such dark, powerful magic to cast a sleeping curse over the entire empire," she explained, her words tripping over themselves as she spoke.

"Nobody knew the truth and instead blamed our father for casting it. He eventually crumbled under the pressure and thought the only way to keep all of us safe was to abandon the throne. Our people...Fates, they *hated* us. We were outcasts from a young age, pariahs in our own home. It took nearly thirty years for the truth to come out and for us to learn that Gayl was behind it all along. He'd practically pushed my father out of the palace."

The look I gave her must have shown my shock, for she smiled darkly into her drink. "Not all of us grew up in fancy palaces and mansions with everything we could want placed at our feet."

I scratched my beard, thinking of my own upbringing. The servants and splendor and riches. "That's quite a story, Empress."

"Well, we all have them."

"I have to admit, it does explain some things."

That earned me a confused glance. "What do you mean?" she asked.

"You're unlike any monarch I've ever met. Or anyone of nobility, for that matter. You're so..." I trailed off, twisting my lips and considering her.

"Confident? Witty? Capable?" She winked and brandished her cup in the air. "Take your pick. I've been told I have a way with words."

"I was going to say earnest." Her head tilted to the side, that playful smile sliding from her face. I couldn't help but chuckle. "Now who's surprised?"

"I'm...not sure how to take that."

I shrugged. "Most people in my world are nobles, lords, and aristocrats, all catering to the crown. They're insincere and shallow, driven by their own agenda or by some sense of duty passed down from the generations that doesn't even mean anything to them anymore. It's just what we're *supposed* to do. What we were born into and can never leave. We're taught what to say and how to say it and to never deviate from the path. But you...you're refreshingly *real*, Empress." Every word drew me closer to her. I barely felt my feet as they took a step toward her.

"You care not only for your own people, but also the ones you've known for all of five days. You want to take action and get things done. And you're not afraid to say what's on your mind." I took a breath, once again all too aware of the effect she was having on me. The fire sparking in her eyes as her features softened, those dark pools swallowing up everything I said.

I needed to rein this in and clear the heavy air forming between us. I needed to put the barrier back up. The one that kept me from drowning.

Because that look...that look could pull me under. I hadn't even known I was close to the edge until now.

I threw my normal smirk onto my lips. "I knew you were different from the moment I saw you walking off that ship looking like a wet, feral cat."

She gasped and faked an angry scoff. "I resent that statement, Lord Reaux," she said, taking a step closer and pressing a finger into my chest. The contact sent lightning through my veins, and I couldn't stop my hand from wrapping around her wrist.

She sucked in a breath. "I'm sorry, I forgot about your injury. Did I hurt you?"

I slowly shook my head. "No, Empress. It doesn't hurt."

Her eyes traveled from the finger that rested against the top of my chest to the locket that dangled from my neck. "I've been wanting to ask...what's this for?"

"It's a marigold," I said, voice rough. "I had it made when she was born."

She brushed her thumb along the chain, a soft hum leaving her lips. Her fingertips lingered against my skin.

Heat unfurled around my chest and into the hand holding hers. I could feel her pulse pounding, could see flecks of gold I'd never noticed in her near-black eyes. I'd touched her before, but only in moments when she needed me. Stepping out of a carriage, working through a panic attack, shifting back into her human form.

Never like this. Never simply because we *could*.

But we couldn't.

Too close. She was too close. She was marrying the king, and we were surrounded by hundreds of people. She—

Her eyes drifted to my lips.

I wasn't breathing. My thumb skimmed the pulse point at her wrist, causing her gaze to snap back to mine. When she let out a breath, I smelled hints of cherry on her lips.

"Dance with me," she murmured.

Fates, this woman.

My fingers itched to grab her waist, to see what her body would feel like swaying against mine in the shadows of the flames. Tucked away where no one could see us, where empresses and kings and curses didn't exist. Where I could slide my lips along her neck, maybe taste the wine still lingering on her tongue—

I threw up yet another wall on those thoughts, then barricaded it with steel. What was I *doing*? She was going to be another man's wife. I had a daughter, a territory to consider, and people to watch over.

It was the alcohol. Exhaustion and stress and alcohol. And that *dress*.

There had to be distance between us. There were lines that couldn't be crossed.

"I don't think that's a good idea, Clarissa," I said softly, releasing her hand and taking a step back. She blinked, and hurt flickered across her features.

Another voice rang out from the center of the festival.

"Everyone gather 'round, gather 'round," a man in overalls cried out. "It's time for the annual sacrifices to the Fates!"

31

CLARISSA

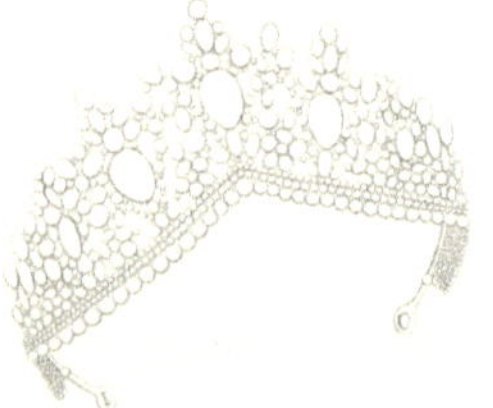

"*I don't think that's a good idea, Clarissa.*"

The tension snapped like a bowstring.

What had I been *thinking*? He was right—the wine was too strong. I could feel it souring in my stomach as he led me to the central bonfire where the sacrifices were to be made.

"Dance with me." My cheeks heated. I was never drinking again.

Perhaps on a subconscious level, I knew this impending marriage to Galen would close as many doors as it would open. Any urge to fill that void of physical touch would have to be done in secret or behind whispers and judgmental stares. I would never be able to give away my affection freely, to love out loud the way someone deserved. Not while I was Empress Clarissa Aris Grimaldi.

I was tired and anxious, and maybe the wine made me cross a line, grappling for some sort of contact, a last-ditch effort to be close to *anyone* before my life changed forever. Before I'd never get the chance to be with someone in any way that mattered.

And now I'd made a fool of myself in front of my fiancé's best friend.

He'd infuriated me in the beginning, but I wasn't lying when I said I'd misjudged him. My mind had been breaking him down piece by piece without me even realizing it over the past few days.

Thorne was kind and understanding, never pushing too far, even when he'd seen sides of me I didn't let a soul see back home. Even when I'd *hurt* him. The love he had for his daughter was palpable. And for all his cockiness, I couldn't help but think he was rather...*innocent*. Something truly difficult to find in this world. But he trusted easily and was quick to see the good in others, to give them the benefit of the doubt—perhaps *too* quick. His heart was so big, so ready to give to everyone around him, and that wasn't something I was used to in a world of secret rebellions and power-hungry Veridians.

I wasn't sure when I'd stopped looking at him as the handsome, privileged, vexingly arrogant advisor and started seeing the protective, compassionate spirit beneath.

But I knew one thing for certain.

I shouldn't have been looking at all.

"While we have faced hardships this year, we've still been blessed by the Fates with good health and a good harvest," announced the same man who had beckoned revelers closer. The festival calmed as people shuffled in, large pockets forming on either side of him, Dion, and Vespera. The three of them stood on a small circular stage, right next to an unlit bonfire. This was the largest of them all, with logs reaching at least three times my height.

"Of course, we want to give thanks to our regent family for watching over our land and making sure we have everything we need to provide for our homes." He nodded to the couple beside him. "To Dion and Vespera Silenus."

The crowd echoed him in a low murmur.

"Every year, we honor the three Fates and show our gratitude for all they've given us by giving a portion of what we've cultivated back to them. Today, we held competitions for the best of our territory, and tonight, we offer each in a sacrifice."

He began listing names of the farmers who had been given first place in the various contests today, having them step forward from the crowd one by one. His voice became lost in a smattering of applause when someone tapped me on the shoulder.

"There you are, Clarissa. I've been looking everywhere for you." Galen stepped between Thorne and me. "Thanks for keeping an eye on her, Thorne."

I bristled but stayed silent. Thorne's nose twitched as he nodded and moved farther away, his eyes landing on Galen's hand at my shoulder before they fell back to the speaker.

"Did you need me for something?" I asked Galen, more curtly than I intended.

"They want us up there." He nodded to the center. "They're going to ask you to light the fire. Hurry, we must go."

Galen and I pushed through a couple rows of people before ascending the small steps to stand next to Dion and Vespera. The latter gave me a warm smile and squeezed my hand as the speaker finished acknowledging each of the winning farmers.

"And now, of course, we must honor our wonderful king, and thank the Fates for his good health and continued prosperous rule." The man held out a hand to Galen. The crowd clapped and cheered as he smiled at my side.

"Finally, we have one more guest to introduce. A gift from the Fates. A savior to breathe life into this dying land." All eyes turned to me as he spoke, and I struggled against the urge to squirm on my feet. "She came when we feared all hope was lost. She rid our land of a terrible blight and brought good fortune back to our homes. We thank you, great Empress Clarissa Aris of the Veridian Empire!"

Thunderous applause followed his words. I smiled and waved, taking in the throngs of people beaming up at me with hope in their eyes. It filled me with pride. They may have started off fearful of me, but these people were still good. All they needed was someone to take care of them.

"Empress, if you would please light the ceremonial fire." The man handed me a torch. Heat licked at my skin as I edged closer to the large pile of logs. When the flames leaped from the torch to the first piece of wood, everyone cheered once more. Several men at the base began lighting small sections to make it go faster, and the timber shifted as more wood caught fire.

Sounds of clapping and hollering mixed with the roaring blaze, almost drowning out a gasp from behind me.

I turned to see Vespera staring at the bonfire, eyes wide as a hand covered her mouth.

I whirled around.

And dropped the torch.

There, in the center of the logs that had moved under the changing weight of flames, was a fox impaled on a spear.

"Clarissa!" Galen shouted, but I barely heard him.

Dead, golden eyes stared back at me from the orange and yellow haze, my vision blurring with smoke as its body was slowly covered by the fire.

I couldn't blink, couldn't breathe, could only stare straight ahead as ice encompassed my body. Hands tugged at my arm, but I shook them off. Noise disappeared, as if a blanket had been tossed over the crowd, muffling their shouts.

Scalding heat erupted on my skin. White-hot pain bit into my exposed ankles, stinging against the icy anguish pooling inside me.

"Empress, *move*," a low voice said, right before warm hands flew to my waist and lifted me into the air, away from the heat. My eyes were still trained on the fading corpse until a new face covered my vision.

Thorne's hand cupped my neck. Sound flooded back to me. The cheers from the citizens had turned to shocked cries as more and more people saw the burning fox. Vespera was shouting at the speaker, while Dion barked orders to his guards surrounding the stage.

"Clarissa, listen to me," Thorne said in rushed tones, his breath skating across my cheeks as pain still licked up my legs. "You need to stand firm. Somebody is trying to scare you, and you *cannot let them.* Hold yourself together until you get back to the manor. Do you understand? Don't let them win."

I met his eyes and blinked once, that fiery blue appearing as dead gold and back again. My lungs struggled to draw breath, but my face remained impassive. Unhearing. Uncaring.

All emotions had burned away with the charred, limp body of the fox.

Another hand, this one cloaked in leather, tugged at my arm. "I've got her from here, Thorne. Let's go."

I didn't even protest as Galen whisked me away into a pool of guards for the second time that day. When I took my first step, blinding pain shot up my leg, and I looked down to see deep red welts on my ankles and calves, the skin bubbling and splitting where fire from the torch had landed. A guard rushed to lend me his shoulder, but I shook my head.

"No," I said, my voice cold and distant.

I took another step across the stage, then another, forcing a wince away from my features.

"Clarissa, please—" Thorne said from behind me.

"Get away," I said to the guards, who glanced at Galen questioningly. When nobody moved, I raised my voice. "Get. Away."

Galen intervened. "We need to get to the carriage. They'll make sure—"

"*No*," I said again.

My gaze swept over the guards and the crowd beyond, now shouting and moving forward to get a better look at the bonfire. It was chaos, voices blending with the crackling of fire and shuffling of feet on grass and straw.

"They wanted to watch me burn," I said, straightening my shoulders. "So let them."

32

THORNE

"Did you see the animal?"

"Who would do this?"

"Is it another attack?"

Frantic citizens scattered throughout the festival, all sacrifices entirely forgotten. Galen and Clarissa disappeared in a swath of guards and smoke.

I pivoted on my heel to face Dion Silenus, clutching his collar and yanking him toward me. "Did you do this?" I hissed.

"Why would you think I had anything to do with it?" he bit out.

"Oh, I don't know. Perhaps the fact that you've been against their engagement from the start."

"That was before. It wasn't me, Reaux. I have no idea who was responsible, nor how they managed to get the animal inside there. Now, unhand me!"

"Thorne, dear, what has gotten into you?" my mother exclaimed as she charged up the steps of the stage.

My thoughts churned. She had *promised* me she'd stop her scheming. She'd agreed that having Clarissa here was a good thing for Galen, and that we needed their marriage to happen.

I trusted her.

Yet I hadn't seen her since we exited the carriage tonight when we got here. She was another person I knew had been opposed to Clarissa this whole time.

I shook my head to clear my mind, but a seed of doubt had taken root.

"Mother, where have you been?" My tone was cold—as cold as Clarissa's had been after she'd seen the fox.

I would never forget the look on her face. I was standing at the base of the stage, unable to see the center of the bonfire when she'd dropped the torch right at her feet. Her face froze, lips parted, chest caving inward as if every ounce of air had been ripped from her. Like one breath would make her crumble.

In the blink of an eye, it disappeared. She went utterly still, features blank. Empty. Hollow. Covering her emotions with that blanket she knew how to use so well.

It wasn't until I barged onto the stage that I saw the fox.

It was despicable. A targeted attack not meant to physically wound, but to send a message. A warning. To break her down after everything she'd done for this territory.

My mother gestured to a middle-aged woman at her side. "I was with Lady Vespera's mother. What in the world is going—" She inhaled sharply when she finally looked into the fire and saw the fox.

Her eyes widened. "Thorne, you can't possibly believe I would be behind any of this."

"I don't know, I think it's pretty believable," I muttered under my breath, making sure none of the others could hear.

Dion appeared beside me, wiping the sweat from his face with a handkerchief. "I must see that this is taken care of and everyone gets out safely. There's a carriage waiting to take you three home," he said, nodding to Vespera, her mother, and my own.

Two of the noblemen who had been at dinner the other night approached, along with a young guard. "Lord Silenus, we've apprehended someone who may know more information about the...offense," the tall nobleman said.

Dion nodded. "Good, good. Keep them detained until we can speak with them."

"Why would someone do this?" Vespera asked, voice shaking as she glanced back at the bonfire. "Clarissa has done nothing but help us."

The tall nobleman looked over the anxious crowd still mulling around the festival grounds. "Some are not so convinced, my lady."

"What do you mean?" I asked. "What have you heard?"

"Just...mumblings. Most are in awe of her magic, but some question the lengths she'll go to." His cheek twitched nervously under the weight of my piercing glare. "A—A person with enough power to take away this blight can surely give it back tenfold if she wished."

"Clarissa would never do that," I growled.

The second nobleman spoke. "Many say she's a gift from the Fates. But there are whispers of her being our damnation."

"This kind of power is unknown to us," the first one added. "It's difficult for some to trust blindly."

I was beginning to wonder how many more agreed with these sentiments. How many of the citizens here secretly despised Clarissa, even after the tremendous show of support the last few days? Could they not see what I saw in her?

I stepped forward, words of defense on the tip of my tongue, when Mother placed a hand on my chest. While the others kept discussing the attack, she lowered her voice and said, "You cannot force them to trust her, Thorne. It's evident not everyone feels the same way you do about her. She *is* still a foreigner, however benevolent she and her magic have been."

My mouth fell open. "So you think what happened tonight was acceptable?"

"Of course not!" She reared back in offense. "I would never condone the actions of radicals. I'm simply saying I can see *why* they may feel this way. Don't try to fight this battle when tensions are high, dear."

I curled my fingers into a fist at my side. "Fine. Then I'm going after them. I want to make sure she's alright."

As I turned to bound down the steps, her cold fingers grasped my wrist. "That's a job for her future husband, Thorne," she warned. "And that man is not you. You're only going to hurt yourself more if you keep this up."

"I don't know what you're talking about," I said through gritted teeth.

She smiled grimly at me. "Yes, you do, dear. And it's time you let her go."

THE
BALL

33

CLARISSA

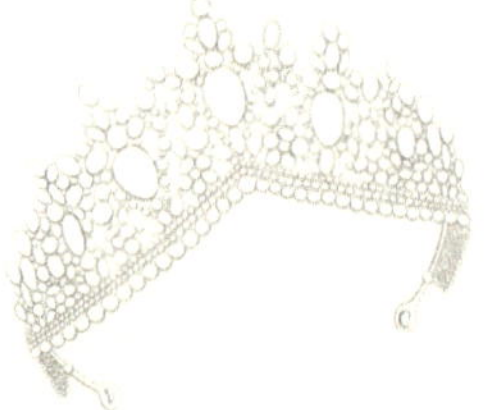

My goodbye with Vespera when we left the Mid Territory the following morning was quick. She was the only one I bothered saying farewell to.

She grasped me tightly and whispered how sorry she was, how she wished she could help, how much she was going to miss me. I patted her back but kept a firm hand on the wall in my mind, the one I feared would shatter like glass if I so much as breathed on it.

And then we were off. I stared out the carriage window as we rode south.

And rode.

And rode.

The Penworth Estates in the South Territory were a two-day journey from Silenus Manor. I requested to share a carriage with my mother, Devora, and Katrine, knowing I wouldn't be able to handle the conversations I was sure would occur with Thorne and Galen after what happened at the Harvest Festival.

Mia got her energy out playing with Katrine and a ball of string in the small confines of the carriage, then napped in my lap as I watched the hills and wide fields of the Mid Territory transition to silver, burgundy, and teal-tinted mountain peaks, green country-side broken up by stone pathways and jutting rock formations.

Mother and the maids chatted throughout the long ride, but they seemed to know to leave me alone. Every once in a while, Mother would rest her hand on my knee, a quiet sign that she was thinking about me. When we stopped at an inn halfway to our destination, I headed straight to my room, avoiding Galen's concerned look and Thorne's hand as it stretched out to graze my pinkie, a question in his eyes.

The next day, we did it all over again.

I was so tired.

The kind of tired that sleep couldn't fix. Which didn't matter, considering the pain from the burns on my ankles and calves kept me from sleeping, anyway. I wasn't even going to bother with them that first night after it happened, but when Devora saw the burns, she was so distraught that I let her apply a topical ointment and bandage the worst of them just to calm her down. She was there every morning and night, cleaning the wounds, adding more ointment, and replacing the bandages.

Every time she touched them, it made me think of the fire.

It made me remember the spear shoved through the fox's limp body.

It made me remember the flames running along its fluffy white tail until it consumed it whole.

The pain wasn't only in my legs. It tore through my chest like a jagged knife, leaving behind an infection that oozed a dark sludge of rejection and betrayal.

I tried to block it out. I tried to cover it with bandages the way Devora covered my burns. But I'd never been good at suppressing such strong emotions—just hiding them. While inside I was thick, viscous darkness, on the outside...I was cold and detached.

Perhaps that was the kind of queen and empress they wanted. Perhaps that was who I needed to become to avoid growing these attachments that ended up as ash in the wind.

I had always put others first. *Always.* Their interests, their feelings, their voices, their safety. And it still wasn't enough. Not for people who were so burdened by fear and grudges. Not for people so blinded by their own misconceptions of me and where I came from.

I knew only a few were behind the crime, and it was wrong of me to blame them all. But it didn't matter. The damage was done, and I'd learned my lesson.

Good intentions couldn't undo a history of hatred. A few days of charm, smiles, and pleasantries couldn't outweigh centuries of suspicion. I'd been a fool for thinking I could wipe the slate clean.

"We should be there soon," my mother said after almost two full days of traveling. I nodded absentmindedly, running my fingers through Mia's soft fur as she stood and circled my lap to find a better position. I'd been silent nearly the entire journey, too lost in my own thoughts and trying to mentally prepare myself for the second leg of the tour.

I dreaded meeting the Penworth regent family. They were the other ones Galen's council said were opposed to my arrival, and I didn't have the energy to put on the face of Empress Clarissa Aris. The idea of having to impress these people after two days of being crammed in a carriage, stewing in my own anger and pain, made me want to launch myself out this small window.

The sun began to set behind the mountains, and even I had to admit how beautiful the scene was. Deep red, gold, and subtle hints of blue painted the sky. The mountain peaks shone above the darkening horizon, and when the carriage slowed to a stop and the door opened, a refreshing breeze brushed my skin.

I closed my eyes and breathed it in, thankful to have left behind the humid heat. Katrine took Mia's leash as she and Devora climbed out of the carriage to get our bags. Mother paused, shut the door behind them, and sat back on the bench with a sigh.

"I hate this," she said softly, gazing out the window at the enormous estate to our right. "I hate watching you go through this and not being able to do anything about it."

"It's not your job, Mother," I said, my voice dull and tired. "I'll be fine."

"We did our best to shelter you from the worst of it, you know," she said. "You and Leo both." I furrowed my brow, and she continued, "Back in the early days of the sleeping curse, when people first began to believe it was your father's fault, we knew we had to protect the two of you from it all. I know you and Leo both faced hardships, but we tried...we tried to keep the worst of it from you. To give you as *normal* of a childhood as we could, all things considered. I never wanted you to see this sort of hatred."

"Has something like this happened before?" I asked.

She nodded. "People did...*horrible* things in the beginning. Born out of fear and the need to blame *someone* for their loved ones being taken from them in the curse. They knew my Shifter form, and the skin of a wolf was once nailed to our cottage door, along with various pieces of the animal being left on our doorstep over time. Countless death threats toward your father were tied to bricks and thrown through the windows. The first time it happened, glass shattered all around you and your brother, and Leo cut his foot. That was why we never let the two of you play by the fireplace when you were toddlers."

My lips parted on an exhale. "Mother, I—I'm so sorry. I never knew."

She smiled grimly. "That was the point, sweet girl. We didn't want you to. And I wish I could keep you from this, too. I wish I could take the brunt of it as your father and I did back then. You're so strong, my Clarissa, but a mother never stops wanting to protect her children."

You're so strong. People kept saying that. First Thorne, now her. I just wished I could believe it myself sometimes.

Knuckles rapped on the carriage, and Mother reached across to pat my cheek. "I may not be able to carry this burden for you, but I will always stand by you."

"Thank you," I whispered, kissing her palm and taking a deep breath.

The carriage door opened. Hiding a wince from the swelling in my leg, I descended the short steps and landed on a paved walkway leading to a miniature palace, with high wrought-iron gates between two imposing stone walls. Galen stood by my side, and together, we silently walked along the path, through the gates, and to the entrance.

The instant I caught a glimpse of Lord and Lady Penworth, I knew I was in for a long few days.

The looks on their faces could have cut glass. Sharp and pointed, his green stare and her dark gray one followed me as we met them at the top of the steps to the grand entrance. They were both a little older than my mother, somewhere in their late sixties or early seventies. He had a full head of bright gray hair that looked so slicked back, it was stiff. He glared down at me over his hooked nose, not so much as inclining his head when we approached.

Lady Penworth was no better. Her silver hair was pulled into a tight bun at the top of her head, her piercing gray eyes even larger behind thin spectacles. She raised an eyebrow when I smiled politely, her frail shoulders moving up and down with a sigh.

"I'm surprised you two bothered to come at all, if the rumors from the Mid Territory are true," was Lord Penworth's way of greeting Galen and me.

Galen's charming grin faltered, but he righted it at once. "My carriages travel quickly, but it appears gossip travels even faster. It's good to see you, Rhys."

Lord Rhys Penworth's simple *hmm* was the most judgmental sound I'd ever heard. "Likewise, Your Majesty. It's been long enough." He looked at me out of the corner of his eye. "So, this is her?"

The sneer in his tone grated on my nerves, and it seemed I wasn't the only one. A large shadow appeared at my side. I glanced up to see the thick, strained jawline of Thorne glaring back at Lord Penworth with a look that would make even myself back away. I reached behind me to discreetly place a hand on his, warning him against doing something stupid.

"I *do* hope you don't plan to bring that kind of scandal to *our* territory, Your Majesties," Lady Penworth said, eyes flitting between Galen and me.

I bit down on the inside of my cheek so hard, I tasted blood. Whether she spoke of the multiple assassination attempts or the display at the festival, I wasn't sure. But either way, she acted as if we had asked for those things to happen. As if I hadn't spent *days* in the trenches with the people of this kingdom, doing what I could to give them back their healthy land.

My fingers curled at my sides, the ghostly imprint of my claws scraping against my palms. If I had to deal with these pompous pricks for the next five days, I was going to lose my mind.

I inclined my head toward her. "It was never our intention to upset anyone, Your Grace. I assure you, this visit will be nothing but respectful. We just want to get to know the people of your territory better and see how we can best serve them."

Her pale lips thinned. "We'll see."

"For the love of the Fates, Mother. Give it a rest. Nobody's scared of you," an unfamiliar voice said from behind the Penworths as the massive black doors opened. The speaker was a young woman leaning against the doorframe with a smirk. Her chestnut-brown hair came to her chin on one side of her face, and was shorn close to the scalp on the other. Silver piercings glittered along the edges of both ears, with one long silver bar through her eyebrow as well. She was only a year or two younger than me, if that.

Lady Penworth rolled her eyes, and the strange woman shot me a wink.

I liked this girl immediately.

"Ah, Taryn," Lady Penworth said on a heavy exhale. "I was wondering when you'd show up."

"Couldn't miss the fun," Taryn said, uncrossing her arms and jumping from the threshold to the landing below.

"Taryn?" Galen asked, giving her a bewildered look. "You're finally back?"

"Hey there, Gale. Nice to see you too," she said with a grin, and I quirked an eyebrow at the nickname. She held out a hand to me. "And nice to meet *you*, Empress Aris. My name is Taryn Penworth, and I have something you may want to see."

34

CLARISSA

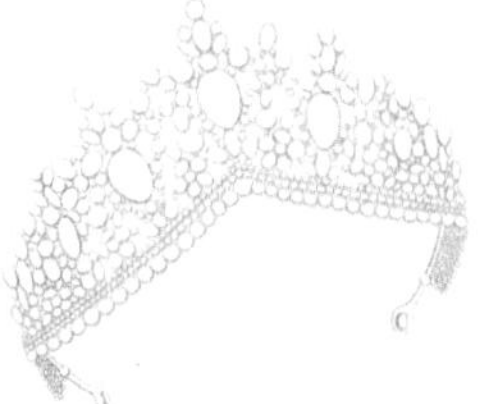

I followed Taryn into the mansion, barely noticing the pain in my leg with my mounting curiosity. I took in the gray stone walls, brown baseboards, and dark floral paintings decorating the long corridors. She stopped before a pair of large double doors. I exchanged a wary look with Galen before he, Mother, and Thorne followed me inside the drawing room.

Where I let out an ear-piercing squeal. "Rose? *Leo*? Emperor's tits, what are you *doing* here?"

My brother beamed back at me, that loose curl of dark hair I knew so well hanging haphazardly across his forehead. When he held out his arms, I barreled into them. Mother let out a laugh of surprise before she wrapped her arms around Leo and me.

"Oh, Leo, we've missed you." She rubbed both of our arms as she backed off to let us breathe, and my heart felt lighter than it had in weeks. Months, even.

"Come here, Rose," I said with a sniff. I squeezed my friend tight. Memories of last fall flooded me, when she'd fallen into the lap of the Sentinels and helped us with our mission to take down Emperor Gayl. Late nights at the Drakin's Lair, dress shopping for the capital's masquerade ball, plotting and planning in between drinks as we slowly peeled back her tough layers.

I pulled away and gripped her forearms. "How have you been? How are you *here*? When did you finish curing everyone in the provinces?" She and Leo had left Veridia City shortly after Gayl died to travel across the six provinces and wake those who had fallen to the sleeping curse. We'd exchanged some letters and kept up-to-date on important matters, but I hadn't seen them in almost eight months.

"One question at a time, sister. It's been a long trip," Leo said with a chuckle as he slipped an arm around Rose and kissed her forehead. She leaned into his touch, her bright green eyes sparkling when they met his.

A fist clenched around my heart. I loved seeing them like this, so at ease with one another. So safe and comfortable. Something my brother never really had before her.

Something *I* would never really have.

The drawing room doors shut with a loud click. I looked back to find Taryn leaning against the wall with Galen and Thorne standing next to her.

"Fates, I'm sorry, I wasn't thinking. Rose, Leo, I'd like to introduce you to Lord Thorne Reaux and His Majesty, King Galen Grimaldi." I motioned to the two men as they stepped forward. "Thorne, Galen, this is my brother, Leo, and our friend Rose Wolff."

"Your Majesty," Rose said, dipping her head in a bow.

Leo, on the other hand, sized Galen up with a hint of that scowl I missed so much. "You're the one my sister has agreed to marry, I take it?"

I rolled my eyes, but Galen smiled. "I'm just as surprised as you are. Speaking of surprised..." He glanced at Taryn. "Bring back some strays, did you?"

"Not that I'm complaining, but what's going on?" I asked as I looped my arm through Rose's.

"Well...that's a bit of a long story," Rose said.

"And some not-so-good news," Leo added.

"*But*," Taryn jumped in, clapping her hands, "how great are family reunions, am I right?"

I propped my free hand on my hip and leveled her with an expectant stare.

Taryn sighed and kicked off the wall. "Relax, it's not that big of a deal. Has he always been so dramatic?" She nudged her head toward Leo, and I chuckled. She added, "Let's sit down. And probably get a drink or two."

"You had me at 'or two,'" Galen said as he made his way over to the armchair by a fire in the center of the drawing room. Two large couches and one smaller armchair surrounded the ornate stone fireplace, with a glass liquor cart next to the wall.

Taryn claimed the other chair, while Leo, Rose, and my mother got comfortable on one of the couches. Heat radiated from Thorne's body behind me before his fingers pressed into my lower back and he murmured, "How's your leg?"

I twisted my neck to meet his gaze. "It's healing." Not as quickly as it would with my Shifter abilities, but still.

"What about the rest of you?" he asked, concern lingering in his gaze. "Are *you* doing alright?"

"I'll be fine. Especially now," I whispered, sweeping my eyes over the couch full of the people I loved most in this world. I caught Rose staring at Thorne's hand on my back before she quickly looked away.

Thorne took a seat on one end of the free couch, and I sat opposite him, keeping distance between us. "So how do you two know each other?" I pointed between Taryn and Galen.

"Taryn is an old friend," Galen started. "We'd spend time together whenever my parents would visit the South Territory. And when hers sent her off to a trade school in the north eight years ago, we reconnected."

"I didn't last six months in that place," Taryn added. "But dearest Mother and Father would've had an aneurysm if they knew. What you saw tonight was them being *nice*. Try growing up with that. It's a miracle I made it past childhood."

"So, I convinced my parents to let her work for the palace. She's done odd jobs here and there—mostly as a courier, delivering messages to and from the territories," Galen said.

"But I've always had my sights set higher. I'm *real* ambitious, you know." Taryn tapped her nose.

Galen snorted. "Ambitious, or bored?" She stuck her tongue out at him. "She was on the correspondence team we sent back and forth to Veridia. Their last scheduled trip arrived at your capital city a couple of weeks before you left to come here, so they should've been back long ago. What *happened?*" he directed to Taryn. "We thought you were lost."

"Close. We got beached in Tenebra. Those cliffs are a nightmare," Taryn answered.

"Thankfully, two *incredibly* gifted Alchemists with unresolved hero complexes just so happened to see the accident," Rose said, raising her glass in the air toward Taryn. "We got some help to repair their ship and restock their supplies."

"In exchange for about a dozen favors," Leo grumbled as he settled further into the couch. His brown, furry tail slipped out from beneath his cloak and flicked against the floor.

Galen jumped to his feet. "What is *that*?"

"Oh, right," I said. "I forgot to mention he has a tail."

"You get used to it," Rose added.

Galen cleared his throat. "I thought your magic didn't work here."

"Did you think it would fall off?" Leo asked with a snort. "I can't access my other Shifter or Alchemist abilities, but this one is permanent, unfortunately."

"It's not so unfortunate," Rose said with a wink. "For me, anyway."

"You two are worse than I remembered," I said, but my shoulders relaxed as we fell into our familiar banter.

Fates, I missed this. I missed *them*. I hadn't realized how much more difficult this last week and a half—truly, the last eight months—had been trying to keep up appearances with hardly any moments to relax.

"So what, you two just decided to hitch a ride back to Mysthelm?" I asked Rose and Leo.

Rose nodded. "Just got in a couple nights ago, actually. We heard this was your next stop."

"I told my parents they're friends from trade school," Taryn said. "Figured that was better than two refugee Veridians."

"Why did you come?" I asked them. "Besides the fact that you missed me so much."

Leo's lips melted into a thin line. "Well, that's the not-so-good news. We spent some time in Drakorum right before and heard rumors of Scarven sending a small group of Shifters to Mysthelm. Some sort of undercover operation."

"We were worried they were going after you," Rose added. "After your one letter mentioned you thought he was hiring assassins to take you out, the timing was just too suspicious."

"Wait, who is this Scarven person?" Thorne leaned forward and gripped his knees. His forearms strained beneath his shirt as his neck snapped to me. "And why is he trying to kill you?"

I sighed. "He's the governor of Drakorum, the Shifter province. He hasn't exactly been receptive to me taking over the empire and all the changes I've been trying to make. I guess he liked the way things were run before. There have been a couple of...incidents."

"Incidents?" Mother scoffed. "She's been the target of two assassination attempts in the past two months. Both of which we believe were done on Scarven's orders. Not to mention, the note."

"What *note*?" Thorne growled.

I closed my eyes and squeezed the bridge of my nose. "Thank you, Mother."

"I'm guessing it wasn't the fun kind of note," Taryn said.

My fingers traced the middle of my palm. "One of the assassins shot an arrow into my hand. There was a note attached to it that said *'you can't run.'*" I curled my hand into a ball. "Look, he was just trying to scare me from coming here. I don't think he wants an alliance with Mysthelm."

"Well, now it sounds like he's followed you," Thorne said. Irritation lined his voice.

"Could this Scarven be behind everything that's happened?" Galen asked.

Rose and Leo exchanged a confused look. "What do you mean? What's been going on?"

My mother and Galen took turns telling them about the carriage driver and the fox in the fire. I stayed silent, running my fingers over my lips as I thought through what they'd said.

Had Scarven really sent Shifters here for *me*? It was an extreme move, even for him. This whole time, I thought it must be someone in this kingdom out to get me. I hadn't considered that he would go this far to carry out some vendetta against me.

"Then what are we supposed to do?" Rose asked. "If he has Shifters here trying to kill you, maybe you should come back to the empire."

"What, just for him to keep targeting me at home?" I shook my head. "This doesn't change anything. Besides, we don't know if it's even true. You said it yourself—it was a rumor. Whether it's *actually* Veridians or someone from here coming after us, I'm not going to walk away."

"We'll increase the security detail," Thorne said firmly. "Make sure all attendants at public events are inspected. Any suspicious activity, and we'll have them apprehended."

I rubbed my forehead with the heel of my hand. As if this trip didn't have enough challenges, now *this* got added to the mix. It raised so many questions. How was Scarven sending men across the ocean without either one of us noticing? Was this a common occurrence?

I was now facing threats from every front, and it was only a matter of time until someone else was caught in the crossfire. Just like the woman at the Drakin's Lair.

"All of this can wait till tomorrow," Mother said. I glanced up to see her eyes trained on me. "It's been a long few days, and even longer since I've had my children under one roof."

Gratitude washed over me. She always knew what I needed, even if I wouldn't voice it myself.

I got up and walked with Thorne, Galen, and Taryn to the exit. Taryn and Galen were already deep in conversation. I put my hand on the door to shut it behind them as they exited with Thorne on their heels, but at the last moment, Thorne turned. He looked like he wanted to say more. He planted a palm on the door to stop it from closing, his thumb barely grazing the edge of mine. Those concerned eyes searched me like they were looking for answers to some unspoken question.

Neither of us said anything.

After another heartbeat, he finally moved his hand. "Good night, Empress."

"Good night, Lord Reaux," I breathed.

And then he was gone.

35

CLARISSA

"So, Leo and I were climbing the mountains by the fjord in Tenebra—cold as balls, might I add—and an enormous moose came up behind us, and his antlers caught around my charms pouch. It ripped off my jacket, and Leo chased after him, but he slipped on a patch of ice, and I had to use a levitation spell before he fell off the side of the mountain." Rose grinned over at Leo, who was stoking the fire with a poker. "You should have seen him chasing this thing. I was laughing for weeks."

A pillow from the armchair by the fire flew through the air and landed on Rose's face. I snorted into my drink when Leo's tail flicked back behind him.

"It reminds me of that time several years ago when Chaz pranked Leo when they were stationed in the west sector," I started, laughter already creeping up my throat. "Leo was bathing in the Scarre River—"

"Because I had *horse dung* all over me—"

"And Chaz stole his clothes, but then a group of raiders attacked and chased Leo butt-naked all the way to Westhaven," I said, snickering at the glower on my brother's face.

"Yes, let's just all team up against me tonight," he said with a shake of his head.

"Oh, I would *never* team up against you, sweet boy." Mother reached out a hand to him. He took it and smiled at her, until she said, "Well, there was this one time when he was a boy, he wanted so badly to be a Shifter like me. He thought he was finally growing a tail, but it was actually his—"

"And that's enough for tonight," Leo interrupted as Rose and I doubled over with laughter.

Our mother's eyes twinkled with mischief. "Alright, alright. Well, I want to hear about the *non*-embarrassing adventures. What was your favorite part?"

Rose and Leo took turns telling us about their escapades in the Veridian Empire over the last eight months, how they crossed through jungles of Emberfell to reach citizens who were under the sleeping curse, to daring the outskirts of the Shadowmere Wastelands in Tenebra, to sleeping in boats under the stars in the tropical inlets of Iluze.

I couldn't help but smile at how animatedly they spoke, how seamlessly they wove their tales together. I remembered the closed-off, wary version of Rose we'd met last fall, who was so hesitant to open herself up to us. So convinced she wouldn't be able to trust. And now here she was, pestering my brother and laughing with my mother like she'd been part of this family her entire life.

And Leo...I thought he was happy last year when they first met, but *now?* He was a whole new man. Still pensive and broody at times, but eager to share these parts of his life with us. Before, he was always so focused. He had his mission with the Sentinels: to avenge our father and take down Gayl. Not much else mattered. I loved seeing him like this—untethered from thoughts of vengeance, free to do what made him happy. To find a purpose that fulfilled him instead of crushed him.

"What about *you*, Rissa?" Leo asked. "Are you really going to marry this king?"

"Empress *and* queen," Rose added. "That's two more titles than you, Leo."

He gave her a bland look, then turned back to me. "How did that even happen, anyway?"

"It's what's best for everyone," I started. The words were routine at this point. "We've been cut off from them for long enough. This will create peace between us. Solid ground to move forward on, instead of always wondering what our future may look like or if there will ever be another war. It's not like it'll change much for me," I said with a shrug. "I'll still be in Veridia City, ruling the empire, while he's here in Mysthelm, with the added assurance of aid and protection if we ever need it."

Leo crossed his arms. "And that couldn't have been accomplished with a peace treaty?"

I glanced at Mother, who raised an eyebrow at me over the rim of her teacup.

"What else is going on?" Rose asked in a suspicious tone.

I sighed. "It's a little more complicated than that." Over the next ten minutes, I told them the truth behind mine and Galen's engagement and the curse, how it manifested as the blight, and how this marriage was the only way it could be stopped for good.

When I finished, Rose let out a slow exhale. "Now who's got the hero complex?"

"I know it's crazy, but...I don't really have a choice. And I want to help. I had my doubts about Galen at first, but he's learning. Without this curse hanging over him, I think he could really thrive here. We can always sever the marriage later down the line if one of us falls in love and doesn't want to keep it up anymore," I joked.

Rose hummed. "Speaking of which, who was that other man?"

Clearing my throat, I asked, "What other man?"

"Don't play dumb; it doesn't suit you."

I stood and took my empty glass to the liquor cart, pulling off the stopper on another bottle. "Oh, Lord Reaux? He's just a friend of the king. One of his advisors."

"Okay," Rose said. I glanced over to see her sipping her drink, and I narrowed my eyes. "What?" she asked innocently. "If that's all you say he is, I believe you."

"Don't. It's a trap," Leo whisper-yelled to me from the couch.

I put the bottle back on the cart a little too roughly, and a *clang* rang through the drawing room. "There's nothing going on between Thorne and me."

"I never said there was," Rose shot back with a shrug.

"Good." I took a drink. "Because there's not."

Rose continued to stare at me while I held my glass, drinking it far too quickly in an effort to escape the awkward silence that had fallen over us.

Mother rose to her feet. "Well, on that note, I think it's time for me to go to bed. Leo, will you help me find my room?"

"Of course, Mother," he said, his tail flicking against Rose's ankle as he stood. Leaning over, he pressed a kiss to her temple. With a nod in my direction, he said, "I'll see you tomorrow, Rissa."

"Good night, little brother," I called after them.

The second the door shut, Rose rounded on me. "Sit."

I chuckled. "Yes, ma'am."

"You can lie to yourself all you want, but you can't lie to *me*. I saw the way you two looked at each other. The way he was ready to tear the room apart at the idea of you being targeted. You're not being very discreet, you know."

I rolled my head back and let out a sigh that turned into a groan. "I don't know, Rose. He's very…"

"Hot?" she suggested.

Against my will, the memory of us at the hedge on the Silenus property popped into my head. His forearm caging me in, that rough beard hiding the edge of his smirk as he gazed down at me.

My cheeks heated. "Nothing's happened between us. He's just…not what I expected. He's been there for me in moments when nobody else was. A friend, that's all."

A friend I wanted to climb like a tree.

I pushed away the unfiltered thought and quickly put my drink down. That was enough for one night. So much for "never drinking again."

"There for you, how?" she asked.

I bit down on my bottom lip, thinking through all the little moments with him this past week and a half. "I'm sure Leo has told you about my—my panic attacks, yes?"

She nodded but said nothing as she rested a hand on top of my knee.

"Thorne was there for one. And he helped me through it with no judgment. Just sat with me, steady and calming. He's been one of the only honest ones and wasn't afraid to call me out when I was being...difficult." Rose nudged my shoulder at that. "He saw right through me. I don't think I've ever been able to trust someone as quickly as I trusted him."

She gave me a small smile. "That sounds like he could mean a little more to you than a simple friend, Rissa."

I swallowed hard. "There was a moment before we left the Mid Territory that I thought..." Exhaling, I squared my shoulders. "It doesn't matter. This isn't like you and Leo. I'm marrying someone else, and we both know that. If I don't, then this curse won't break, and I can't leave Galen and his kingdom to that future. That's not even an option. Nothing can happen between Thorne and me."

"What about Galen?" she asked. "Do you think you could ever love him?"

"No, but I think I can grow to respect him. And that's good enough."

Rose pursed her lips, then grabbed my half-empty drink from the table and downed the rest of it. "Oh, Rissa," she said with a sigh. "I can't say I envy you. But I do *admire* you. I always have. I want you to get everything you want, but I get that this is bigger than you. It feels so...final."

I took her hand and squeezed. "Thank you, Rose."

"For what?"

"For not giving me some fake sense of encouragement and telling me to 'follow my heart.'"

"You know I don't do well with all that mushy stuff." She waved a hand in the air. "Besides, I think it's *because* you have such a good heart that you choose to do right by others. Not everyone would do the same. I want you to be happy, but there's no magic spell I can say to make it all turn out the way we want. We have to make our own happiness with what we're given."

Her words wrapped around me, soothing my turmoiled heart. I put my head on her shoulder. "Never thought I'd see the day when Rose Wolff spoke in platitudes."

She rested her head against mine. "What can I say? I'm a changed woman."

I smiled. "It's good to see you, Rose."

"You too, Rissa."

We stayed like that for a little while, watching the last of the flames slowly turn to embers, until I no longer saw the shadow of a fox in them.

36

CLARISSA

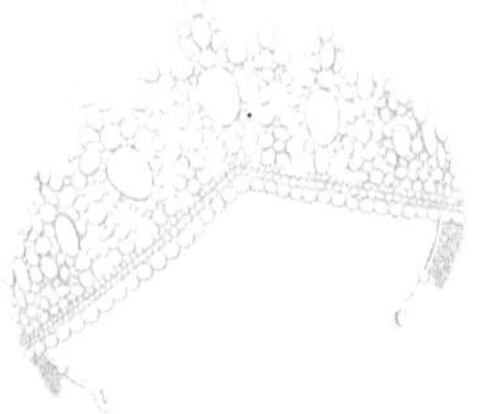

*K*nock. *Knock. Knock.*

I opened my eyes a fraction, surprised to find my room still bathed in moonlight.

Knock. Knock.

Was it the middle of the night? Who was coming to my door so late?

Throwing my legs over the side of the bed, I grabbed my silk robe off the door to the bathing chamber, wrapped it around my nightgown, and padded across the floor.

When I opened the door, I sucked in a breath. "What are you doing here, Thorne?"

"I couldn't sleep," he said, his normally light blue eyes now a dark navy, tired and urgent. There was a deep crease in his brow, and his long hair was disheveled. He was usually so calm. So sure of himself. But tonight, he looked...distraught.

"Is everything okay?" I asked. "Did something happen to Marigold?"

"No, she's fine. It—it's not that."

"Then why are you here?"

He scrubbed a hand down his face. "Because I'm worried about you. About all of this. And I can't stop thinking about you."

I could have sworn my heart stopped. I was barely breathing, my fingers clutching the doorknob so tightly, they turned white.

His gaze flicked from my eyes to my lips. "Being down the hall from you, knowing you're in here alone after everything you've been through, after that night at the fire...I don't know how much longer I can do this."

"Do what?" I whispered.

"Stay away from you." He stepped forward. "Stay in control."

My pulse pounded erratically as a flush crawled up my neck. "I—I don't know what you're talking about."

Thorne let out a low growl and moved into the room, shutting the door behind him. I gasped and backed into the wall, only for his large body to hover over me, his scent that was so distinctly *him* filling my senses. Sweet grass and leather. Late nights in the garden. Masculine and heartfelt, all at once.

"You lie so beautifully," he murmured. He lowered his head so his beard brushed against my neck. "Tell me you don't feel this." His nose skimmed the column of my throat, breathing me in. My eyes fluttered shut as my neck rolled to the side. "Tell me you're not fighting against every instinct in your body when we're near each other."

Lips grazed the sensitive spot below my ear. A shiver raced down my spine, that simple touch sending my heart through my chest. My hand flew to his shoulder, whether to keep him there or push him away, I wasn't sure.

This was wrong. He shouldn't be here, not like this, not with Galen mere doors away. But I couldn't think clearly with his chest pressed into mine. With his hands gripping my waist, strong fingers digging into my skin, the feel of his shoulders so tense with restraint beneath me.

"Thorne," I breathed out. "We—we can't—"

"Please, Empress," he said. I sucked in a breath when he kissed my neck, then my jaw. His lips met the edge of mine as he said, "Just one kiss. One taste. One night I can call you mine."

My mouth parted on an exhale, and his other thumb came up

to press into my bottom lip, his eyes focused on the contact like it was the only thing keeping him tethered.

He moved his thumb away to cup my chin, drawing me closer. "Clarissa," he whispered, right before his lips met mine.

I jolted awake with a gasp. My fingers were clenched around the bedsheets, my legs so tangled, I could barely move. Mia stirred in her sleep and stood to stretch, her tail thumping at my cheek as if saying, "It's time to wake up." I squeezed my eyes shut to block out the morning sun coming from the window and buried my head in the pillow to muffle my groan.

This is going to be a problem.

I could still feel him, the ghost of his lips and hands and body pushed against mine. Fates, I had to pull it together. Take a cold bath. Throw something through a wall. *Anything.*

There were three things that were abundantly clear. Non-negotiable.

I had to marry Galen and break this curse.

I had to go back to the Veridian Empire. Back to my home, my people, my throne.

And I had to stay away from Thorne Reaux.

So I would bury it. Whatever this fleeting pull to him was. Shove it down so deep, it had no air to breathe. Forget the way his voice soothed and his touch heated, forget the thrill of our banter, the light in his eyes when he looked at his daughter. All of it.

I would not let Thorne Reaux steal a single piece of my heart. Not when it could never fully be his.

———

To my not-so-surprise, Lord and Lady Penworth were nowhere to be found that morning as the rest of us loaded into carriages to begin our exploration through the South Territory. Taryn had been appointed our guide, which I was more than happy with. She, Rose, Leo, Mother and I squeezed into one carriage, while Galen, Thorne, his mother Azura, and Marigold rode in another.

Marigold had raced across the grounds when she saw me, throwing her hands around my waist and giving me that adorable, gap-toothed grin. Her father had made the last-minute decision to let her come, and she was so excited to join us on a tour through the jewel mines that she was practically vibrating.

The rocky landscape of the territory passed by the window as we traveled west. Jagged mountains rose in the distance, the sunlight making the deep red and turquoise of the rocks shine even brighter against the gray stone. I'd never seen rocks with colors like that. They blended together in beautiful waves, the peaks of the mountains looming nearer as we ventured farther into the heart of the mining district.

Taryn told us how the South Territory was known for its plethora of caves, with various precious stones and metals that the entire kingdom used. The workers here mined jewels for decorations and jewelry, but also copper, iron, and other metals to make weapons and tools.

Dozens of small communities cropped up as we got closer to the first mine. Wooden homes with slate roofs layered up and down the hills and dips in the terrain, with small paddocks for animals and many wagons full of supplies. The homes were spaced far enough apart that each had plenty of land, even leaving room for a stream to wind its way through the neighborhood. Our carriage rolled onto a paved path, and I could see the reflection of the peaks in the clear water as we came upon the side of a mountain.

Groups of men and women in hard hats and overalls with pickaxes and chisels hanging from utility belts meandered around us, getting ready for their day in the caves. Devora had prepared me for what to wear, and I was thankful for her guidance as I glanced down at my thick boots, black pants, and dark blue vest over a tight-fitted shirt. The black pants bulged slightly at the bottom where bandages still covered my burns, but walking was no longer as painful as it had been the past couple days.

"This is Kol," Taryn said once we'd all gathered around her and a tall man in a helmet. She stretched to prop her elbow on his shoulder and patted the top of his head. "He'll be showing us around the Devil's Mine today."

"That name bodes well for us," Rose muttered in my ear.

"It's an honor to have you join us, Your Majesty," Kol said to Galen, bowing low to the ground. "My crew and I have worked hard in these caves, and it's one of the highest-producing jewel mines in the territory."

"We're excited to see it. Thank you for having us. And may I introduce to you Empress Clarissa Aris?" Galen nodded toward me, and I dipped my head, smiling at Kol and the workers waiting behind him. Some of them sneered when they caught my eye, while others lowered their gaze.

"Your Majesty," Kol said as he bowed once again. "Pleasure to meet you. I have a cousin in the Mid Territory who met you early in the week. She told me how you saved their farm. Our family is in your debt." He lowered his voice and added, "Even if not everyone here feels the same."

"I'm happy to help," I said, ignoring the last part.

He led us under a large stone archway and deeper into the opening of a vast tunnel, easily the size of a house. Lanterns hung every few feet to illuminate what the natural sunlight couldn't reach. Shelves were affixed to the wall, storing all kinds of shovels, helmets, vests, and belts for the workers. People stopped and stared at us as we passed, many bowing or uttering a greeting to Galen but glaring at me. Their faces became hesitant when they spotted several members of the King's Guard flanking us on all sides. Increased, as Thorne had promised.

He hovered nearby, blocking out the onlookers. It seemed he was as attuned to the scathing looks and uncomfortable interactions as I was and, ever since the incident at the bonfire, wanted to shield me from them in any way he could. He had this way of being protective while not overbearing, attentive to my emotions while not trying to control them.

I found that wildly attractive.

Which was why I ignored him the entire time.

Kol instructed a few of us to grab some of the hanging lanterns, then went through safety tips and gave a generic background on the Devil's Mine. It was one of the more recently discovered mines and had been in operation for about forty years. They had drilled deeper and deeper into the side of the mountain and uncovered several caves rich with precious jewels that were in high demand in the wealthier areas of the four territories. He proudly stated how many of the jewels from this very mine made their way back to the Mysthelm palace and had a place in the Grimaldi treasury.

I listened and observed the workers as we traveled down the wide tunnels, catching glimpses of jewels as they used chisels and pickaxes to carefully carve them out of the stone. Soon, Kol's words became drowned out by the echo of metal on rock. Clangs and vibrations filled the caves until we reached a set of rough steps.

"Down here is one of the newer sections," Kol shouted over the noise. "There aren't as many people assigned there, so it'll be quieter."

We made our way down the steps, the air growing colder and staler the farther we went. A little hand snaked its way into mine, and I looked down to find Marigold perched at my side. She stopped moving and bit her lip with a frown on her face.

"I don't like the dark," she whispered up at me.

I glanced around at the others as they kept filing through and pulled Marigold to the side. Thorne shot me a look, but I quickly shook my head and gestured for him to keep going. Once everyone moved on, I knelt to face her, keenly aware of Thorne lingering not far out of sight.

"I used to be scared of the dark too," I said. "But we'll all be down there with you. Me, your daddy, your grandmother, Uncle Galen. We won't let anything happen to you."

"It's not *me*. What if something happens to *you*? All of you?" she said, her bottom lip trembling.

I remembered Thorne had mentioned his daughter suffered from anxiety too. I wondered if this had anything to do with it.

Some deeply rooted fear she couldn't shake—not necessarily for herself, but for those around her.

"Can I tell you a secret?" I asked, and she nodded. "Did you know that where I come from, we have *magic*? And that some of us, like me, can even turn into other *animals*?"

Her brown eyes widened in shock. "You *can*?"

I smiled. "When I'm back home in my empire, I can become a fox." Her mouth fell open. "Do you know anything about foxes?"

"They're soft. And...they have sharp teeth."

"Yes, that's true," I said with a chuckle. "But they can also see in the dark. Everything looks bright, even when all the lights are off. What if we both pretend to be foxes? They aren't afraid of the dark because they can still see."

She looked at me for a second, then propped her hand on her hip. "You know *I'm* not a fox, right?"

A snort escaped me. "It's called *pretending*, little girl," I said as I tickled her sides and underneath her arms. That earned me a giggle.

"Okay, I'll pretend. And if anything tries to hurt me, I can bite them." She mimicked biting the air.

I ruffled the top of her head and stood. "I feel safer already. Do you want to go now?" She nodded and tucked her hand back in mine, and we followed the path the others took deeper into the new cave.

Thorne emerged from the shadows a short distance from us. "Thank you," he said under his breath, holding his hand out to touch mine.

I pulled away and stepped ahead of him. "Of course," I said, more briskly than I meant to. That look in his eyes was already threatening to draw me in, and I had to put distance between us.

"These caverns are a bit smaller than the ones out front, so we'll split you into two groups to explore these areas," Kol was saying when we reached the rest of them. Azura saw Marigold's hand in mine, and her sharp eyes narrowed before turning back to

Kol. "You four can come with me"—he pointed to my mother, Leo, Rose, and Taryn—"and the rest of you will go with Amalia."

A young woman who had been on her knees inspecting part of the wall stood up, brushing dirt off her hands and smiling at us. Her eyes caught on Thorne, and they slowly scanned down his body.

Something coiled in my stomach.

"It's such a pleasure to meet you, Your Majesty," she said to Galen, giving a quick bow. "And who else do we have joining us?"

"Empress Clarissa Aris of the Veridian Empire," he started, gesturing to each of us in turn. "My close advisor and Regent Lord of the North Territory, Thorne Reaux, his daughter Marigold, and his mother, Lady Azura Reaux."

Amalia shook each of their hands, ending with Thorne. I didn't miss the way she glanced at his left hand.

She flashed him a coy smile. "So nice to meet you, Lord Reaux," she purred.

I turned my head and rolled my eyes.

"Right this way." She placed a hand on his upper arm as she guided us down the opposite tunnel from Kol's group. She spoke of the mines and what a day in the life for the workers looked like, but I wasn't listening. My gaze was homed in on her fingers as they brushed down his arm, the way she threw her head back in laughter at everything he said, how she flicked her golden braid over her shoulder and batted her eyelashes like some lovesick teenager.

"It seems my granddaughter has taken a liking to you," a voice said behind me as we walked, and I twisted my neck to find Azura smiling down at Marigold. "As has my son, although he's always had a fondness for pretty things. Until the next one comes along." Her blue eyes glanced at him and Amalia ahead of us.

I clenched my teeth but said nothing, simply nodding and returning her smile.

A moment later, she let out a sigh. "I believe we started off on the wrong foot, Your Majesty. I would like to apologize."

"Oh?"

We both stopped walking, and she slowly bent down to rub Marigold's back. "Why don't you run along and catch up to your father, dear," she said, then straightened as we watched her trail after Thorne and Amalia.

"You have to understand that Galen is like a second son to me," Azura went on. "You must see how difficult it is to trust others who walk into his life when we can only guess where their interest lies."

"I have no *interest* beyond securing an alliance with your kingdom, Lady Reaux. One that would strengthen both Mysthelm and my empire."

She tilted her head to the side. "I understand that now. Forgive me if I wasn't sure of your true intentions in the beginning. But it has become obvious what your purpose here is."

None of this sounded like an apology to me. She hadn't done or said anything overtly antagonistic or untrustworthy, but something about her rubbed me the wrong way. However, I was nothing if not diplomatic. "I'm glad we can work together to move forward. All I want is to help King Grimaldi and your people."

"At least we have that in common, dear," she said, patting me on the shoulder. "I was terribly sorry to see what happened at the Harvest Festival. I hope you've since recovered."

"I appreciate your concern. I'm getting better."

She hummed. "Let's pray to the Fates that the rest of the tour goes smoothly. I'll be here if you need anything." With one more firm pat to my shoulder, she sauntered off ahead of me to take Marigold's hand, her black skirt trailing behind her in the dirt.

"I'm sure you will be," I muttered under my breath.

A few seconds later, the tunnels opened into a new cave with a low ceiling. The rocks jutting down from above were close enough that I could reach out a hand and touch them. Thorne and Galen had to stoop to avoid hitting their heads on the points.

Galen pulled Amalia to the side to speak with her and another miner stationed at the entrance, while Marigold dragged Azura to a wall full of glittering rubies. I averted my gaze from Thorne's and wandered to the back of the cave, taking in the array of silver, red, green, and purple jewels still covered in grime, waiting to be shined to perfection. I skimmed my fingers along the sharp edge of a diamond.

"Something catch your eye?" Thorne asked.

I looked over my shoulder to see Amalia still standing with Galen across the cave. "Well, something has certainly caught *yours*," I said without thinking.

A smirk toyed with the edges of his lips. "Is someone jealous?"

I gave him a bland look. "Hardly. You're allowed to spend time with whoever you want."

Propping an arm against the cave wall above my head, he spun a strand of hair that had come loose from my bun around his finger. "If you wanted my attention, Empress, all you had to do was ask."

I slapped his hand away, sudden irritation flaring through me. This was the Thorne from the hedge maze that night, the one who used his cocky grins and flirtation to get whatever he wanted. Not the Thorne from the bonfire. The one who let me glimpse the emotions hiding behind that mask, who was genuine and warm and felt like both sin and safety at the same time.

"Don't play games with me," I snapped. "You know I'm not that girl."

I didn't know where this bitterness came from, only that my tongue was saying the first thing that came into my head. The desire to push him away was equal to the desire to pull him in, and I was sick of how twisted it made my thoughts.

I was a *master* of control. But this man got under my skin and ripped that control from me without even trying.

His roguish smile dimmed. He lowered his arm back to his side. "I never meant to play games with you, Clarissa. This is who I have to be."

I shook my head. "That doesn't make any sense."

He ran a finger along his lips while the crease between his eyes deepened. "I can't let you be anything other than just another woman."

A scoff left me. "Well, *thank you*, Lord Reaux. That clears things up." I moved to slip away, but his hand closed around mine.

"You don't understand," he said, voice low. "If I let you become what you are to me, if I let you become *anything* other than the woman marrying my best friend, I..." He trailed off, his eyes resting on my fingers clutched in his.

The rest of the cave faded around us, save for the sound of my pounding heart and the heat spreading from my hand all the way to my core.

"And what am I to you, Thorne?" I whispered.

His thumb rubbed against the inside of my palm, sending a shiver down my spine. Images from my dream slammed into me. His lips on my neck, fingers at my thigh, my pulse racing to the warm breath below my ear.

He swallowed. "Clarissa, I—"

A thunderous crash rang through the cave. The floor shook violently, the force of it throwing me into the wall. Small rocks and dust fell from the ceiling as a rumble echoed all around us.

"Thorne! Clarissa!" Galen shouted from across the space, and the last thing I saw was Marigold's big brown eyes widening in horror as she shrieked for her father.

Then the ceiling collapsed.

37

THORNE

Dust and debris hung heavy in the air, so thick I could barely see.

"Clarissa?" I choked out, trying to rise from my knees but disoriented from the fall and the ringing in my ears.

My throat tightened as the dust began to settle. She was crouched to the floor with a hand on the back of her head and another gripping her leg. We were trapped in a small corner of the cave with no light other than a single torch burning to my right. The ceiling between us and the others had caved in, leaving a solid wall of rock.

Marigold.

I scrambled to the pile of stones. "Marigold! Mother!" I roared as I clawed at the jagged boulders, willing them to part. I just needed to see her face. Hear her voice. Know they were safe.

My movements barely dislodged two rocks. I ripped them away and pounded into the barricade. My fingernails split with a sting, but still, I kept going. We had to get to them. We had to get out of here. We—

We were trapped.

A fist squeezed around my lungs. I struggled to breathe, drawing in a single, gasping breath before my vision flickered. I couldn't move my fingers. Slowly, I fell down the mountain of boulders, sharp edges snagging my skin and clothes. Gray spots appeared in my line of sight, and I blinked them away with another ragged inhale.

"Thorne. Thorne!" a distant voice yelled. Soft hands found my neck, but all I could see were gray stone walls closing in, crushing me, crushing *her*, crushing my daughter...

Blonde hair haloed by the glow of the torch hovered before me, blurry and glimmering like a mirage. Lips moved, and while I couldn't understand what she was saying, I kept my eyes focused on her. Her, and not the image of the mountain slowly collapsing. Her, and not the idea of my little girl stuck behind layers of solid rock. Her, and not the air being sucked from my body with every labored breath.

Just her.

"Thorne, can you hear me?" Clarissa asked.

I nodded as a cough racked through me, making my vision sway. But her hands kept me upright.

"Listen to me. You're alive. You're okay. *We're* okay. We're going to get out of here, but you need to breathe." She wasn't panicked, only resolved. A safe, strong beacon in a sea of darkness.

I took a deep breath, and suddenly it was as if I couldn't breathe fast enough. My chest expanded and contracted as my lungs tried to catch up. Air swooped in and out of my nose faster than I could control it, my pulse pounding to the rhythm of half-formed thoughts flying around my head.

Marigold.

Breathe.

The cave.

Breathe.

Not enough air.

Breathe.

Crushing.

The back of my legs hit the floor as my spine crashed into the wall of rock. My hands grappled for anything, *anything* to hold on to, and they landed on something soft and smooth.

"Thorne, please. Please look at me," Clarissa pleaded, her voice now lined with a hint of fear. "I'm trying to help you. I need you to stay with me." A weight landed on my thighs. Her face came back into focus, those dark eyes glittering like onyx in flames, beautiful lips turned down, with tendrils of blonde waves framing her cheeks. Hands cradled my neck as she breathed in and out, motioning for me to copy her.

"If you can hear me, tell me three things you can see," she said shakily. "Just three things. Nothing else is here."

I took another breath, slamming my eyes shut and opening them again to clear the haze. They landed on the lit torch to my right. *Just three things.*

"The fire," I rasped, then forced my gaze onto the wall behind her, drowning out everything else. "A—A diamond." It was peeking out from the edge of a rock, caked in dirt but giving off a faint shine.

My eyes flicked back to her. "You."

She nodded. "Good. You're doing so good. It's going to be okay. Tell me two things you can feel," she said in a whisper, her hands trembling at my neck and cheek.

I slowed my breaths, and my heart steadied with it. A sensation that had been dull before now sharpened at my back. "A sharp rock." I shifted to get away from it and realized what the weight on my legs was. What I'd grabbed when I couldn't see.

Clarissa was straddling me on the cave floor, two thighs wrapped around my waist with her chest mere inches from mine. My hands rested on her lower back. My fingers had crawled up the fabric of her tight shirt, her smooth skin hot beneath my fingertips. Without knowing what I was doing, I trailed my hands around her waist, and she let out a gasp when they skimmed over her stomach.

My panic began to slip, only for something else to take its place. Something just as unsteady, just as uncontrollable. One hand squeezed her waist while the other traced a path to the top of her thigh and gripped it tightly.

"I feel *you*," I breathed out, pulling her closer, pressing into her. She was all I could feel, all I could see, all I could think about as I tried to force away the fear.

I thought she was going to push me off. She'd been ignoring me for days, ever since what happened at the bonfire, and I couldn't blame her.

But she didn't.

She melted into me. A sob broke free as she buried her face in my neck. Her body shook with small tremors, and I held her against me as I guided us to a seated position against the stones.

"You scared me," she said on an exhale. Her breath hovered at my neck, sending a shiver through my body and making my fingers clench around her legs. "I thought...you weren't breathing, and then you fell, and I couldn't get you to... I didn't know what to do."

"I'm fine, Empress," I said hoarsely. "I'm with you. Don't be scared."

She pulled back an inch, still close enough that I could see a tear lining her eye. When she blinked, it fell from her lashes and rolled down her cheek.

"I'm always scared," she whispered.

I didn't think. I pressed my lips to that tear, its salty taste bursting on my tongue.

Fates, she felt good. Her legs wrapped around me, my hands covering her back, our chests pushing together with each shared breath. I let my lips linger on her cheek, then the column of her throat, inhaling her scent like I could draw her into me. Like I could keep her golden light with me wherever I went.

She made everything brighter. She took away the gray.

When she let out a small moan and tilted her neck to the side, I nearly lost my mind.

I placed another kiss on her throat, murmuring her name against her skin. A small part of me knew I shouldn't be doing this. There was a reason this was wrong, a reason this felt like temptation and pain all in one. But I couldn't remember the last time I felt so *right*.

The sound of rocks shifting above us caught our attention. Clarissa's face snapped up, and her body tightened as she started to move away from me.

I pulled her closer. I *needed* her. She was the thing that kept me grounded. The pulse in her throat beat to mine, steady and sure and safe. "Please, Clarissa," I begged, sliding one hand up her back and the other gripping her thigh hard enough to leave a mark.

"It could be someone trying to get through." Even as she said the words, she sank back onto me, as if she was also caught in whatever haze I was in. Like a string tied her to me, and we couldn't rip ourselves from it even if we wanted to.

"I don't care."

"Thorne, it could be Marigold."

The string snapped. *Marigold*.

Her name pulled me back to reality. I nodded and dropped my arms, and we both scrambled from the ground.

"Clarissa! Thorne! Are you there? Are you alright?" Galen's muffled voice sounded from the top of the rock pile. If I squinted, I could see a small hole someone had cleared away, enough to let us hear through to the other side.

"We're fine!" I shouted. "How are you? Where's Marigold?"

"She's safe," he responded, and my shoulders dropped in relief as my head rolled onto my chest. "She and your mother went back to the entrance. They've got some miners here with equipment to get you two out, don't worry. It shouldn't take long. Shout if you need anything."

Clarissa's hands were steepled in front of her face. I instinctively reached for her and pulled her into my side. "We're going to be fine," I said into her hair, more to reassure myself than her. "They're all safe."

When she pushed away from me, I knew the moment had burst. This fragile bubble we'd found ourselves in, where the outside world didn't exist, where for a single heartbeat, she was mine.

It was gone.

"Thorne, we—we can't," she said quietly. She crossed her arms over her chest as if trying to make herself smaller as she took several steps back.

"I know." I scrubbed a hand over my beard. "I'm so sorry. I don't know what I was thinking."

"It's the stress," she said. "I feel it too. Everything is chaotic, and we don't know what we're doing. It doesn't mean anything."

My hand flexed at my side, where the imprint of her skin still seared into me. "You're right." The lie tasted like ash in my mouth.

She slumped against the wall and slid to the ground. "Has that ever happened before?" she asked. "Your panic attack?"

I shook my head. "Not to me. But like I said before, Marigold gets them sometimes. I think they started when her mother died, although she doesn't really remember it. They happen whenever she's scared someone she loves might be in danger." I crouched to the ground and closed my eyes. "I hope my mother kept her calm. I hope this didn't—that me being trapped here didn't trigger another one."

"Me too." Clarissa's eyes found the small hole at the top of the wall. "Hopefully it won't be long."

We sat in silence for a moment until she said, "You don't have to talk about it, but...how did your wife die?"

I brushed my fingers through the dirt to give myself something to do. "Heart disease. It was inherited—her father died of the same thing not long before her. It happened four years ago."

"I'm sorry, Thorne," she breathed out.

I nodded. "Thank you." Fire crackled from the torch as echoes of steel chipping against the rock wall filled the air. "She was... incredible. Not afraid to speak her mind, like someone else I know." I gave Clarissa a pointed stare.

"But *unlike* someone else, she wasn't great at hiding her thoughts. You could read her from a mile away." I chuckled.

"Which caused some problems with my parents, seeing as they didn't get along in the slightest. You don't know how many fights I had to break up between them. Marigold entering the picture helped with that a little."

"I can imagine," Clarissa said with a grin. "It's impossible not to love that girl."

A pang shot through my heart. "And Iris did. So much." I stared at the rock wall, aching to be able to see through the stone and find my daughter. "I wish she could see how much she's grown."

"I'm sure she would be proud of her," Clarissa said. "And you. You've done such a good job raising her."

I swallowed hard. "Anything I am is because of Iris. She changed me. I don't think you would have liked the man I was eight years ago."

"I highly doubt that," she said, looking down at her hands.

"What about you?" I asked. "The night at Silenus Manor when you...when you were so panicked. Has that been happening your whole life?"

She shook her head. "No. That's a more recent development, actually." She turned her head to the side and bit down on her bottom lip.

"You don't have to tell me anything you're not comfortable with," I said.

"That's not it." She took a deep breath. "It's just that I don't talk about it with many people. It...it started last fall. After everything that happened with Emperor Gayl. He—he tried to kill me the night he died. Me and a close friend." Her voice quieted. "He would've succeeded, but my Shifter abilities heal me too quickly."

I moved closer to her on instinct. "What happened?"

"He cast a spell to break most of the bones in my body."

My eyes widened. I closed the distance between us and knelt at her side, covering her hand with my own. "He *what*?"

She closed her eyes. "It was...the worst pain I've ever felt. And hearing it happen to my best friend at the same time..." A single tear tracked down her dusty cheek. "We're both alive, but I haven't been able to escape that day. Not fully. I'm not sure I ever will. It's like I'm this...this fragile little girl who can't even control her own mind. Any time I hear something that sounds like the c-crack of a bone—" She inhaled sharply and shivered. I wrapped an arm around her shoulders, tucking her under it.

"I'm so sorry, Clarissa." I couldn't even imagine. To endure such trauma and live to tell the tale...to *relive* it, over and over like some nightmare taking over her body. And here she was, leading not only her own empire but doing everything in her power to save my kingdom. Putting on the confident, capable, brave face she wore so beautifully to hide the pain lurking beneath.

"You're the strongest person I've ever met, did you know that?" I asked.

She looked up at me. "Then you haven't met many people."

I took her chin firmly between my thumb and forefinger. "Stop that," I said. "Stop downplaying the kind of person you are. How everything you've gone through has shaped you into who you are now. You shouldn't hide from your past and how you got here. You shouldn't hide from the way those memories make you feel. It doesn't mean you're out of control—it's exactly what makes you so *strong*. Because you take what's happened to you, all that you've seen, all that you care about, and you turn it into this passion for your people. For *everyone*." I brushed my thumb along her jaw. "Your emotions are what make you *you*. Don't ever apologize for them. Don't ever push them away."

Her dark eyes held mine as her tongue flicked against her bottom lip. "I have to push some of them away," she said, her voice barely a whisper.

My gaze fell to her lips.

A few rocks tumbled from the hole at the top of the wall. I stiffened and put my body in front of hers when a muffled voice sounded. "Get out of the way, you two!"

We rushed to the far corner as the mountain of stones trembled, and, in the next second, half the wall came crashing down.

We were free.

But it felt like I'd found myself in an even more dangerous trap.

38

CLARISSA

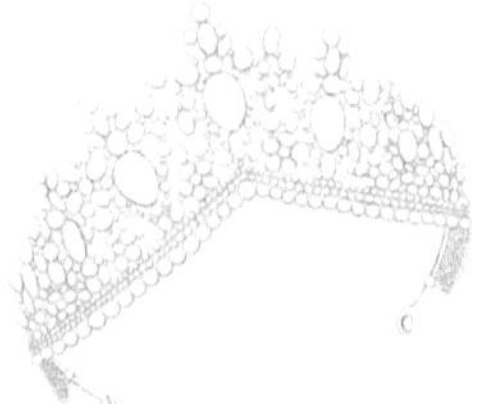

The cave-in was evidently the final straw. For my family, at least. I was now treated like porcelain, not allowed to go five feet without someone glued to my side. They begged me to keep my head down. To stay quiet and not alert the attention of whoever was after me—be that a hired assassin from Veridia or a wronged, bitter citizen of Mysthelm.

I hated it. It went against every instinct in my body. But between my mother's pleas and my brother's glowers, I did what they asked. I let Galen do the talking and try to woo his people back into agreement. I let the King's Guard follow me around like lap dogs. And I did quite a bit of avoiding a certain lord, who had an annoying habit of making nightly appearances in my dreams.

Word had spread of our series of unfortunate incidents across the kingdom, and gossip ran *wild*. Especially the exaggerated stories about the cave-in and how "close to death" their dear king had been by *my* side three times now. There were whispers about me and whether or not I was secretly trying to have Galen murdered so I could take his place, and it made me want to scream.

So much for a quick, easy, painless tour. It felt like I was walking on eggshells everywhere I went.

The only thing I could do was keep the peace. Visit the markets and mountains on Galen's arm as the dutiful woman these regent families evidently wanted me to be. Sit back during dinners and nod politely, and absolutely do *not* make a scene. Let Galen meet his citizens, show them we were a united front, smile, and look pretty.

Lord Stryker would be pleased with how things were shaping up. My *purpose*, as he put it.

But I couldn't stand aside and watch Galen's curse continue to ravage Mysthelm. During our days in the South Territory, I kept an eye out for the blight. Mother, Rose, Leo, and I healed as much of the land as we could. We found fields and forests covered in the familiar black death, riverbanks and streams full of decaying fish that had risen to the surface like bubbles. There was no telling how long some of it had been like that. Just another sign that Galen's curse had taken on a life of its own.

When we weren't off touring the territory, our little group made a nightly habit of commandeering the drawing room once Lord and Lady Penworth went to bed. It had become my favorite part of the trip so far, being able to unwind and relax with people I felt comfortable with.

"What I want to know is why he thinks he can just send people across the Avonige Ocean without either of our councils being aware," Galen said after dinner on the third full day we'd been in the south. A common topic of discussion the last couple nights had been Scarven and his Shifters.

Taryn was sprawled across one of the armchairs with her feet straight in the air, trying to balance a half-empty glass of wine on the soles of her shoes. Rose lounged with her head in Leo's lap on the couch, and Mother sat next to him with her nose stuck in a book. I'd claimed the other armchair while Galen paced in front of the fire.

Thorne was lost in the shadows of the curtain, the moonlight illuminating him every once in a while when the breeze from the open window fluttered the drapes and revealed his form. As far away from me as possible, as had been our unspoken agreement since the cave-in.

When we were forced in the same room together, we stayed on opposite sides. He'd made up excuse after excuse to avoid our daily excursions, and I'd requested to be with my mother instead of joining him and Galen for whatever activities Galen kept inviting us to.

But I always knew he was there. I could *feel* him. His gaze on my back, his warmth in the night, his low voice that rumbled like thunder over me no matter how far away we stood.

Something had changed in that cave. There had been no one around to see. No one around to care that I'd had my legs around his waist, his hands on my skin, both of us a single breath away from crossing a line we couldn't come back from. I'd told him it didn't mean anything, that it was stress and panic manifesting itself in some form of comfort, but we both knew that wasn't true.

I was constantly aware of him and this cord stretched between us, pulling tighter and tighter each day. Its edges frayed and splintered with every passing glance, every accidental touch, every time we caught each other staring from across the room.

I feared the day it would snap entirely and send both of us flying backward.

"Scarven's powerful. And arrogant. Thinks he's untouchable. Like most men who lack self-awareness," Rose said with a yawn. "Present company excluded, of course."

"The rumors we heard made it sound like he's been doing it for a while," Leo said, tapping his fingers on Rose's shoulder. "I can't believe we hadn't heard about this in all our years with the Sentinels. None of the scouts in Drakorum ever breathed a word of it."

"Yes, well, they didn't know dragon Shifters existed either, so I wouldn't put too much confidence in that," I said.

Galen's eyes widened. "*Dragons?*"

I waved a hand in the air. "Long story. The point is, who knows what they could be up to? They're practically invisible. I'll have to have Scarven investigated once I get back to the empire." Reaching for my glass, I added, "Or better yet, I can draw out his Shifters *here* and take them out while they don't have access to their magic."

I'd said it offhandedly, but it actually wasn't a bad idea.

"You can't be serious," Thorne said from his corner of the room, breaking his silence for the first time that night.

I kept my gaze away from his. "Nothing I haven't handled before. And it's a smart move. They wouldn't expect it, and without their magic, they're not nearly as strong. It would take care of all our problems."

"Clarissa, you're not going to dangle yourself as bait for a bunch of would-be assassins," Thorne growled, taking a step out of his hiding place.

I took a sip. "It would be my choice, Lord Reaux."

"What do you expect the rest of us to do, sit by while you run headfirst into danger unprotected? *You* don't have *your* magic, either."

"And how would you recommend I be *protected?*" I snapped, finally meeting his stare. His eyes were like the raging sea. "As you can see, I'm not exactly *safe* anywhere I go, despite all of your best efforts. If I let them wander free here, what about when I go back home? Are the two of you going to come all the way to the Veridian Empire to rescue me?"

I threw a hand out to him and Galen. "I can take care of myself. I'm not saying I'm going to do anything rash, but we need some sort of plan in place."

Thorne stalked closer, putting a hand on the back of the couch as if that kept him from leaping across the room to me. "This man has already made two attempts on your life, if not more. If he's truly as dangerous and powerful as you all say he is, it sounds like he won't be stopping anytime soon. Do you think you can go up against that alone?"

"Do you think I can't?" I challenged.

He glared back at me but stayed silent. Leo's eyes flicked between the two of us. If anyone in this room was going to be on

Thorne's side, it was my brother. He was protective to a fault, often recklessly endangering himself if it meant keeping me or those he loved out of trouble.

"I agree with Thorne," he said. "We still don't have definitive proof that there even *are* Shifters here. Rissa, I get that you want to take action. I get that you feel sequestered here," he brandished an arm, "but you're not a Sentinel anymore. Don't go looking for trouble that may not be there. You have more important things to worry about right now."

Thorne tipped his head and pointed to Leo as if to say, *See? I told you so.*

I pursed my lips and crossed my arms. Tension crackled as I shifted my jaw, knowing Leo was right. I was itching for something to do, and when someone told me I couldn't, it made me want to prove them wrong.

Galen shook his head with a sigh. "Calm down, you two. Look, it's been a very quiet three days. Perhaps all of this worrying is for nothing. Let's just get through the rest of this tour, yes? Starting with the ball the Penworths have planned for tomorrow evening."

Taryn made a disgruntled noise in the back of her throat. "Ah, yes. Mother can't resist any chance to throw a *ball*."

"Even when she hates us?" I asked.

"She hates everyone," Taryn shot back. "But she loves pretty things and showing off this ridiculous house more."

The others rose from their seats and stretched, picking up empty glasses as they made their way to the door to retire for the night. Galen approached me and said, "Speaking of pretty things, I wanted us to take a break from everything in the morning. Get away for an afternoon, just the two of us. And the guards. The South Territory has these beautiful seaside cliffs I remember from my childhood, and I wondered if you might want to go with me to see them."

"Sure," I said with a tired smile. "That sounds great."

"Wonderful. We'll leave after breakfast."

———

"Does this work for today?" I asked Galen upon greeting him in the breakfast hall the next morning. I swished my sundress around my feet, the muted tones of burgundy brushing against my calves.

He glanced up at me with a piece of toast halfway to his mouth. "I'm sorry?"

"My dress," I said. "For the cliffs. You didn't tell me what we'd be doing, so Devora picked something easy to walk in." He cursed, and I raised an eyebrow. "You forgot, didn't you?"

"No, no, I didn't," he rushed out. "But Lord Penworth pulled me aside and asked if I would meet with him this afternoon. Some South Territory business."

I sighed. "That's fine. I'll take Mia for a long walk around the estate or something."

"Nonsense. Just because I can't take you doesn't mean you shouldn't get to go." His eyes snagged on something behind me. "Thorne! Come here," he said, crooking a finger.

My smile fell.

"Clear your schedule. I'm stuck in a meeting with Rhys, so you're going to take Clarissa to the Aurelia Cliffs for the day."

"No," both Thorne and I said at the same time, exchanging a glance out of the corners of our eyes.

"That won't be necessary," I continued.

"I'm busy today, Galen," Thorne spoke over me.

Galen chuckled. "I know you two aren't fond of each other, but honestly. This won't kill you." He spun between us and put a gloved hand on both of our shoulders. "And besides, you need to get used to working together. Think of this as a bonding experience."

I ran my tongue along my teeth. *Bonding* with this man was the last thing I needed. I pictured his hands gripping my waist the way he had in the cave, and my dress felt too tight.

"Really, Galen, it's not that," I tried again. "I don't think—"

"No arguing, it's already done. I'll have a carriage waiting for you in the next ten minutes, along with a couple of guards, just to be safe. You're going to love the cliffs, Clarissa."

Thorne opened his mouth, and Galen shoved his half-eaten toast into it. "I'll see you two this evening for the ball," he said as he walked toward the hallway doors. "I'm sure you'll be fast friends."

I watched the door shut. Behind me, Thorne said, "I'm sorry. I had no idea he was going to do this. I can find someone else to take you."

Turning to face him, I smoothed my hands along my dress. "It's fine. Why wouldn't it be? We'll go see these cliffs, placate him for a bit, and come back in a couple hours. There's nothing to worry about."

His eyes flickered between mine before he slowly nodded. "As you wish, Empress."

39

CLARISSA

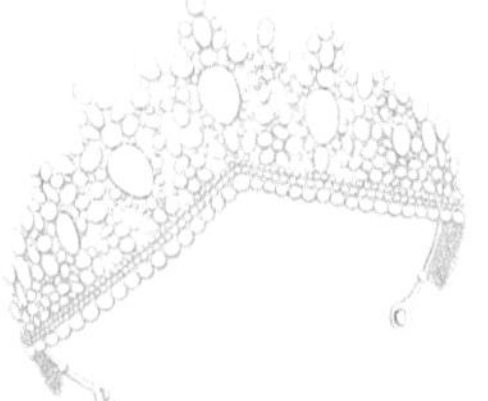

The ride to the southern shores was silent, save for Thorne's occasional commentary on the landmarks we passed and our hurried apologies when the carriage would jostle and make our knees knock against each other.

It took about an hour to get from the Penworth Estates to the Aurelia Cliffs, and most of that time was spent traveling up winding mountain paths. I took my attention off Thorne by staring out the window, catching views on one mountainside of the territory growing smaller and smaller as we ventured higher, and of the rocky coastline and white spray of waves on the other side.

This shore wasn't like the one I knew in Veridia City, with the dense tree line opening up to a short stretch of sand before it met the ocean, nor the Port of North Pine in the North Territory that we'd arrived at—which had golden sand and palm trees as far as the eye could see. The shore here at the south was rugged, layered with sharp boulders jutting from dark sand that extended from the base of a long strand of green cliffs and white-capped mountains. Strong winds coming from the ocean pushed against the carriage, and water formed into waves as it rushed toward the sand, racing and tumbling while the next ones approached.

It was beautiful and wild and dangerous, and somehow, it made my anxious nerves settle.

The carriage rolled to a stop. There was a soft tap on the door before the driver opened it. "We're here, Your Grace, Your Majesty," he said, bowing to Thorne and me in turn. He gestured to himself and the two guards in the box with him. "We'll be waiting here if you need anything."

I stepped onto the rocky ground and gasped.

We were stopped on a mountain pass overlooking the ocean. On either side of us stood two mountains that glistened like gold in the light, while before me was a grassy cliffside leading to waves crashing far below. The midmorning sun hovered on my upper left, shining across the water and making it sparkle like thousands of little diamonds.

Wind whipped through my hair and lifted the skirt of my burgundy dress. I inhaled deeply, closing my eyes to the scent of salt and the feel of the ocean breeze brushing my sun-kissed cheeks.

It was peaceful. No stodgy lords. No stone walls. No masks and forced smiles and secrets. Just...me.

And *him*.

"He figured you wanted to get away," Thorne said from behind me. "Galen, that is. Nobody lives up here, and when the weather is nice, it's a perfect—"

"Escape," I finished on an exhale. Grinning, I spun to face him. "Yes, well, he was right. I can finally hear myself think."

He nodded and then sighed, bracing himself. "Look, I'm sorry about yesterday. I'm not trying to be...overbearing, but I worry about you. I don't like the way that governor sounds. I—"

I cut him off with a dramatic groan. "Your apology is accepted as long as we don't discuss it anymore. We're coming here to *escape*, yes? I don't want to hear about assassins and regent families and governors." *And marriages.* "I just want to be *here*."

I turned to the cliffs again, taking a few steps forward until I burst into a run. I spun in the grass with my arms flung out to my side and the wind blowing my hair in all directions.

"Forget all of it," I shouted to the mountains, laughter bubbling in my throat. "Forget you're Thorne Reaux, Regent Lord of the North Territory. Forget *I'm* Clarissa Aris—soon-to-be Empress of the Veridian Empire. Let's just be...us."

A smile stretched across his face where I'd left him. "And who are we, exactly?" he called out above the wind and waves. "Without all the titles?"

"Whoever we want to be!" I yelled back.

He walked across the grassy terrain toward me, his brown locks swaying in the wind. As he drew nearer, I saw a sparkle in his blue eyes, the slight upturn of his lips, the smooth skin at his forehead where wrinkles of concern normally lived. He, too, looked freer out here. As if the weight of what waited for us down below disappeared the higher we climbed.

"How about," he took one more step forward and pushed back a strand of blonde hair that had gotten stuck on my lips, "we just be Rissa and Thorne."

I was breathless from running, but perhaps from something else too. My heart picked up speed as the tips of his fingers skimmed my jaw when he pulled his hand away.

"Rissa and Thorne," I repeated softly. "They sound nice. What are they like?"

He took a moment to think, squinting in mock concentration. "Well, *he* is charming and smart and very, very handsome."

"Naturally."

"And *she* thinks everything he says is perfectly witty."

I snorted. "Since we're pretending, then *she* is elegant and funny but doesn't care what people think—in a non-pretentious way, of course." I walked across the grass, kicking a stone and leaping from large boulder to large boulder. "And she's a wonderful baker. With a cute little bakery—or perhaps a bar, right beside the ocean where she can hear the waves and the seagulls and have an acceptable place to toss rude customers when they annoy her." I shot him a wink and jumped off the top of a rock.

"Perhaps he owns a bookshop next door. Where he often sneaks pastries or drinks when she isn't looking." Thorne picked up a handful of stones and threw them off the cliffside down into the ocean.

"Oh, a *bookworm*," I teased as I stole several rocks from his grip. "How very studious of him."

He gazed off into the waters with a small smile on his lips. "Maybe he'd rather read of far-off places where people get their happy endings than open his eyes to his own life."

I swallowed hard and threw a rock off the side of the cliff, watching it fall and crash into the waves. "He seems like a romantic."

"I think she is too," he murmured.

"Maybe she wants to be." I shrugged. "Maybe she wants to be someone who isn't so bound to her duty. Someone who can take life into her own hands, snap the reins, and go anywhere it takes her."

"She could be," he said.

"Well, of course you think so—we've already established you're a romantic."

"*He's* a romantic," he corrected me. "This fictional Thorne with his bookshop and stolen baked goods."

I chuckled. "Ah, yes, how could I forget?"

He collected more rocks from the ground. "*He's* not the type to boast, but his throwing skills do seem to be far superior."

With a scoff, I said, "And *she* definitely doesn't make everything into a competition, but she may have to prove him wrong."

"Probably not a good idea." He stepped closer to me, his gaze roving to the stones clenched in my hand and back to meet my stare. "He would never want a lady to embarrass herself."

His hair tangled with mine in the fierce wind. He was so close now, I had to angle my head up to take him in, those blue eyes the exact color of the swelling waves below.

"Don't worry, she doesn't back down from challenges," I countered.

"And he's not falling for the woman destined to save his kingdom," he said, so quietly I could barely hear him.

The breath left my lungs with a *whoosh*. My lips parted, but no sound came out.

"Come with me." He took my hand before I could even *think* of a response. "I want to show you something."

I let him lead me, my legs numb as they carried me across the rocks and grass and back to the mountain pass. My curiosity won out over my shock when he didn't stop at the carriage, instead heading toward the looming mountain to our left.

"It's not far. Just on the other side here." He pointed ahead of us where a path disappeared around the mountainside. We walked for several minutes in silence, a light layer of sweat forming on my skin. The closer we got, the louder the wind picked up—it was now rumbling in my ears like someone had dropped us inside a cyclone.

When we followed the thick expanse of trees around the bend, I realized it wasn't the wind at all.

An enormous waterfall poured from a drop-off on the side of the mountain. It cascaded from one edge down to the next, rippling over rocks and boulders until it landed with a resounding crash in a pool at its base. Mist rose from the water in a thick fog. Sunlight filtered in and caught the haze, making it glow like a rainbow suspended over the pool.

"It's beautiful," I said, although I wasn't sure he could hear me over the noise.

Without a word, he tugged me forward until I felt the cool spray on my skin. The sound of the tumultuous water was a roar, vibrating all around me with every breath I took. It was invigorating and mesmerizing at the same time, watching the rush of water freefall from such great heights only to collect itself and slowly, calmly, peacefully wind its way downstream.

Thorne released my hand and strode headfirst into the base of the waterfall.

"Thorne!" I yelled. "What are you—"

"Do you trust me, Empress?" he asked, eyebrow raised.

I eyed the cliffs above us, with its surging waves that could draw me under and lose me completely.

"Yes," I replied.

He held out his hand.

I placed my palm in his, and we walked forward. But he wasn't leading me *into* the waterfall—he was leading me *behind* it, to a hidden alcove invisible from the front. I rushed beneath a small deluge of water with a squeal and exited into a dark, dank nook on the side of the mountain, both of us spluttering and drenched.

It was like someone had dulled all sound. The pounding of the waterfall on the other side of the rock wall was muted, barely a drumbeat in our little haven. I could still see the trees through the thin cascade we'd walked under, but other than that, it looked as if we'd left everything behind.

I realized why he'd brought me here.

We stood there panting, water dripping from our skin and clothes as we stared at each other.

I pinched my brows together and blinked at him through the drops on my lashes. "You—you're falling for me?"

His shoulders dropped with his next exhale. "How could I not?"

My head spun. Before the cave-in, I thought this was all in my mind—every heated glance, every grazing touch, the crackle of lightning I felt when he was near.

It wasn't supposed to happen this way. It wasn't supposed to happen *at all*. I had a responsibility. A duty I proudly bore, so long as it would help our nations. People counted on me. *Believed* in me. Expected me to do the right thing.

He was never supposed to matter.

He was never supposed to be the balm to my storm. The one who inexplicably knew how to soothe the fringes of my panic. The one who crawled his way under my skin and made a home in the corner of a heart I'd sworn I couldn't give away. The one who saw parts of myself I hated and didn't turn his back.

"How did this happen?" I breathed out, more to myself than him.

He combed his fingers through his wet hair and rested a hand on the base of his neck, his forearm flexing when he squeezed it. "Trust me, I didn't plan for any of it."

I leaned back until my spine hit the damp rock wall behind me. "I don't know what we're supposed to do."

"Nothing, Empress," he said quickly. "This is for me to bear, and only me. It has *nothing* to do with you. I would never do anything to jeopardize the plans you have."

I glanced at him with wide eyes. "You think this has nothing to do with me?"

"I only mean that—"

"You think I'm not falling for you too?"

His words evaporated on his lips, his chest swelling as he took a shuddering breath. He didn't even seem to notice his feet moving toward me. "You are?"

This was possibly the worst mistake I'd ever make. Nothing good could come from today. From opening my heart and telling him the truth—telling *myself* the truth—because I was going to be Empress Clarissa Aris, and it didn't matter what I wanted. Not if people would suffer for it.

But right now...

Right now, we were just Rissa and Thorne.

His hand came up to cup my neck, tentatively at first. When I didn't push away, his thumb brushed along my bottom lip. My eyes fluttered shut.

"Clarissa..." He trailed off, waiting for my answer as his warm breath washed over my cheeks. Something hot and longing coiled in my core.

"Yes," I said, voice trembling. "I think I'm falling for you too." He dropped his forehead to mine, a tremor going through his body. "And I don't know how to stop."

His thumb traced my chin and over my jaw, then down to the pulse point above my collarbone. His hand wrapped around the back of my neck. He pulled his forehead away, his eyes so close, I could see water droplets dripping from his lashes with every blink. They fell onto my cheek and rolled down my neck.

"Then we fall together," he murmured, pressing his thumb into my pulse as he brought his lips to mine.

I gasped, bringing my hands around his upper arms to pull him in. I pushed onto my toes until my chest met his, and I could feel his thundering heart. His hand weaved to the base of my skull and his fingers tangled in my hair with bruising, desperate force.

He tasted like every kind of desire I wasn't supposed to have. Sweet and fresh and free with a jagged edge begging for me to cut myself on, to bleed out the reasons this would never work until all that was left was us.

Rissa and Thorne.

For a moment, I let myself *take*.

I trailed my fingers down the drenched fabric of his shirt, feeling corded muscle flex at my touch. My hands made their way to his hard chest where the ridges of four claw marks strained against his shirt. I sucked in a breath and broke the kiss. My fingers trembled as I took in the faint outline of the scars beneath the wet material.

"It's my fault," I whispered.

He gripped my wrists. "I will gladly bear your mark, Clarissa. It's a part of me, as you always will be."

I swallowed and slowly rested my palms on the top of his chest, looking back up at him. His other hand fell to the small of my back while he angled my face and brought my lips to meet his again, moving urgently against me. Feverishly. As if he knew this dream would have to come to an end soon.

He was everywhere. His hands, his fingers, his scent. He clung to me the way our wet clothes clung to our skin until I couldn't tell where I stopped and he began.

Breaking away, he traced a path of fire with his lips on my neck, his rough beard biting into the sensitive skin. "I've been dreaming of this since the day I met you," he said, lips fluttering against me with every word.

"Then we've come full circle," I said with a breathless laugh. "What did you call me? A wet, feral cat?"

He pulled back slightly to gaze down at me, my hands still pinned between us. "You are the most stunning creature I've ever seen, Clarissa." Kissing my forehead, he then lowered his face to brush his nose against mine, his words pouring over me like hot oil.

"It doesn't matter where you are. Soaking wet and spitting fire, running through a field as your fox, or hugging my daughter with flowers in your hair." His fingers swept a strand of hair behind my ear, and unexpected tears burned the backs of my eyes. "Because it's *you*. And all of it is beautiful. All of it is powerful and captivating and *good*."

A tear fell down my cheek, my heart swelling with so many strong emotions I typically tried to hide. But that was his point, wasn't it? I didn't have to hide them from him. I didn't have to pretend to be the perfectly poised empress, always in control, always calm and collected. As if there wasn't a wild, untamed fox usually bursting beneath my skin. He'd seen that side of me, the side that made people turn away in horror or disgust, and he thought it was beautiful.

He thought it was *good*.

"Please don't cry," he whispered, kissing away the tear rolling toward my chin.

I raised myself up to burrow my face in his neck, unable to bear the thoughts and feelings swirling like a storm inside me with no outlet, no way to shift and let them be free.

"It's not fair," I said quietly. I closed my eyes and inhaled him, the scent of sweet grass and leather and river water and warmth.

Would he ever hold me like this again?

Would *anyone*?

"To find you, to find *this*, and have it ripped away. It's not fair," I repeated.

His heart beat beneath my palms, and I could feel how much he wanted this. How much it pained him too. With every heavy breath, every wave of heat rolling between us, I wanted to make up for all those hours I'd spent keeping my distance, forcing my gaze away and clenching my fingers to my side.

I turned my neck until my lips grazed his skin. When I pressed a kiss below his ear, he let out a low hiss, gripping my waist tighter.

"Lie to me, Empress," he rasped. "Tell me none of this is real." His thumb brushed right above my hip, making my breath hitch. "Tell me you haven't thought of me every night as I have you. Tell me it won't hurt to watch you walk back to *him*."

"This isn't real," I breathed into him as I wound my arms around his neck, kissing the column of his throat. "I never think of you." I skimmed my lips up the other side of his jaw. "And if this is pain...then let it come. I'd rather feel this than nothing at all."

He silenced me with another punishing kiss, his lips and tongue and teeth devouring me like a starved man. I slid my fingers into his hair, exploring every inch of him I could reach.

"I loathe you," I said into his kiss, pulse pounding and fire spreading down my spine.

"And I loathe you," he repeated back to me in a growl.

I lost myself in him. For the first time in perhaps my entire life, I didn't think about the consequences. I didn't think about what waited for us on the other side of this mountain.

I just *felt*. Truly, deeply, wildly. Unrestrained. Uncontrolled and imperfect, the way I never could be.

Hungry kisses turned to sweet caresses until we broke away panting. As our breaths slowed, a heavy weight descended between us, thick and hot and suffocating.

"Thorne..." I whispered, my voice breaking at the end.

"Don't say it, Empress. Please."

I swallowed and rested my forehead against his as he held me.

"I don't…I don't know how to do this." The words were barely a whisper, the tears I'd forced back earlier now flowing freely and silently.

I'd let this man, this soft-hearted, idealistic, romantic man cloaked under the cocky mask of his youth worm his way into my heart. Him and his daughter both. I'd lied to myself for days that it was mere attraction, that it was far too quick to feel anything meaningful. My life was tied up in my responsibilities, and I could never be deterred by a handsome man and his pretty words.

But he was so much more than pretty words. He was the compassion of a father, the grief of a lover, the unconditional loyalty of a son and friend. A steady, immovable rock and a gentle summer's breeze. Red-hot passion and lightning hidden behind cool blue eyes. There was so much I still didn't know, so much I wanted to learn, so many layers I wanted to peel back. To see what made Thorne Reaux tick.

Perhaps in a different life, I could.

In this life, however, I was marrying another man. I was leaving this kingdom for my own. I would never be able to be with him.

It was selfish of me to want this time with him after everything I knew I had to do. Putting us in this position would just make it more painful when I left.

There was only one way this would end. And it wasn't at his side.

Mustering every ounce of self-control I had, I pulled away from him until he lowered me to my feet.

I gazed up with my fingers still intertwined in his shirt. My teeth worried at my bottom lip, so many words threatening to burst to the surface. "If things were different, I—"

"I know, Empress," he murmured, wiping a tear with his thumb. "Me too."

40

THORNE

Devastation often happened on beautiful days.

The day my Iris died was the most pleasant autumn day Mysthelm had seen in months. Bright sky, warm sun chased by a chilly breeze, the smell of changing leaves and fresh soil mixing with the crisp fall air. I'd been walking with three-year-old Marigold along the palm trees bordering our mansion when the servants rushed to us, bearing the news that Iris had suffered another heart attack.

One she never recovered from.

Mere months before that, we'd had the wettest spring season in recent history. Multiple floods in the North Territory, villages overrun with rainwater, and hardly a dry day in sight. Until one morning, we woke to birds chirping and the sun peeking through the never-ending clouds, bringing with it blooming gardens and a reprieve from the storms.

That was the day my father abandoned us.

He took three quarters of the gold we kept in our treasury and disappeared without a backward glance. He left no note, no warning, no explanation. Just a legacy to uphold and a new title added to my name.

I stared out the window of the carriage with Clarissa, taking in the sunlight over the rugged horizon of mountain peaks. The water had kept our clothes cool in the mild summer heat. It was the perfect day.

And as it so often went, its beauty was deceptive.

Across from me, Clarissa gave a little shiver and rubbed a hand over her bare forearms. I picked up the cloak I'd brought this morning, just in case, and leaned forward, undoing the clasp to tuck it around her shoulders. Her dark brown eyes caught mine as I pulled away, and I swear, it was as if something that had been locked inside me had burst free ever since our kiss. A raging, burning, ruinous desire I'd suppressed from the moment I met her. And for good reason. We both had more important things in our lives that needed our attention—her with her empire and marriage alliance, and me with raising my daughter and overseeing the North Territory.

The old Thorne would think nothing of instant attraction, of getting it out of our systems and going back to our normal lives. The old Thorne never felt much beyond the surface. Anything pleasurable or joyful was there for a moment and gone once I'd had my use for it.

My life was shades of black and white before Iris and Marigold. They taught me how to see beauty and love the way it should be— deep and enduring, not as a tool or distraction.

For four years now, the brightness had been slowly fading, with my daughter as the only beam of light in a graying world.

And in fourteen short days, Clarissa had brought the color back. It exploded before my eyes, vivid hues and tones I'd long forgotten. Peace like white clouds drifting across a pale blue sky. Anger like red and orange flames dancing in the wind. Passion like the deep pink of her cheeks, her swollen lips parting beneath mine. Strength and steadiness like the brown eyes staring back at me, or the unshakeable dark mountains drenched in sunlight at our backs.

Fates, maybe she was right. I *was* becoming a romantic. Or I'd always been one. A fool, as my mother called me, to once again even consider the idea of *love* being a force strong enough to conquer the darkness.

I didn't know what might exist between Clarissa and me. It could've been something beautiful. Something to rival the Fates themselves.

I supposed the Fates were the only ones who would ever know.

———

THE HALLS of the Penworth Estates seemed darker as I watched Clarissa make her way to her room, my cloak pulled tight around her shoulders. I ached to follow her, but I knew the best thing for me—for *both* of us—was to keep my distance before my heart could travel even further down this path.

I rounded a corner in the corridor where my daughter's room lay when voices behind my mother's cracked door caught my attention.

"...promised me you had this under control," my mother whispered, her tone cold.

"I'm sorry, Your Grace. Things didn't go as planned." I couldn't place the second person's voice, but it was definitely female. Through the small open sliver in the doorway, I could only see Mother's frame and half of her dark purple gown. Her back was to me, her body hiding any hint of the person she was speaking to.

"Obviously. I want it done before we get to the island. Or do you not understand what I..." Mother moved farther into the room, and her voice grew so soft, I could no longer make out what she was saying.

I shuffled closer to the door, and the tip of my shoe bumped against the frame. I cursed under my breath as their whispers ceased, followed by the sound of a skirt ruffling and footsteps tracking across the wooden floor. When I pushed the door open, my mother stood alone.

"Who were you speaking to?" I asked.

"A servant," she responded with a shrug, adjusting the bun at the top of her head.

"That wasn't a servant." I took a step toward her. My mind raced through the few words I'd heard, doubts I didn't want to face growing with each second. I'd barely spent any time with my mother since our disagreement at the Harvest Festival. I hadn't wanted to be around her much. She didn't particularly approve of the empress *nor* Galen's reign, but I thought she'd agreed to stop plotting against them after learning the truth about the curse.

I didn't want to believe she had anything to do with the terrible things that had happened to both Clarissa and Galen in the past weeks. But after what I'd just overheard...

"What are you planning, Mother?"

"I'm not planning anything, *son*," she said, drawing out the word as she crossed the room to her vanity. "I asked a servant to fetch me some more decent clothing for this territory, and they failed to deliver. I was expressing my disappointment."

"That's a terrible lie, even for you."

She whipped her head toward me. "Watch your tone," she snapped.

"Then tell me the truth. What hasn't gone to plan?" I clenched my hands at my sides, paranoia causing new, unthinkable suspicions to come into the light. "Do you know who's behind what's happened to Clarissa and Galen?"

She turned to her mirror and picked up a makeup brush. "Why does someone have to be 'behind it' at all? They are merely coincidences, Thorne. Terrible coincidences that have thankfully seemed to stop." She dabbed blush along her sharp cheeks. "You've always had such an active imagination. Just like that woman you married."

I'd often been frustrated with my mother, but I'd hardly ever felt the kind of anger that burned beneath my skin as it did now. She'd never been this *cruel*. Condescension seeped from her pores, and for the first time, my rose-colored glasses toward the woman who gave me life began to lift.

Was this how she'd always been? Scoffing at me, hurling underhanded insults toward the people I loved?

"I could have you arrested," I said. "Conspiracy against the king is treason."

She rolled her eyes and threw the brush down. "For Fates' sake, Thorne, I'm not *conspiring* against anyone. And even if I were, you'd do well to remember that *you*, my dear son, were once in agreement with me about the Grimaldis." Standing abruptly, her chair went skidding along the floor. "If you're going to throw around allegations of treason, you better be prepared to face the consequences."

"Are you *threatening* me?"

She took a deep breath as she closed her eyes, rubbing her fingers in a circle at her temples. When she opened them again, the anger had left her features. "Of *course* not, Thorne. I would never do anything to put you or Marigold in danger. You caught me at a bad time. I'm frustrated, and I've taken it out on you. I'm sorry, dear."

I let my breaths even out, trying to force aside my momentary rage. I crossed my arms over my chest. "Then tell me what that conversation was about."

She paused, then said, "Your father."

My lips parted as I took a step back. That was the last thing I expected her to say. "What does he have to do with this?"

"I've been looking for him. I've paid several people to uncover his whereabouts and track him down. *That's* what you heard. My latest informant was unable to bring me anything helpful."

My features screwed in confusion. "Wait, how long has this been going on?"

"Several months. But he's certainly made himself difficult to find."

"He could be dead, for all we know," I muttered, combing my fingers through my hair as I tried to take in this revelation.

"Yes, well, based on what little I've discovered so far, that's very possible."

"What have you found out?" I was irritated with myself for how much I cared. I thought I'd put that man behind me. I thought we *both* had.

She let out a sigh. "Your father had a gambling problem. It was always one of his vices, but even I didn't know the extent of it until I found some of the people he owed money to. It was worse than I thought. They threatened him, and when it hit the breaking point, he drained our funds to pay some of it off and—"

"And left us with next to nothing." I had no idea he was a gambler. My father was always so disciplined—to a fault. Everything had to be precisely how he liked it. His food, his clothes, his son. If anything was out of line, there were punishments. If his breakfast was overcooked, if the tablecloth had a stain, if there was a single coin missing from the North Territory treasury.

"Why do you even want to find him? He's not worth any more of your time, Mother."

She ran her tongue along her teeth. "Call it curiosity. Or retribution. After the way he treated both of us, I just—" Her shoulders fell as she paused.

"I simply want to know, Thorne. There's nothing I can do about it, but perhaps it would give me peace of mind." She moved closer, the hard lines on her face softening slightly as she held out a hand to me. "I'm sorry I didn't tell you. I didn't want to bring you back into this."

I hadn't realized this was on her mind at all, but it shouldn't have surprised me. Both my father and Iris had entered my thoughts more often than usual in the last couple of weeks. Maybe she was feeling the effects too. We'd been traveling among all the other regent families that she'd once spent so much time with at my father's side, and now she had to watch me carry on that role.

A sliver of guilt crept in as I let her take my hand. I'd been so quick to assume the worst in her. No wonder she didn't want to admit the truth.

"I understand," I said. "And I'm sorry for accusing you of

anything else. I had a hard day too, and I guess I was also taking it out on you." Before I could talk myself out of it, I added, "Will you let me know if there are any updates?"

She squeezed my fingers. "Of course, dear. Now, let's get ready for the ball."

41

CLARISSA

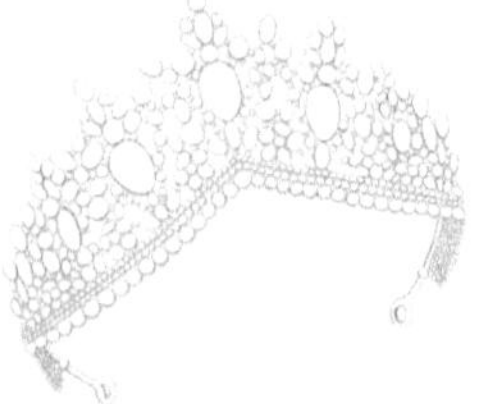

Tonight was my first ball.

It felt strange to say, considering I was technically the heir to the Veridian Empire. In another life, I would've grown up attending balls, galas, and fancy dinners with silverware more expensive than a small house. But up until eight and a half months ago, I was more used to dirty leggings and daggers than gowns and slippers.

I savored any reason to get dressed up, and tonight felt like the first time in a while that it was okay to be excited. Giddy, even. Getting to laugh with Rose as Katrine and Devora helped us with our hair in my large suite, picking out beautiful dresses and putting on far too much makeup while we sipped sparkling wine and watched Mother try to teach Leo how to dance properly. Rose kept tickling the underside of his tail to distract him, and he'd step on his own feet or crash into the couch. Eventually, he whipped away from Mother, grabbed Rose and hauled her over his shoulder, then threw her onto my bed before going back to his lesson. Katrine nearly had a fit over Rose's messed-up curls, but the rest of us were laughing too hard to care.

Things felt right. *Normal.*

And I welcomed the distraction from the ache in my chest that hadn't disappeared since this afternoon. I knew going to the cliffs with Thorne was a bad idea, but I wasn't prepared for how much having everything I could ever want in that little alcove would crush me.

I slipped into my gown behind the partition in the bathing chamber, and my shoulders sagged when I shifted the fabric on my hips. I remembered the way his hands felt there. I bit down on my bottom lip and could still feel his teeth dragging against them, the memory both heating my skin and causing my heart to constrict.

"Do you need help tying up the back, Your Majesty?" Devora asked as she walked around the partition.

I cleared my throat and nodded. Her steady hands made their way up the intricate laces of the back. It was a beautiful sleeveless gown the color of dark rubies at the bust, then fading into an ivory at the bottom. Red gems and pearls dotted the full tulle skirt, while the top half was made of a soft satin that clung to my chest. While Devora worked, I pulled on a pair of matching red gloves that came up to my elbow.

I took one look at them in the mirror and instantly tugged them off.

"Is something wrong?" she asked.

"No, I just...I'm not a fan of gloves," I said. She averted her gaze from mine when I tried to smile at her, then tapped my shoulder to indicate she was done.

"You look beautiful," she said softly, taking in the dress and my hair that she'd pulled into an elegant knot at the back of my head. Several curls hung loose to frame my face.

I reached out and grabbed her hand. "Are you alright? You've been quiet lately." I'd noticed she'd taken to hanging back while Katrine chatted away with us at all hours of the day, the mischievous girl from the beginning of the tour now hidden behind a cloud.

"I haven't been feeling well." She tucked a strand of red hair behind her ear. "Don't worry about me—you're going to knock them dead tonight." She finally gave me a grin, then clamped her lips shut. "Poor choice of words. For the record, I'm pro-nobody being knocked dead."

I snorted. "There she is," I said. "I'm also pro-nobody dying. Well, I could take or leave Lord Penworth."

A noise of disgust sounded in the back of her throat. "He's the worst. I saw him kick his page yesterday for bringing the wrong carriage around."

"Fates, what a miserable man. I hope his bed is always lumpy."

"I hope his bed is always *empty*."

I chuckled as Devora's grin broadened. "Thank you, Devora. I needed that. I hope you start feeling better soon."

Her face quickly fell before she righted it again and nodded. "Come on, you don't want to be late to the ball."

"An empress is never late," I said, shooting her a wink. "Everyone else is simply early."

———

I HAD to grudgingly admit that the Penworths knew how to host a ball.

Given that the South Territory was known for its jewel mines, the entire ballroom was decorated in shimmering, dazzling gemstones. The floor, walls, and ceiling were all silver, while every piece of decoration in sight was covered in jewels. The wine glasses, the serving trays, the candelabras. All dotted with hundreds of miniscule stones. Anytime the candlelight caught one, it glittered and cast its refracted light onto the nearest silver surface, and before long, the ballroom was lit like a rainbow.

Galen waited for me at the bottom of the grand staircase, looking as handsome as ever in his navy-blue suit, the official color of Mysthelm. His jacket even bore its crest—a tree with four branches and a sword and sickle crossed at the trunk. He'd switched out his black leather gloves for a pair of dark brown, and they felt like silk when I took his outstretched hand.

"You're radiant tonight," he said, bowing low. "May I have the first dance?"

I nodded. He led me past a tabletop fountain of pink wine with jewels lining the outer rims, and several tables full of more plates of food than I could count. Sweet, heavy scents of chocolate and cream wafted to me, along with a salty hint of breads and meats.

On the furthest side of the circular ballroom, near a pair of double doors that led to a balcony, was a string quartet playing a smooth, lively song. Couples flew across the dance floor. The sounds of glasses clinking and heels clacking against the floor made my lips tilt into a smile as I watched the guests enjoying themselves.

The song ended, and a moment later, the band struck up a slower ballad. Galen faced me and placed a hand on my hip, and I couldn't help but scan his arm for any sign of exposed skin. I put one hand on his shoulder, and he grabbed the other, and we fell into step with the other couples.

The space between us was strained and awkward. I tried not to think about Thorne. About how mere hours ago he had me pushed against the wet stone wall. How I now knew exactly how the column of his throat felt beneath my lips, or how his shirt had looked clinging to his skin, with droplets of water falling from his beard.

"So how was your day at the cliffs?" Galen asked after a long moment of silence.

I cleared my throat. "It was fine. You're right—they're very beautiful."

"I'm sorry I couldn't go. Maybe next time."

"How was your meeting with Lord Penworth?"

He sighed. "It was about what I expected. Him complaining about all of the things I haven't been doing that he's had to take on for his territory. Budget constraints, amendments he wants made to Mysthelm's ordinances, things like that. I'm thirty-two years old, and he talks to me like I'm a child." His grip on my left hand tightened. "It doesn't help that they've all watched me grow up. I just want to prove I'm more than these last eight months have shown them."

I gave him a placating smile. "You will, as long as you don't give up and get so in your head about it."

"You make all of this look easy, you know that?"

I scoffed. "If by hiding behind you and your guards for the past three days to avoid someone trying to kill me again is 'making it look easy,' then sure, it's a breeze."

"You're not *hiding*. You're staying safe. Protected."

"Now you sound like Thorne."

"Well, he has become the rational one of the three of us. As long as you're over here plotting ways to use yourself as bait for potentially nonexistent Shifter assassins, I'm happy to sound like him."

I rolled my eyes. "You two are no fun."

The humor slipped from his face as his eyes fell to my elbow, then up to where our hands met. He twisted the engagement ring on my finger with his thumb. My arm involuntarily flinched at the movement.

"Really, Clarissa. Promise me you won't try to draw them out? I don't—I can't risk something happening to you. Not before we're married."

The easy banter we'd fallen into dissipated in the blink of an eye. I dropped my arms to my sides, my body heating for an entirely different reason than it did with Thorne.

"Don't worry, Your Majesty," I said coldly. "I'll be sure to keep myself perfectly intact. What good am I if I can't *save* you?"

His eyes widened. "No, Clarissa, that's not what I meant." I shook my head and turned to walk away, but he grabbed my hand. "Please, let me—"

I yanked my arm away, then looked around the crowded ballroom and schooled my features. I didn't want to cause a scene, but I also didn't want to be around him.

He furrowed his brow and took a step toward me, reaching for me again. This time, however, he didn't get the chance to touch me.

A hand landed on his shoulder.

"Is there a problem?" Thorne asked, his voice low and with a hint of danger.

Galen straightened his jacket. "No, Thorne. Just trying to talk to my fiancée."

My cheek twitched at the word. "We have nothing more to talk about. You should make your rounds, Galen. Your people are expecting you."

He let out a noise of impatience. "You're being difficult. If you would just let me explain—"

"You don't need to explain. I understood you perfectly," I said, keeping my voice calm. "I know what my value is to you. What my purpose is. Let's not pretend this has to be anything more."

He looked like he was about to argue when a messenger approached. "Your Majesty, a letter has arrived for you from Palace Grimaldi." He held out a silver platter with a folded piece of parchment to Galen.

Galen batted the tray away. "Not now."

The messenger shuffled on his feet. "It's urgent, Your Majesty. About your mother."

That got his attention. He looked over at the messenger, then down at the envelope. Grabbing it, he gave me one last look and said, "I need to see what this is about."

I didn't respond. He turned on his heel and strode out a side door in the ballroom. I let out a breath and felt my chest deflate, along with all the tension I'd been carrying.

"Are you alright?" Thorne murmured, stepping closer.

"I'm fine." I waved a hand in the air. "Just another day of never knowing what side of him I'm going to get." Over Thorne's shoulder, I spotted the doors leading to the balcony. "Excuse me, I'm going to get some air."

The ivory bottom of my gown brushed across the floor as I made my way through the crowd and opened the double doors. It was a beautiful stone balcony, with dark vines twisting around the rails and over the edge. I took a deep breath and closed my eyes. I missed being out under the stars whenever I wanted. The night's breeze was a cool reprieve against my skin, and I rested my elbows on the stone rail to take it all in.

When I opened my eyes, they landed on the sprawling grounds of the Penworth Estates several stories below. The tall hedges bordered acres of beautiful gardens, with winding paths and fountains that glistened in the moonlight. And on the very periphery of my vision—

A shadow.

I squinted. It looked like a cloaked figure running along the trees on the edge of the property, heading toward the entrance—

Before I could focus on the dark image, a scream burst through the ballroom.

"Come quick! It's the king!"

42
THORNE

I bolted toward the servant girl who came running from the door Galen had exited through. Members of the King's Guard were already stationed there, preventing hordes of people from clambering past.

"I'm Regent Lord of the North Territory. Let me through," I commanded.

They moved aside, and I heard my mother following closely on my heels. When I turned the corner down the hallway, a small kitchen came into view.

And at the entrance lay a body.

I sprinted the short distance, my heart lurching into my throat. *Galen.*

"What happened?" I asked the servant girl still shuddering behind me. She stumbled and reached down toward him, but I leaped forward to grasp her arm. *"Don't touch him,"* I snapped. The last thing we needed was a rotted corpse wasting away with no explanation.

She reared back in fright. "I didn't hurt him, I swear!" she cried, a sob racking her body. "H—He asked me to bring him a glass of whiskey, and wh—when he took a drink, he just—he fell!" Tears poured down her face as she pointed to the broken glass on the floor at Galen's side.

"What's going on?" Clarissa's voice sounded, followed by a gasp. I whirled to see her, Taryn, Rose, Leo, and Evadine gathered at the door. Evadine grasped Clarissa's arm.

More sets of footsteps clicked against the wood floor.

"What is the meaning of this?" Rhys Penworth boomed. He and his wife pushed through the others.

"I think His Majesty has been poisoned," my mother answered. Her face was drained of color, her fingers clutching anxiously at the pendant around her neck.

"*Poisoned?*" Lord Penworth exclaimed.

Galen lurched, and his upper body seized violently. His eyes were closed, but I could see them fluttering beneath the lids. A thin line of white foam formed on his lips as he spasmed.

My heart raced. I didn't know what to do. We couldn't touch his skin, or we'd die. But if someone didn't help him, *he* would die.

"Fetch a healer," I shouted to the distressed servant.

To my surprise, Rose stepped forward and reached for a strange leather pouch hanging from her belt. She knelt at Galen's side, and Leo hissed, "Rose, what are you doing?"

Her emerald eyes shone determinedly. "Helping him. My magic may not work here, but my tonics might."

Clarissa's sharp cry rang through the air, "Rose, don't!"

I lunged for Rose's hand as she reached for Galen's bare neck.

I was too late.

The moment her fingers touched his skin, her entire body jolted backward like something had slammed into it. She sucked in a sharp breath and snatched her hand away, staring at it in alarm.

"What is it?" Leo asked, instantly at her side.

"I can—I can feel it. My magic."

I glanced at Clarissa. Before we could ask questions, Rose grabbed her little pouch and began pulling out stems and leaves I couldn't identify. I watched in bewilderment as she pressed each to her tongue, mysterious words flowing from her lips. Slowly, Galen's seizures subsided until he was still once more.

"What are you doing?" Lord Penworth thundered behind us, making his way to Rose and Galen. "Get away from His Majesty!"

I rose to my feet and put a hand on his chest. "She's *saving* him."

"She's a *witch*!" he snarled. Whirling on his daughter, he pointed a finger at her and said, "You told us these were companions from school. How *dare* you bring these people into our home?"

Taryn crossed her arms over her chest. "This probably isn't a good time to tell you I never finished school, is it?"

Clarissa stepped forward. "Lord Penworth, your daughter is—"

"And *you*." A vein in Rhys's wrinkled neck bulged. "You're the one behind this. Coercing my daughter into your schemes, sneaking your repulsive kind to my land, to *my* house? The rumors from the Mid Territory were right. You're plotting against us. How many more are there, hmm?" His nose screwed in disgust as he stepped closer and spat at Clarissa's feet. "What else are you hiding, you manipulative little—"

"*Enough*," I said through gritted teeth. Red appeared at the edges of my vision as rage flooded me. I grabbed his outstretched wrist and twisted until I felt a small pop, and his snarl turned into a hiss of pain.

I'd had enough of these people treating Clarissa like vermin when she had done *nothing* but help them. Nothing but try and earn their approval, when they should be the ones begging for hers.

"Kneel," I commanded, still gripping his wrist.

"Excuse me?" he spluttered.

I stepped closer to him and lowered my voice. "You've always been a despicable man, Penworth. You don't deserve to touch the ground she walks on. I said *kneel*, and beg that she doesn't wipe you from this kingdom like the rightful empress she is." I thrust his arm back at him, and he staggered into his wife, who glared daggers at me.

Lord Penworth met my gaze, a sneer pulling at his lips. The entire room held their breath as my anger coiled like a snake ready to strike.

A cough sounded from the floor.

I jerked toward Galen, who gradually propped himself up on an elbow, his arms shaking.

"Are you alright? How do you feel?" I asked, bending low.

"Wh—what happened?" he replied in between coughs. He looked around the small kitchen in confusion. "And if you're going to start fights, Thorne, I want to be there." His voice was frail, but he chuckled weakly.

My shoulders sagged as my panic and wrath dimmed. Until Rhys Penworth's voice rang out.

"This has gone on long enough." He pulled himself up to his full height, still clutching at his wrist. "Grimaldi, I've chosen to respect you out of loyalty to your father, but I will *not* be offended and lied to in my own home. And I absolutely will not tolerate terrorists under this roof."

Galen narrowed his eyes. "You're toeing a very dangerous line, Penworth. You forget that I am your king."

Rhys shook his head, his slicked-back gray hair catching the light. "The great King Orion would never have approved of the company you keep. Marrying an outsider? Letting our kingdom fall into ruin?" He scoffed. "You claim to be a king, but you are a *boy* trying to step into his father's shoes."

Galen grasped the back of the couch and shakily hauled himself to his feet. His normally combed hair was ragged and loose around his ashen face, and his voice was rough as he glared at Rhys. "There will be consequences for your disloyalty, Penworth."

The older man chuckled. "Attempt anything, and see what happens when a quarter of your kingdom turns against you, *Your Majesty*." He took a step closer to Galen, and I moved on instinct, ready to get between them. "You are nothing without your regents. You speak of disloyalty? When have you ever been loyal to *us*, Grimaldi?"

Tension swelled and heated in the silence between the two. My muscles were drawn tight, unsure what the next move would be, barely daring to draw breath.

Rhys's cloak billowed along the floor as he spun on his heel, taking his wife by the arm. He didn't bother to face us when he said, "I want all of you out of my house by morning. You are no longer welcome in the South Territory."

THE
HUNT

43

CLARISSA

The faint silhouette of the mountains receded behind us as we sailed east into the rising sun. A full day aboard the *Queen Mignonette* awaited us on our journey from the South Territory to the elusive Island Territory.

I'd hardly slept. By the look of the motley crew surrounding me at the table in the quarter deck, neither had the others. Leo's arm was thrown around Rose's chair, her head resting on his shoulder. He kept tipping forward and backward on the legs, and I glimpsed his tail winding and unwinding around Rose's ankle beneath the table—a sign of his unease.

Devora brought my mother a cup of tea, and the two of them sat next to me. It took Mia all of five seconds to rouse from her nap at my feet to prop her little paws on Devora's leg, begging to be let into her lap.

Galen had gone straight to the captain's cabin to continue sleeping off whatever toxin he'd ingested last night. Katrine was preparing a medicine for him that Rose had taught her, and the Reaux family...well, I wasn't sure where they'd settled on the ship. I tried not to think about them. *Him.* With everything else going on, my complicated emotions for a man I couldn't have didn't need to muddy the waters.

I sighed and scrubbed at my eyes. Apparently it wasn't just *me* someone was after—it was Galen too. I'd known from that very first dinner at Palace Grimaldi that there were people opposed to my coming here, and Galen hadn't exactly established the best reputation among his kingdom. Plus, Scarven's Shifters had entered the picture. The threat could literally be anywhere at this point. We had no idea who to trust, no idea what lurked around the next corner.

I'd tried to find the Penworths and tell them about the strange figure I saw running through their grounds last night, but they refused to see me. I settled for Taryn and hoped she'd be able to get through to them. Not that it mattered anymore.

Every single person aboard the *Queen Mignonette* had been examined. The assassin hadn't left the South Territory with us. I prayed they wouldn't follow—or worse, that there weren't more waiting for us on the island.

I was curious about this next regent family. If Scarven *wasn't* behind the attacks, then the regent families had plenty of motive too. Especially if they were working together. Even if Dion Silenus had changed his mind at the last moment, that didn't mean he wasn't at one point part of some larger plan. And the Penworths *definitely* hated us. They all had the power to do anything they wanted in their territories—bribe carriage drivers, pay security guards to let a man with a weapon through at the Harvest Tournament, rig a bonfire, poison a bottle of whiskey, even cause an explosion to bring down the roof of a small cave.

"You look like you could use this," Devora said next to me, breaking me from my thoughts. She slid her teacup across the scratchy wooden table. Mia's head peeked up at the motion before she settled back into her lap.

I gave her a look. "Tea?"

"Sure. *Tea.*" She fingered the top of her shirt, and the metal tip of a flask peeked out.

I snorted. "Devora, it's not even eight in the morning."

She shrugged. "I won't tell if you won't."

"Devora, dear, did you put that in my tea?" my mother asked, leaning over in her seat next to me and raising an eyebrow.

Devora's eyes widened. "Of course not, ma'am, I—"

Mother's cup scraped against the surface. "Top me off."

"Mother," Leo said with a chuckle. "Rough night?"

"I believe we've all had better," she replied.

Devora glanced at the captain's quarters, where Galen rested beyond. She pursed her lips, a crease appearing on her forehead as she took another sip of her spiked tea. I knew she was concerned for him. She'd had a relationship with him in the past, however fleeting it might have been.

"He's going to be alright," I said softly as my mother, Leo, and Rose continued their conversation.

"I know." She gave me a tight smile. "This tour has just...not been what I expected."

"You and me both."

"I really admire you, you know," she said, then raised the cup to her lips and drained the rest. I tried not to smile—I could tell this sort of conversation didn't come easy to her. "The way you've handled it all. I—I thought you should know that."

I squeezed her arm. "Thanks, Devora. I don't think anything I've done has made much of a difference, but I appreciate it."

"No—no, it has," she said, brow furrowing. "You don't hear the way the servants talk. They know how you've saved their fields and livestock. They know you've done more for this kingdom than those regents ever have. Some people are afraid of your magic, maybe, but they also realize what it can do." She paused, and her eyes flitted across the table to Rose. Her voice lowered. "That's how she saved him, isn't it? Magic?"

I nodded. "Rose is an Alchemist. That means she can use the nature around her to do spells and things like that. She's also very good with healing charms. We were lucky she had some of her herbs on hand."

"But...how? I thought the only time you can use your magic

here is when you touch the blight. Like at that dinner at Silenus Manor."

I licked my lips but kept my tone casual. She was shrewd and observant, and was stepping far too close to the truth. "I think Rose had just helped clear it from someone's land nearby before the ball. She must've still had some of the magic lingering."

Devora nodded thoughtfully. "All that power at the tips of your fingers...and nobody to control you," she murmured, more to herself than to me. "Your empire sounds so free."

"Nothing is free. There's always something to run from." I pushed back from the table and stood, the abrupt motion causing the others to glance up at me. "I'm going to check on Galen."

Turning toward the captain's quarters, I glimpsed the orange sun slowly rising above the horizon. Its shadow left a trail of shimmering gold across the waves, making its way ever closer to the hull of our boat. A light breeze swept over my nose and cheeks, the kind that smelled like salt and warned of a humid summer day ahead.

I knocked on the cabin door and waited for a garbled "Come in," before pushing it open and entering the dim room. Curtains were closed over windows overlooking the deck. Galen sat in the bed, dark circles rimming his eyes, his cracked lips pulling into half a smile when he saw me.

"How are you feeling?" I asked stiffly.

"Like someone tried to kill me."

I couldn't help but roll my eyes. "You get used to it."

"You of all people should know there's only so many ways we can handle things like this." He swung his legs over the side of the bed and motioned for me to join him. "Go crazy with paranoia, or pretend it doesn't bother us."

"We've gotten very good at that, haven't we?" I said as I sat next to him. "Pretending."

He let out a loud breath. "Clarissa, I'm sorry. I shouldn't have said what I said last night."

"It's fine, Galen. We both know how big of a deal this marriage is. I get it."

"No, you don't. You mean more to me than just someone who can break this curse." He started to move forward, and my muscles tensed. I stood and scratched the back of my head, searching for something to fill my discomfort.

"Do you remember anything?" I finally asked. "From before you were poisoned?"

His shoulders fell. "You saw the courier deliver a letter from the palace. I was... It was bad. I needed a drink. I had the nearest maid in the kitchen fetch me a glass. She came back, I took the drink, and—well, you saw the rest. The room began to spin, and the next thing I knew, your friend Rose was staring down at me."

"The message was about your mother, right?"

Looking down at his gloved hands, he nodded. "She's taken a turn for the worse."

My eyes widened. "Then why are we going to the island, Galen? We should be heading back to Palace Grimaldi. You need to be with her."

"Trust me, I want to. But they said she insisted I stick to the tour. We only have one territory left, and the respect of the regents is barely hanging by a thread as it is." He twisted his hands in his lap, his actions betraying the surety in his tone. "She isn't as sick as my father was. There's still time."

"Fates, Galen..." I huffed out a breath. "Are you sure?"

He met my stare, red veins hovering around tired hazel eyes. "No. But I've always balked from the hard decisions. It was time I finally made one, even if it ends up being the wrong choice."

I nodded. "I'm sorry. I hope she'll be alright."

"Thank you. I'd like for you to meet her before this is all over with," he said. "She's always been intrigued by Veridians and your magic. And here I am, having been saved *twice* by one of you. First you with Tovar Printh, and now Rose..." He trailed off, the edges of his eyes crinkling as his forehead creased in thought.

"What's wrong?"

He shook his head. "Nothing, it's just...it must have been a figment of my imagination, but when I go back to last night, I keep thinking that—that Rose *touched* me. My skin. But that can't be possible, because she's still alive."

I hesitated, running my finger along my lip before I said, "She did, Galen."

His neck snapped up. "What? But—but *how*?"

"I don't know for sure. The only explanation I can think of is that Veridians are immune to your curse—not only the objects you curse, but your *actual* touch too. The magic in the curse that the Fates gave you must be similar to the magic we have, so it doesn't affect us. It seems to do the opposite, actually. It *gives* us our magic back. It's how Rose was able to use her Alchemy to heal you in a way your healers here wouldn't be able to."

He swallowed hard as he took in my words. "So, you think I—you think I could...I can *touch* you? Because you're Veridian?"

I nodded once, the air in the room suddenly heavy. I could feel his desire, his breaths coming faster as the reality of physical contact hit him.

"Clarissa..." He pulled at his bottom lip with his teeth. "Can I touch you?" he whispered. "Please?"

I held my breath and scanned his features, his wrinkled forehead, his pale cheeks, his dilated pupils. I didn't fear his curse—I knew in my bones that I was right, that I couldn't be hurt by him. It was a wonder I hadn't figured it out before now. But what I *did* fear was something that had been lurking at the edges of this king since the day we met.

Desperation.

I was still angry with him. But part of me felt sorry for him. He was hurting, and after months of never having the most basic of human contact, I could give him that. One touch.

I cleared my throat. "Alright."

I moved back to the bed. Slowly, he tugged off the glove of his right hand, finger by finger. Raising a trembling arm, he halted before his skin touched mine, a question in his eyes. I gave a small nod. His lips parted as the tip of his finger grazed a loose strand of my hair, hovering there for a moment before brushing it behind my ear. Clammy fingers skimmed my ear and down to my cheek.

That same bolt of warm magic I felt when I touched the blight liquefied in my veins the second his skin met mine. It was fainter this time, barely a whisper, but still…it was there. My magic.

"Did you feel that?" he whispered. I nodded tightly. We both sat in silence, the clock on the wall ticking to the sound of our hearts.

Waiting for his curse. For the rot to take hold.

But nothing happened.

His eyes widened. "It's real. I can touch you."

His grip became firmer, more confident, his thumb running along my cheek to my jaw, then his other hand cupped the side of my neck. I fought the urge to lean away from him, from the unfamiliar, uncomfortable touch of his hand.

A different man appeared in my mind. The way Thorne's rough skin felt holding me, his soft lips punishing against mine.

I clenched my jaw when Galen scooted closer. "This—this is amazing. It's been eight months since I could *touch* someone, Clarissa. You have no idea what this means to me." His breath hit my face as he leaned in, awe in his voice and wonder in his eyes. His hold on my neck tightened, and a spike of uncertainty slithered down my spine. My eyes flitted to the closed door across from us.

His thumb continued to trail the side of my neck and to my collarbone, running back and forth across my skin. My limbs locked.

Before I could blink, he moved forward and pressed his lips to mine.

The shock of his movement made me gasp. I flinched, but he merely gripped the back of my neck harder, pushing himself into me. I put my hands on his chest and shoved until I could rip away, almost falling off the bed at the motion.

He reared back. "Clarissa, I—I'm sorry. I don't—I don't know what—"

"Stop," I said, my cheeks burning. I ran my fingers through my tangled hair, shivering at the sudden chill. My fox half pulsed beneath my skin.

"I shouldn't have kissed you. I just—I thought this was a good thing." He swallowed and stood to face me. I jerked away instinctively. "That we could touch each other. I thought you'd want that too."

My legs shook, my heart racing as my adrenaline slowly faded. Fates, it would be so much easier if I wanted him. But if these past days had shown me anything, it was where my heart truly lived.

Not that it mattered.

"Galen, this marriage, it—it's only for show. *You* were the one who made that clear in the beginning. To build an alliance and break the curse. I'm going back to my empire after this—you know that."

He looked at the ground. "Things could change."

"No, they can't. Look at me," I said. "You don't want this. You don't want *me*. You're enamored by the idea of me saving you. I have the power to break this curse...to give you your *life* back. And I'm one of the only people you can touch without hurting. That's where all of this is coming from. It's what I represent to you."

His gaze searched mine, and I wondered if he could see right through me. If he could see the icy blue eyes that lurked in my subconscious.

"You're right," he finally said, turning away from me. His voice was void of emotion, that longing and amazement he'd held now gone. "I'm sorry I made you uncomfortable."

"Galen, I—"

"I'm tired. I should rest before we reach the island."

I stared at his back for a moment longer, then twisted the door handle and stepped onto the deck, now arrayed in bright sunlight, my skin still cold and yearning for the touch of someone else.

44

CLARISSA

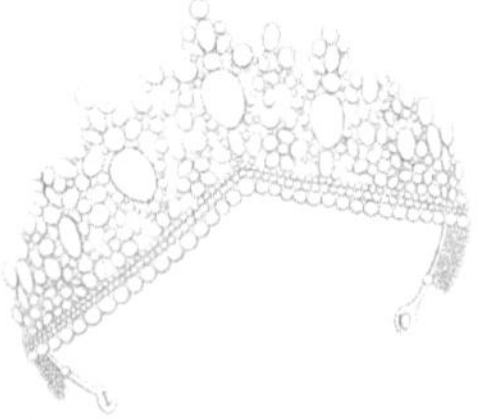

"Holy Fates." Devora slumped into the seat next to me, her eyes trained on a sight at my back. "I've never seen it up close."

"Seen what up—" I turned around and cut myself off.

We'd arrived at the Island Territory.

Straight ahead loomed two enormous green cliffs on either side of the ship, with bright, glassy turquoise water lapping and winding through the space in between. I kept craning my neck up, up, up to take in the beautiful, towering cliffs as we sailed farther into the bay. My eyes followed their sloping peaks until they descended to meet the shore, which was littered with tall trees and broad leaves. I could barely make out the tiny crowds of people milling about, and even farther back stood buildings covered with grassy roofs and plunging waterfalls scattered across the terrain.

"It's beautiful," I said.

Devora nodded. "I've always wanted to visit."

"Let's just hope *these* regents don't try to kill one of us."

"Third time's the charm."

I smiled, then jumped in my seat when a voice behind us said,

"I wouldn't worry about that too much. The Zeloria regent family isn't like the others."

I turned to face Thorne. My heart thumped louder when his eyes lingered on me.

"Empress," he said softly, inclining his head.

"Lord Reaux," I replied.

Devora's sharp eyes flitted between us. "I'm...going to go make sure your bags are ready to go, Your Majesty." She gave a quick bow before handing me Mia's leash and darting off toward the cabins. The pup wagged her tail and let out a high-pitched bark as a seagull swooped close to the railing.

I shook my head. "I swear, I tell them to call me Rissa, and it's like they don't even hear me."

Thorne chuckled. "Habits are hard to break, I'm afraid." Shuffling his feet, he glanced down at Mia, then at the table between us. He cleared his throat. "Are you...are you well?"

"Yes, very. Thank you," I said. "And you?"

"Good. Yes, I'm—well, you know, as good as we can be." He brandished a hand in the air. "With everything."

I twisted my lips, shifting my gaze out to the approaching shoreline and back again. An uncomfortable silence wrapped around us as I ran my finger along the edge of the wooden table.

He stepped closer and lowered his voice. "Is this awkward for you too?"

I instantly let out a breath. "I thought it was just me."

"It doesn't *have* to be like this." He took another step toward me. "We were friends, yes? That doesn't have to change."

I nodded. "Yes. You're right, we're friends. Of course." When I realized I was still nodding, I abruptly stopped. "I don't even know if I'd go that far. You're rather cocky, you know."

His eyes sparkled back at me. "So I've been told. Alright, then. How about 'allies'?"

"Perfect," I said, voice breathless as he set his hand on the table next to mine. "Allies."

I stared up at him, neither one of us willing to move. The air stretched taut between us, the rocking of the boat seeming to guide our limbs closer.

The captain called for the crew to prepare to anchor, snapping our attention back. Thorne took a step away. As he silently brushed by my side to leave, his little finger came out to curl around mine. A single heartbeat, and it was gone.

I closed my eyes and took in the sound of seagulls cawing overhead, the fresh air tinged with salt blowing through my hair and nostrils, and Mia's soft fur rubbing against my legs.

Just one more regent family. This would all be over soon.

As the island's shores were too shallow for the ship to dock at, we anchored out in the bay and took dinghy boats up to the sandy banks. The closer we got, the more vivid all the colors became. Bright pink and blue flowers dotted the leafy trees. Large, lush fruits hung from branches all across the shore—brown coconuts, orange mangoes, ripe bananas. Clouds like pillows hung over the very tops of the cliffs, opening to sloping green hills and crystal waterfalls.

A handful of men helped pull our little boats ashore, their feet splashing through the water as they hauled us in. Groups of islanders passed by with curious looks. Some waved and smiled at us, while others lingered with baskets or wheelbarrows before going off to their tasks. The pulse of island life washed over me as I sank into the white sands—the flapping of wings, rush of wind through trees, steady beat of feet on the earth. Mia tugged on her leash, eager to join them.

"Ah, Thorne, my friend! It's good to see you!" a man with thick black locks hanging to his large waist called as he strode toward our line of boats. I looked to my left to see Thorne helping Marigold and his mother out of their dinghy, his tan face splitting into a grin when he saw the man.

"Daelan. Still getting up to trouble?" Thorne said by way of greeting as they clapped each other on the back.

"More so than you these days, I daresay," Daelan remarked. "The last time I saw you, Iris was ready to pop." His amber eyes fell to Marigold, who stood a few paces behind Thorne, holding a stuffed doll in her hand. "Is this..." He trailed off, eyes widening as he looked back at Thorne. "She looks just like her," he said, his voice quieter.

A look passed between them, one that spoke of a deeper friendship. Thorne smiled softly and nodded, then turned to his daughter. "Marigold, I'd like you to meet Daelan Zeloria. He's one of the regent lords of the Island Territory, just like I am back home."

My lips parted. *This* was the regent lord?

Daelan grimaced. "Please, Thorne. Do I look like a *lord* to you?" At that, Marigold giggled, and Daelan got to his knees with a chuckle. The sand shifted beneath his hefty weight, his dark braids swinging and twirling with the colorful beads he wore around his neck over his exposed broad chest. "Hello there, Marigold. It's nice to meet you."

She gave him the most precious curtsy I'd ever seen, with her little blue dress skating the tips of the sand. "I like your necklace," she said shyly.

"This old thing?" He fingered the red beads. "Here, you can have it, sweet girl," he said, taking it off and draping it over her neck.

"Two minutes and you're already wrapped around her finger. Pathetic," Galen teased as he approached from our left. He looked stronger than he had in the early hours of the morning when I'd seen him.

Thorne scoffed. "You're one to talk."

"Oh, wait till Hector shows up. He'll hand over the entire island to her," Daelan countered, standing to give his king a bow before Galen patted him on the back.

"Who is Hector?" I blurted, and all eyes turned to me. I bit down on the inside of my cheek, feeling like I'd interrupted some private moment.

Daelan wiped his hands on his tan breeches, and sand flew off them with the movement. "Well, well, you must be the infamous Veridian." His eyes scanned mine, but it didn't feel threatening. Merely curious. Observant.

"You can call me Clarissa." Then I motioned to the dog dancing around our feet. "And this is Mia." When I held out my hand, Daelan took it, a smile brightening across his dark features. His palm was callused, with gritty grains of sand rubbing against mine as he pulled away. A regent who wasn't afraid to get his hands dirty, it seemed.

"Oh, she'll be well-loved here," he said as he knelt to scratch behind Mia's ears. "We have plenty of animals wandering the island." His lips tilted into a smirk. "So, I hear my counterparts have been giving you a rough time."

I glanced back at Galen, who averted my gaze. "It's been...interesting," I said.

"Well, we don't run things the same way around here." Daelan shot me a wink. "And thank the Fates for that."

"Careful now, Zeloria. Some of us are still a bit traditional," Thorne's mother said as she came up to take Marigold's hand.

"Lady Azura." Daelan gave a dramatic bow. "Always a pleasure."

"Where is that brother of yours?" she asked, raising a sharp eyebrow. "He was always my favorite."

"Hector's around here somewhere. Probably entertaining our new friend. Who just so happens to know you, Clarissa."

I leaned back, startled. "Me?" I didn't know anyone in this *kingdom*, much less this small island.

He shrugged, but there was mischief behind those amber eyes. "Come!" he said, clapping his hands together. "Let's show you around."

We all shouldered our bags and trudged after him in the sand. We must have been a sight to behold—nearly a dozen of us plus our guards and a dog carving a path across the shore, earning the stares of many islanders as we made our way onto the paved road of tightly packed rocks.

Daelan, Thorne, and Galen chatted like old friends, and I wondered how they knew each other. Daelan appeared to be several years older than the other two, perhaps in his late thirties. He was certainly unlike any of the other regent lords we'd met— Thorne aside, I supposed. Much more relaxed and carefree.

The tall trees surrounding the path opened up to a wide clearing that looked like a town square. Huts of various sizes with moss growing on the roofs were scattered across the large patch of land. A stream trickled through the center and off to the right. Men, women, and children played at its edges, carrying buckets of water or scrubbing clothes on washboards. Others were up at the tops of the trees gathering fruit, while more still passed by with fishing gear and hunting knives strapped to their backs.

A large round building came into view. The walls were made of bamboo with carvings etched into the thick stems—I spotted drawings of animals, the elements of nature swirling around land-scapes, and the face of a woman embedded in the walls. Waiting at the entrance was a tall, dark-skinned man with a shaved head, his arms crossed over his thin chest and a pleasant smile on his lips. A rod of bamboo leaned against his side.

"Heard you coming all the way from the shore. You're a loud lot," he called out in a rich, deep voice.

"Sorry to disturb your evening, old man," Daelan teased back.

"Seven years older, and I'll never hear the end of it." The new man shook his head. "Welcome to the Island Territory, friends." Grabbing his walking stick, he spun to the door, leading us inside the hut.

"Hector Zeloria," Thorne whispered in my ear. "Daelan's brother. They oversee the island together."

"The two brothers are *both* regent lords? Did neither of them marry?"

Thorne shrugged. "Not yet. It hasn't been their priority. If one of them bears an heir one day, then they'll be happy, but it's not like the other territories. The islanders often opt to elect their regents."

"Not a bad idea, honestly."

Thorne tilted his head in agreement as we walked through the first building and out the back door, where more than a dozen huts made up a circle around a large courtyard. Everything was lit in a hazy glow from the light of the setting sun.

"We call this the Base," Daelan explained, sweeping an arm toward the rest of the buildings. "Hector and I live here, and we have plenty of guest houses for you all. The main market for this side of the island is a short walk west. We islanders love our nightlife, so things may get a little loud around here," he finished with a chuckle.

I could see evidence of said nightlife in the enormous courtyard where we now stood. Leftover campfires littered the space, and benches and chairs made out of logs formed U-shapes around them, perfect for little pockets of community.

Daelan and Hector led us around the guest houses at the perimeter, stopping at each one to show our party their assigned living space for the next few days. Lady Azura was next to Thorne and Marigold's hut, then Galen, my mother and me, and lastly Rose and Leo. A couple of larger ones beside them were reserved for our maids and guards.

When only Rose, Leo, Mother, and I remained as the others settled in, the brothers stopped in front of a little house with flowers hanging from a red awning.

"Your palace, madam," Daelan said, bowing low before me.

"You'll find a welcome gift has already made itself at home," Hector added.

I glanced at them. "What are you talking about?"

Daelan shrugged. "He said to tell you that."

Exchanging a curious glance with my mother, we stepped inside. It was a small suite with a low ceiling and walls painted midnight blue at the top, then fading into a light sky blue at the base. I could see almost the entirety of the hut from the front door. There was a round table with a couple of chairs near the entrance, a hallway to the right opening into a room with two beds, and straight ahead was a tan couch facing wide, floor-to-ceiling windows.

And on that couch sat a lone figure watching the sunset beyond the mountains in the distance. Something about his dark blond waves and the rings glittering on his fingers as he twirled a glass of amber liquid had my brow furrowing. Mia sensed his presence and yapped loudly, pulling hard on her leash.

Next to me, Leo sighed. "You have *got* to be kidding me."

The *welcome gift* craned his neck to look at us. Familiar navy-blue eyes twinkled as he smirked.

"It's about time," he said, raising his glass. "Did you miss me, darling?"

45

CLARISSA

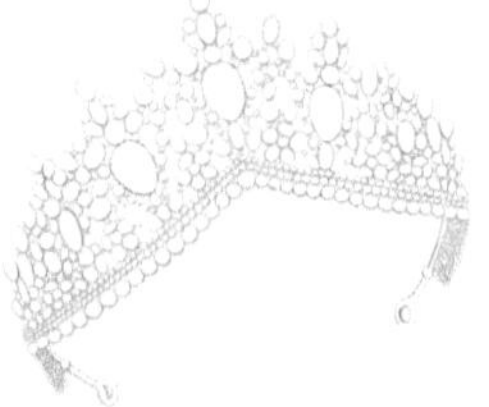

"Nox Duma," I said with a chuckle. "Are *you* here to kill me?"

He raised an eyebrow. "That's an interesting way to say 'hello, Nox, it's good to see you,' after five months."

"Hello, Nox. It's good to see you."

He grinned and stood from the seat, a lock of dark blond hair falling over his eyes. "It's good to see you too, Rissa."

I smiled as he pulled me in for a hug. I hadn't seen the cheeky, silver-tongued dragon Shifter in months after sending him to Mysthelm as an ambassador last fall. He'd been the first Veridian to meet with the Mysthelm council on my behalf, under the condition that he stay confined to the palace. It was how we'd sent messages back and forth between Mysthelm and Veridia in those first few months.

But then he fell silent. The last I'd heard from him, he had some personal business he needed to take care of in his home province of Drakorum.

His eyes landed on Rose and Leo. "Ah, the love birds. How long has it been?"

"Too long," Rose said, stepping forward to embrace him. Mia

was still going crazy, making me stumble as she followed Rose and barked her cute head off at Nox.

"Not long enough," Leo answered under his breath. I held back a laugh. My brother had always been a little short with Nox, but I knew the dragon Shifter had grown on him.

"We'll leave you all to catch up," Daelan said. He and his brother exited our hut, making their way back to the courtyard.

Nox knelt to hold his hand out to Mia. She instantly began sniffing every inch of him. He laughed when she let him pet her, her tail wagging so fast, it was almost a blur. "I have that effect on women."

Rose rolled her eyes. "Same old Nox, then."

"Rissa, darling, why have I never met this beautiful woman?" Nox asked as he stood and faced my mother.

Mother's lips tilted up. "You seem far too clever to know that will never work, but charming enough for me to like it anyway." She held out her hand. "Evadine Aris."

"Nox Duma, Your Grace. It's an honor to meet you." He took her hand between his and kissed her knuckles. "Your children have told me so much about you. And while I'm not old enough to remember much of yours and your husband's rule, my parents always spoke highly of you."

Mother's brow wrinkled. "Duma...as in, *Caius* Duma? The former governor of Drakorum?"

A small flinch passed over Nox's face before he smoothed his features once more. "My father, yes."

Her face fell. "Oh. I—I heard about what happened to him. I'm very sorry for your loss. Your father was a good man."

"It was a long time ago, Your Grace."

"Some pains do not age," she murmured back.

Nox's father was the governor of their province until Kane Scarven challenged him for the position when Nox was merely a teenager. And when Shifters issued challenges, it was to the death.

I didn't know much about Nox's life. He was captivating smiles and pretty words and loyal to the end, but he kept his past locked down deep. I suspected it was more in an effort to hide it from himself than others. All I knew was that he was taken from his family at a young age because of his rarity as a dragon Shifter and used as Scarven's secret weapon. He had a much younger sister, but they kept her locked away as collateral for him to do their bidding. She was still in captivity, as far as I knew.

Having a dragon Shifter on their hands after our entire empire thought his kind to be extinct for centuries was nothing short of a miracle. One that Scarven would do anything to keep for himself.

Those of us in this room were some of the only people to know Nox's *true* Shifter form...the most dangerous, most powerful beast known to man.

My order for him to be my ambassador in Mysthelm was issued in part because I knew it would be the only way to get him out from under Scarven's thumb. Nox wouldn't be able to disobey a direct command from the empress-elect. But it turned out my attempts to save the dragon Shifter landed him right back in the lion's den anyway.

"What are you doing here, Nox?" I asked.

"Am I not your faithful ambassador?" he replied, lazily swirling his half-empty glass in the air. "I'm...ambassador-ing."

I crossed my arms. "You haven't written me an update in months. You're not here on *my* orders."

"Leo and I heard rumors of Scarven sending a group of Shifters over here from Drakorum," Rose added. "We never thought it would be *you*."

"Which brings me back to my initial question," I said.

Nox let out a disbelieving laugh. "No, I can confidently say that I am not, in fact, here to kill you."

I shrugged and gave him a smirk. "Had to check. What about the others?"

"What others?"

My brow pinched. "Are there not more Shifters with you?"

"No. I'm the only one. Why?"

I licked my lips. "We just...I thought Scarven was having me followed. That he'd sent more assassins after me all the way from Veridia."

"I'm afraid it's just me. And I don't know about any plans to have you killed." Nox cocked his head. "Why does it seem like that disappoints you?"

"Because someone *has* been trying to kill her," Leo interjected.

"And it would've made things a lot easier if it was Scarven," I said with a sigh. "Now I'm back to having no clue who's behind everything."

Nox blinked. "You've lost me. What, exactly, has been happening?"

I quickly recounted both assassination attempts back in Veridia City, plus the various incidents in Mysthelm over the last two weeks. How Rose and Leo had come all the way to the kingdom because they thought Scarven was sending more Shifters, and they feared for my safety.

"You never answered the question though, Nox," I said when I'd finished. "Why *are* you here? Is it for Scarven?"

"It's nothing you need to worry about," he replied, taking a sip of his drink. "Just some small project he has me working on."

Leo scoffed. "Rather secretive."

"Darling, the number of secrets I have would make even your pretty tail curl," Nox drawled. The nonchalance in his eyes faded as his gaze fell to his fingers, which were clenched around his glass. He lowered his voice and looked at me. "You know there are things I can't tell you, Rissa. I'm doing the best I can."

His sister. The reason he had to toe such a fine line with his loyalty, and the reason Scarven could keep the only dragon Shifter in centuries on a leash. They still had his sister under their control, and Nox would do anything to keep her alive. I knew his priorities when I recruited him to join my Sentinels last year, and again when asking him to work for me.

The truth was, I didn't blame him for his secrets. I snuck a glance at Leo. If anyone took my twin, there wasn't much I wouldn't be willing to do for him.

"I know, Nox," I said. "Just...tell me you're safe."

Those navy-blue eyes met mine with a sad smile, but he didn't respond.

The muffled sound of laughter filtered through the closed door at my back, along with a distant drum roll and steady footsteps. In the window facing the mountains and the dimming sunlight, small bursts of fire appeared in the darkness, like torches being lit.

Nox's gaze flicked behind me, and his smile widened. "I think we all deserve a little break to taste the island life, yes?"

———

AFTER I FED MIA, our small group—minus Mother, who wanted to rest—made our way out of the hut to find the massive courtyard already full of laughter and music. People were gathered around small campfires smoking meats over the open flames, passing bottles of drinks while some played music on small drums and flutes. It was as if the entire island came alive with the setting sun —animals shuffled in the nearby brushes, birds flitted from tree to tree, and insects joined in with their melodies.

I gazed around in awe at the broad leaves covering the land like a canopy, smoke curling through the sky and into the deep blue starry expanse. A large path lit by standing torches led from the courtyard of the Base out to the rest of the island beyond, and Nox nodded for us to follow him.

Daelan, Hector, Galen, and Thorne were already sitting on some logs around a campfire a ways from the Base, and several other islanders with them were cooking what looked like rabbit legs and pineapple on a spit. I was surprised to see Marigold up so late, but there she was, playing with two other little girls by her father. When she saw Mia and me, a grin split across her face, that dimple making my heart swell.

"Rissa! Rissa!" she called with an excited wave. "Can I play with Mia?"

"Of course." I handed her the leash, making sure she had a tight grip on it. Mia smothered her and her two new friends with kisses, the four of them dancing around the sandy dirt and leaves.

A small pang shot through me. Fates, I was going to miss her.

Leo and Rose were drawn into another fireside with the promise of a strong chocolate drink I hadn't heard of but that smelled fantastic. Nox and I took a corner log facing the others, with Marigold and Mia nearby. My eyes kept straying to them and, inevitably, to Thorne right behind. I tugged my cloak tighter around my shoulders as I stole another glance.

He'd always been casual compared to the men of nobility back home, but tonight...tonight he was an entirely different Thorne. Barefoot with his sleeves rolled up, beads like Daelan and Hector's strung around his neck—along with that same marigold necklace he always wore. I didn't think he'd stopped smiling since we got here. A *real* smile, not that smirk he often had when he knew others were watching. Those blue eyes sparkled in the firelight, little creases appearing at the corner of them when Hector said something that made him laugh.

I imagined sitting next to him, his arm flung around my shoulders with Marigold and Mia playing between us, the drum roll and lively music and chatter of the island wrapping us in its cocoon.

"Can't stop watching your king?" Nox crooned to my right. Shooting him a bland look, I leaned back on my hands and stared up at the moon, taking in the night.

"Or perhaps not the *king*," he added.

"No idea what you're talking about."

"Ah, so I'm just imagining the ruggedly charming blue-eyed man who's been staring at you since we walked up."

I jerked forward. "What?"

Nox chuckled. "You're too easy, darling. I knew it had to be one of the two."

"I don't know why you assume there has to be anyone at all."

"You're right, there doesn't. And you don't owe me any explanations." He leaned back to match my earlier position. "But if I turn up dead because Handsome over there skewers me through the heart for sitting too close to you, I'll start asking questions."

I rolled my eyes. "You're just as ridiculous as I remembered."

"Probably more so."

Propping my chin in my hand, I turned to face him. "How long have you been here, Nox?"

"About a week." He shrugged. "You tend to lose sense of time here."

"I can see why you like it. The island suits you," I admitted.

He twisted one of his rings on his pointer finger. A moment of silence passed between us before he said, "Truthfully, the first time I came to this kingdom months ago under your orders, the loss of my magic shocked me. But then...it was freeing, in a way. Knowing nobody could use me for what I could do because I simply *couldn't* do it here. In Mysthelm, I'm just a man. No secrets or ulterior motives."

"Nobody to control you," I said softly. It reminded me of what Devora said on the ship.

"I am *so* close to getting Vera out, Rissa." His voice was low and strained, at odds with his usual composure. "So close I can taste it. I just have to hold on for a little longer. Do what he wants a *little* longer."

I rolled my lips together. "Will you tell me if there's something I can do? Some way to help you?"

"Yes," he said with a quick nod. "I'm still trying to figure things out, piece together exactly what's going on and what Scarven is up to. You just have to trust me. I'm on your side, Rissa. But I *have* to get her out."

"I understand," I whispered. "Just please, take care of yourself. Be careful."

He nudged my shoulder. "Always knew you had a soft spot for

me. But *you*, my dear future Empress *and* Queen of Mysthelm, have other things to worry about. Have you heard about the Hunt?"

I shook my head. "No. What's that?"

"Oh, boy," he said, letting out a whistle. "Are you in for an adventure. These islanders are very keen on their traditions. And also very superstitious." His eyes flashed with humor. "You know, maybe I'll let you find out for yourself."

I smacked him on the arm. "You can't set me up like that. Now I have to know."

He ignored me and scanned the passersby. "Ah, here we are," he said, reaching behind me and tapping someone's elbow as they walked by with a tray full of drinks in tall glasses. "We'll take two."

To my surprise, Devora spun around, her red hair sweeping over her shoulder at the motion. She raised an eyebrow as Nox gave her his charming smile.

"Excuse me?" she asked.

"The drinks. We'll take two, if you don't mind," he said, motioning to the tray.

"And what makes you think I'm serving?"

Nox blinked. "Oh, well, I—I suppose I just assumed—"

"Yes, you did, didn't you?" Her blue-green gaze gave him a once-over, and I had to hide a grin behind my hands. Devora glanced at me and said, "Your Majesty, would *you* like a drink?"

"I'd love one, Devora. Thanks." I reached out to take a glass, my hand brushing right past Nox's bewildered expression.

"Anytime." With that, she turned on her heel and headed toward a campfire several yards away, where Katrine and a few other women were chatting. I watched as all of them took one of the drinks. Katrine said something that sent the group into laughter. A smile tugged on my lips at the sight of them getting the chance to relax. This island had that effect on people.

"And who is *that*?" Nox asked, his eyes still fixed on Devora as she pulled her long hair into a strap of leather, the firelight glinting off her glasses.

"If I tell you, will you tell me what this Hunt thing is?"

"Can't. I've been sworn to secrecy." He pinched his lips shut with his finger.

I rolled my eyes. "She's my lady's maid. And a friend."

"Well, then, here's to friends," he said, holding his cup in the air.

I tapped mine to it. "To friends."

46

THORNE

"Here, try this," Galen said, handing me a skewer. "Best fish I've ever had, and that's saying something."

I took a bite of meat hanging off the edge. He was right—the skin was the perfect crispiness, seasoned with rosemary and a hint of spice. It fell apart in my mouth as I chewed and groaned my approval.

It had been a long time since I'd been to the island. My father used to bring Mother and me when I was a teenager, which was when I met Daelan and Hector. They were several years older than me, but they were still willing to give a scrawny, annoying adolescent the time of day. I was instantly awestruck. They were everything I wanted to be—confident, untroubled, likeable without even trying. An air of lax importance that made others respect them and want to be their friend at the same time. Their father was the Regent Lord of the Island Territory back then, so they would often visit the North Territory when meeting with King Orion. The two of them, Galen, and I became instant friends.

It was always like this when we saw each other again. Laid-back, indulgent, burdenless. Laughing and drinking around a fire like nothing had changed.

But this time, something was different. This time, all four of us bore titles and positions of power we hadn't before. And this time, we had secrets we couldn't share.

Too much was on the line, and there were too few people I trusted after multiple assassination attempts and all the other strange incidents. I thought Galen knew the urgency of the situation. I thought he understood how careful he needed to be to get through the rest of this tour, considering not twenty-four hours ago, he was seizing on the floor with poison coursing through his veins. But tonight...

"I'll take another, beautiful," he slurred to the woman passing by on his right. She and a couple other islanders had been bringing him drinks all evening. I'd lost count of how many he'd downed.

Perhaps things hadn't changed as much as I thought.

"Galen, you might want to slow down," I muttered.

"Why? We're on island time now," he said. "If someone's gonna try to poison me again, at least it'll taste good." He threw an arm out wide to grab his fresh drink. His sleeves had ridden up his forearm a couple inches, exposing bronze skin that had me instantly flinching away.

"Because you get careless when you're drunk," I hissed, pointing to his skin.

He rolled his eyes. "I'm not drunk."

"Trust me, friend. You're drunk," Daelan said as he swung his arm over Galen's shoulders. I tensed, then relaxed a fraction when the high collar Galen always wore held true, blocking Daelan's skin from touching his. During Galen's drunken stupors, I had to constantly be on alert.

A glorified babysitter. Except the *baby* was a grown king who could kill someone with a single touch.

"Shouldn't your *fiancée* be with you tonight?" Daelan hinted suggestively, nudging Galen's shoulder.

On instinct, my gaze found Clarissa. She was sitting at a nearby fire with a man who looked familiar, but I couldn't place why I knew him. Clarissa, however, seemed to be *well* acquainted with him.

Something hot and acidic boiled in my chest. It didn't matter how casual or friendly it was—every time the man's hand grazed hers, every time I heard her laugh fill the air, my fingers squeezed tighter around the edge of the log beneath me. The thought of others being able to touch her the way I did...

She may be engaged to my best friend, but Fates, she felt like *mine*.

And I couldn't stand the sight of her with someone else.

A piece of the log splintered under my grip, breaking my glare. I looked down to see blood welling on the pad of my thumb and hastily pressed it to my lips to stem the flow, careful not to wake sleeping Marigold. She and Mia had both passed out sitting between my legs. Her head rested against the inside of my knee, while the little pup was curled in a ball in her lap. Mia had only been with us for a week, but she'd already grown enough for her paws to hang over the edge of Marigold's legs.

Galen sighed dramatically, drawing my attention back to him and the brothers. "Don't save us a private suite just yet, if you know what I mean. Especially after today."

"What happened today?" Hector asked.

Shrugging, Galen leaned back on the log, precariously close to tipping right off. "She wasn't exactly *receptive* to my advances."

My stomach sank to my feet, that same searing heat snaking its way across my chest as Daelan chuckled and said, "Well, Fates, if the *King* had no luck, nobody will."

"What did you do?" I asked Galen, my voice shaking with an attempt to rein in my rage.

"Kissed her."

"You *what?*" I growled. "And she—she didn't—" I glanced over at her again, needing proof that she wasn't a rotted corpse. That his curse truly *didn't* affect her. I'd wondered last night when Rose touched his skin. It shouldn't come as a surprise that he'd wasted no time *testing* that theory on his future wife.

"She's fine, Thorne. Obviously." For a split second, the alcohol-induced haze disappeared from his eyes, and his brow furrowed as he looked at me. Something like suspicion shone from the hazel depths. It was gone just as swiftly, his eyelids drooping and a grin slipping easily onto his lips. "I s'pose we have different ideas of what this marriage will look like. It's a shame. Would love to see what I'm working with."

Anger tore through me as Daelan and Hector both smirked. Was this what I used to sound like? What I used to *be* like? Viewing women as nothing more than objects at my disposal, expecting them to cater to my every whim?

"You're disgusting," I muttered, shoving my long hair out of my face. "She's doing this to save you, you know. Show her some respect."

Daelan and Hector exchanged confused glances, and Galen narrowed his eyes. I was dangerously close to the subject of the curse, something nobody outside of those closest to him knew of, but I didn't care.

The image of him running his fingers along her skin the way I had slammed into me. Of him pushing her against a wall, sliding his lips over hers as she tried to get away.

My jaw was clenched so tightly, I thought my teeth would crack. "I need to get Marigold to bed," I spat out, avoiding their eyes as I scooped my daughter in my arms before they could respond. The movement made Mia jump off and shake her body. Her leash dragged on the ground when she followed me, running in wide circles around my legs.

"I'm sorry, Thorne," a breathless voice said from the side. "I didn't mean to leave her with you for so long."

Clarissa drew nearer and knelt at my feet to grab the pup, then paused to look up at me. Her cheeks were pink from sitting near the fire, and her windswept blonde hair pillowed on the shoulders of her black cloak.

My heart stuttered.

My black cloak. The one I'd given her on the way back from the Aurelia Cliffs.

"Are you heading to the huts?" she asked as she stood.

I merely nodded, not trusting my own tongue. Burning rage and jealousy paired with the sight of her on her knees with my cloak wrapped around her neck ignited some territorial instinct that I needed to get rid of.

"I'll walk with you," she offered. "I'm getting tired, anyway."

"Was the company not riveting enough?" I blurted, jerking my chin toward the man she'd been with all evening. He was watching us and had the nerve to *wink* at me when my stare met his.

She glanced back at him and rolled her eyes. "That's just Nox. He's a friend from home. My ambassador for Mysthelm, actually, although he didn't get the chance to do much before he was called back to his province."

Nox. *Nox Duma.* The Shifter. It all came back to me—he'd been sent to establish communication with Galen's council after their former emperor died eight and a half months ago. We'd met with him a couple of times, but in the wake of King Orion's death and Galen's new curse, I barely remembered him.

"What's he doing here?" I asked, the iciness melting from my voice as we walked. Marigold settled against my chest, puffing warm breaths of air in her sleep.

"Apparently, he's the 'group of Shifters' Rose and Leo heard Scarven was sending here. Only, it's just him, and he's definitely not here to kill me." She shrugged. "We were wrong. They aren't the ones after Galen and me."

I made a disgruntled noise in the back of my throat. "So we're back to no leads."

"My money is still on the regents. After everything Rhys Penworth said, I wouldn't be surprised if he was working with others to make them look like accidents. And Dion Silenus wasn't exactly my biggest fan in the beginning." She eyed me. "You seem close to the Zelorias. How well do you know them?"

"I highly doubt they're hiding poisonous snakes in your bedsheets, Empress," I said with a chuckle.

"Well, thank you for giving me *that* new fear."

"They're good people. We were much closer when we were

young. Their family would come up to the North Territory all the time to meet with King Orion. Daelan was actually the one who taught me how to flirt with women," I said, laughing as memories came back to me. "The second they could sneak Galen and me into the taverns, we were there every night. His favorite line when meeting a beautiful woman was always, 'I was enjoying my drink, but then I saw you. Now I think I need something stronger.'"

Clarissa snickered. "Did that actually work on anyone?"

"It did for him. But when I tried it once, she swung her satchel at me and said, 'Here, is this strong enough?'"

She burst into laughter. I had to control my shaking shoulders so as not to wake Marigold.

"Alright, fine. If you say I have nothing to worry about with the Zelorias, I believe you," she said as our laughter subsided. "The good thing is, it sounds like your shot with women improved over the years. Galen mentioned you being rather 'wild' once upon a time." She quirked a mischievous eyebrow at me.

"I suppose I was. But thankfully, I figured out who I wanted to be." We reached the door of my hut and turned to face each other.

"And who is that?"

I looked down at Marigold. "A father. A *romantic*," I said teasingly, then my eyes met Clarissa's and my voice softened. "A better man."

Sounds of the island filtered in around us—the chirping insects, the wind through trees, the distant laughter and crackling of fire. Her stare lingered on me before flitting to Marigold.

"I should let you get her to bed," she whispered.

Those dark eyes traveled back up to mine, and that same territorial instinct from earlier pounded like a drum in my chest. I bit down on my tongue before I said something that would only be a mistake, but every muscle in my body yearned to reach for her. She swallowed, the edges of her lips falling slightly as she tapped on the doorframe with her knuckles and turned on her heel.

Fates help me.

"Do you want to come in?" I asked.

She froze and slowly faced me again. "Are you sure that's a good idea?"

I shook my head. "No."

My eyes caught on her mouth as her teeth pulled at her bottom lip, indecision warring across her features. I held my breath and willed my pulse to slow. Blood rushed through my ears like a tidal wave when she took a hesitant step forward.

And another.

And another.

And then she opened the door and walked into the house.

47

THORNE

She turned in a wide arc to take in the space, which I imagined looked similar to her own little hut. Tall windows along the back wall facing a forest just outside, several couches and one table, a small hallway leading to a single bedroom.

"I'm going to put her in bed," I said quietly, dipping my chin down at Marigold. Clarissa nodded and looped Mia's leash through one of the chair legs.

I slipped into the room. Marigold stirred as I carefully shifted the blankets on the bed and set her down. Her lips puckered into a pout, and I smiled when she burrowed into the pillow and let out a sleepy sigh. Peeling her hair away from her forehead, I kissed her temple and turned to head back out.

Clarissa leaned against the doorframe, her shadow darkening the few feet leading to the bed. She smiled softly at us. "My father used to tuck me into bed like that. He'd find me passed out by the window or outside in the garden under the stars and carry me inside. I don't think he knew that I remembered, but I always woke up. Just for a split second. Long enough to hear him tell me he loved me."

"She usually begs me to read a story." I glanced back at

Marigold as she turned on her side. "She's had so much anxiety from such a young age that she's never been the adventurous type, but I think her books are how she lives out her fantasies."

"She'll have her adventures one day," Clarissa murmured, straightening and backing out into the hallway.

With one last look at Marigold, I followed and shut the door with a soft *snick*. We stood there, the narrow space barely leaving room for the two of us. My shadow encompassed Clarissa as she pressed her back into the wall. My eyes trailed from her neck down to her waist. I remembered what it felt like to grip her there, to have her legs wrapped around me, her warm breath on my skin.

"I shouldn't have asked you to come in," I said.

"Then why did you?" she whispered, eyes searching mine.

I felt myself giving in, felt that undeniable pull that always emerged around her. I slowly placed my palm on the wall at her head and leaned down, my fingers burning with the urge to hold her again. She angled her head up to me and parted her lips.

A soft whimper behind the closed door at my back made me pause, followed by a muffled cry of "Mommy!"

I let out a breath, my shoulders sagging. "It's the night-mares," I said. "They happen sometimes, and she...she doesn't know how to handle them. How to tell the difference between them and real life." I pushed off from the wall and turned to open the door, finding my daughter thrashing in the blankets. She kept calling for her mother with terrified whines, her little chest heaving.

Clarissa put a hand on my arm when I moved toward the bed. "Can I try?"

I looked between her and Marigold, then cleared my throat and nodded. She padded across the floor and climbed in on the other side of the bed. Marigold's arm swung out as she cried. Clarissa scooted in next to her and cradled her head against her chest, running a hand down Marigold's bronze hair.

"It's okay, sweet girl," she whispered, gently rocking from side to side. I had to strain to hear her next words as Marigold's moans rose and fell. "You're safe. Your daddy is safe. The nightmares aren't real, I promise."

"I want my mommy," Marigold whimpered, her eyes screwed shut to where I couldn't tell if she was still asleep or not.

It felt like an arrow was digging beneath my ribs. The backs of my eyes burned as I watched her cry, knowing there was nothing I could do.

"I know, I know," Clarissa repeated in her soft voice. She pulled Marigold closer to her. "I bet your mommy loved you *so much*, Marigold. Do you want to know what mine used to do when I got scared?" Clarissa paused, and Marigold let out another sniff.

A few seconds later, Clarissa began humming a quiet melody I'd never heard before. The hums turned to soft words as she sang my daughter back to sleep. It was a beautiful lullaby about green meadows and sweet dreams in the stars. Marigold's body slowly relaxed, her moans becoming fewer and farther between as she settled back into sleep.

I stared at them for what felt like hours. Clarissa's gentle hands swept up and down Marigold's side, a small smile forming on her lips when she looked down at her. Clarissa's shoulders rose in surprise when Marigold turned toward her, burying her head in her side.

It was beautiful.

It was painful.

It was like something bursting in my chest, spreading instant warmth that turned to lead, sucking the air from my lungs. I took a step back and out the door to try and catch my breath.

The bed shifted with a subtle creak, then Clarissa appeared at my side, carefully shutting the door. Her brows pinched together as she faced me. "I'm sorry, Thorne. I just wanted to help."

I shook my head. "Why are you apologizing?"

"Because I..." She trailed off and licked her lips, a shyness I wasn't used to seeing now bleeding onto her features. "I'm not her mother. And I—I wasn't trying to be. I know how the nightmares can be, how scary it is to lose a parent. But I'd never try to—"

I let out a breath that released some of the tension building in my spine. "No, Clarissa. That's not what I thought at all. Please don't apologize. It's not—" I scrubbed a hand down my face. "It was exactly what she needed. Thank you."

"Then why did you look so upset?" she asked. She reached out a hand and threaded her fingers through mine, and I was so distracted by the display of affection that I didn't take time to over-analyze my words.

"Because it's hard to watch," I blurted out. "It's hard to watch something I can never give her back. And it's hard to watch *you* with her, knowing we both need you. Knowing that..."

You're leaving us.

I didn't finish the thought. I swallowed the words and squeezed her fingers.

"She'll be okay," she said. "She's a strong little girl. She'll get through it, even if she'll always carry some of the loss with her. And she has so much love in her life, Thorne." She raised her other hand to my cheek, soft fingers skimming my beard. "You're everything she needs."

But what about what I need?

I merely nodded, the emotion clogging my throat making it difficult to respond. I dropped her hand but my fingers traveled up her arm, stopping when I reached where the cloak was clasped around her neck.

"You wore my cloak," I murmured as I fingered the edge of the fabric.

Her breath hitched. "It smells like you."

My thumb ran along the neckline of the cloak, my eyes fixed on the goosebumps my touch elicited on her skin. "I was jealous tonight, you know," I confessed.

"Of Nox?"

I tilted my head as my thumb landed on the pulse at her neck. "And Galen. He said he kissed you."

She swallowed. "He did."

"And?" I was drawing closer to her again, that string pulling me tight. My hand now cradled the base of her neck, but I wasn't sure if it was to push her away or reel her in.

"And I wished it was you," she breathed out.

I dropped my forehead to hers with a groan. "He said you weren't...*receptive*," I bit out. "Did he hurt you?"

"No," she replied, and my muscles relaxed slightly. "It wasn't like that. He stopped. I just...I was thinking about you. About the waterfall."

Closing my eyes, I rolled my forehead back and forth across hers. The air tightened and pulsed between us. I clenched my jaw against the image of them together. "The idea of him kissing you, of him *touching* you..." My hold involuntarily clenched at her neck, and she sucked in a breath.

"I don't want him, Thorne." She tilted her head up so the edge of her nose brushed mine. "I've never wanted him."

"Then tell me why I still feel so guilty," I rasped out. "Why I still feel like I want something that isn't mine to take?"

"I can't." The way her throat constricted under my touch as her fingers grazed my ribcage made my hands tremble. "Because I feel the same."

The heat coiling around my chest snapped. "If we're going to feel guilty about something, it should be this."

And I pressed my lips to hers.

Our kiss at the waterfall was urgent and blazing. Consuming, desperate need. But this...

This one stopped time.

This one froze me to my core.

This one shattered within me, obliterating every ounce of denial and self-control I had left.

I grabbed her waist and moved us back out of the hallway, cursing against her lips when I stumbled over the leg of a chair. A chuckle rumbled up her throat, and I devoured it, my heart pounding with each stroke of her tongue, each intake of breath.

Every second with her was a mistake.

But every moment with her gave me life.

Lifting her with ease, I set her on the small table toward the front of the house, ignoring the shake it gave at the pressure. She wound her arms around my neck and pulled me lower. I rested my hands on either side of her to balance myself, a groan leaving me when she caged me between her legs.

Fates, she was so beautiful. So strong and brave and powerful. I would never get my fill of her, of the way she made me feel like I was enough, like I was *worthy*. Like I could live again.

She bit down on my bottom lip, and I curled my hand around the edge of the table.

Crack.

The center gave way as the supporting beam broke, and I wrapped an arm around her waist to lift her off before it fell. A breathless laugh escaped me. I opened my mouth to make some joke about breaking the table and waking up Marigold, but the look on her face stopped me in my tracks.

All the blood had drained from it, leaving her shell-shocked and pale. Her eyes widened—and that was when I remembered.

The sound. Like cracking bones.

"Clarissa, listen to me." I took her chin in my hand. "Stay with me, okay? Tell me what you need."

She shook her head and blinked rapidly. "I—I'm okay. I just...it surprised me." She gripped my forearms and took a deep breath, like she was trying to ground herself. When she leaned her head against my chest, I instinctively weaved my arms over her shoulders and kissed the top of her head.

"I'm glad you're here," she said faintly.

"There's nowhere else I'd rather be, Empress."

We stood like that for a moment as her breaths evened out and her shaking limbs finally relaxed into my hold.

But the second she lifted her gaze, a muffled scream rang out from outside.

Both of our necks snapped to the door. I bolted toward it and yanked it open, searching for signs of danger. Clarissa gasped when Devora, her maid, sprinted across the dark courtyard.

"Rissa, you have to come! Please!" she cried out, staggering closer.

"What is it, Devora?" Clarissa demanded.

"Katrine. It's Katrine," Devora said, her voice wavering. "He— the king. He was kissing her, and then she—she just—"

Horror ripped through me. Clarissa and I shared a glance before we both took off at a sprint.

48

CLARISSA

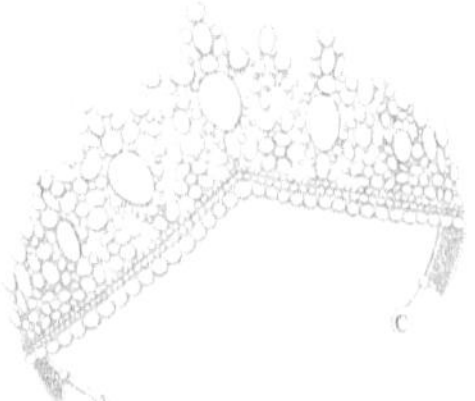

*W*e're too late. *We're too late. We're too late.*

There was no way we'd get to Katrine in time. Galen's curse was too fast, too deadly.

Thorne and I dashed to the campfires, him only pausing long enough to yell back at Devora to stay at the house with Marigold and Mia. Thankfully, many of the islanders had already gone home, given the late hour, and only a handful were crowded around the firepit Galen had been sitting at. The Zelorias, my brother and Rose, and Nox were among them. I pushed my way through and stopped in my tracks.

We were too late.

Katrine's body lay crumpled on the ground. Her dark skin was dried and flaking, the flesh almost peeling from her like thin paper.

"No," I breathed out, falling to my knees. The memory of the woman who'd died in my arms at the Drakin's Lair mere weeks ago flashed through my mind. I'd been too late to save her too. Both of these women had trusted me, put their faith in me, and I'd failed.

When I glanced up, I saw Galen's shaking form leaning against a tree in the shadows, eyes bloodshot and mouth open in silent terror.

Whispers of confusion swirled around me from the islanders.

"How did this happen?"

"Did anyone see her fall?"

"What's wrong with her?"

Perhaps nobody saw Galen kiss her—or didn't connect the dots.

Nox knelt at my side. "Did you know her?"

I didn't realize I was crying until a tear landed on my arm. "She was my maid. She was a sweet girl." Trying to hold back a sob, I reached out an arm to cup her cracked cheek, and her skin felt like sandpaper rubbing against mine.

And then...

I felt my magic.

I sucked in a breath. It was like when I touched the rotted land or Galen's skin. The same sensation stormed through me, lighting me with warmth and power and *home*. Golden magic filled my veins, and my fox half purred deep in my chest.

Distantly, I heard Nox call my name.

But all I could see was Katrine.

Inch by inch, painstakingly slowly, the color returned to her skin. Cracks filled in on her flesh, no longer flaking but smooth and vibrant once more. I watched as it spread from where I touched her face, all the way down to her exposed leg.

She opened her eyes with a shuddering gasp. "Your Majesty?" she croaked, her gaze unfocused and brow furrowed.

"Emperor's tits," I murmured. Without thinking, I leaned down to pull her into a hug. "You scared me, Katrine."

"Wh—What happened?" she asked.

"Yes, I'd like to know the answer to that as well," Nox said.

"You fainted, that's all," I assured her as I helped her sit against the log. Nox glanced at me but didn't argue.

"What in the ever-loving Fates just happened?" Daelan Zeloria hissed. He and his brother approached as Nox and I stood, their once friendly stares now suspicious.

"Was anyone else around to witness it?" I asked urgently.

Daelan hesitated, then shook his head. "Most people had already gone home at that point. I saw him talking with the girl by the fire, but the flames were dwindling. It was too dark to make out much."

Good, I thought to myself. "She fainted," I repeated, more firmly this time. "My maid has a tendency to get woozy when she hasn't had enough to eat."

"What?" Katrine croaked. "Your Majesty, I—"

I shot her a look, and thank the Fates, she shut her mouth and swallowed. "Perhaps I—I was feeling a little lightheaded," she confessed.

Daelan narrowed his eyes. "But your skin. I saw it—"

"You heard the empress," Thorne said as he appeared next to me. His towering frame shadowed the brothers. "She fainted. Clarissa revived her, and now she needs to rest."

The few islanders remaining dispersed once they saw that Katrine was alert, brushing off the incident and going back to their night. Daelan looked over my shoulder to where I knew Galen still slumped against the tree, barely visible to onlookers.

"Thorne, what's going on?" Daelan tried again.

"Not right now, Daelan. Please," Thorne said in a low voice. "Just get your people home. The girl will be fine."

A beat passed. Finally, Daelan nodded, and the tension in Thorne's shoulders released. Daelan and Hector backed away to help the rest of the islanders pack up their things.

"Are you going to try and convince me she *just fainted* as well?" Nox asked at my side, his head turned away from Katrine so she wouldn't hear.

Rose and Leo joined us, the former crouching to the forest floor to check on Katrine. I licked my lips and faced Nox. "In the week you've been here, have you noticed anything strange? Areas of the forest rotted and blackened, fish in the water or birds in the sky dropping dead out of nowhere?"

He scratched the back of his neck. "You mean the blight? Yes, I've heard whispers. People have been talking about how it's getting worse."

"Well, it's not just a blight. It's a curse. The *king's* curse." As quickly as I could, I summarized the story of the Fates cursing the Grimaldi line and how Galen's rotting power fell onto his shoulders several months ago, as well as how a marriage between our two lands would break the curse once and for all.

"Nobody knows about it except us and a few of those closest to him," I whispered. "But that's why Galen insisted on marrying me. It's the only way to end his curse and stop it from carrying onto his descendants."

Nox exhaled and ran a hand through his wavy locks, his dark rings glittering in the faint firelight. I could see him processing the information behind those keen navy eyes. "If I'd known that's all it took to marry you, darling, I would have made up some curse long ago," he quipped, but his tone fell flat.

I rolled my eyes and snorted. "Oh, shut up." This man would flirt with a brick wall. "That's not all."

"Good, it was getting rather boring."

"Veridians are immune to the curse."

That got his attention. His forehead creased as his spine straightened.

I continued, "I figured it out by touching one of the rotted fields, and—"

"Of course you did."

"—sort of sucked the blight right out of it. And when I did, I got my magic back. Just for a little while, though. It isn't permanent."

"That's how you saved her," he said slowly, glancing back down at Katrine and Rose. "You took the magic of the curse out of her."

I was about to bend down to help her back to her room when Galen approached from the tree line. I'd seen him look worse for wear before, but this...he was like a ghost of himself. A tortured, devastated ghost. His clothes were covered in dirt and leaves, his arms trembled at his sides, and his hair looked as if he'd been clutching at it and pulling hard.

My fox half writhed with anger beneath my skin at the sight of him.

He did this.

I strode the distance between us before he could reach the group. Extending my arm, I willed my hand to shift into a paw, red hair and sharp claws forming as I grasped his neck and shoved us both back into the shadows, several yards out of sight.

"How *dare* you?" I snarled, slamming him into a tree.

He struggled to breathe and grabbed at my forearm, but I held firm. His voice was strangled as he forced out, "Clarissa, I—"

"Not so happy I can touch you now, are you?" I snapped. "What were you thinking? You almost *killed* her, Galen. In front of all those people. What is *wrong* with you?"

His hazel eyes pleaded with me, the veins around his irises growing redder. With a growl, I eased my hold on him slightly so he could breathe. One of my claws dug into the side of his neck, and he winced as I drew blood.

Good.

I'd forgotten how much wrath my fox side brought. How it heightened all emotions, making it difficult to control or keep my head clear. And now, all I saw was red.

"I'm so sorry. I wasn't thinking," he rasped. "Please, let me talk to her—"

"Absolutely not. You will stay away from her, unless you want me to cut the skin from your lips and see if your curse still works then," I seethed. "Everything I've been doing is to help you and your people, Galen, and you can't keep it together for *one night*." I pushed him out of my hold as the small burst of magic faded and my paw went back to a hand once more. He stumbled to the ground and scrambled farther away from me, rubbing at his neck.

The soft crunching of leaves came from behind me. I turned to see Thorne, who eyed the scene before him, his gaze landing on Galen with a flash of rage.

"Get up," he said across the forest floor to Galen, his tone icier than I'd ever heard it. While Galen groaned and rose to his feet, Thorne lowered his voice toward me. "Rose is with Katrine. She's going to be alright." His fingers grazed my arm, and I moved closer without thinking. "You saved her. That was amazing, Empress."

Galen let out a scoff. "I should have known."

His eyes were locked on Thorne's hand still brushing mine. I hastily backed away, but it was too late.

"You always did want what was mine, didn't you, *friend?*" Galen said. "Even as boys."

I winced. "Galen, don't—"

"What, was I not good enough for you? You won't let *me* touch you, but you'll lift your skirts for *him* and let him—"

Before I knew what was happening, Thorne lunged at Galen and punched him in the jaw, knocking him flat on his back.

"*Thorne!*" I cried. His chest heaved as he glared down at Galen, his long hair whipping wildly in the wind, eyes churning like the sea.

And then he blinked.

His lips parted, and he took a step farther away, the tan color of his skin already fading.

A crack like crumbling stone appeared on his cheek.

I rushed across the gap between us and grabbed his neck, my heart pounding in my chest. When the magic spread through me once more, I let out a sigh of relief.

"You're an idiot," I said, my voice wavering. "Why would you touch him?"

The crack slowly seamed itself together, and the color returned to his cheeks. "Knew you'd save me," he grunted with a small laugh.

"And if I hadn't been here?" I shoved his chest. "Don't you *ever* do something like that again."

"I promise," he whispered. We both glanced down at Galen, who was knocked out cold several feet away. Thorne sighed. "Well, that's a mess we're going to have to deal with."

I shrugged, my adrenaline still racing. "Maybe he's so drunk, he won't remember any of this."

"Your optimism is inspiring."

The edge of my lip quirked up. "How are you going to get him back to his hut?"

Thorne looked around. "Do you have any spare rope?"

I chuckled, surprised I could find humor in anything tonight. But he had a way of making the burdens not seem so heavy. "Let's see if Nox and Leo can help. We won't have to worry about them accidentally touching his skin."

He nodded, then took a deep breath. "The things he said, Empress, I—"

"Don't." I shook my head. "It doesn't matter. He's drunk and angry and an idiot. I won't waste two seconds caring about what he says about us, Thorne. All that matters at the end of the night is that you and Katrine are okay."

"We are, thanks to you." With his thumb, he tilted my chin up to meet his eyes. "You don't have to go through with this, you know. Marrying him. After everything he's done, nobody would expect you to uphold your end of the alliance."

"It's never been about him, Thorne," I whispered. "What kind of a person would I be if I left your people defenseless against this curse?"

He let out a breath. "We don't deserve you, Clarissa. *He* doesn't deserve you."

"It's not about what they deserve. It's about doing what's right for those who can't help themselves." I covered his hand with mine and squeezed. "If I'm in a position to do good and don't use it, *I* don't deserve the power I've been given."

He stared after me, his eyes searching mine so deeply, I wondered if he could see into my soul. I squirmed under his gaze and forced a smirk on my face. "Let's go, Lord Reaux. We have a mess to clean up."

———

THE BOYS GOT Galen to his bed while Rose and I helped Katrine to the hut I was sharing with Mother. Devora urged me to let her take Katrine back to the servants' quarters, but I refused. Nothing like this had ever happened before, and I wanted to make sure there were no lasting side effects. And after seeing how frightened the poor girl was, I didn't want her out of my sight.

I could tell Devora was shaken too, despite how nonchalant and coy she always tried to appear. Her gaze kept bouncing back to Katrine, her fingers fidgeting in her shirt or adjusting her glasses.

"Come on," I said to her after I got Katrine settled on an extra cot in the living room. "You're staying with me too, Devora."

Her eyes shot to mine. "Your Majesty, I—"

"For Fates' sake, if you call me that one more time, I'm leaving you on this island," I said with a laugh as I grabbed her arm and pulled her into the living room. I set up two pallets of blankets and pillows on the floor next to Katrine and patted the spot beside me.

Katrine tugged the blanket to her chin and rolled on her side to face us, her dark brow furrowed as she met my gaze then quickly glanced away. "I'm so sorry," she choked out with a whisper. "I—I don't know what I was thinking. You're *engaged* to him, and I—I fell for his charm. I didn't know he was going to k-kiss me." She hiccupped at the last word, and my heart squeezed.

I reached out to take her hand. "It's alright, Katrine. I don't blame you. Please, get some rest. You'll feel better tomorrow."

"You're very kind, Your—*Rissa*." She yawned wide, black curls framing her tired features. "Much better than who we worked for in the past."

"We?" I asked, tilting my head.

"Katrine—" Devora said in a voice of warning.

"Devora and I used to work for Lady Reaux," Katrine said with another yawn as her eyes fluttered closed. "Devora brought me with her when His Majesty hired her." She opened her eyes again and gave me a look of concern. "You promise you're not upset with me?"

I smiled and said, "I promise. I'm just glad you're okay."

She nodded slowly as her eyes shut again, and she was asleep within moments.

"I'm sorry, Rissa," Devora said quietly. "She shouldn't talk like that about our former employers."

"You never told me you worked for the Reauxs."

She shrugged and took off her glasses, placing them on the side table nearby. "It wasn't for very long. Lady Reaux hired me when she saw me working at one of the taverns in the North Territory. It's how Katrine and I met—she was barely fifteen." She averted her gaze as she crawled back under the blanket. "Like Katrine said, we're much better off now."

"What did Lady Reaux do to you?" I asked, forehead creasing. "Was she—"

"Nothing," Devora said quickly, then closed her eyes and took a deep breath. "She was fine. It doesn't matter." She turned to face me, her red hair spilling onto the pillow beneath her. Her voice was softer when she said, "You've been so good to us. And the way you saved her tonight... She's like a little sister to me, Rissa. That's something I can never repay."

"I didn't save her," I whispered back. "She just fainted."

Devora gave me a look that spoke volumes. "You can tell the others whatever you want to, but I know what I saw."

I searched her stare, and I knew arguing with her would be a lost cause. Devora wasn't like the others. She was perceptive, far more so than I'd given her credit for. "Why didn't you say anything?"

"Maids are taught not to ask questions. It's how we survive." She shifted to lying on her back and gazed up at the dark ceiling. "I don't need to know everything, Rissa. Just that she's going to be alright."

"She will be. And, Devora...I'm sorry for whatever you may have faced in the past. For how people may have treated you. You didn't deserve that."

The room went quiet, save for the sound of Katrine's steady breaths, and I thought Devora had fallen asleep.

Just as I was drifting off, I could've sworn I heard her say, "It's *you* I don't deserve, Rissa."

49

CLARISSA

Eighteen days. That was how long I'd been in this kingdom. Like the others, the Island Territory held its own unique beauty—lush, dense jungles with creatures crawling and squawking about, stunning shorelines with water that lit up like diamonds, and towering mountain peaks in the distance that cast the whole island in shadows at sunset.

The regents filled my time with so many activities at all hours of the day and night, in between touring the island and meeting the people. Everywhere I went, I kept wondering when this evasive "Hunt" that Nox mentioned was going to pop up, but the people were just as tight-lipped as he was. Whenever I asked about it, they would give me a smirk and pretend they didn't hear me. It was starting to make me a little nervous.

However, I barely had time to worry about that or assassins with the hours spent hiking in the massive jungles, rock climbing off the side of Mount Tivalor, weaving fishnets at six o'clock in the morning, and my least favorite—deep sea fishing well past sundown, with nothing but lanterns and the moonlight to guide our way.

Foxes were *not* meant for water, and those dinghies they took us out in did little to ease my skittishness.

I'd seen more, *done* more, than I had in my twenty-eight years in Veridia. It was incredible. But it was also exhausting.

Almost three weeks wearing this mask of diplomacy and knowing I was both placed on a pedestal and under a magnifying glass at the same time was wearing me down. *Especially* after everything that had happened. Before, I was determined to gain the approval of the people and the regents so Galen and I could get married and be done with this without any pushback.

Now...the idea of being shackled to him in any sort of union made bile creep up my throat.

It's for the people, I reminded myself over and over.

Two days had passed since he almost killed Katrine, and he hadn't emerged from his hut. Every time I checked, the curtains were drawn, and one of his personal guards was stationed at the door to ward anyone off.

I knew he was spiraling. That was what he did—something bad happened, and he burrowed so deeply in his guilt that he cut everyone off. And he *should* feel ashamed. But a leader couldn't hide the way he did. His instability and flightiness were infuriating...yet part of me still felt sorry for him.

Galen was genuine but misguided. Able to sway people with a smile, but unable to trust in his own self. His past made him crave affection and approval so desperately that it crippled him. I understood now why Thorne continued to defend him after everything they'd been through.

I'd hardly seen Thorne since that night, either. Our group would gather for dinner in the evenings with the Zelorias, and shortly after, he and the brothers would go off together, or he'd try to get Galen to talk to him. I finally had my first free morning since we got here, and I was hoping to go find him, but to my surprise, Hector Zeloria was waiting outside my hut when I left for breakfast.

"Good morning," I said.

"Morning, Clarissa. Up for a little target practice?"

"That depends. Am I the target?" I asked, and he raised an

eyebrow. I cleared my throat. "That was a joke. Poorly timed. It's just been a few days since anyone tried to kill me."

"Yes, Thorne has filled us in on the *adventures* of your tour. I'm sorry it's been so difficult." He held his hand out in a motion for me to follow him, and we made our way through the main courtyard of the Base. "And, no, I planned on using *actual* targets. Unless you have a better suggestion."

"What exactly are we practicing for, Lord Zeloria?"

He chuckled. "You know, I rather like that title. Far more than my brother does. Don't tell him I said that." Instead of heading down the main path like I expected, Hector curved around the Base and to a clearing near the campfires we'd spent our first night at. "We're going to get you ready for the Hunt."

"*Finally*," I said. "Nobody will tell me anything about this ridiculous Hunt. I started to think it meant *I* was being hunted."

A devilish grin worked its way onto his dark features. "I apologize for the cloak and daggers, but it's a tradition our people are very fond of here. A rite of passage, if you will. And we're not allowed to speak of it to outsiders until they're ready to be considered *true* islanders."

"And how do I be considered a *true* islander?"

"You must succeed in hunting the elusive blood stag, found only on the island."

"Sounds...anticlimactic. What's the catch?" I asked. Tracking wasn't exactly a challenge for me—even without my magic, my hunting instincts were strong.

He stopped walking when we reached a tree with a bow and a quiver of arrows leaning against it. About thirty yards ahead of us was another row of trees, with wooden targets painted red staked into the ground in between them.

"You have forty-eight hours to find and kill a blood stag. We'll leave you alone in the jungles on the eastern side of the island, where it backs up into the mountain range." As he spoke, I looked to the east, where I could see the far coastal range rising into the clouds. "You can take only what you can carry—including the ceremonial bow and arrow you have to use to shoot it. Bring back a piece of its red antler, and you're an official islander of Mysthelm," Hector finished, flourishing the end of his walking stick in front of him.

I picked up the bow and slid my fingers along the handle. "And if I don't catch the stag?"

"You and your family will be cursed to the end of time." He grinned, and I snorted. "You'll face some ridicule, but nothing you can't handle. It's simply a fun tradition among the islanders. To prove your worth and your place in our world, especially as our future queen."

"So, no pressure."

"My brother and I have faith in you, after everything Thorne has told us." The edge of his lip quirked up, but I ignored what he was implying.

"When does the Hunt start?"

"Tomorrow just after dawn."

I dropped the bow to my side. "*Tomorrow*? Fates, you don't waste any time, do you?"

He shrugged. "It's tradition. But now you know and can get a little practice in before tomorrow."

"What makes you think I need any practice?" I teased.

"Maybe you don't. It wouldn't surprise me." He handed me the quiver and gave me a knowing look. "But perhaps I also thought you needed some time to yourself."

I took the quiver, then looked across the clearing at the targets. The midmorning sun was bright on the green grass, its heat comforting against my skin. It was small, but his gesture meant more to me than he probably realized.

"Thank you, Hector," I said softly. "There haven't been many to show me true kindness here. Most of the people are wonderful, sure, but they haven't really taken the time to get to know me. To care about what *I* need. So, I guess...thank you. For noticing. And for being the only regent to not hate me," I added with a small huff of laughter.

"That's not the way we run things here. We don't care about the rumors and speculation and whatever grudges the rest of them hold against Veridians." He waved a hand in the air. "That was all in the past. We think this alliance with you is the best decision Mysthelm has made in decades. Besides, it's impossible for my brother and I to hate a woman our best friend has fallen madly in love with."

My hand clenched around the bow. I swallowed and forced a nonchalant smile on my face. "Oh, Galen isn't in love with—"

"We both know I'm not talking about Galen."

I bit down on my tongue. "I'm...not sure what you want me to say."

"You don't have to say anything. Just shoot straight." He patted the quiver. "Good luck tomorrow. I'm sure if you follow your heart, it will lead you where you need to go."

He gave me one last smile and took off in the direction we'd come, his walking stick stomping through the grass and dirt.

I sighed. His words left me feeling so...unsure. Like I was floating aimlessly, an arrow launched toward a target that never found its mark. Like I was standing before the path I'd always known, and a veil had been lifted from my eyes to reveal a second.

I needed to throw sharp objects at something.

And if I was to complete the Hunt, my archery *could* use some practice. It had been years since I'd shot a bow and arrow. I much preferred the twin daggers I kept strapped to my thighs.

I hadn't been professionally trained with weapons by any means, but since we'd lived in the underbelly of the capital for most of our lives, Leo and I had grown up knowing basic defense. Our magic could only get us so far in a place like the south sector. And once I'd formed the Sentinels, I knew we'd need to be proficient in using weapons. We trained together for years and were lucky enough to have recruits like Chaz and Horace, who came from backgrounds with more formal combat training, who could teach us. After a year of working with them, I was able to shoot apples straight off my brother's head with almost any weapon of choice.

A pang of longing shot through me at the thought of my friends back home. Both the ones waiting for my return, and ones I'd never seen again.

What would they say about all of this? The danger we'd faced on the road, the hate crimes, the curses and secrets I'd had to uncover. The choices I had to make. Lark would be torn between scolding me for not keeping more protection around, and diving into her analytical nature to try and solve problems. Chaz would say to screw it and come back to Veridia.

Horace…Horace would be our ever-faithful grumpy guard. Doing what needed to be done and sacrificing his time and energy to keep me safe. He was also secretly a teddy bear. He'd grunt, pretend to be uncaring, and then tell me I was blind. That everything I never knew I wanted was right within my grasp.

I exhaled loudly and set my small bag and the quiver of arrows on a large, flat stone. I started with my daggers, pulling them from their sheaths at my thigh and twirling them in each of my hands as I sauntered closer to the trees and targets across from me. I hadn't had the time or freedom to train in a while. There wasn't much of a reason to, ever since Gayl died and I took over as empress-elect. I was no longer the one patrolling the streets at night, taking down bandits and terrorists and stopping violence before it reached those who couldn't defend themselves. I had *people* to do that for me now.

I tossed one of the daggers into the air and caught it with my right hand, quickly taking aim and sending it flying into the trunk of a tree fifteen feet away.

People I *commanded.*

I spun and launched the other dagger to my left mid-leap, watching it land right below the first with a satisfying *thwack.*

People who *relied* on me.

The image of the woman with the arrow through her neck

who'd died in my arms flared back to life, followed by Katrine lying ashen and rotted.

I stalked to the tree and wrenched the daggers free, then repositioned myself in the clearing. Gripping one, I aimed for a trunk farther away from the first and pulled my elbow back.

I always catered to what everyone else needed. What everyone else asked of me.

Like my council.

I flung the dagger with a grunt, and it zipped through the air to find its mark.

Or Galen.

I sent the second one following close on its tail.

And I did it willingly, because that was who I was supposed to be. For the longest time, that was who I *wanted* to be. The one others came to, whom they trusted in, because so many people needed that constant in their lives. They needed to feel safe. And I loved being that constant piece they could cling to.

But what happened when they took those pieces of me with them? What happened when there was nothing left for *me* to hold?

I strode to the trees and yanked the daggers out with more force than I intended, bringing bits of bark showering down onto the forest floor. Spinning on my heels, I took up the same spot and fired dagger after dagger, envisioning a different moment of the last four weeks with each twirl of the blade, each glint of steel.

Everen Stryker and his bigoted mouth. *Strike*. The assassin at the bar. *Thump*. The carriage driver. *Thwack*. Galen's secrets.

Dion Silenus. Rhys Penworth. The wary, judgmental eyes of people afraid of what they didn't understand.

The fox burning at the stake.

Galen's hands on my face, his lips on my skin.

Katrine's lifeless features staring up at me.

I threw a dagger again, but this time it fell to the ground at the roots of the tree. I leaned forward with a gasp and steadied myself. The hole I'd made in the trunk had become too wide for the blade to find purchase.

My shoulders fell with a sigh. It was in these moments of seclusion when I could let my emotions through. The overwhelming ones I kept locked away for fear of unleashing the animal, of being unable to control my actions or words.

Thorne had said they made me strong. But he didn't see what a mess I was half the time.

Except...he had, I supposed. When I shifted and hurt him, and when he'd watched me try and pick up the pieces. How I'd almost fallen apart on multiple occasions from panic, from memories and fears I couldn't get rid of.

Who is strong for you?

"What did that poor tree ever do to you?" a low voice said from behind me. I whirled and almost sent a dagger straight into his chest before I stopped myself with a sharp exhale.

"It's not wise to sneak up on a girl with daggers in her hand, Lord Reaux."

He held his hands up in mock surrender. "Consider me warned. You're quite handy with those blades."

My heart skipped a beat at the sight of his long hair pulled back in a strap at the nape of his neck, his loose shirt with rolled-up sleeves, that familiar necklace swinging against a smattering of dark chest hair. The very top of a red, jagged line peeked out, and I remembered how my claw marks felt beneath his shirt.

"How long have you been standing there?" I asked.

"Long enough to see you mutilate island property." He motioned to the wrecked tree trunk.

"Well, I didn't like the way it looked at me."

He chuckled, that deep rumble sending waves of heat across my skin. "I think you've taught it its lesson." He glanced down at the bow resting on the boulder off to the side. "Are you as adept with this as you are with your daggers?"

I smothered the sly grin that started to work itself onto my face. *This could be fun.*

I shrugged. "I'm not sure. It's pretty new for me. I figured I should learn since they're sending me on this Hunt tomorrow."

He frowned. "A what?"

"Some top-secret mission where I have to kill a wild stag, or my family is cursed for all eternity," I said dramatically, then winced. "Probably too soon for jokes like that, in hindsight. Hector just got done telling me about it. Tomorrow morning, they'll leave me in the eastern jungles until I can find and kill the island blood stag."

"You'll be alone?" he asked, his frown deepening. I nodded. "Are you sure that's the best idea? Someone is still trying to kill you."

"And we left them on the mainland," I said. "Nobody else came aboard our ship, and you have the docks being watched for any newcomers, remember? There's been nothing suspicious in over three days."

He took another step, and I had to look up to meet his gaze. "I still don't like the idea of nobody being there to protect you."

"I think I can handle it," I murmured.

"I know you can. But I wish you didn't always have to." He held my stare, and after a heavy moment passed, he looked at the bow. "Do you need help?"

I bit the inside of my cheek to suppress a smile. I nodded, blinking up at him with wide, innocent eyes. I could practically see his spine straighten and his chest broaden with masculine pride as he reached down to pick up the weapon, then led me to the center of the clearing.

Men. They were too easy.

I followed him, letting him position me with my feet shoulder-width apart. "You want a solid base," he said, then tapped my feet with the tip of his shoe. "Point your toes slightly out for better balance, but keep your hips and shoulders facing your target." His hands fell to my waist, gently guiding them forward. My breath hitched when his thumb slipped beneath the edge of my shirt, his skin grazing the ridge above my hip bone.

"Good," he murmured. My eyes met his, and the whisper of wind through the trees and birds chirping in the distance grew faint. I licked my lips, my mouth suddenly dry, and his gaze latched onto the motion.

"What now?" I asked softly.

His eyes lingered on mine a moment longer before he backed away, knelt to grab the bow, and stepped behind me. "You favor your right hand, yes?" he asked, and I nodded. "Then take the bow like this"—he placed it in my left hand—"and hold the grip here. Make sure your hand is relaxed."

He stood with his chest to my back as he reached out and covered my left hand with his, those corded arms flexing at the motion. His quiet words brushed along my neck, making the hair there rise. The heat left me for a moment when he bent down to pick up an arrow and nocked it onto the bowstring.

"Draw the string back like this as far as you can go," he said, leaning in closer. Warm lips skimmed my ear as I pulled the bowstring back. His other hand wrapped around my elbow and carefully lowered it. All I could feel was his body pressed to mine, his warmth seeping into my back.

"How does that feel?" he asked in a whisper.

"Perfect," I breathed out.

"Then let go, Empress."

At the last moment, I shifted my aim ever so slightly and released the string, watching as the arrow embedded itself into a tree to the left of the red target.

"Oops," I said.

He chuckled. "No, that was good. Let me go get it, and we can try again."

He strode off toward the line of trees, and I let out a breath to clear my head. I quickly grabbed another arrow from the quiver, nocked it, and closed my left eye, steadying my breaths. Muscle memory from all those nights spent practicing came back to me as I smirked.

I pulled back the string and let it fly.

The arrow zipped through the air, cutting the feather off the first one and sinking an inch above it, right before Thorne's hand stretched out to grab it.

He cursed and whirled to face me.

"Was that one better?" I called out.

His features morphed from shock to exasperation, a laugh slipping free as he shook his head. "Let me guess—you never needed help."

I shot him a wink. "You were adorable, though."

He stalked toward me with a predatory gleam in his eyes and a grin curling on his lips, abandoning the arrows. "You could have taken my hand off, you know."

"Don't you trust me?" I asked, tilting my head.

His smile faded as he drew nearer, and my own dropped as the air became heady and weighted. "With everything I am," he said softly. He moved a strand of hair behind my ear, so close now that his chest brushed against mine.

Voices and footsteps crunching on leaves reached our ears from the path at my back, and his eyes shot up as he took a step away from me.

"Can I see you tonight?" he whispered.

I bit down on my lip. "Thorne, I—"

"Please, Empress. One last time."

My heart hammered so loud, I could hear it in my ears. Every beat whispered *yes*. Every thump of my pulse murmured his name.

Before him, I never listened to my heart. It was always the most selfish part of me, and a leader couldn't be selfish.

But perhaps one more time, I could be.

Swallowing hard, I met his gaze and nodded.

"Yes."

50

THORNE

A knock came from the door of my hut as I was packing a small bag for Marigold. "Come in," I shouted, and it opened with a click.

"Thorne, dear?" Mother's voice called.

I finished buckling the strap on the bag. "You're early, Mother." She had agreed to take Marigold for the night since I was expecting Clarissa. I'd told my mother I'd be out late in meetings with the Zelorias—I figured she wouldn't be too approving of the truth. But we were on the last days of this tour, and the thought of never having another moment with Clarissa...

I needed to say goodbye.

"I know. But you said you wanted to be updated on any progress," Mother replied, her voice a bit breathless. I peeked my head out into the hallway to see her standing with a small piece of parchment in her hand.

"Progress?"

"On your father."

My muscles immediately tensed. I strode across the floor to meet her, keeping my voice low to not disrupt Marigold playing with her dolls by the window. "Has someone found him?"

I wasn't even sure what I wanted to hear. Did I *want* to find him? Did I want him to be alive, or for the last remnants of him to be buried somewhere deep in Mysthelm soil?

She shook her head, and relief mixed with uneasiness stirred in my gut. "No, but it's more than I had last time. There are records from a cargo ship ledger stating a man by the name of Armand R. was aboard four years ago, but no mention of when he disembarked."

Armand Reaux. My father boarded a cargo ship but never got off?

"Where was the ship heading?" I asked.

Her eyes shifted from the parchment and back again to my face. "Unclear." She handed it to me.

> *The passenger in question, a man by the name of Armand R., paid thirteen gold coins to gain passage on the cargo ship transporting goods from the Island Territory to four other regions, one of which is unnamed. The ledger doesn't clarify which region he stopped at, and anything past this point is untraceable.*

My brow furrowed. "Four other regions? There are only three other territories it could have gone to. Unless—"

"It went to Veridia," Mother finished the thought for me.

"You think Father is in the Veridian Empire?"

Her shoulders fell, frustration lining her face. "I don't know what to think, Thorne. It shouldn't be possible. You would think we would know if people were going to and from the kingdom back then, but there's no other record of him. He can't have simply disappeared into thin air."

I thought about Nox, and how that Scarven governor could so easily send his own people to Mysthelm. What if we'd been shipping people and cargo over there as well, with nobody knowing about it?

"That would be just like him," Mother said with a sneer. "To leave us with his problems and run for the hills, starting a new life with *their* kind. As if he could get any lower."

Over the last three weeks, I'd developed defensive instincts toward the empire. So many people here spoke about Veridians with such contempt, and it made my hackles rise. "It's not their fault if he messed up his life so completely that he had to get away from Mysthelm," I countered. "Not everything about their empire is bad, Mother."

"Evidently your father would agree with you. Perhaps they will brainwash you next, if they haven't already," she snapped, ripping the parchment from my grip. "Come along, Marigold; it's getting late!" Mother moved away from me to help Marigold gather her toys, leaving me rearing from the sudden turn in conversation.

A gentle tap at the window behind them made my neck snap up. A flash of blonde hair appeared for a split second before vanishing just as quickly.

Mother looked back with a raised eyebrow.

"Grandma's right, it's time for bed," I said, drawing her attention away from the window.

Mother held my stare for a second longer, then looked down at Marigold to take her hand. A genuine beam—one only reserved for that little girl—split across Mother's stern features. "We're going to have so much fun tonight, sweetheart."

Marigold jumped up and down in excitement. "Can I have some of that chocolate candy we tried yesterday?" she begged.

"Maybe. But we can't tell your daddy, alright?"

Marigold put her finger over her lips and nodded, and the strange tension from before began to melt away as I watched them together.

"You two have a good time," I said softly. They waved back at me, my mother's gaze lingering on the window before they walked out the front door.

I let out a sigh and rubbed my temples. These moments with my mother lately left me confused and disoriented, never knowing quite how to read her anymore.

Those thoughts faded when another tap sounded behind me.

I smiled as I unlatched the window, ushering Clarissa in through the small opening.

"Was the front door not good enough for you?" I asked with a chuckle as she straightened and brushed leaves off her leggings and tight black shirt, her cheeks flushed and hair windswept.

"I figured I should be discreet." She shrugged, then eyed the door. "Plus, your mother kind of scares me."

"I know the feeling," I muttered.

Her forehead pinched. "Is everything alright?"

"Yes, it's just...she gets in these moods." I shook my head, needing to talk to someone about it. Galen was the person I always confided in, but he was currently refusing to speak to me.

I motioned for her to follow me to the couch. Its weight shifted as we both sat, and she tucked her feet under her, leaning her elbow on the back of it. She tilted her head to the side, those big dark eyes alert and attentive. I resisted the urge to draw her closer, resisted the thoughts of how right this felt. The two of us settling in after a long day, so mundane and casual.

In another life, perhaps.

"I haven't told you much about my father," I began. "He left us four years ago with no explanation, and we haven't heard from him since." Her eyes widened, but I brushed away her concern. "Trust me, it was ultimately for the best—he was a bad husband, and an even worse father."

I looked down at my hands. I'd never spoken these next words aloud, even to Galen. "For a long time, I never wanted to have children. Not when the only example of a father I had was the man who raised me. I refused to be anything like him, but was afraid I'd turn into him, anyway." I fingered the chain hanging around my neck. "I was more of an heir to him than a son. The child he was responsible for carving into some predetermined image he had in his mind of the future Lord Thorne Reaux, Regent of the North Territory. Someone like *him*. Cold, principled, strong."

I chuckled darkly and tightened my grip on the locket swinging at the end of the chain. "Well, *his* version of strong. To him, being a leader meant forming no attachments. Nothing that could get in the way of accomplishing your goals. I wasn't allowed to make friends, not unless they were approved by him—which is why Galen and the Zelorias were the only ones in my life up until a certain point. Even something as simple as a pet..."

I trailed off and snuck a glance at her, watching her lips curve down with every sentence. I thought back to that formative memory of my childhood, the one that finally snapped the tether on whatever affection I might have still had for the man.

"I found a rabbit once," I said. "Tucked away in our front gardens. It was so small, I could fit it in both of my hands, even as a ten-year-old. I made it a bed of hay in the corner of my room and fed him vegetable scraps from the kitchen. It was the first thing that had ever felt like *mine*. I named him Nutter, because the first time I saw him, he was chewing on nuts from the tree." Clarissa laughed softly at that. "I would watch him scuffle around my room or the kitchens, excited to see him exploring. In my head, I was giving him a good life. That made me proud, in a way.

"My father found out about him. He took me into his study and punished me, telling me how I needed to value only that which could make me stronger. Make me *greater*. Anything else was worthless. And then he stormed up to my room and took Nutter from his bed of hay."

Clarissa leaned in closer as I spoke, and her hand came out to rest on my knee, fingers digging in as if bracing for the rest of the story.

"I ran after him, crying and pleading to let the rabbit go, just let him be *free*, but that only solidified his point. He said I was weak for becoming so attached to something so inconsequential. I tried to argue that Nutter didn't make me weak; he made me happy— how could that be bad?" I swallowed thickly. "So, Father took him to his study, where he kept a large tank with his pet snake. Fates, I hated that thing." A shudder left me.

"He opened the lid, put Nutter inside, and said if he was strong, then I had nothing to worry about." My voice lowered. "He made me watch as his snake attacked and ate the rabbit."

Clarissa's fingers gripped my knee harder. "Thorne, that's—"

"It's the first time I knew what hatred felt like," I said, needing to get these thoughts out. "I hated him. But I also feared him. I feared *becoming* him. It wasn't until I got older that I realized he needed me as his heir, so he couldn't truly touch me. That sparked those rebellious years with Galen at my side, doing any and everything we could to drive our parents crazy. But still..." I paused and scrubbed my hand over my face, the roughness of my beard scratching my palm. "I don't know, I guess I've always held on to that fear. Even when he left us."

Eyebrows furrowed, Clarissa wrinkled her nose in disgust. "Thorne, you're *nothing* like him. He was cruel and vile. A coward hiding behind some archaic view of what men are supposed to be, only to run away in the end. How is that strength?" She scooted closer to me on the couch, forcing me to meet her eyes. "You are *warm*. You're gentle. Compassionate. You held on to that ten-year-old boy, no matter how hard he tried to force it out of you."

On instinct, I reached out to cover her hand that still rested on my knee. "I was thankful he left. I didn't want Marigold growing up seeing him and the way he treated those around him. Mother, however..." I grimaced. "She's been searching for him. I think she wants answers. Or even vengeance, for what he took from us. And if I know her, for the blow he dealt her pride, too."

"Has she found him?"

"That's what we were just talking about before you got here. Apparently, he was a gambler and got himself into massive debt right before he left. He took most of our life savings to pay off part of it, then disappeared. The last sign of him was a ledger from a cargo ship here on the island indicating he was on board, but no clue about where he got off. We have a sneaking suspicion it was the Veridian Empire."

"Four years ago?" she asked, straightening. "But that doesn't make sense. Gayl wanted nothing to do with Mysthelm back then. There's no way he would've allowed people to cross our borders."

I shrugged. "Maybe he didn't know about it. Didn't you say your friend Nox was sent here just this last week? Do you really think he and his governor got *permission*? Who knows how long travel between our lands has been going on undetected."

"Well, who knows if your father made it very far, either. After the way Gayl made outsiders look like the enemy, nobody back then would've been particularly receptive to the idea of your people just washing onto our shores. If they came to the wrong place, it would've been a bloodbath. I've seen them do *terrible* things to our own kind...but someone without magic? They'd rip you to shreds. You don't stand a chance against angry Veridians."

She glanced over at me. "Sorry, I'm not trying to sound morbid. It's just a very dangerous gamble to make." Standing, she began to pace in front of the couch. "Do you think it's still happening? People crossing between both our borders unprotected?"

"I suppose it could be. We both know Galen wouldn't have done anything to stop it."

"Of course he wouldn't. That would've required taking action. We all know how quick he is to do that."

I raised an eyebrow. "I sense some repressed anger coming to the surface."

She threw her hands in the air. "Yes, I'm angry. I've been angry for a long time, Thorne. And it's not just about the border cross-ing." Her shoulders rose and fell as she took a deep breath, her bare feet padding back and forth across the carpet.

"We keep saying we just need to get through this marriage, that once the curse is broken, it'll all be over. But breaking the curse isn't going to change anything, is it? This is just who he *is*. I know he's your best friend, and I know you want to defend him. Trust me, I keep doing the same thing. We can't change the kind of king he is. He claims to care about his people, but what he's doing now?" She flung a hand to the right, in the direction of his hut several doors down. "Hiding away for days, refusing to talk to anyone? *That* isn't what leadership looks like. He's *failed* you, Thorne. All of you. He shouldn't be your king."

I sighed and took her hand, making her stop pacing and turn to me. "But he is," I said simply.

Clarissa stared down at me, her chest heaving and eyes bright with resolve. Fates, she was beautiful like this. She was beautiful all the time, but so often when I looked at her, I saw that pacifying mask she wore. The one she thought others wanted to see, of the controlled, peaceful woman with a submissive gaze, instead of the fire I knew could burn them to the ground. She felt the need to hide her strong emotions, but something in my chest swelled at the thought that she'd never hidden them around *me*.

I pulled her to stand in between my legs, caging her in. She rested her hands on my shoulder as I gazed up at her. "I know it's hard for you to watch him fail his people when you've grown so attached to them. Because you *know* how they should be treated. I told you that day in the hedge maze that we'd be lucky to have you as our queen, and I meant it. But we shouldn't be your burden to bear."

"I just want him to be better for all of you," she whispered. "I wish I could *make* him better."

I chuckled softly. "If anyone could do it, it's you. By sheer will alone."

She bit down on her bottom lip. "I may have a control issue."

"You just feel deeply. That's not a bad thing, Empress," I said, brushing a strand of hair behind her ear.

Something darted across the window behind her, and I stiffened.

In one motion, I stood and pushed her behind me. I could have sworn I saw a dark cloak swish against the window, but it vanished as quickly as it came. Striding to the wall, I peered through the glass and into the night. A slight breeze brushed through the trees several yards out, and leaves skittered across the sandy dirt. I glanced down to find we'd left the window cracked after Clarissa crawled inside.

"I think it was just the wind," I said, closing the window and latching it tight.

"The last thing we need is someone running back to Galen telling him they saw us together," she said with a sigh. "I shouldn't even be here after what happened the other night."

"He was drunk," I said as I made my way back to her. "Probably making things up in his head to assuage his guilt over being an idiot."

She tilted her head and gave me a look. "We both know he's not making anything up, Thorne."

The memory of that night burned inside me, heating my blood with anger once again. "He shouldn't have said those things to you. No matter what the truth is," I said through clenched teeth.

A grin worked itself onto her lips as she took a step closer. "Usually, *I'm* the one knocking others out. It was nice to have someone else do it for a change."

Our chests brushed, and I let out a low hum, feeling it vibrate through our bodies. "You have a bit of a violent streak, don't you?"

"I blame the fox half," she murmured, eyes drifting to my mouth.

I pressed my thumb to her bottom lip and tugged it down, relishing her soft intake of breath. "Remind me never to get on your bad side, Empress." I released her lip, and her tongue darted out to swipe against it. "Or else you may threaten to cut the skin from *my* lips."

She scrunched her nose and shook her head with a laugh. "Fates, did I really say that to him?"

"Yes, you really did." I dipped my head to her ear. "And you have no idea what seeing you like that did to me."

A shiver went through her. "Perhaps *you* have a bit of a violent streak too, Lord Reaux."

"Only when it comes to you." I gently kissed her temple, the desire to take her and tuck ourselves away from the rest of the world so strong, it nearly took my breath away. But the image of that stray cloak against the window kept tugging at me, and the idea of someone watching us—watching *her*—made my protective instincts kick in.

"You should go, Clarissa," I said quietly. "We need to be more careful."

She rested her forehead against my chest, wrapping her arms around my waist. I held her tighter and propped my chin on the top of her head. The Hunt began tomorrow, and as soon as that was over, we would head back to the North Territory for the wedding.

And then she would be gone.

"Clarissa—"

"No, don't say anything," she whispered. "Just hold me."

There was nothing words could say that we didn't already know. Nothing that could fix this or make it right. Nothing except the feel of her against me one last time, of her heart beating to mine as the world around us kept moving forward.

I held her in my arms as long as time would allow, and then I watched her slip back into darkness, taking a piece of me with her.

51

CLARISSA

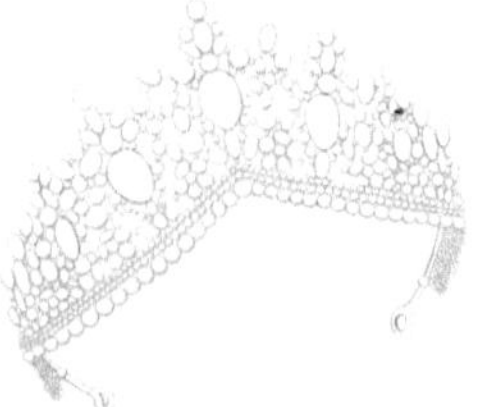

I was dragged from sleep well before dawn by two islanders and Devora, who gave me a grimace and a quick "I'm sorry," as the three of them ushered me out of the Base and to a strand of bamboo buildings about a mile east.

Sleep still clogged my eyes, my brain in that foggy, in-between stage where everything felt heavier. Devora shoved tea and a hot biscuit in my hand while the other two women took my measurements and disappeared into the back room of some sort of supply shop and armory all in one.

"To get you ready for the Hunt," one of them said.

I probably should've been more concerned about being dropped in the middle of a jungle for two days, but after everything I'd seen in my life, it didn't faze me. Nothing to really worry about.

But as the older of the two women passed me a pair of fighting leathers and placed numerous weapons into a large rucksack, I wondered what kind of a mess I was about to walk into.

"Do they expect me to fight an army of monkeys?" I muttered to Devora as she helped me pull on the leathers. There was a thick padding along the chest and shoulders, but the material was a stretchy, supple black fabric that melted into my skin.

"You can never be too careful," the older woman said from

several feet away. "It's more than animals haunting those jungles, girl."

The younger one let out a sigh as she tied the laces on my boots then looked up at me, her light blonde hair swinging over her shoulder at the motion. Hints of red dye were sprinkled throughout her braid, matching the beads around her neck. "Yvette's always been rather superstitious."

"Spirits never lie," Yvette countered, wagging her wrinkled finger.

I glanced down at the bag full of weapons. "And what exactly are these going to do against ghosts?"

"Oh, those are for the wild animals." Yvette shrugged. "There's nothing that can protect you against the spirits."

"Comforting."

The younger woman—I thought her name was Thalira—rolled her eyes. Yvette swatted at her with a stick of bamboo. "Don't disrespect them, girl. They've been around much longer than you."

"As have you, you quirky old bat," Thalira shot back.

"What are these spirits you're talking about?" I asked. I didn't necessarily believe in ghosts, but it was always interesting to hear the lore of the kingdom.

"Back in the War of Beginnings, the island was a common battleground between our two lands," Yvette started.

Thalira made her way to the back room, tossing an exasperated, "Here we go again," over her shoulder.

"It was mostly unoccupied and easy to get to from Veridia. Many battles were waged here on the northern and eastern coasts. Legends say there was so much bloodshed, the river waters ran red." There was a hint of eagerness in the elderly woman's voice. *Quirky old bat is right,* I thought.

"The number of lives lost on these shores is countless. Their spirits still rest among the sand and the leaves, a warning to those greedy for power. Some even think the Fates left a bit of their magic in the land to help the weary souls eventually find their rest." Yvette edged closer to me, her green eyes gleaming. "Others say it's cursed. Not everyone who enters the Hunt makes it out alive, girl."

A shiver crept down my spine, but I met her gaze, willing my face into nonchalance. "Well, I've had enough curses to last a lifetime."

Thalira strode back across the small room. "Oh, don't listen to her. Only one person has ever died during the Hunt, and it's because they accidentally stabbed themself in the hand, and it got infected. Quite the scary story," she said, wiggling her fingers mockingly. "There are no spirits or curses. Now, here." She held out the most beautiful bow I'd ever seen, smiling when my eyes widened. "All you have to worry about is hunting the blood stag."

I fingered the upper limb of the bow, which was a light wood painted gold and inlaid with delicate etchings of vines. The grip fit perfectly in my hand when I took it from her. She passed me the quiver, and I looked back up.

"There's only one arrow," I said.

"Hope you're a good shot," she responded.

We made our way out of the shop to the lines of people waiting outside, all ready to send me off. Hector and Daelan Zeloria stood right outside the shop entrance.

"I told you our people are very fond of this tradition," Hector said to me.

Dozens and dozens of families gathered on the busy street, waving colorful beads and torches above their heads. Excited smiles and lively conversation filled the morning air, charging it with anticipation that stirred in my gut.

Mother, Leo, Rose, and Nox all stood several feet away, looking just as taken aback by the buzz. Thorne was with Marigold and his mother off to the side. I felt his lingering stare on me as my eyes passed over him. A faint smile pulled at my lips until my gaze landed on Galen.

I hadn't seen him in three days. His hazel eyes gave away nothing. They simply held mine for a moment before he nodded tightly, then turned away.

I let out a sigh. I'd deal with him later.

Rose approached, her eyes narrowed as she looked over at the crowd. "These people are crazy," she whispered under her breath. I held back a snort. "How long do you have to stay out there?"

"Two days," I responded. "Or however long it takes for me to find the stag and kill it."

"I give it till tonight," Nox cut in. "I bet you'll be back before dark."

"No, it will take her at *least* a day without her Shifter half," Leo argued.

Nox studied my brother. "Willing to put your money where your mouth is?"

"How does three silver coins sound?" Rose interjected.

"I can tell you're all really going to miss me," I said with a laugh.

"If you don't come back, does that mean I get to be emperor?" Leo asked as he flung an arm over my shoulder. The heat from his cloak made me sweat just thinking about it, but I knew he had to hide his tail somehow. "Go get your prize, big sister," he said, pulling me into a hug.

The others wished me good luck as Hector and Daelan urged me toward a chariot pulled by a large golden-brown horse. Devora hurriedly stepped up to my side and handed me a second bag, this one full of imperishable foods, a canteen of water, rope, and a fishing hook. I shot her a quick smile of thanks before the roar of the crowd drowned out everything else. A chant worked its way down the street, faint at first, then stronger as more people joined in.

I squinted as I strained to make out the words. "Are they saying—"

"*Bring us blood! Bring us blood!*"

Devora and I exchanged a glance. These people *were* crazy.

She gave me a wry grin. "Good luck. Don't die."

This time, I couldn't help but snort. "Thanks, Devora. Always helpful."

I swung the golden bow across my back with the quiver, hooked both bags of supplies over my arm, and grabbed the handle of the chariot.

Two days. I could do this. Honestly, some time away from the secrets and pressure and *people* didn't sound too bad.

"Let's get this over with."

———

THE CHARIOT DRIVER left me at a waterfall just west of the entrance to the jungles. He told me someone would check in here every eight hours to see if I was ready for them to take me back to the main village square.

And then he was off.

The sound of rushing water, of birds whistling through the broad leaves and insects chirping along the thick stream mixed with the humidity of the island. It pushed against my skin, making my head buzz.

I took a deep breath of the warm, muggy air and faced east, toward the series of mountaintops in the distance and the canopy of low-hanging trees. I yearned for my Shifter senses—my heightened sight in the shadows, my ability to hear heartbeats in the distance, my speed and reflexes.

This must be what normal people felt like.

As I trekked through the jungle, my boots sloshed against shallow pools of water and vines tangled in my loose braid. I thought the island had been teeming with life back in the main village, but *here*...it was bursting. Monkeys swung from branch to branch, barely pausing to give me looks of curiosity as they chittered and picked at the tree trunks for bugs. Colorful birds swept in and out of the leaves with wide wings that came so close, they brushed my cheeks. The occasional snake slithered in the underbrush, and frogs leaped from beneath fronds when I crossed over the streams.

All four territories of Mysthelm were beautiful in their own ways, but this...this was my favorite. The wildness, the colors, the sounds. Knowing I was alone with no one to lead, no one around to see my masks, no hidden agendas lurking around the corner.

Even if my fox half wasn't here to enjoy it with me, I still pretended I could feel it just under my skin. I imagined claws pressing from my fingertips, felt sharp ears fluttering to every sound, and saw my black nose lifting in the wind.

I turned my eyes to the mountain range in the distance and began the Hunt.

52

CLARISSA

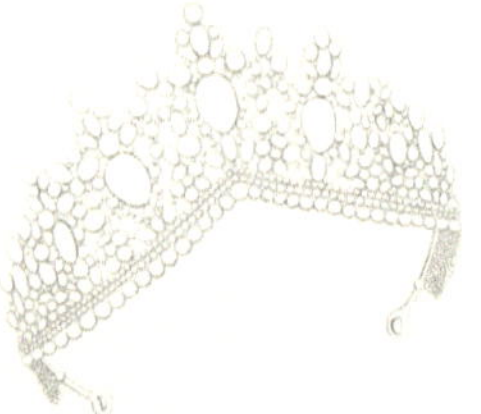

I went ten hours before catching a single sign of the blood stag. But then, I found tracks.

At the base of an enormous tree several miles from where I started were two faded hoof marks in the clumpy, wet dirt. I followed them through the underbrush until they disappeared into a thin flow of water in between bushes.

With a groan, I leaned against a nearby tree and took out a piece of dried meat from my rucksack, allowing myself a small capful of water. The sun was beginning to set behind me, highlighting the upcoming mountains in a dark golden glow.

I'd need to find shelter for the night soon. Without my ability to see in the dark, I'd be useless in the next hour or so.

As the sun continued its descent and the stars winked into existence, so did the evening creatures of the island. The cheerful swishing of animals through the leaves became more sinister in the fading light. Each snap of a twig made my muscles jolt; each brush of some unidentifiable object made me suck in a breath.

My fox would be laughing at me right now. Half of me was nocturnal, and here I was, afraid of the dark.

Or what could be hidden in the dark.

The wind carried whispers of rustling leaves and trickling water. The sound morphed as it flowed around my ears, a faint, breathy chant echoing in my mind.

Bring us blood.

Bring us blood.

Bring us blood.

A disembodied howl ripped through the air.

I jumped back, and my heel caught the end of a log. My ankle buckled, sending me to the damp ground. A grunt of pain escaped me as I tried to calm my racing heart. I reached out to grip the edge of the log and haul myself forward when my fingers closed around smooth, wet scales.

A snake darted away from my touch. I scrambled backward on my hands, letting out a string of curses.

It wasn't alone.

At the base of the log swarmed a nest of snakes, their tan and dark brown speckled scales gliding over one another, squirming in unrest. I froze, still leaning on the palms of my hands as my eyes darted across the scene.

Letting out a breath, I leaned forward with painstaking slowness to crouch on my heels. When the snakes stayed in their nest, I rose and took a single step back.

Then another.

And another.

The adrenaline racing through my veins evened out as I put several feet of distance between us. My eyes shut in relief when I felt for both my packs and the arrow, finding them all intact.

Something brushed against my knee.

I opened my eyes and glanced down to see a brown, scaled tail winding up my thigh.

Before I could blink, the snake lunged.

Sharp fangs sank into my neck. An ear-splitting scream flew from my lips as I wrenched it off my body by the head, but its lower half was still wrapped around my leg. It thrashed and writhed, coiling even tighter in defense, and my thigh throbbed with loss of circulation.

With a shaking hand, I yanked a dagger free from its sheath and plunged it through the snake's neck. Its body went limp. I flung the head as far from me as I could, and with a frightened sob, I unwound its lower half from my leg and kicked it aside.

Blood trickled from my wound and darkened the front of my leathers. I lifted a hand to my neck, pulling back fingers coated in blood.

My breaths came out in short spurts. I had no clue what kind of snake it was—what kinds of snakes even inhabited this foreign island. Was it poisonous? Had it nicked something vital? How deep had it bitten?

The sun had completely vanished. Moonlight filtered in overhead, giving barely enough light for me to see the trees in front of me. I turned, searching for any sort of shelter to stop for the night.

To my right was a slow stream, its water lapping gently as it flowed toward the coast.

Up ahead was the shadowed outline of the mountain range.

To my left was a pair of bright yellow eyes.

I screamed and launched myself backward, only to realize it was an owl resting on a low branch.

Gazing up at the tree, I saw several nearby branches and one thick, sturdy one several yards above my head. My limbs were shaking, but I gripped the first branch as tightly as I could and pulled myself up. I took it one branch at a time until I reached the largest one, then dragged my legs over the curve of the rough bark.

I was panting by the time I straightened my back against the thick trunk. Either I was woefully out of shape, or that snake bite was getting to me.

I gingerly felt for the two small holes in my neck, wincing at the stab of pain that shot through me. The wound had begun to clot at least, which I told myself was a good sign.

Taking the rope from my bag, I tied myself to the branch so I wouldn't slip off in the middle of the night, then tugged my weapons close to my chest.

Exhaustion and adrenaline warred inside every crevice of my body, making my head swim and throb. Pain pulsed from my neck with each heartbeat.

I hope I'm not dead by morning.

With that bright thought, my exhaustion won out, and I slipped into a restless sleep.

———

Well, I was still alive.

But when my eyes opened to the balmy island morning, my entire body was racked with shivers. A sweat had broken out on my forehead, and my temples, chest, and neck pounded like someone was hitting them with a boulder.

I winced as I turned my neck to undo the rope around my waist. When I reached up to feel the snake bite, raised, bumpy flesh met my fingertips. I pulled them back and grimaced at the pus and dried blood.

A wave of nausea hit me. I swallowed hard, shoving back the fear and panic that threatened to overwhelm me.

I probably had a fever, but I could still move.

I *definitely* had an infection, but if I could get back to the Base within the next few hours, a healer could help.

The sun was rising from the east, so I made my way down the tree with my supplies and faced west, back toward the waterfall I was dropped off at. With each passing step, sweat dripped from my neck and head, the sunlight searing my eyes while chills continued to travel down my back. After a few minutes, my legs were trembling so badly, I had to use a broken branch as a walking stick.

"I hate this island," I muttered in an effort to distract myself from my hazy vision. "And I hate snakes." I kicked aside a large rock.

My mind wandered to the story Thorne had told me about his father feeding his rabbit to the snake. Thinking about *him* helped to keep me from spiraling. He grounded me, even when he wasn't here.

I thought back to that night in the hedge maze. I'd barely known him and had *no* reason to trust him. But he'd trusted me. He went against his king's wishes to tell me about the curse. He knew I deserved more than to be left with half-truths, something I wasn't sure I ever truly thanked him for.

He saw my panic attacks. He saw the side of me others ran from in disgust. He saw my uncertainty when all I gave others was their idea of perfection. He saw my anger, my fear, my clumsiness, my desires, my pain...even when I tried to force him to stop.

He had *always* seen me.

Without even knowing, without *trying*, he'd helped me stop fighting the idea of needing someone. Of leaning on them. I'd always thought that to be a good leader—a *powerful* woman—I couldn't show vulnerability.

He was right—that wasn't true at all. My emotions weren't a weakness.

I hated it when he was right. I hated that I couldn't stop thinking about him.

And I hated that I had to leave him.

I let out a sigh, blinking hard against the sun as I made my way through the jungle. "This is why we don't talk to handsome men" —I swiped a vine away from my face—"with handsome hair"—I kicked a rock out of the path—"and handsome teeth." I stomped through the thick grass and leaves, ignoring the dull ache in my neck and the way the ground swayed before me. "It doesn't matter if I'm in love with him, I have to—"

I stopped in my tracks.

Oh, Fates.

I was in love with him.

A twig snapped behind me.

I whirled around, but there was nothing there. The bushes to the right rustled as the sound of steps padding against dirt reached my ears.

"I don't have time for this," I mumbled, cupping my hand around my neck to feel pus slowly oozing from the wound. I gripped my dagger in my other hand. "If you want to be the first thing to try and kill me this morning, come on out," I called.

The jungle stilled, with nothing but the sound of my ragged breaths to break the silence.

When nothing moved, I took a step forward.

A blade swished through the trees, narrowly avoiding my left ear.

"You missed," I shouted, then grabbed the other blade at my thigh.

A masked figure in all black came lunging from the bush. I staggered out of the way before they could crash into me, the sudden movement making my stomach lurch.

Fight it. You have to fight it, Rissa, I screamed at myself, willing my muscles to work. Adrenaline kicked in and fought against the sluggish fever, but my motions were still choppy.

My assailant came at me again with another knife. They threw a punch at my head with one hand and swiped at my waist with the other. I ducked and blocked their arm, slicing a thin line at their wrist with one of my twin daggers. They let out a low hiss and snatched their hand back. I aimed a kick at their stomach, but my balance was so off that I barely nicked their side. With a grunt, they grabbed my extended foot and yanked me forward until I was sprawled on my stomach in the dirt.

The force rocked a gasp from me. *Get up!* I ordered myself, blinking away the fog from my mind. I quickly flipped onto my back as my attacker jumped on top of me, straddling my waist. They wrapped their hands around my throat, and I let out a strangled cry at the pain that reverberated from my wound.

From this close, I could tell it was a man. While the rest of his face was hidden by the mask, gray-blue eyes stared down at me from beneath bushy brows. They narrowed as he pushed harder, causing my vision to go in and out of focus.

I thrashed against his hold and brought my knees up to shove into his back, but that only made him press his fingers deeper into my neck. Searing pain shot through my chest when I tried to draw a breath. My shouts came in croaked bursts as the fight swiftly faded from my limbs.

I should be wondering how the assassin got here when we'd been so careful. I should be thinking through his motives and his weak points, searching for clues on how to read him.

But all I could think about was how tired I was. How every part of me begged to rest.

And of course, I thought about Thorne. *Always him.* How I'd never get to see him again. How I'd never get to tell him I loved him. Not that it made any difference in the end, but still...he deserved to know. He deserved to know he was more than enough, and he didn't have to live in the shadow his father cast over him.

Fight for me, Empress.

His voice wafted through my mind, caressing me, filling the painful spaces that hurt too much to lift on my own.

Come back to me.

I let out a whimper and flexed my outstretched hand. My fingers dug into the dirt at my side. As the man leaned in closer, I wrenched my arm up and threw a handful of sand into his eyes.

He fell backward with a howl. I sucked in as much air as I could, tears stinging my eyes and lungs burning in my chest. Wiggling out from beneath him, I snatched his dagger along with mine and kicked him in the head, sending him to his back. My vision swam as I tried to right myself and took off in the opposite direction.

Find the waterfall. Find the waterfall. I could hardly keep one foot in front of the other, but I thought I was heading west. *Just keep going.* He had to have gotten here somehow. Maybe he'd left a horse somewhere nearby I could use.

I tripped over a log and caught myself before bashing my head on a rock. I wiped away the hair from my face with shaking, sweaty hands.

Focus. You're not dying. You're just tired.

Sure, Rissa. Let's go with that.

Fates, now I was talking to myself.

Footsteps sounded behind me. I let out a weak growl and cursed myself for not killing him the first time.

The man let out a sharp cry.

With a wince, I craned my neck back to find him. This time when I stumbled, I fell straight to my knees.

I saw death.

Rotted, blackened death. And it was moving. Just like the hill in the Mid Territory.

The curse crawled like a slow tide across the jungle floor. The once vibrant, green, leafy trees that hovered above me were now sucked into its path, instantly rotting before my eyes. Black rot overtook the trunks from the roots upward, as if someone were twisting their branches into gnarled lumps.

Small streams dried up, birds and snakes and other animals fell dead from the branches, and green grass crumpled to dirt. The magic pulsing from its depths was a hundred times stronger than the rotted fields and rivers I'd healed before.

It was still many yards behind me, but my attacker was mere feet from its edge.

"Help me!" the man pleaded, eyes locked on me. He pumped his legs and stretched out his hand, his arm straining for rescue.

It was too late.

The black edge of the curse brushed against his heel, and in a single breath, his body went still. He crashed to the ground as the rot spread from his ankles to his head. The small space of skin around his eyes was the only thing I could see before it went ashen, pieces of him flaking off and drifting in the wind.

I blinked back my disgust and took a few unsteady steps forward until my hands crossed over the curse. My magic swept through my body, filling me with relief and strength as it immediately worked to fight against the poison.

I expected the edges of the curse to stop, to disappear and heal as it had back in the Mid Territory.

But...it wasn't stopping.

It was slow, but still, it kept moving past me, covering anything in its path and killing it instantly.

Fear barreled into me, mixing with my flood of magic. I had to get back to the village. I *had* to warn the others.

If we couldn't stop it, it was going to take over the entire island.

I squared my shoulders and shifted.

53

THORNE

"Thorne, can we talk for a moment?"

I turned at the sound of Galen's voice, pausing on my walk back to my hut. He hadn't been willing to speak with me since the night I punched him. I hadn't even seen him until everyone gathered on the outskirts of the village to send Clarissa off on the Hunt early yesterday morning. It appeared he'd finally chosen to come out of hiding.

"Of course," I said.

He motioned for me to follow him, and we walked to the stables on the far end of the Base. Two horses were waiting for us, and we mounted them before taking off and tracing a path down to the now-familiar markets and shops of the main village.

"Where are your mother and Marigold today?" he asked.

"With some of the families farther inland. Marigold has made quite a few friends here."

Out of the corner of my eye, I saw a faint smile on Galen's lips. "That doesn't surprise me."

We fell into silence once more as we trotted along, discomfort shifting around us. We passed the village square when he finally said, "Thank you for helping to cover things up after the...incident the other night." He cleared his throat. "I was out of line. I'm sorry for the things I said to you and Clarissa, and for what I did to the maid…" A sigh left him as he scrubbed a hand down his tired face. "I wanted to find her to apologize, but Clarissa warned me not to go anywhere near the maid again. Between you and me, that woman terrifies me."

I hummed in casual agreement, keeping my eyes straight ahead. "She is rather extraordinary," I murmured.

Another awkward pause followed until Galen asked, "You're in love with her, aren't you?"

An ache formed in my chest at the words. I'd been expecting them. I knew this conversation would be coming if he remembered anything from his drunken stupor that night, and I'd already promised myself I wouldn't lie to him. Things were far too strained between us as it was.

"Yes," I said simply.

He didn't respond, merely nodded. We rode past small buildings and open markets with people selling their wares, the scents of nearby taverns and food stalls opening for lunch filling the air around us. Soon, we left behind the street Clarissa had departed from yesterday, making our way farther east. A small hill appeared before us, with a strand of bamboo buildings visible at the top.

"You know why I have to marry her, Thorne," he said.

"I know."

He nodded again, as if that were the only way we knew how to communicate anymore. "And the things I said that night, I wasn't—"

"Galen." I tugged on the reins to stop my horse, and Galen halted abruptly, turning to face me. Clarissa's heated words from when she'd finally let her true feelings show the other night came back to me, and I hated how accurate they were.

"I'm through listening to your excuses," I said. "And I'm through defending you. I've done that our entire lives. That woman is the best thing that could ever happen to you *and* to this kingdom. You *will* respect her, even if you don't love her."

"I know, Thorne." He looked down at his gloved hands wrapped around the reins, then back up at me. "I—I don't know what's wrong with me. But I'll be better. Once this curse is broken, I'll—"

"It's not about the *curse*, Galen; it's about *you*," I snapped. Clarissa was right. "You've been using it as an excuse for almost nine months to hide from your responsibilities as king, but when that's gone, what will you blame next? If you can't figure out how to rule your people in the hard times, what makes you think you deserve to in the good?"

Galen's eyes sharpened as he met mine. He opened his mouth to respond when a handful of men came riding down from the tall incline in front of us with shouts of terror and galloping hooves.

"It's the blight!" one of them yelled, his voice ragged. "Coming from the jungles!" He pointed to the east, beyond the hill.

"Everywhere," another wheezed. He kept glancing over his shoulder. "It—it's moving. Got one of our hunters."

"It's *moving*?" I snapped my gaze up to the jungles they pointed to.

Where Clarissa was currently alone.

I leaned over and gripped Galen's elbow. "She's in there," I said through gritted teeth. "And this is *killing* people."

His hands shook as he twisted them in his reins. "I don't—I can't *control* it, Thorne. I've never been able to. You know that."

"It's heading this way!" one of the men shouted. "We have to move!"

I held Galen's stare for a second longer.

"Show us," I commanded the man.

Galen and I followed them up the hill, urging our horses as fast as they could go. I wasn't sure how far out Clarissa had gone, but every passing moment caused terror to swell in my gut. We reached the top of the grassy incline and crested the hill, the buildings I'd seen before now clearly in sight.

The hunters led us past the small community and to a ledge overlooking the jungle and mountains beyond.

That's when we saw it.

Below us and miles to the east crept darkness, almost as if a blanket were covering the land. It spilled over the jungle floor like ink.

And everything behind it…rotted.

Dead and shriveled, with the signs of the curse I'd come to recognize in the past nine months evident in the blackened trees and decaying branches.

Galen cursed under his breath. "They were right. It's moving."

I'd only seen that happen once before. Then, it stopped when Clarissa touched it. Where was she now?

Our horses must have sensed our apprehension, for they anxiously pawed at the ground and tossed back their heads.

A small crowd had gathered at our backs at the commotion. Several gasps echoed around us as people began to see the curse.

"What's going on?"

"How did this happen?"

"It's the blight! Is that even *possible*?"

Whispers quickly turned to panic. Some of the people found Galen at the edge, and hope flared to life in their features.

"King Grimaldi!"

"Are you here to help us?"

"We need to get out of here! What should we do?"

His ashen face swiveled between them, then his eyes found mine in desperation. He blinked at me as his lips fell open and shut again. "I—I don't—"

"It's getting closer," one of the hunters rushed out. "What will you have us do, Your Majesty?"

Galen's hands clenched around his reins, his eyes locked on the curse heading toward us.

"Your Majesty?" the man prodded. Those nearest glanced around in wariness.

These people were looking to him to lead. To save them.

His forehead creased, but no words came out.

I pulled at my reins and shifted the horse to face the hunters.

"One of you, gather every able-bodied rider and horse up here and—"

A sharp cry sounded from my right, and I turned to see them pointing at the jungle.

Where a red fox sprinted from the dense, green expanse.

54

CLARISSA

I smelled them before I saw them.

Up on the hill ahead stood Thorne, Galen, and a small crowd of islanders, dismay etched on their faces as they gazed upon the oncoming curse. I bounded my way up on all fours, then shifted midair, only pausing to catch my breath.

The strangers backed up in alarm. A couple of them clutched one another's arms, their wide eyes and frozen expressions taking in me and my magic.

I didn't have time for their fear.

Thorne immediately grabbed my shoulders, his eyes frantic and searching. They roamed over my body, the tick in his jaw giving away his panic. "You're covered in blood, Clarissa. Please tell me it's not yours." His hold on me tightened, and my heart leaped. "Actually, I'm not sure if that would be any better."

"It was a snake bite, but I'm fine now, I promise," I assured him. "Shifters heal fast. It's already gone."

I didn't want to tell him how close to death I would've been if I hadn't absorbed the curse's magic in time.

I squeezed his hand once before pulling away and facing everyone. All eyes locked on me as I raised my voice. "We need to get to the western shore. You, you, and you"—I pointed to the three men on horseback behind Thorne and Galen—"round up every horse, carriage, or wagon you can find and get the people up here down to the main village. And we have to warn the Zelorias. Someone needs to find them so we can coordinate ships at the port for departure. Thorne—"

"I'm sorry, did you say *departure?*" one of the islanders asked.

I leveled him with a stare. "Unless you know of a way to stop this," I brandished an arm at the still-moving edge of the blight, "I'm afraid your island isn't safe anymore."

Stunned outbursts rustled among the crowd, but thankfully, the three men I'd given orders to began to take charge and gather everyone.

"Why didn't it stop when you touched it?" Thorne whispered.

"I don't know," I said, forcing back panic. "It's strong. Stronger than anything I've felt before."

He closed his eyes and clenched his jaw. When he opened them again, determination shone back at me. "What do you need from me, Empress?"

"We need to get my family and Nox," I rushed out. "If we can't slow it down, then at the very least, we can save anyone who might get caught in it. And Nox can get a better view from up above of where it's impacted so far."

Thorne tilted his head. "Why? What can Nox do?"

"He's a dragon Shifter."

He blinked. "Of course he is."

Galen cleared his throat. "How can I help?"

My eyes slid to his, my voice cold. "Not hiding away in your room would be a great start."

Thorne stepped between us. "We don't have time for this. Do what she says. Let's go back to the village and find Daelan and Hector."

I held Galen's stare for another moment. It was a battle of wills —the King and the Empress. I knew he wouldn't take my barging in here and giving orders to his people—to *him*—lightly, but he had to realize what was at stake.

And that he wasn't strong enough to save them.

His jaw stiffened as he gave a single nod, then mounted his horse once more. "We'll meet you at the docks," he said before snapping the reins and galloping off in the other direction.

When everyone was out of eyesight, Thorne reached for my waist and pulled me closer. "Find my family, Thorne," I whispered, cupping his cheek. "We can't let this hurt anyone else."

"I will." He quickly kissed my palm. "What will you do?"

"What do you think?" I gave him a small smirk and pushed away to give myself enough space. "I'm going to lead them."

In the blink of an eye, I launched myself into the air and shifted.

———

THE NEXT HOUR WAS A BLUR.

I ran to the Base as quickly as I could to find the island's guard station, where I shifted—to their utter shock—and relayed the situation. I ordered them to split up among the neighborhoods and businesses to inform the citizens of the evacuation plan and get as many people as possible to the western shore.

At the docks, Galen and the Zeloria brothers were already working on getting the ships ready. Deckhands were tossing as much cargo as they could onto the shore to make room for the mass of people the ships would have to carry. Smaller dinghies were being pulled from storage sheds, along with any and every vessel that could be used to make it across to the other territories. I'd suggested the Zelorias send a couple of messengers ahead on a swift fishing boat to deliver word to the Silenus and Penworth regent families about the incoming horde of people. It was going to be a nightmare to figure out accommodations, but that could be sorted out once everyone was safe.

An enormous burst of wind almost knocked me off balance as I started to head back to the Base. Screams ripped through the air behind me, and I spun around, expecting to see the curse having already reached us.

It wasn't the curse.

The summer sun glinted off navy-blue and silver scales. The air shook as two wings, each three times as long as my body, beat in tandem. A spiked tail slashed over the tips of trees, slowly descending until four paws landed in the sand with enough force to make the ground tremble.

At least a dozen people jumped off the back of the dragon and staggered away, mixed expressions of terror, awe, and relief on their faces. In the next breath, Nox shifted back to his human form and ran toward me.

"I see you found the curse."

"It's incredible," he breathed out. "Well, not the curse. But my *magic*. It's really back."

I motioned to the frightened villagers who'd climbed off him. "How did you convince those people to let you carry them?"

"Told them it was either get on, or I'd burn them to a crisp."

"Can you really do that? Breathe *fire*?"

He shrugged. "Wouldn't you like to know?"

I rolled my eyes. "How far has the curse spread?"

"I got a view of the entire island before I found this group fishing off the south coast." He motioned to the people he'd carried here. "I think it started over in the eastern mountains, and it's already gotten that entire coastline. It's about halfway across the island now. And it's picking up speed." He swallowed. "Clarissa, this—this is unlike anything I've ever seen."

"I know," I said grimly.

Halfway across? Fates, that was worse than I'd expected. I thought through courses of action, weighing my options. "Look, the priority is getting everyone off the island. Can you circle around again and pick up anyone who may be lingering too far out of the way?"

He nodded, but before he could shift back, I grabbed his arm.

"The magic won't last forever. Don't forget to absorb more if you feel it waning."

"I know, Rissa."

"Be careful!" I called out as he strode off, jumped into the air, and shifted back into his dragon form. "Show-off," I muttered under my breath.

I spent the next few minutes updating the Zelorias and Galen on the status of the curse. Urgency mounted with every passing moment. Panic clawed just beneath my skin and in the rustling wind around me, pressing in on all sides. But as more people came up to me with questions, problems, and requests for instruction, I had to rein it in. I couldn't lose control, couldn't let them see me crumble. Not when they were looking to me for guidance. For hope.

That was all I'd ever wanted to bring them.

I shoved aside the anxiety and stayed their solid anchor, unmoving despite the clouds of fear billowing in.

Until I heard his voice.

"Clarissa!" Thorne shouted from the tree line behind me. I whirled around, my stomach lurching up my throat at the sheer despair in his tone.

I rushed to meet him. "What's wrong?"

"It—It's Marigold," he choked out. His dark hair hung limp around his face, his blue eyes ragged and lips parted. "I can't find her."

55

CLARISSA

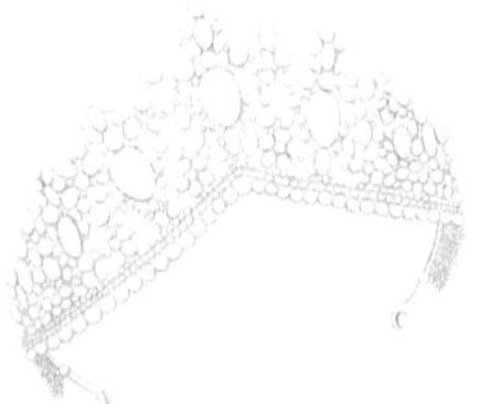

My forced composure threatened to snap. Alarm swept through me like a tidal wave, terror breaking the surface and gripping my heart.

"Nobody knows where she or my mother went," he said. "I—I have to find them. I can't—"

"Thorne! What is it?" Galen asked from my left.

I swallowed hard. "He can't find Marigold or Azura."

Galen staggered backward with wide eyes, as if the words hit him like a blow to the chest. I knew he loved that little girl, and the guilt of it—of *all* of it—was probably crushing him. It was only a matter of time until he broke.

Blood drained from his face, but he sucked in a breath and straightened his spine. "We'll find her. I'll help." His gloved hands gripped Thorne's shoulders tight. "We *will* get her back, Thorne. I promise you."

"Where were they seen last?" I asked.

Thorne ran a shaking hand through his hair. "In a forest a little northeast of the Base."

Another spike of panic shot down my heart. That was close to the hill near the eastern jungle, and Nox said the curse had already spread halfway across the island.

425

"Get on your horses and follow me." Without another warning, I shifted and took off.

I tore through the island, faintly aware of two sets of horse hooves pounding on the ground behind me. It was difficult to track Marigold since I hadn't been around her in my fox half and didn't have a great idea of her specific scent, but I recalled her as best I could, searching for any sign along the terrain.

When we passed the Base, my magic began to fade. That golden light dimmed to a flickering candle, leaving a chill in its wake that spread from my chest and out into my limbs.

Come on, I thought to myself. *Just a little farther*.

I pushed my legs as fast as they would carry me, whipping through trees and jumping over logs. Holding on to my magic was like trying to cup a stream of water in the palm of my hand—it kept slipping between my fingers, draining inch by inch.

For a split second, my body involuntarily shifted to human, then back to a fox once more, like a stuttering heartbeat. I tripped over my tangle of limbs and barely managed to stay on my feet.

But then...

There.

The faintest scent of dirt mixed with florals, like the perfume I'd smelled on Azura over the weeks.

And blood. So much blood.

I put on a final burst of speed and lunged through a copse of bushes and into a nearby clearing, shifting to my human form with my last ounce of magic.

I followed the trail of dark blood and crushed grass until I found Azura leaning against a tree trunk.

"Please!" she cried out when she saw me. "You have to find her!" Her voice shook, her face streaked with tears and dark kohl. I glanced down to see her ankle caught in some sort of animal trap.

"What *happened?*"

"The others—they ran when it...when the blight came, and she —" Azura cut herself off and gritted her teeth. I knelt down and tried to wrench the jaws of the trap open, but it was shut tight, its teeth digging into the muscles of her ankle and calf.

"She ran. I think she was—was afraid," Azura continued, breath labored. "I tried to chase her and—got caught." Hooves sounded at my back as Galen and Thorne entered the clearing. Thorne didn't even wait until his horse stopped before he leaped to the ground and sprinted over to us.

"Mother! Mother, are you alright?" He immediately reached for her ankle, wrenching the jaws apart just enough for her to slip her foot out. "Where is Marigold?"

With a quaking finger, Azura craned her neck and pointed to the jungle behind her.

Darkness crawled from the trees in the back, the edge of the curse making its way toward us.

"Thorne, get your mother out of here," I said on an exhale, my eyes fixed on the approaching black line. It was maybe a quarter of a mile out, and Nox was right—it had picked up speed.

"Clarissa, you—"

"Go!" I shouted, whipping back to face him. My eyes pleaded with his, a desperation I'd hardly felt before pushing inside my chest. "It can't hurt me. But it can hurt *you*. I need you to leave, Thorne."

It was bad enough that Marigold was in danger, and I couldn't focus with him here, knowing at any second he could get sucked into the curse. Knowing I may not be there to save him.

He stood. "That's my daughter, Clarissa. I can't leave her." His head shook as he clenched his fists at his sides. "That's my little girl," he whispered, his voice breaking at the end. Those blue eyes bore into mine as his entire body trembled.

I gripped each side of his head, forcing him to meet my stare. "I know, Thorne. I *know*. And *I will bring her back*." I pushed my forehead to his. "Do you trust me?" I'd asked him that once before, but this...this was different.

His hand lifted to cup the back of my neck. "With her life."

"Then go." I released him. "Get your mother to the docks. We'll meet you there."

"I'm going with you." To my surprise, Galen stepped forward, quickly averting his gaze from mine and Thorne's display of affection. "It can't hurt me either. Not when I created it."

Azura grabbed my hand. Her eyes, identical to Thorne's, held mine, and for once I didn't see the coldness that so often lingered there.

"Thank you," she whispered.

I nodded. With one last look at the two of them, Galen and I turned on our heels and ran for the jungle.

"This is hunting land," Galen said, breaths uneven. "There are traps and snares everywhere. Watch your step."

"I'm more concerned about Marigold," I huffed out, but made sure to keep an eye out for any potential traps.

We rounded the nearest tree, and that was when I heard it.

A scream.

Horrible visions flew across my mind. A snare cutting into her little leg, rot seeping into her skin, animals snatching her in their jaws.

"Daddy! Daddy, help!" her scared voice rang out.

Galen and I picked up speed, leaping over logs and knocking branches and vines from our path. We careened around another corner, and—

There she was.

"Marigold!" I shrieked.

She was suspended midair inside a net that swayed from a large tree branch. Her hands clawed at the material as she sobbed, her brown hair filled with twigs and tears streaming down her cheeks.

Galen inhaled sharply. "Clarissa, *look*." He pointed a finger, and I followed it until I saw the line of black several trees away.

Heading straight for Marigold.

"Come on!" I shouted to him. We clambered to her, but she was hanging too high up for us to reach. I ran to the trunk and dug my fingers into the bark, searching for any foothold to grab on to. Slowly, *too* slowly, I scaled my way up the tree and hauled myself over the limb holding the net.

I wasn't fast enough. The curse was so close, I could throw a rock and hit it. Birds fell like dead weight from the sky mere feet away, the canopy of trees caving in on themselves as they succumbed to the rot.

"Hold on, Marigold!" I yelled, climbing on all fours across the wide limb. When I reached the net, I pulled one of my daggers from the sheath on my thigh and started sawing through the material.

The curse crept closer.

My breaths were sharp in my chest. Sweat beaded and fell from my forehead onto my outstretched hands.

"Clarissa, hurry!" Galen shouted below.

There wasn't enough time. We weren't going to be able to escape it.

"Marigold, as soon as I get this loose, I need you to grab my hand," I instructed her. Her wide eyes stared up at me in horror, but she nodded, already reaching out her arm to grasp mine.

The jungle floor below her turned black.

"Are you ready?" I asked, making one final swipe at the net.

The skin on her right arm began to flake.

She nodded.

A crack appeared on her cheek, and her body swayed.

Snap. "Now, Marigold!"

The net fell open to release her to the ground. I lunged for her outstretched hand.

I let out a cry as her weight hung limp in my grasp, but still, I held on. The curse siphoned from her and barreled into me, igniting my magic. In the next second, she sucked in a strangled breath, kicking her legs as she realized where she was.

"Marigold, hold still!" I shouted. With a burst of my Shifter strength, I lugged her onto the branch with me and cradled her to my chest. A sob tore from my throat as I weaved my fingers through her hair.

"You're okay. I've got you, sweet girl. You're safe," I kept murmuring into the top of her head, soothing her tears and the cries that racked her body.

"Where's my daddy?" she finally said with a hiccup as she pulled back to look at me.

"He's waiting for you. He and your grandmother. Uncle Galen is there down the tree—do you think you can be brave and climb down with me?"

She swallowed and wiped at her eyes with the back of her hand. I made sure to keep a steady grip on her other arm. With a sniff, she nodded.

"Marigold, I need you to listen to me." I tapped her chin to look up at me. "No matter what happens, you *have* to keep touching me, okay? I know it sounds strange, but do you see this scary darkness that's spreading?" I gestured over the branch to the curse that had now passed us. To my relief, Galen was right —it didn't seem to affect him, for he stood below us, looking up with a deep crease on his features. "You know how I come from the Veridian Empire across the sea? Well, that gives me special powers. And the scary darkness doesn't hurt me. As long as you're touching me, it can't hurt you either. Do you understand?"

She nodded again as she leaned forward and clung to my neck.

Thank goodness I had my Shifter strength and agility back, or I might not have been able to climb down the tree with her in my arms. We made it to the bottom, and I switched her to my back, making sure she held on to my neck tight before Galen and I sprinted back the way we came.

We quickly passed the edge of the dead, rotted land and kept going into uncursed territory, and I thanked the Fates we were still faster than it. For now.

Although, I supposed it was their fault we were in this mess in the first place.

When we reached the back entrance of the Base, I let out a growl as Thorne scrambled out of the circle of huts.

"I told you to go to the docks!" I shouted, glancing behind my shoulder to see if the curse was gaining on us yet. I couldn't see it, but that didn't mean it wouldn't appear soon. Marigold slid down my back and grabbed my hand when she saw Thorne nearing.

"Turns out I'm just as stubborn as you, Empress." A tear tracked down his cheek as he collided with us.

His arms wrapped around me and Marigold at my side, pulling her in between us in a hug that threatened to squeeze the life out of me.

"Your family is safe at the docks, ready to go. And they have Mia," he reassured me. "But I couldn't wait with them. I had to know you were alright." He bent to kiss the top of Marigold's head, all while keeping a hand on me. Marigold jumped up to embrace his neck, and he scooped her into his arms. Still, she clutched my thumb in her small hand.

"*Thank you*," Thorne mouthed to me over her head.

All I could do was nod. I thought my heart was going to burst out of my chest.

Tears streamed down my cheeks as I took in a shaky breath. We could have lost her. If we'd been only a couple minutes later, the curse would have gotten her. I couldn't imagine life without this little girl. Without *both* of them. They were so deeply embedded inside me, so twisted in the fabric of my being, I couldn't untangle them even if I wanted to.

Was this what Leo and Rose had? The kind of love that made it hard to breathe, that made every heartbeat call out for them. That had you throwing caution to the wind and leaping heart first when your head had always been the one to take the lead.

The words bubbled on the tip of my tongue.

The words I ached to say, even if they wouldn't change anything.

"Thorne, I—"

"Clarissa," Galen's voice rumbled behind us.

I quickly released my hold on Thorne and Marigold and spun to face him, wiping the tears from my dirt-covered cheeks. His lips were set into a thin line.

"Clarissa, this—this is all because of me. Everything that's happened to these people, that *could* have happened to Marigold... it's my fault." He choked on his words as he swallowed hard. "There's only one way to stop it." His eyes flitted between Thorne and me. "You know what we have to do. And we have to do it as soon as possible."

A dead weight settled in my stomach.

He was right. I always knew it was coming, but a part of me never let myself dwell on it. Never let myself peel back the curtains that separated dreams from reality.

Galen let out a breath. "We have to get married. Tomorrow."

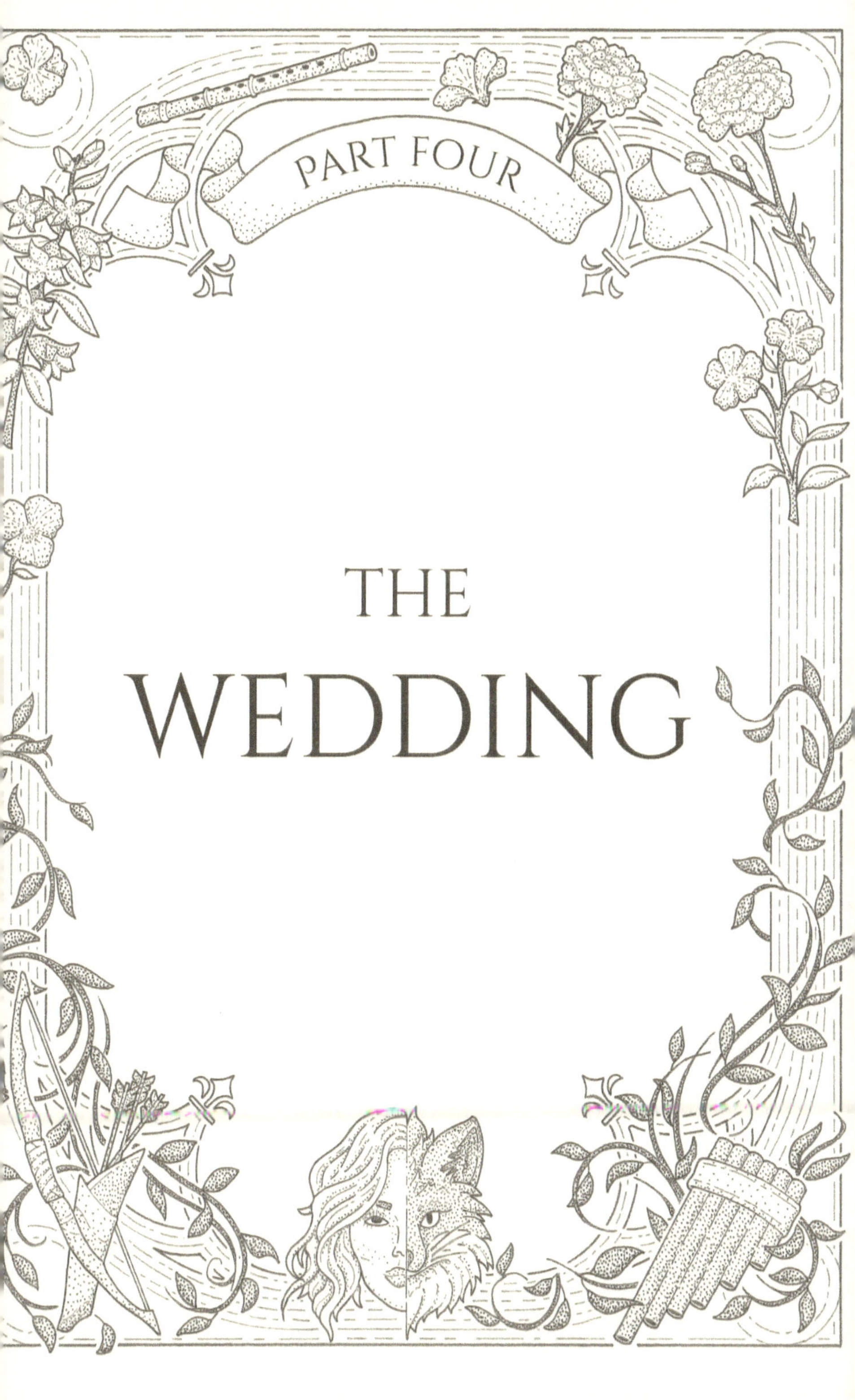
PART FOUR
THE
WEDDING

56

CLARISSA

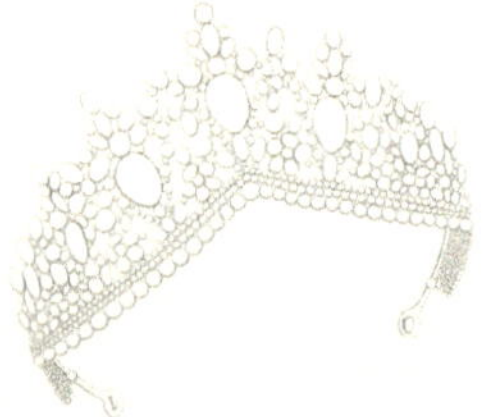

I stared at the reflection in the gold-plated mirror. The delicate blonde curls, the deep brown eyes, the pink-stained lips and kohl liner.

The dark circles hiding an anxious mind.

The pale cheeks, the down-turned mouth.

The white dress.

It was a beautiful dress. Handmade by Katrine, of course. I had to admit it was something I would've picked for myself, had it ever been my choice. It had a delicate lace bodice and a deep V-neckline, with floral embroidery in the lace and along the sheer, lightweight sleeves that extended to my wrists. It cinched at the waist before cascading into a long train that billowed around my feet as I sat at the vanity in my suite back at Palace Grimaldi.

I couldn't care less about having it all—the dress, the flowers, the false grandeur. But Galen said we had to keep up appearances for the kingdom. The rest of them didn't know the only reason we were doing this was to break the curse that had taken an entire island captive in a single day.

Nox stayed behind to make sure we had gotten everybody off the island, while the rest of us organized travel routes and passage. It was about a full day's trip to the nearest ports in each of the three territories on the mainland, so we split the ships up so as not to overwhelm them. We docked on the eastern side of the North Territory in the middle of the night and spent the next ten hours waiting for the others, unloading and finding refuge for the displaced islanders.

It was an absolute mess. I hadn't slept since…I didn't know how long anymore.

We wouldn't have an accurate count of survivors until the other territories were settled and got an idea of numbers, but I was hopeful we'd done all we could to get as many of them to safety as possible.

It was evening now, and I'd barely had a minute to myself since we made port.

Despite everything that had gone wrong, every obstacle in the road, every nightmare that had come to life…it all still came down to this moment.

I was about to marry Galen Grimaldi.

And I was in love with his best friend.

Tap tap came a small knock on my door. "Come in," I called out.

My mother, Rose, and Leo entered the suite. Mother held up a hand to her lips when she saw me, letting out a soft, "You look beautiful, my dear."

I gave her a half-smile as I stood. "Thank you, Mother."

Rose enveloped me in a hug. "Are you alright?"

"I'm fine." I swallowed. "Just ready to get it over with."

Leo pulled me into his side, and I leaned against him, thankful for the quiet, steady reprieve with my family.

Another knock on the door had all four of us turning. A middle-aged woman in a wheelchair being pushed by a servant appeared in the doorway.

The servant cleared his throat. "Isabella Grimaldi, the Dowager Queen Mother, would like to see you, Your Majesty."

My eyebrows flew up. *Galen's mother.*

I hadn't met her yet, since she hadn't been feeling well when we were last here. I took in her golden-brown skin, her graying hair flowing in brittle waves down her shoulders, her thin, sunken cheeks. Her hazel eyes were so hooded, she could barely meet my gaze when I stood before her.

"It's a pleasure to meet you, Your Grace," I said, bowing low.

She opened her mouth to speak, but a hacking cough came out instead. With shaking arms, she raised a yellow, bloodied rag to her lips, her shoulders bobbing with each cough. She waved her other hand in the air while clearing her throat, and the servant rushed forward with a small silver box.

"For you," Isabella Grimaldi rasped. It looked like it took all her energy just to get those two words out. The servant opened the box to reveal a strand of pearls and matching earrings, with a single diamond on each.

"Your Grace, they're beautiful," I murmured, fingering the pearls.

Another coughing fit overtook her. My heart sank as I thought about how it must feel for Galen to have watched his father and now his mother succumb to such a terrible disease. When she looked back up at me, I saw a haze covering her tired eyes. She swallowed thickly and pointed to her throat, then the jewels, then to me. She wanted me to wear them.

I nodded. "It would be an honor. Thank you, Your Grace."

Her thin lips split into a faint smile, and she reached out to take my hand. "Thank you," she choked out. "For...for saving him."

I bit down on my bottom lip and nodded before taking the box from the servant. Isabella slumped back in her wheelchair, and he pushed her out of the room.

Rose stared at their retreating figures with a puzzled expression on her face. "What kind of illness did Galen say she had?"

"He didn't specify," I said with a shrug. "Just that the same one eventually took his father's life. Some lung disease, maybe."

Her brow furrowed, and Leo grazed her arm with his finger. "What are you thinking, little wolf?"

"I don't know," Rose responded slowly, toying with the pouch of herbs she always kept strapped to her. "But I want to go see about something. I'll meet you at the wedding, okay?" She kissed Leo and gave me another hug before starting off after Isabella.

"Rissa, there's something I want to give you too," my mother said as she crossed to the door and shut it softly. She held a book in her hands—the same book she'd had in the Mid Territory the night of the Harvest Festival, with a letter sticking out the top. I gave her a quizzical look when she pulled it out and ran her fingers over the worn edges.

"What's that?" I asked.

"It's a letter. From your father," she added, and my eyes widened. She took my hands and placed the envelope in them, giving me a squeeze as her eyes lined with silver. My mother so rarely cried—a product of everything she'd been through, everything she was "supposed" to be as a former empress. But there was a slight tremble of her hands, a shake in her voice. "He wrote this for you when you were born. I had always thought he would be the one to give it to you when he felt the time was right, but the Fates had other plans."

The paper was wrinkled and faded by time, with the edges curling in on themselves. I slowly opened the flap to pull out the yellowed pages inside.

"Bad timing. You should've given this to me *before* my makeup was on, Mother," I joked through the lump forming in my throat.

She cupped my cheek and gave me a small smile. "We'll give you some time alone. I love you, sweet girl. Your father would be so proud of you."

"I'm just glad you're here," I whispered when she pulled me in for a hug.

As she backed away, Leo took her place. His tail flicked out from beneath its hiding spot under his thick cloak and curled anxiously around his ankle.

"I know this probably isn't how you imagined this day would go," he started. "But I was wondering if you'd let me walk you down the aisle?"

Tears stung at the backs of my eyes. "Emperor's tits, *both* of you could have done this earlier," I said, hurriedly swiping at my cheeks. I scrunched my nose to hold back the wave of tears and sniffed, then tugged at my brother's neck to bring him down to me.

"I'd love that, little brother," I murmured.

He cleared his throat and released me, nodding as he met my mother at the door to my suite. "We'll see you down there," he said.

Once they had both gone, I tossed myself into the vanity chair. I took a deep breath and fingered the folded letter, feeling each crease in the thin parchment. When I opened it, my eyes scanned the words and instantly recognized my father's cramped scrawl.

> *My dear Clarissa,*
>
> *Tonight, we welcomed you into this world. I have yet to stop thinking about the moment I laid eyes on you—nestled in your mother's arms, your little fingers and toes peeking out, eyes as deep and endless as our love for you. I knew in that second our lives would be forever changed.*
>
> *I'm in disbelief that this perfect creature is mine. That I get to watch you grow up, to live your life, and one day take my place and lead our people. This is my vow to you, Clarissa, that I will always do right by you. I will take care of this family and this empire so that when it is left in your hands, you have the strength and foundation to rule them well.*
>
> *I cannot guarantee the path forward will be easy, as much as I wish I could protect you from all that will come your way. My hope is that you will be infinitely better than I have been. Just remember that people are not led only by force, but by wisdom, courage, and most importantly, compassion. You may bend, but I know you will not break. Never forget, my dearest daughter, that even the strongest of steel was once softened by fire. And you will be the strongest of them all.*
>
> *With all my love,*
> *Your father*

A tear dripped and landed on the bottom of the page, leaving a dark splotch that spread along the edge. I closed my eyes. Memories of those childhood years before he died came flooding back— every time he took me in his arms and swung me in the air, every time he held Mother in the kitchen as she tried to cook, every time he let me watch as he and Leo practiced Alchemy. The nights our family spent under the stars, the stories read by a dying fire, the pride in his eyes when I shifted for the first time.

Even the strongest of steel was once softened by fire. I wondered if he knew back then how difficult it would be to allow myself to feel any hint of weakness. If perhaps he was the same—always needing to meet expectations, to present himself as the perfect emperor, full of strength and power.

The thought soothed me as I folded the letter back into its envelope and tucked it into my vanity. I took one last look in the mirror and reached for the delicate lace veil atop a pillow to my left. I stared at the large diamond in the centerpiece, the light refracting my own image in its reflection.

I pinned the veil to the top of my head.

It was time to save this kingdom, once and for all.

57

CLARISSA

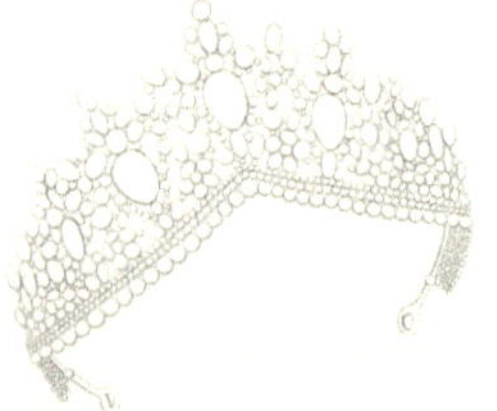

Drums echoed down the corridor as I descended the stairs to the entrance of the banquet hall. At first I thought it was the sound of my own heart beating in my ears, but then a violin joined the chorus. The royal symphony played a hauntingly beautiful tune that wound around me and set my nerves even more on edge.

Four members of the King's Guard stood at attention at the doors, and my brother waited for me at the bottom of the staircase. I took his outstretched arm as he leaned in to kiss my temple. To my left, Devora handed me a bouquet overflowing with greenery, white wisteria, larkspur, and violets. She offered me a small smile and squeezed my wrist for support before trailing behind me to fluff the train of my dress.

It was like every second increased the pressure building on my chest, until the guards opened the doors and I let out a breath.

The scene before me was something out of a fairytale. Even with such limited time to pull this wedding together, the palace had outdone my wildest expectations.

The walls of the hall were lined in gold pedestals, each holding flower arrangements that matched my own bouquet, with greenery cascading over the edges and onto the floor. Cream-colored tapestries hung from the ceiling all the way down the aisle to the two golden thrones at the end, behind the altar. Chandeliers lit the space every few feet, along with candelabras mounted on the walls. A light blue and gold rug covered the aisle from the entrance to the altar, where a royal priest and Galen were stationed.

Countless heads turned as the guests stood. Their eyes burned a hole through me.

My feet locked into place. I blinked, wetting my lips as I fought to draw breath.

Leo tightened his grip on my arm. I felt him looking at me, could picture that familiar crease in his brow, but I couldn't move.

My eyes took in Galen's form at the end of the aisle—his dark blue royal robe, the sash across his chest, the black leather gloves, the crown on his head.

My future husband.

A weight slammed into me, keeping me planted to the floor. Until I glanced to his side and met Thorne's eyes.

I'd never seen him so…put together. He wore the same color of deep blue pants with a matching fitted jacket, and a sword sheathed in a gold scabbard at his waist. His dark brown hair was pulled back with a strap of leather at the nape of his neck.

His gaze seared into me. I felt him everywhere—his fingers running across my skin, his lips on my neck, his chest pressed into my back.

I wanted this to be him. I wanted to be walking to *him*. My breaths came out in shaking spurts as the flowers in my hand suddenly became too heavy to bear. I couldn't spend the rest of my life tied to another man, not when all I wanted was to be in *his* arms. I couldn't—

Thorne slowly dipped his chin into a small nod, his eyes never leaving mine. *You can do this, Empress,* I could hear him whisper.

He was there, giving me strength. Even when I knew this was crushing him. He was always there.

I took a step forward.

I kept my eyes on him as Leo led me down the aisle. Those icy blue pools were the only things anchoring me to the palace, that allowed me to move forward when my entire body screamed to run away.

When Leo set my hand in Galen's, I finally shifted my focus to the king. He gave me a thin-lipped smile and turned to face the priest. I quickly scanned the front rows to find Lady Reaux and Marigold on the left, with her nanny at her side. Isabella Grimaldi was front and center in her wheelchair, an elegant tiara of twisted golden vines resting on her head. To the right sat my mother, Rose, and Katrine, with Leo joining them. Devora took my flowers and sat next to Katrine. The regent families were unable to attend, what with us moving up the date and the sudden arrival of all the island refugees. But what looked like the entire North Territory filled the seats behind our families.

"This evening, we are gathered together by the will of the Fates to witness His Majesty Galen Theodore Orion Grimaldi, Sovereign King of Mysthelm, unite in matrimony with Her Majesty Clarissa Valienne Aris, Empress-Elect of the Veridian Empire," the elderly priest began, his voice ringing through the hall.

As he performed the ceremony, speaking words of unity, love, and devotion to a prosperous Mysthelm, my mind spun with the events of the last three weeks. Those stolen moments with Thorne echoed around me, piercing my heart.

"Breathe, Empress."

"We would be lucky to have you as our queen."

"Don't be afraid of me. You're safe."

Galen slid a ring onto my finger, repeating meaningless words after the priest.

"You're strong for everybody else in your life, Clarissa Aris. Who is strong for you?"

"I feel you."

I took the ring from a pocket sewn into my dress and pushed it over the leather glove of Galen's ring finger. I barely heard the words coming from my mouth as I pledged my loyalty and fidelity to him.

"Then we fall together."

"Lie to me, Empress."

"If we're going to feel guilty about something, it should be this."

The priest cleared his throat. "Your Majesty, you may kiss your bride and Queen to seal this bond of marriage."

Galen gripped my hand as he faced me and leaned in.

My eyes slid over to Thorne's.

I love you.

Galen's rough lips met mine.

Familiar magic sparked at his touch, flowing over me like a breath of fresh air.

But something was off this time.

When I pulled away, the priest spoke over the smattering of polite applause. "I am honored to present to you the King and Queen of Mysthelm, Galen and—"

His words faltered.

Galen's lips parted as he stumbled backward. When he looked up at me in confusion, I almost screamed at the sight.

A crack appeared on his cheek.

The brown skin at his neck slowly faded to gray.

"Clarissa—what—" he croaked out, before his lips turned to ash.

Flakes of skin peeled away and drifted to our feet as I surged forward and gripped his cheeks.

He fell to his knees, and I went with him. The entire room burst into screams.

"Galen!" I shouted, urging my magic to siphon the curse from him.

But it wasn't working. It wasn't like the last times—I couldn't feel anything. No magic coursing through me. No sudden jolt of power. The curse wasn't leaving him.

What was *happening?*

"Galen, come on!" I shook his face, cradling him in my lap as he slumped over. "It's not working!" I yelled when Thorne knelt at my side.

My heart hammered in my chest as I ripped Galen's gloves off to get access to more of his skin, only to let out a gasp at his decayed hand. It was gray and cracked, bits of his fingers already breaking off and crumbling.

Bile crept up my throat. Thorne grabbed me by the shoulders and pulled me away as guards stormed the altar, but my eyes never left Galen's body.

I watched in horror as the curse overtook him.

His frozen gaze was fixed on mine until his lids finally shut and his body crumpled into dust.

58

THORNE

He couldn't be...*dead*. My best friend wasn't dead. Our *king* wasn't dead.

But there he was, his body rotted and turned to dust by his own Fates-forsaken curse.

Clarissa clung to me, but I could barely feel her over the pandemonium of the palace. People screamed and clambered from their seats. The priest fell over in alarm. And Isabella...

Galen's mother threw herself from her wheelchair, clawing at the ground as she tried to crawl her way to her son. A coughing fit overtook her, blood splattering the floor and her blue gown.

I didn't think I would ever forget the sound of her choked wails as she watched her son die.

My vision homed in on the dust, still in the shape of his body, and all sounds of chaos from the wedding faded. Until a voice split the air.

"Seize her!"

A knot twisted in my stomach.

It was my *mother's* voice.

My neck snapped to find her pointing a wrinkled finger at the woman in my arms. The King's Guard immediately surged forward.

"What?" I snarled, forcing Clarissa behind me. "No! Stand down. Empress Ar—*Queen Grimaldi* had nothing to do with this." The title made me wince, but it was the truth. And it might be the only thing that could save her now.

The guards faltered and glanced at my mother as she stormed the raised platform, the cane she had to use since her injury on the island tapping viciously against the wood floor.

"Back away, Thorne. She has murdered your king and must answer for her crimes," she said in a low voice of warning. She nodded again toward the guards, and they plowed behind me to grab Clarissa. I gripped one of them by the forearm and swung my fist into their jaw with a satisfying *crunch*.

"Stay away from her," I seethed, keeping my hold on Clarissa's wrist. The other guard reached for his sword, but I was faster. I unsheathed mine and held the point to his throat.

"Thorne, please," Clarissa whispered at my side. "Don't make this worse for you."

"I'm not going to let them touch you," I snapped.

"I raised you to be smarter than this," my mother said, gathering her thick skirt in one hand. "We have all witnessed the assassination of King Grimaldi at *her* hands. Justice must be upheld."

"Lady Reaux, you know I didn't do this," Clarissa said. Her eyes flicked between the rest of the crowd and my mother, knowing she couldn't say the full truth in front of everyone—why would she kill him when she was trying to break his curse?

"Mother, what are you *doing*?" I urged.

She ignored me. "Do you deny that you've been working against him? Against our *kingdom*?" she asked Clarissa. "My son heard you utter the very words for himself. That your people would *rip our kind to shreds*. That Galen Grimaldi should not be King of Mysthelm. That sounds dangerously close to treason, *Your Majesty*."

It was like a bucket of ice water had been thrown over me. Those were the same words Clarissa said to me the night before the Hunt. How could Mother have possibly known?

Clarissa slowly met my stare, betrayal shining in her eyes. She pulled out of my grip and took a step backward.

My breath caught in my throat. Did she believe I had any part in this? That I would do *anything* to hurt her?

"Clarissa, no—I didn't tell her—" I tried to reach for her, but she recoiled at my touch. My heart pressed against my chest, cracking and shattering at the look on her face, the wide eyes, the furrowed brow, the parted lips.

"You see?" Mother gestured between the two of us. "I speak the truth. It's been her the entire time. She's the one behind the failed assassination attempts, and she's finally succeeded." She moved forward, motioning once again for the guards to seize Clarissa. Out of the corner of my eye, I saw Rose and Leo leap from their seats, but more guards held them back.

"What about Lord Reaux, Your Grace?" the head of the King's Guard prompted. "Is he involved in this as well?"

Mother stopped when she reached me, placing a cold hand on my cheek. I jerked away from her.

"My son is loyal to Mysthelm." Her blue eyes lanced through me like a dagger. "You've done beautifully, dear. Thank you for your help to the crown."

"You're lying," I snarled. The guards yanked Clarissa's hands behind her back. "Stop! You can't take her." I struggled to get to her, but one of them blocked me, shoving me farther back. All Clarissa did was stare at me in defeat. My mouth went dry, every muscle in my body fighting against the guard. "Clarissa, I promise, I—"

"Not only has she been plotting against our king," my mother interrupted me, raising her voice to drown out my plea, "but she has brought a new threat into our kingdom." She waved her cane toward the front row, where Rose and Leo were still wrestling with guards. "*Veridians.* They have crossed over our borders, without permission from the king, to hide among us, spying on our people."

Gasps rose in the crowd. Members of Galen's council seated on the second row exchanged angry glances.

"The regents were right—they're invading our land," Lord Sadim barked. "Penworth was afraid of this. There could be more of them. Spies, entire *armies*, and there's no way to protect ourselves—not when they have magic."

Some of the guests nodded in agreement, anger evident in their features.

"How do we know she's not the reason the blight came?" my mother called out, and my mouth fell open in shock. She was *blatantly* lying. She knew exactly how this "blight" happened, and it had nothing to do with the Veridians. "Did our land not suffer exponentially more when she agreed to ally with our king? When she set foot on our soil? Look at what her mere touch has done to him."

Many in the crowd were now standing and hurling accusations toward the front of the hall. Mother was riling them up. Priming them to attack, to demand retribution. They looked as if they wanted to tear Clarissa apart.

"Mother, stop this!" I grabbed her hand and spun her to face me. "What are you doing? You know none of this is true!"

"I'm doing what I should have done long ago." She stepped closer, icy hatred blazing in her eyes. Her features were set in sharp determination. "Putting someone worthy of the title on top of that throne. And if you want your little plaything to live, you'll keep your mouth shut."

Her words sent a chill down my spine. This...this wasn't my mother. This wasn't anyone I recognized. Cold, calculating, *vile*.

I couldn't believe I'd ever trusted her. *Believed* her. After all the years of her standing by my side, the nights she would rock Marigold to sleep as my little girl cried for her mother, the way we were there for each other when our worlds fell apart. Everything had been a lie.

Every consoling word she used to soothe me, to manipulate

me…it was all for this. So *she* could have the power. So *she* could sit on that throne. As if this had been her plan all along.

She whipped back to the guards still holding Clarissa captive. "Take her to the dungeons to await trial. May the Fates have mercy on her soul."

59

THORNE

I made sure Marigold was safely tucked away with her nanny in the servants' quarters before following my mother outside the grand ballroom.

"You've gone too far, Mother," I said. "You have no authority in this palace. With Galen dead—"

"Well, I certainly don't see the Dowager Queen doing anything to stop me." She slowly turned, keeping her weight on her good leg as her gown swirled across the floor. "And do you truly think that *foreigner* has any power here? After that sham of a wedding? Please, dear." She scoffed. "Nobody in this kingdom would follow her rule."

"And you expect them to follow *yours*?" I spat.

"With the support of our fellow regents, I'm sure the kingdom will come to an agreeable solution."

I let out a derisive laugh. "How diplomatic of you, Mother. Why don't you say what you really mean? That this was what you wanted from the beginning—yourself on that throne, even if you had to wade through bloodshed to get there."

"No blood has been shed. You're being dramatic, as always." She pursed her lips as she stepped toward me. "You were involved in this from the start, Thorne. Do not forget that."

I stood my ground. "No. You will *not* keep manipulating me. You know I refused to play along once I realized what an asset Clarissa would be to this kingdom. How she could *save* us."

Mother threw out a hand toward the ballroom. "And what would you call what just happened? Galen is *dead*!"

"She did not kill him!" I roared. "Blame the Fates, if you must. But I *know* she wouldn't hurt him. You're putting an innocent woman behind bars."

She let out a sigh. "You have always trusted so easily, my son. So freely." With a shake of her head, she said, "You don't know what those people are capable of."

"Is this some sort of twisted revenge for what Father did to us? Because he left us for Veridia?" I ground out.

She narrowed her eyes at me. "This has nothing to do with that man. I'm making the most of the situation and salvaging what I can of our kingdom."

When she turned away from me, my anger morphed to desperation. "Please," I said, voice cracking. I reached for her hand, clinging for any scrap, any morsel of compassion in the woman I'd loved for so long. The woman who raised me. "I love her, Mother. Don't do this."

Her eyes held mine, and the wrinkles on her forehead smoothed. "You do, don't you?" she breathed out, cocking her head to the side. "Just as you loved your Iris." Her shoulders fell, and hope soared in my chest.

"That was always your downfall, Thorne. But you will not make it mine."

She tore her arm away.

As her decision settled over us, I straightened my spine. Resolve coursed through me. This world had taken Iris away from me. It had taken my father, my freedom, my identity.

I would not let it take *her*.

"Then I'll get her myself," I muttered, resting a hand on the pommel of my sword.

Mother's eyes flicked to something behind me as she *tsked*. "I was afraid you might say that." With a wave of her hand, two guards grabbed me by the arms. I tried to yank out of their hold, but their vise-like grip pinned me down.

"What are you doing?" I asked through gritted teeth.

"I love you, son, but as I said...I won't let your heart get in my way." She gave a swift nod.

Something slammed into the back of my head, and the world went black.

60

CLARISSA

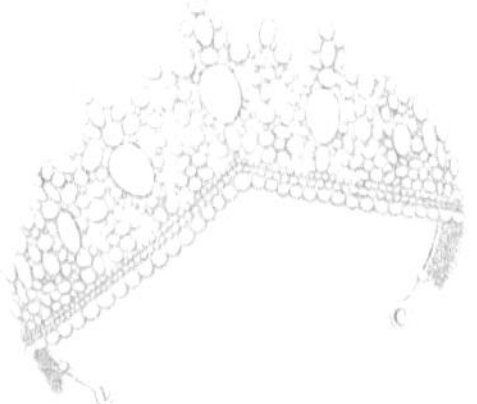

The last time I'd been in a dungeon, I was the one interrogating a Shifter on the other side of the bars. The cells in Veridia were nicer, I had to admit.

Staring at the dark, dank stone wall, I listened to the *drip drip drip* of a leak in the ceiling above me. The sound echoed through the cell as a chill sank into my bones.

It was safe to say this dress was ruined. I'd been sitting on this dirty stone floor for hours, with only the Fates-knew-what-else seeping into the fabric. It smelled like musty piss, the staleness of the air making it difficult to draw a full breath.

The only light came from a couple of swinging lanterns placed along the wall on the opposite side of the bars. Every once in a while, I'd hear an occasional whistle or scuffle from some inmate deep within the dungeon, but other than that, I was left with my own thoughts.

A dangerous place to be.

Galen was dead. My family was in trouble, Azura was framing me, and there was *nothing* I could do about it. Not when I was stuck in a foreign kingdom without my magic to protect me.

How could he have died? Our marriage was supposed to break the curse. That was what the Fates told his ancestor. That was what we'd based this entire alliance on. Had we done something wrong? Misunderstood the curse? Pissed off the Fates?

I groaned and held my face in my hands, then winced at the grime on my fingers. I had to figure out a way out of here. Mother, Rose, and Leo were just as defenseless as I was. Azura could be doing *anything* to them right now, all because she had some vendetta against me. Against all Veridians, I supposed. It was far too easy to make an entire throne room full of guests turn on us with a few simple lies.

And Thorne...

I closed my eyes and rested my cheek against the cool stone. I couldn't even think about him right now. I didn't know what to believe—Azura was a manipulative liar, but how else could she have known the things I said about Galen that night? She was Thorne's mother. It would make sense for his loyalty to be to her. She cared for him and Marigold, in some twisted way. If she had this grand plan to obtain power for her family, it wouldn't be a surprise if he'd been part of it.

I thought I *knew* him. After everything we'd been through, everything he'd said...

He was either as skilled of a liar as his dear mother, or she was playing all of us.

I just didn't know which was true.

A draft blew through the cell, sending a shiver down my spine. The flames in the torches outside the bars flickered. Something light and airy pressed against my skin, and the hair on the back of my neck rose in warning.

"Who's there?" I called out. I felt along the floor and grabbed a small, sharp rock as I slowly rose to my feet.

A faint giggle reached my ears.

"My, this one is brave, isn't she?" a high-pitched voice crooned.

I jumped and slammed my back into the corner, holding out the rock as if it could do anything to protect me. Scanning the shadows, I craned my neck to listen for footsteps, but there was nothing. No movement, no bodies, just darkness.

"Who said that?" I asked.

A ripple of wind rolled across my arm, almost as if invisible fingers danced over it.

"*Though not as bright as she seems,*" a second feminine voice said.

Well, that was just rude. "Who are you?" I demanded with a growl. "Show yourself."

"**Haven't you guessed by now, Clarissa Aris?**" The last sound was drawn out like a snake hissing through the grass.

"*You call upon us in your anger,*"

"**Your pain,**"

"<u>Your desperation</u>," said a third voice, rising with the other two as they wavered closer.

"*And we answer in our strength,*"

"**In our glory,**"

"**<u>*In our power.*</u>**"

All three voices blended together, and the force of it sent me staggering to the side. Magic stirred in the air. Old and long-forgotten, like an ancient, primal power that made my own dormant magic raise its head in curiosity.

"The Fates," I breathed out.

"**At your service,**" the first one said, and a faint presence brushed against my skin.

I glanced around the cell, trying to find some form or body to lock onto, but it was still empty. "How—what are you *doing* here?"

"<u>Call us curious</u>," one of them mused.

"*We've been wondering when someone might come along and break this curse.*"

"**It was my favorite one, too,**" the first one purred.

I wrinkled my nose. "Break the curse? The king *died*. I thought our marriage was supposed to save him? Or did you lie about that to his ancestor too?"

"<u>Brave *and* a sharp tongue.</u>" Ghostly fingers gripped my cheeks, pinching them together. I reared back to yank out of their hold, and faded laughter echoed off the stone walls.

"*The curse did break, little Empress,*" the second voice hissed. "*Or is it Queen now?*"

"<u>We did not lie. The blight will no longer touch this kingdom.</u>"

"**We never said *how* it would break,**" the first one said, and I could almost imagine an outline of shoulders lifting into a shrug.

"<u>Nyses Grimaldi's son simply never asked.</u>" A dark chuckle drifted in the cell.

My stomach sank. This was always how they'd planned for it to go. This was always how the curse would be "broken." Galen had based his entire hope, his entire *future*...on a lie. A *technicality*.

And now he was dead.

My forehead pinched. "You...you're supposed to be the Fates. The overseers of our world, the ones people pray to in their darkest hours." I shook my head in disgust. "You're nothing but cruel. Preying on desperation and weaknesses."

Anger boiled inside of me as I thought about the past weeks and all we had worked for. *Everything* was for this. I may not have respected him as a ruler in the end, but Galen didn't deserve to die. He didn't deserve to have one shining millisecond of freedom before his life was snuffed from him.

I clenched my jaw. "You're no better than the tyrants of this world. Do you get off on weaving your little webs and watching us all get caught in them? Does it make you feel *powerful*?"

"*Careful, Clarissa Aris,*" one of them warned.

"Or what, you're going to curse my bloodline too?" I bit down on the inside of my cheek, wondering if I'd finally crossed a line. For as much as I'd learned to control my tongue over the years, my anger still got the best of me.

"<u>Do you know the truth of what happened that night with</u> <u>Nyses Grimaldi?</u>" the third voice boomed.

I swallowed back a retort. "I know he asked for magic out of jealousy for what you gave the Veridians after the war, and you granted it to him. But it wasn't magic like we have—it was devastating." I thought back to what Thorne told me at the hedge maze, how each descendant had a different brutal power. Seeing spirits, inflicting pain, forced to become a beast. "It was a curse."

A myriad of hums echoed around me. **"It seems the Grimaldis have concealed things as well,"** the first one said.

"What do you mean?"

There was a pause, a rustle in the air. And then—

"_Let us show you, little Empress._"

A cold, invisible hand gripped my wrist. I let out a strangled gasp as my body was thrown backward into the stone wall.

The cell disappeared.

I was standing before a burning temple in the dead of night. Smoke and bright orange flames attacked the building, rising like a warning against the dark blue sky. Dozens of men and women in long white robes rushed around the blaze. Some carried buckets of water, while others tucked leather-bound books and old scrolls under their robes as they fled the scene. A particularly terrifying wail caught my attention, and I looked to the right to see a young man—barely out of adolescence—flailing on the ground, flames consuming his legs.

My eyes widened as he screamed himself hoarse, his flesh bubbling beneath the fire traveling higher and higher up his body. I tried to run forward, but my limbs wouldn't move.

"There is nothing you can do but watch," the third voice of the Fates murmured in my ear, and for once, it didn't sound cruel. It sounded pained. Remorseful.

My breath quickened, a whimper escaping me as the inferno overtook the boy.

His mangled cries stopped, leaving behind a scorched body.

A thunderous crash came from the front of the temple. One of the statues resting above the entrance cracked in half. My eyes flicked to the ground where an elderly woman struggled to carry a bag overflowing with scrolls away from the building. I sucked in a breath and again tried to lurch toward her, only to be stopped by the same force.

The statue tipped.

I let out a silent scream as it tumbled through the air and crashed on top of the woman. She crumbled under its weight, not even having time to call out before she was dead. A pool of blood trickled from her head and over the grass, mingling with the ash and dirt.

Tears now tracked down my cheeks. I took in the chaos, the hordes of people running for their lives as flames continued to wreck the temple.

Horse hooves pounded on the ground behind me. I turned to see a large man in a mahogany cloak barreling forward on his horse, the crest of Mysthelm adorned on the saddle. Those familiar four branches with a sword and sickle. A priest rushed to him as he dismounted.

"My King!" the elderly man called out.

Nyses Grimaldi. Galen's ancestor. I could see the resemblance as I squinted—the same golden-brown skin, the dark hair, the chiseled features.

Was this the night the curse began?

I blinked, and my body jerked forward as the temple vanished. In my next breath, I was inside what I assumed was the same building—a high ceiling with marble columns surrounded by burning wood, a raised dais with the king standing at its center. There was a dagger in his grip. Blood streamed from his hand to the stone altar beneath.

The voices of the Fates rang out around me. But they weren't the ones who had spoken to me—they were speaking to *him.*

"Tell us, oh great Nyses Grimaldi,"

"What would make the King of Mysthelm,"

"Burn his own temple to the ground?"

Confusion struck me as they kept talking. *He* had done this? Their own king? That couldn't be true. All those innocent people, dead—

"Setting fire to your people? Letting them burn among the

smoke and flames? You must be truly desperate to summon an audience with us."

The third voice purred, "**Yes, Nyses. So very desperate.**"

Nyses's body jerked, and he tipped his head up as if being clutched around the throat.

"Well, Your Majesty?"

"*What is it that you seek?*"

"Magic," he choked out. His voice was deep and gravelly, full of hatred.

"That's what all of this was for?" the third voice asked. "You desire magic?"

"Yes. Magic to rival that of the Veridian Empire. Magic *you* granted them."

"**Magic they earned, Nyses.**"

"*The Veridian Empire defeated your kingdom over a century ago.*"

"They conquered the power we offered to both of your lands."

"You asked what I sought," Nyses said. "That is my answer. Magic to rule over my people. Magic to conquer my foes. Magic greater than what you have given our enemies."

The smoke in the temple rose as their voices grew distant. My vision wavered, and when I reached up to rub my eyes, my body slammed back into the stone wall of my cell.

I stumbled forward and dropped to my knees. The smell of smoke clung to the walls, to my skin, to the inside of my nose.

"Was—was that real?" I croaked out.

"*Yes,*" the second one hissed. "*Do you see why we did what we did?*"

"The Grimaldis were power-hungry and foolish, desperate for bloodshed without caring who got in their way."

"**Call us liars all you want, little Empress,**" the first one sang. "**But can you truly blame us?**"

I closed my eyes and pinched the bridge of my nose. Galen's ancestor was willing to endanger so many lives, all for the sake of seeking an audience with the Fates. To what, *threaten* them? Bargain with them? To convince them to give him their magic?

And in his greed, he'd condemned his entire bloodline.

A wicked laugh filled the silence. **"Poor Nyses must be turning over in his grave knowing his own flesh and blood put a Veridian on his precious throne."**

I gritted my teeth. "This isn't funny. Galen didn't deserve to die for his ancestor's sins."

"*Perhaps not,*" the second voice said. "*But what's done is done.*"

"You don't even care," I muttered. "You've never cared about any of us. You started an entire war, killing hundreds of thousands of people over this magic, just for what? Your *entertainment*? And now you act as if this curse was some sort of justice against a corrupted king. Where's the justice in *anything* you've done?"

"We did not come here to be lectured by a self-righteous, would-be queen," the third one warned, the feminine voice now deep and laced with irritation.

"Then why *did* you come here?" I demanded. "To watch me die like you watched Galen?"

Frigid air swept over me as an invisible finger swiped along my neck. I froze in place, my legs rigid and breaths shaking. Its touch trailed over my collarbone and my shoulder, then down my right arm.

Quick as lightning, another set of fingers wrapped around my throat.

"We came here, little Empress, because we're not done with you yet," the first voice said sweetly in my ear.

I choked against their hold and reached up to try to claw my way loose, but they released me. With a gasp, I slumped into the wall, struggling to catch my breath.

"What is *that* supposed to mean?" I rasped.

Silence.

"Hello? Are you still there?"

The doors to the dungeon slammed open, and loud footsteps drew nearer, along with the clanking of metal on metal and a cane scraping the floor. Voices filled the cell as shadows came into view.

I recognized Azura's voice. I backed farther into the corner, but something on the ground at my feet caught my eye. I paused and squinted, cocking my head. It looked like a flower. A...marigold. Faded orange petals connected to a stem, their colors beginning to turn gray as if caught in the blight I'd seen so many times.

A warning buzzed in the back of my mind, and before I could think too hard about it, I knelt down and scooped up the cursed flower with the sleeves of my wedding dress.

The door to my cell banged open.

"Clarissa Aris," the head of the King's Guard called out. Azura stood next to him, and I held her stare.

"You have been found guilty of the murder of King Galen Grimaldi and treason against the Mysthelm crown. You are hereby sentenced to death."

61

THORNE

I woke up to a throbbing heat at the back of my head. Wincing, I pushed myself off the ground and took in my surroundings.

Evidently, Mother had deemed me enough of a nuisance to have the guards knock me out, but not enough to warrant the dungeons. I recognized where I was: the guest suite in the northern tower, with its windows facing the Avonige Ocean that I could barely make out in the distance. A large bed, a bathing room, some end tables and a dresser.

I wished it were the dungeons.

I could only imagine what Clarissa was going through. Horrible visions swam across my mind—guards tying her up and beating her, throwing her around those dark cells, grabbing at her skin, her clothes, her hair.

The welt on my head pulsed as indignation shot through me. I would tear them apart if they touched her.

Sunlight beamed across the room from the windows. It had to be midday or later. How much time had passed since the wedding? How long had I been unconscious?

I strode to the door and tugged on the handle, unsurprised when it didn't budge. I threw my weight against it with a grunt, shoving it with my shoulder, kicking it and rattling the knob until I heard a sharp thud on the other side.

"We have orders to detain you if you attempt to escape, Lord Reaux," a muffled voice said.

"Of course you do," I muttered. Changing tactics, I crossed to the opposite side of the room to peer out the window. It was at least a ten-story drop, with nothing to grab on to or jump from in sight.

"The hard way, then," I said to myself. I pulled open every drawer in the dresser and flung the closet and bathing room doors wide, grabbing as many sheets, towels, and pillow cases as I could find. After stripping the bed, I quickly tied all the ends together, thankful to have something to occupy my hands before I spiraled.

I had to get to them. Clarissa *and* Marigold. I trusted Marigold's nanny, but I had no clue what lengths my mother would go to to get what she wanted or to keep my daughter from me. My insides were twisted with anxiety, the urgency of the situation blazing through me like a wildfire.

I gave the last piece of my rope a final tug and dragged it over to the window.

An enormous shadow passed in front of it, and before I could blink, the glass shattered around me.

Rearing back, I shielded my eyes from the blast. A heavy weight landed beside me. "Not the damsel I was trying to save, but you'll do," a familiar voice said.

I blinked against the sunlight and looked over to find Nox Duma standing amid the pile of broken glass.

I cursed. "What are you doing?"

"Rescuing you, of course."

"How did you get here?"

"I siphoned all the magic out of the curse on the island and flew. When I overheard what happened to Rissa, I figured they probably didn't let you go quietly. Are you hurt?"

I shook my head. "I'm fine, but we need to get to her." He

nodded, and I gripped his shoulder. "Duma—did you hear anything about my daughter? Is she safe?"

He gave me a sympathetic look. "I'm sorry, I don't know. As soon as I heard the guards talking about the wedding, I started looking for you and Rissa."

A shout rang out from the hallway, and Nox hurriedly motioned for the window. "Subtlety isn't my strong suit. You ready for a ride?"

I furrowed my brow. "A what?"

He rolled his eyes. "Come on, lover boy. Let's go get your girl."

Taking a running start, he leaped out the window and shifted midair.

My jaw dropped.

I knew what his Shifter form was, but...*Fates*. Seeing it was something else entirely.

His size was unmatched. The claws on his feet alone were large enough to shred this entire tower to pieces. Silver and navy-blue scales shone in the bright sun as he flapped his wings, casting a shadow over the room. If I wasn't in such shock, it would've been beautiful. Like iridescent waves on a darkened sea. His spiked tail flicked back and forth while his head, framed by huge silver horns, cocked at me. I could practically hear him saying, "Scared, lover boy?"

Then the door burst open behind me.

I took a deep breath. If only Marigold could see me now—her daddy, about to ride a *dragon*.

"You better not drop me, Shifter," I warned before launching myself into the air, straight onto his scaled back.

62

CLARISSA

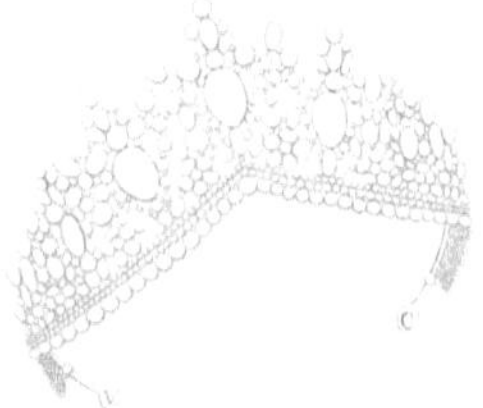

The tunnel dragged on ahead of me, seemingly unending, until a pinprick of sunlight appeared at the end. The chains wrapped around my ankles and wrists clanged together as the two guards on either side of me forced me down the path. I stared at the back of Azura's head, her gray locks tucked into a tight bun, her gold dress flowing behind her.

I looked down at my own gown. The once-white fabric was now littered with dirt and small rips lining the beautiful lace. I couldn't believe this time yesterday I was getting ready for my wedding. That all seemed so trivial now, so...distant.

The lives of my family and friends hung in the balance. Mother, Rose, Leo, Nox. *Thorne.* The lives of my people. Of those who relied on me to come home. What was going to happen to them?

I tripped over a rock in the tunnel, staggering forward before I caught myself on the guard's shoulder. Azura turned her neck with a raised eyebrow.

I licked my dry lips. "Azura, please," I croaked. "Please let my family go. They had nothing to do with this."

"They will each be given a fair trial," she said dismissively.

I scoffed, which sounded more like a cough. "Oh, like I was?"

She trailed her gaze down my body as we kept walking. "*You* killed our king in front of hundreds of people. This is as fair as the law gets, Clarissa."

"You actually think you're doing the right thing, don't you?" I shook my head, and my limp curls brushed over my chest. "For the fiftieth time, I didn't kill him, Azura. It was his *curse*. The one you seem so intent on ignoring. And all these accusations of treason? Of my empire plotting against yours? I wouldn't have come over here to create an alliance if I wanted war. I would have brought an *army*."

The guards tightened their hold on me, and I tugged at my restraints as I asked, "Are you so blinded by power and hatred that you won't see reason?"

She abruptly stopped moving, causing the guards and me to almost run into her. "Leave us," she snapped at them. With a skeptical glance, they both let go of me and sauntered farther down the path.

Azura lowered her voice. "*I* am doing what is best for this kingdom. You and I both know that boy would have run Mysthelm into the ground. We need someone who has the strength to put ourselves first, not bow to some foreigner." She took a step closer. "You may have seduced my son, but make no mistake: you Veridians are all the same. And I will see you hang before I kneel at your feet."

I sighed as my shoulders dropped under the weight of my chains. "You were never going to accept me, were you? You were never going to let this marriage happen."

"I certainly did my best to stop it." She straightened her spine and stepped back. "I didn't necessarily want Galen to die, but the Fates had other plans."

A laugh escaped me. *She had no idea.*

"You think this is funny?"

"No," I responded, meeting her gaze. "I think this is sad. That your prejudice against an entire empire of people has made you so calloused. Thorne will never forgive you for this. You may get the throne you always wanted, but you're going to lose everything you've ever loved."

Her stare blazed through me. "Love is a myth, Clarissa," she hissed. "It will always fail you in the end."

She grabbed my chains with her free hand and led me forward, out of the opening of the tunnel and into the bright afternoon sun.

The light blinded me after sitting in the dark cell for so long. I winced and lifted an arm to cover my eyes. Another guard came from the side, tugging my restraints and making me stumble in the dirt. The sound of a crowd reached my ears, and when we turned a corner, a raised platform in front of a large audience came into view.

On the platform stood an elevated beam with a single noose swinging from the top.

The world faded around me.

I saw Mother, Rose, and Leo on the opposite side of the platform, but it was as if I were watching from outside my body. Watching as Leo thrashed against the three guards holding him back, as Rose gritted her teeth and tried to push forward, as my mother stared at me, lips parted and chest heaving.

I turned my head slowly to take in the crowd, their blended shouts both demanding my execution and begging for my release.

The wooden steps groaned as the guards guided me up the side of the platform. I barely felt the boards beneath my feet. The sounds grew distant and fuzzy, while the violent pumping of blood through my heart filled my ears. As if my body knew what was coming and was pushing itself to the extreme to keep me alive.

My limbs went cold as the noose grew closer.

Azura stood with the head of the King's Guard at the edge of the platform, reading off the list of my crimes. The words buzzed in my ear.

Murder, treason, plotting against the crown. All the lies I'd heard before.

The other guard stopped me once we reached the center. He pulled at the rope until it hung eye-level, then gripped my head and fastened the noose around my neck. Its frayed length scratched my sensitive skin.

The shouts of the crowd grew louder. I spared one last glance at my family as my legs trembled and my vision wavered.

I love you, I mouthed to them.

The guard backed away, and for a split second, all noise ceased. A light breeze kissed my skin, ruffling the skirt of my dress. The faint floral scent of the gardens nearby tickled my nose. Something that smelled like marigolds.

The rope grew taut as its hold tightened. I could feel the pulse at my neck pounding against it.

I took one last deep breath.

Then many things happened all at once.

From the center of the crowd staggered Isabella Grimaldi, no wheelchair in sight and looking more clear-headed than I'd ever seen her. She raised a hand holding a bloody rag and pointed it at Azura Reaux.

"*You!*" she cried.

"Now!" Azura commanded.

The platform at my feet disappeared. My body fell, caught at the neck by the rope digging like a hundred knives into my skin.

"We're not done with you yet," the voice of the first Fate echoed in my mind.

As I choked and swung, suspended in the air, I concentrated on moving my wrists behind my back. My vision began to gray at the edges, the pressure in my head feeling as if it would pop. I tugged on the cursed marigold that I'd shoved between the fabric of my sleeves until my fingers closed around the stem.

The tiniest, almost indiscernible kernel of power spread through my veins.

My eyes were drawn forward by someone screaming my name. Thorne burst through the front of the crowd, lunging toward the platform.

I met his blue gaze.

With my final breath, I shifted.

63

THORNE

Nox saw her before I did. In his dragon form, he nose-dived from the north tower to the western grounds where a crowd had formed at the gallows. His feet had barely touched down before I slid from his back and took off at a sprint, my heart flying into my throat.

I'm too late, was all I could think as I shoved through the throng of people. *I love her, and I'm too late.*

I reached the front and watched her body hang from the rope, her neck bent and her legs flailing. I pushed off the ground with every ounce of strength I possessed, leaping for the raised platform.

She saw me. For a single moment, time halted, and her eyes met mine.

And then she was gone. Replaced by a familiar lithe, furry form as her fox half slipped out of the noose, landed gracefully on the platform, and bounded off to the right with her powerful hind legs.

"Stop her!" my mother screeched. Guards charged after her. I followed, yanking one of them back by their uniform and punching them in the face. Ahead of me, Rose lifted her hand and blew some sort of powder into one of their faces right as Leo dodged two of them and knocked out a third. Together, he and I reached for the nearest weapons and chased after Clarissa's pursuers.

She didn't even make it to the palace walls before she shifted back into her human form. Whatever had allowed her to shift at the gallows must not have had much power.

But it was enough. She was *alive*.

One of the guards closed in on her, but Leo was faster. His tail emerged from beneath his cloak and wrapped around the assailant's wrist, jerking him backward.

I smirked, but Clarissa screamed. My lips fell in confusion until I looked behind Leo and saw a second guard's sword raised at his back.

"No!" I cried.

The blade pierced Leo's shoulder.

I slammed into the guard, and we both fell to the ground as Leo's knees hit the floor.

"Leo!" Clarissa shrieked.

"Take them to the dungeons," a cold voice instructed behind me. Mother approached with more men at her side. I grabbed my sword and stood between them and Clarissa, my nostrils flaring.

"No," another voice said. "You will not lay a finger on them, Azura Reaux."

Mother's forehead creased. We both turned to the side to find Isabella Grimaldi striding toward us.

"Bella?" my mother said in surprise.

My mouth fell open. I hadn't seen Galen's mother so much as *stand* on her own in months, yet here she was, charging at us like a bull.

Evadine and Rose appeared behind Isabella. Rose let out a whimper as she rushed to Leo's side, that pouch of herbs I was so used to seeing on her already open in her hands.

"We need to get him to a healer," Rose said, ripping part of Leo's shirt off and pressing it into his shoulder to stem the flow of blood.

"Bella, this fraud killed your son." My mother ignored Rose and gestured to Clarissa. "His death deserves justice."

Out of the corner of my eye, I saw Devora sneak across the side of the palace wall. Her eyes stopped on my mother, then trailed over to Clarissa.

"Devora!" Clarissa said. "We need bandages and—and something to clean his wound." She gripped Leo's hand. "Please hurry!"

My attention was caught between both Isabella's confrontation and wanting to be at Clarissa's side. I started to make my way to Clarissa when Isabella's next words stopped me in my tracks.

"Don't you dare speak to me of justice, Azura," she hissed. Her dark eyes flashed at my mother. "Not when you're the one who murdered my husband."

I sucked in a breath, all else forgotten. "*What?*" I tightened my grip on the sword. "Mother, tell me that isn't true."

Orion Grimaldi had been sick for quite a while before he died. The palace healers said it was a lung disease, one they suspected Isabella contracted soon after his death. It was unfortunate, but it was an accident. A natural course of illness. That was what we all believed.

"You were clever, Azura, I must admit," Isabella said. "And nobody would have known if it weren't for Rose. One of the Veridians you seem to despise so very much."

My mind spun. What did Rose have to do with this?

Rose hunched over Leo, pouring some yellow oil from her pouch onto her hands. Leo was still conscious and propped up on his good arm, with Clarissa's hand resting protectively on his shoulder. His face was sweat-slicked and pale, wincing with pain at Rose's every motion.

"I thought it was a lung disease," I said slowly, still taking in Isabella's accusation.

"He was truly sick," Isabella admitted. "But he was recovering. And then Azura began visiting and suggested we try an herbal tea, brewed by her own healers." She took another step toward my mother. "You sat there, week after week, watching him lose his life.

Watching *me* lose my senses. Until I was nothing more than a ghost of myself confined to that chair, coughing up blood and waiting to follow him to the grave." Her voice wavered with both anger and despair, those eyes that reminded me of Galen piercing my mother to the floor.

"I don't know what you're talking about, Bella," my mother said, her lips barely moving as she gripped her cane tighter.

"Foxglove and hellebore," Rose gritted out. Her eyes were still locked on Leo's injury. "I found traces of it in Isabella's tea. That's what you've been slipping them." She finally removed her gaze from Leo and stared up at my mother. "Poison."

Leo's pale lips pulled into a tired smile from his slumped position on the ground. "That's my girl," he wheezed out.

The few members of the King's Guard around us shifted on their feet, some weapons aimed at Clarissa while others now strayed to my mother.

Mother's nose twitched. Her eyes narrowed on Rose. "You cannot honestly believe her. We've already seen how adept their kind is at lying. Look at everything that has happened in our territories since their arrival. Why would any of you listen to this?"

"Open your eyes, Azura!" Isabella barked. "She sensed it the moment she met me before the wedding. All it took was one of her herbal tonics to counteract the poison and prove her theory correct." Her arm shook as she pointed to Azura. "I didn't want to believe it, but the instant the haze cleared and I could *think* again, could *breathe* again...I knew." Isabella dropped her arm and whispered, "How *could* you, Azura?"

I stared at my mother, waiting for a response. Perhaps part of me was hoping for some kind of explanation, some scrap of truth that would make all of this disappear. That would bring back the mother I knew before she let her grand ideas of power get in the way of her ability to show compassion.

But she simply stood there, unmoving. Frozen. Except for those eyes, which darted between those staring at her, the gears in her mind turning to think of a way out of this. To lie and manipulate. Deceive, as she always did.

"It's true, isn't it," I murmured, the last shred of confidence I had in her hardening and shattering.

Mother rolled her lips together, then flattened them into a grim line. For a split second, her eyes found mine and softened, that same look of tenderness she reserved for Marigold shining through.

She blinked, and it was gone.

"It was supposed to be me," she said, her voice barely more than a whisper.

"What was supposed to be you?" I asked.

"The throne. The kingdom. All of it." Her gaze swept over to Isabella. "Orion Grimaldi was supposed to marry *me*."

64

THORNE

"What are you talking about?" I asked.

Mother's jaw ticked. "My parents worked in the palace. I was born here on these grounds and grew up with Orion. My family came from a modest background —not of nobility, but my father served the crown well. Eventually, Orion and I became...close." At these words, she looked away, her throat bobbing as she swallowed. "He promised to marry me. He said it would all be ours one day."

I remembered the conversation we'd had toward the beginning of the tour in the Mid Territory, when she told me she'd been in love once.

"It was him," I said. "The man you loved. It was Orion Grimaldi."

Her eyes flicking back to mine was my only answer. Isabella rocked on her heels, her brow furrowed. "I—I had no idea," she said.

"How could you, Bella?" Mother replied. "You were the beautiful daughter of a lord, not the little girl who grew up playing in the kitchens and hiding in the gardens. *You* were the one the Grimaldis wanted on the throne with their son. The one they wanted bearing his offspring. I was simply not good enough." She steeled her voice. "And Orion agreed."

"So that's why you killed him? Why you poisoned me?" Isabella exclaimed. "Because you were *jealous*? Azura, this was decades ago!"

Mother's eyes flashed. "How dare you diminish my pain to a mere emotion, Isabella," she said, enunciating every syllable. "There was no one left to love me. No one left to take my retribution. So I did it myself."

I shook my head in disbelief. "*I* loved you, Mother. *Marigold* loved you. Was that not enough?"

She licked her lips, then bit down on her bottom lip, showing the first hint of regret. "You don't understand," she said quietly. "You don't know what that was like. Being in love, seeing a future with someone, then having it ripped away by people with the power to change my life. All because I wasn't *enough*."

"So you took it out on the entire Grimaldi line," I said.

Her words were like ice. "Do not underestimate the power and wrath of a scorned woman."

"Did you kill my son?" Isabella snarled, moving quicker than I thought possible. She stood nose-to-nose with my mother, her fists balled at her sides.

Mother snapped, "Your son was an immature, apathetic, *lazy* child who didn't deserve the crown he inherited." Her jaw clenched as she swallowed. "But I didn't want him dead, Bella. That, if anything, is the truth."

"You just wanted him gone," Clarissa said from the ground beside Leo. She stood on shaking legs, her white dress covered in dirt and grunge. "You knew you couldn't move against him directly, but he was already one misstep away from driving his entire kingdom away from him. His curse was running him into the ground."

Clarissa took another step toward my mother. "So you didn't *want* him to break the curse. And I was your biggest obstacle. Every 'accident,' every setback, it was all *you*. The carriage driver, the cave-in, the —the fox." She paused to clear her throat, and I instinctively moved to her side. "You say you didn't want him dead, but you poisoned him too, didn't you? And the hunter on the island that almost killed me?"

"The *what?*" I growled.

"The poison was meant for *you*, not Galen," my mother bit out.

I blinked. How had I been so blind? So utterly naive?

"Who are you working with?" I seethed, locking my eyes on my mother. "It's impossible for you to have done this all on your own. I was with you most of the time—*Marigold* was with you." My words turned into a snarl at the thought that I'd allowed this woman to be anywhere near my daughter.

She merely stared at me in silence.

The memory of walking in on her speaking with someone in private right before the ball popped in my mind, as well as the glimpse of a cloak Clarissa and I saw outside my hut the evening before the Hunt.

"You have spies, don't you?" I asked. "That's how you knew the things Clarissa said about Galen. That's who you were speaking with when you told me you were searching for my father." When she still didn't answer, the air grew thick with tension. My anger swirled inside me, readying to lash out.

"Answer me!" I thundered, chest heaving.

"What do you want me to say, Thorne?" she hissed. "You're already going to see me behind bars after all of this. Your own *mother*. What more do you want from me?"

"I want the *truth*. I want you to look me in the eye and tell me you tried to kill the woman I love. That *you're* the one who caused her such pain. That you've been lying to me for *months*."

Clarissa sucked in a breath, and her fingers grazed the side of my hand.

"I told you once that you were a fool," my mother whispered. "Perhaps we both were. But I was doing what I thought was best for our kingdom."

I shook my head in disgust. "No, you weren't. You were doing what you wanted. What best served *you*."

"How did you do it all?" Clarissa asked. "Who was helping you?"

"Someone who owes me a great debt," Mother said. "And who's just as willing to do what must be done to get what she wants."

Her eyes flitted over my shoulder.

I turned to see a flash of red hair and sunlight glaring off black-rimmed glasses. The maid appeared from the side door of the palace with bandages and ointment in hand.

Clarissa inhaled sharply. "Devora?"

Devora's keen gaze found my mother's. Her face hardened. She dropped the supplies and spun on her heel.

"Not so fast, darling," a low drawl echoed from behind her right as Nox wrapped his hand around Devora's wrist.

She gasped like something had burned her, then snapped her neck up at him. A second later, a dark mist seeped from her feet. It almost looked as if it were coming *from* her.

Nox glared down at her, his features shifting from suspicious to downright murderous as he let out a curse and yanked her closer to him.

"*Who are you?*" he shouted, a hint of his dragon form leaking through. His navy eyes held a storm while the veins at his forehead and neck pulsed.

"Nox!" Clarissa said in warning, pointing to the shadows now billowing between Nox and Devora. "What are you doing?"

"That's not me," he said. In the blink of an eye, Nox twisted Devora's arm so her back was pressed into his chest, his arm held tight across her throat.

His voice came out a growl as he said, "It's her. She's *Veridian*."

65

CLARISSA

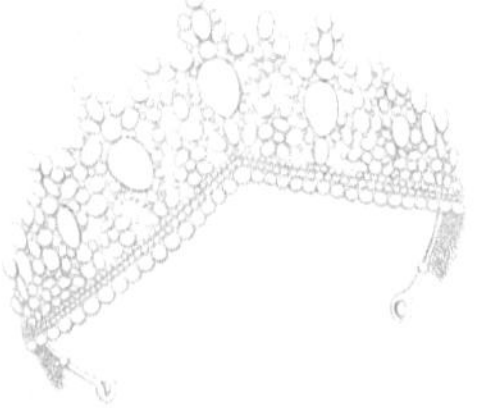

She's Veridian.

My mouth opened, but no sound came out. I blinked to try and wipe away my shock, to make sense of the impossible. Because it was *impossible*.

"How do you know?" Thorne asked.

Nox strengthened his hold on Devora, who glared up at him and tried to pull away. "My magic," he answered. "I still have some left from the island, and when I touched her, she siphoned it from me." He turned so his nose grazed the side of Devora's face, baring his fangs to her. "Tell me how you got to this kingdom, *Shadow Wielder*."

She struggled against him. "I don't know what you're talking about," she snapped. "Let *go* of me."

"You're lying," Nox shot back.

"I'm not," she seethed. "I never knew my family, okay? I don't know what this," she jerked her head toward the shadows dissipating at her feet, "is. Nothing like that has ever happened before. I'd never even met a—a Veridian until Clarissa."

Her eyes found mine, and their voices melted away. All I could do was stare at Devora, at the familiar face of the woman I'd come to know these past few weeks. The woman I'd called my *friend*. I

478

didn't care where she came from. I didn't care if she was Veridian or not.

She'd betrayed me.

Those blue-green eyes held my stare, and to her credit, she didn't back down. She was never one to tuck her tail between her legs—this was the girl with daggers under her uniform and liquor hidden in her chest. Honest, authentic, unfiltered.

Except...it had all been a lie.

"How could you?" I whispered.

Her gaze fell to her feet.

I took a step forward, my voice rising. I could still see the charred red fur staked in the middle of that bonfire, only this time, Devora's form flickered next to it. "The fox in the fire? Was that you?"

She swallowed. "I didn't have a choice. I know it doesn't seem like it, but I was trying to protect you."

"Protect me?" A chuckle full of mirth bubbled out of me. "That's the best you've got? After trying to kill Galen and me, trapping us in the mines, *humiliating* me?"

"I never tried to kill you," she rushed out. "That wasn't me, I promise."

I paused, searching her features. When I gave a quick nod to Nox, he reluctantly released his grip as I stood toe-to-toe with her. My fingers itched to close around her throat, the violent streak of my dormant fox half longing to rise to the surface. "I trusted you. I let you into my life. I don't know what she has on you, but I would have done anything to help you, Devora."

"I know," she said. "But Lady Reaux promised to give me information on my family. You have no idea how long I've been trying to find them, Rissa, and—"

"*Don't*," I snarled. "Don't you dare call me that."

She blinked and rolled her lips together. "I'm sorry, Your Majesty," she finally said. "I didn't want any of it to happen this way. Lady Reaux threatened to have you killed, to make it easier for her to ruin the alliance. But after I met you, I knew I couldn't let that happen. I begged her not to. I—I told her I could get you to leave willingly, to abandon the marriage and go back to your empire. I didn't want anyone to have to die."

Her voice lowered, remorse shining in her guarded eyes. "Lady Reaux agreed. She told me to do what it took to convince you to leave. *Whatever* it took."

"You could have warned me." I was angry at how choked my words sounded—how my emotions bled through even when I tried so hard to hold them back. "You could have said something. *Anything*."

"I know," she whispered back. "I'm sorry. But she—she gave me a job, a home, when nobody else would. I owed her a debt. And she knows about my family, things I've been searching for my whole life. The answers were *right there*. All I had to do was—"

"Betray me," I finished for her.

Her shoulders slumped, that wavy red hair swaying across her chest. "She was going to get her way no matter what. I tried to protect you the only way I knew how."

I didn't respond. I took a step back and straightened. "I hope it was worth it," I finally said, forcing ice into my tone. "I hope you got your answers."

"I think today's revelation made things a whole lot more complicated." Devora's eyes slid behind me to meet Azura's. "How could you not tell me my parents were Veridian?"

I turned and saw Azura bristle. "I had no idea," she admitted. "I don't know who your parents are, Devora. All I know is that you were found on the shores of the North Territory as an infant."

Devora's eyes flashed. She jumped forward, and I could have sworn wisps of shadows appeared once again where she stood. "You *lied* to me? You promised if I helped you, you'd tell me!"

"And you were desperate enough to show your hand, dear. I knew you'd do anything to get what you wanted, just as I would. We're not so different, you and I," Azura remarked.

"I am *nothing* like you," Devora spat, then spun to face me. "Riss—Your Majesty, I'm sorry. I never wanted to hurt you, but I—

I made a mistake. So many mistakes." Her voice hitched. "I'll tell you anything you want to know."

I crossed my arms over my chest. "Start from the beginning."

She nodded. "I was hired by the Reaux family four years ago. I served as Lady Reaux's handmaiden, and she grew to trust me. She made up a plan to have me transferred over to the palace's staff so she could have eyes and ears on the Grimaldi family, although she wouldn't tell me why. So I...got close to the prince." She averted her gaze from mine.

"As Lady Reaux knew he would, he eventually brought me to the palace. I worked there for two years, spying on the crown, delivering information back to her. Nine months ago, when King Orion died, things became...different. Galen would disappear for weeks on end. Lady Reaux stopped communicating with me, and everyone was quieter, more secretive. I couldn't figure out what was going on. But when word came about *you* arriving"—she gestured toward me—"she reached out again. Told me what she needed me to do, in exchange for information on my family.

"Katrine and I were assigned to be your lady's maids. She had no idea about any of this, of course—I didn't want her involved. After we met you, after we heard about what you'd been through over in your empire, the way you were changing things for your people..." Her shoulders fell. "I couldn't do it. I told Lady Reaux I refused to go along with her plan. I thought she would give up, but then I found out about the attack on the way to the Mid Territory, and I *knew* it was her. She was serious. She was willing to do anything to get you out of the way, even kill you. So I went back to her and offered my deal: I'd do what I could to drive you off, if she swore not to hurt you again.

"I'd heard rumors about one of the citizen's daughters winding up dead in the palace several months ago. I found her father and told him Galen would be at the Harvest Tournament. Then I bribed the guards to let Tovar Printh through with his weapon. I hoped if you saw the kind of man Galen was, you'd be scared away. Or pissed off—it didn't matter, I just wanted to give you a reason to bolt."

Devora paused to rub a hand on the back of her neck. Her cheeks paled as she took a deep breath. "When that didn't work, I —I remembered how upset you'd been about shifting. How the people were scared of you. I thought—I thought if nothing else could convince you to leave, *this* would. So I found the fox."

I gritted my teeth against the pressure mounting in my chest. She'd seemed unlike herself that night. Almost as if she didn't want to go to the Harvest Festival. And when I was burned, she dropped everything to take care of me, with an urgency I'd thought was compassion but turned out to be guilt. All the signs were there, but I'd been too blind to see them.

Her eyes swam with silver as she met my stare. "I hate myself for what I did to you." She swallowed. "But it was better than watching you die."

"Were you behind the mine collapsing as well?" Thorne asked, stepping to my side.

Devora shook her head. "No, that wasn't me. I wasn't the only one working for her. When I didn't succeed, she turned to other means. She must have paid someone in the South Territory to cause the cave-in."

Thorne rounded on his mother. "*Marigold* was in those caves, Mother. Have you lost your mind? If anything had happened to her, if a *single* hair on her head had been—"

"I didn't know she would be there!" Azura cried out. For the first time, she looked desperate. True fear crossed over the hard lines of her face. "She wasn't *supposed* to be there, Thorne. I would have never gone through with it had I known. I made sure she wasn't caught in the collapse. She was *safe*."

Thorne's jaw flexed beneath his thick beard. "Then I guess it didn't matter that your 'accident' almost killed me too, as long as it got Clarissa. It's all collateral damage to you."

Azura reached forward to cup Thorne's cheek, but he shoved her hand away. "That was a mistake," Azura whispered. "Clarissa was supposed to be alone while Galen was distracted by the miner girl. You and your ridiculous heart simply couldn't stay away from her."

I turned back to Devora. "The poison, then. Our last night in the South Territory. Who was that?"

"I didn't find out about that until after," Devora said. "Lady Reaux spiked the whiskey, thinking you and your friends would have a few drinks after the ball, like you had the other nights."

I hummed. "Take the Veridians out all at once."

"But the girl who brought him the whiskey had no idea," Devora finished.

"Another mistake, I assume?" Thorne snarled at his mother. "Your *mistakes* seem to be hurting everyone you claim to care about, Mother."

Devora glanced between him and me. "She had me spy on you," she confessed. "One last time. Before the Hunt. I—I told her what you said about Veridians. And about Galen." She twisted her lips. "I thought it could look like cause for treason, and if Galen found out, he would send you away."

I looked up at Thorne and found his eyes already on me. It wasn't him. A small trickle of relief mixed with the sea of emotions that had flooded me in the last twenty-four hours. I didn't know if I would've been able to handle him betraying me too.

"I guess it was your hunter in the jungle, then," I said to Azura, my voice sharpening. "It was a good attempt, considering I was already half-dead, but I'm sorry to tell you that your little *friend* didn't make it."

At my side, Thorne muttered, "Fates, what *happened* in that jungle?"

"How did you ever think the regent families would accept this?" Isabella asked Azura incredulously. "That our kingdom would accept *you* after what you've done?"

Azura's shoulders clenched. "The regents had all made their apprehension of Galen known. I was doing this to bring about a better reign. A *stronger* reign. Not some petulant boy who used his crown as a toy while he ignored the cries of our people."

"You may have convinced yourself of some noble cause, but that doesn't make it true," Isabella said, shaking her head. She coughed into the bloody rag still in her hand. When she looked back up, her eyes were filled with fire. "You did this out of revenge. And because of that, I've lost my entire family." She pointed a finger at Azura's chest, waves of hatred rolling from her. "You have taken my husband's life, and you may yet take mine. But you are *done* harming this kingdom."

She snapped her fingers without looking away from Azura, and two guards stalked forward. "Take her," she commanded.

"I want to see my granddaughter," Azura said as the guards grabbed her wrists, making her drop her cane. She tried to pull away from them. "I want to see Marigold."

A scoff of contempt left Thorne's throat. "You can't be serious." He screwed his face into a look of disgust, but I could see him hiding the pain. "I swear to you, Mother, you will *never* see her again. Not after this."

Her features fell as she pleaded with him. "Please, Thorne. I— I'm so sorry. Just one more time. I love her, you have to know that."

His shoulders sagged, and despite how much I hated the woman before me, my heart hurt for them. For the bone-deep ache I knew Thorne must be feeling, for the past he once had with his mother. Besides Marigold, she was the only family he had left. I couldn't imagine how much this decision was warring within him.

"You once told me that love couldn't rescue me," he started, his voice wavering. "And yet here you are, using it as a crutch. As a bargaining chip." He stepped backward, putting more space between the two of them. "You don't know what love is, Mother. I'm not sure you ever did."

He looked at Isabella, dipping his chin once. She moved forward and signaled to the guards.

"Azura Reaux, for the assassination of King Orion Grimaldi, attempted assassination of myself, and treason against the crown,

I sentence you to a lifetime in prison." She narrowed her eyes. "It's for the sake of your son and granddaughter that I don't have you executed on the spot. Consider this a mercy—something you failed to show me and my family."

The guards led Azura away, her gown trailing in their wake.

Isabella turned to Devora, who squared her feet and lifted her chin, saying, "I know I have to answer for my crimes, Your Grace. I'll accept whatever punishment you give me."

Isabella raised an eyebrow. "Actually, what I was going to say is that, given your heritage, you're no longer under Mysthelm jurisdiction."

Realization bolted through me, and I let out a sigh. I really didn't want to deal with this. I would be *dead* right now if it weren't for the Fates and their little gift. I needed air. I needed time and space away from all of this.

I closed my eyes, feeling the weight of their stares on me, and tried to push past my emotional response to find the diplomatic part of me that would make the right decision.

"She'll come with me," a voice said. My eyes popped open at Nox's statement. "She can serve out her punishment in Drakorum."

"I'd rather you stuff me in a cell," Devora muttered.

"And here I was, thinking you wanted to learn about your family," Nox drawled, but venom seeped from him. "So much so that you put the life of my friend and Empress in danger. So, yes, you'll be coming with me. Whether you like it or not."

Shifters were loyal creatures, and it pricked something in my chest to see how protective he was of me.

Devora's jaw shifted, her eyes burning with defiance, but she stayed silent.

"Nox, are you sure this is a good idea?" I asked slowly.

"You have enough problems on your hands," he said. "Besides, there are plenty of ways we can make her answer for her crimes." A dark glint of a challenge appeared in his navy eyes.

I had a feeling this would not end well.

I looked at Devora again, those placid features hiding so much more than I ever imagined. Memories of the last few weeks flitted through my mind—our talks every morning as we got ready for the day, adventuring through the Mid Territory and healing the land, going to the Harvest Festival together. Watching her come alive around the campfires, surrounded by music and laughter. How terrified she was for Katrine the night Galen kissed her, how attentive she was when taking care of my burns.

Burns *she'd* inadvertently caused.

I turned away. "Fine. Get her back to the empire, and she's your responsibility, Nox."

Nox took her by the shoulder, and they made their way to the palace, followed by Rose and Evadine, with Leo supported between the two of them. Thorne, Isabella, and the head of the King's Guard began discussing logistics and damage control, how they needed to get the regent families to the palace as quickly as possible to figure out a plan of action.

It all made my head spin.

The reality of the last twenty-four hours settled into me, and it was like that noose was back around my neck. Pulling, straining, tightening.

"Excuse me, I—I have to go," I said as their puzzled expressions shifted to me.

I pivoted on my heels and ran.

66

CLARISSA

"I see you've found my favorite hiding spot," Thorne said from behind me.

I craned my neck to watch him climb through the trap door of the secluded rooftop, a little sanctuary tucked away between two of the taller towers on the west side of the palace.

"Katrine told me about it." I turned my attention back to the view in front of me. "I think she knew I needed to get away."

When I'd found her in the servants' wing and told her the news about Devora, she'd broken down crying. I knew they were like sisters, after having worked at Reaux Mansion and then the palace together. I wasn't the only one who'd been affected by her betrayal. And now Devora was being carted off to a different land, with no telling if she'd ever set foot on Mysthelm soil again.

We faced the sunset, its orange and pink glow casting the palm trees and winding, sandy roads of the North Territory in a golden hue. A light breeze rifled through my hair and the plain tunic I'd changed into as soon as I could get out of that wedding dress. I sat with my knees tucked into my chest, my arms wrapped tight around them, breathing in the evening air.

"I used to hide here all the time when Galen and I played hide-and-seek," Thorne admitted. "Found it by accident when I tripped and ripped the tapestry covering the stairs to get up here." His voice softened. "Galen never found it. I won every time."

Guilt needled beneath my ribs. *His best friend was dead*. And while I'd argued for my innocence, part of me couldn't help but wonder...*had* I killed him? Something in the curse broke and consumed him when I'd kissed him. When the marriage was sealed. If I hadn't gone through with it, he'd still be alive.

Did Thorne blame me? I was the reason his best friend was gone, the reason his mother was behind bars, and everything he'd known had been torn from him. Dread and fear trickled down my chest and into my stomach like hot wax.

I pulled my knees in further. "Thorne, I—I'm so sorry." My words came out a whisper. "I don't know what to say. This is all my fault. He's dead because of me, and I—"

"No, no—Clarissa, this is *not* your fault." He strode to my side and fell to his knees before me, cupping my face in his hands. His body blocked the sunset. His shadow consumed me, blanketing me in his steady presence, a cool reprieve from the anxiety curdling in my gut.

He gently stroked away a tear I didn't even know had fallen. "You went into that wedding wanting to break his curse. To save him and our entire kingdom, no matter what the cost. This was all some twisted game of the Fates. There was nothing you could have done."

I swallowed and nodded, sniffing back more tears. His gaze fell to my neck and the faint red scratches that hadn't yet healed from the rope rubbing against it. Slowly, he moved his thumb to graze along the raised skin, and I closed my eyes.

"I'm sorry too," he said. "For what my mother put you through. When I saw you up there, when I thought—" He cut himself off, his voice low and raspy. Pressure built in my chest, my lungs, my throat. "I thought you were gone. I thought I'd lost you. I would have done anything to take your place, Clarissa." He dropped his forehead to mine, and I let my knees fall so he could lean in closer.

"I would rather die a thousand deaths than watch a single moment of your suffering."

I sucked in a shaky breath as another tear fell, landing on the space of roof between us. A rush of humid wind blew across the side of the palace. Our long hair twisted and twined around us, blonde against dark brown.

"So, I guess you sort of love me," I whispered.

He kissed my forehead, and his small smile pressed into my skin. "Ah, you heard that part, did you?"

"It must have slipped out."

I want you to look me in the eye and tell me you tried to kill the woman I love.

Time had frozen in that moment. Just for a second. Amidst the chaos and outrage and secrets, my heart soared.

He pulled away and brushed a strand of hair behind my ear. "Before I met you, I thought I was happy. As happy as this life could make me, at least. Marigold was my sun. She was all I ever needed in a world full of gray. I smiled when I was supposed to smile, went where I was supposed to go, checked my duties off an ever-growing list. I didn't *want* anything more for myself. I'd wanted enough in my past life, and I hadn't been able to hold on to what it had given me."

He gave a subtle shake of his head, his brow pinching as if thinking through his words. "And here you come, beauty and grace and strength all bottled into this fiery, stubborn woman, and I *wanted*. I wanted your resolve and conviction. I wanted your heart of gold, your ability to give such light and magic to the world. I wanted *you*."

His blue eyes searched mine with an intensity that made my breath catch in my throat. "From the moment I saw you, I knew I couldn't have you. But I wanted you anyway. I wanted to be a better man because of you. For my daughter, for my kingdom, and for *myself*."

His hand shifted to the back of my neck. "You bring life to everything you touch, Clarissa. Not just with your magic. With your *compassion*. With your selflessness. How could I not love you?" He brought his other hand up to graze my jaw, my lips, my cheek. "All that you are is all I have never let myself want before. And I am desperately, deeply, maddeningly in love with you."

I couldn't even try to stop the tears from flowing down my cheeks. I turned my neck to tuck my face into his hand, kissing his palm and tasting my own salty tears. It was too much. What he saw in me was too much—it made my heart swell to the point of bursting, made me want to cover the strong emotions I'd learned to chase away under pressure.

"Don't you dare," he whispered, leaning in so close that his lips skimmed the top of my cheek. "Don't hide from me, Empress."

"Has anyone ever told you that you're quite the romantic?"

That same smile melted along my skin again. "Someone might have mentioned it before."

I pulled back so I could see him. That rough, tan skin, that dark beard that felt so good against me, those eyes that swallowed me whole.

"I told you once I wished I was like that," I said. "I don't know if I'll ever stop being bound by my duty. For as long as I can remember, I've had people I needed to look out for. People who relied on me. It always felt like one small mistake and so many people could get hurt. I think I stopped caring about whether *I* got hurt in the process. It's like you said—I thought I was happy. If those I loved were happy and taken care of, I had no reason *not* to be." I let out a small laugh. "You know, you're not the first one to call me out on that."

He chuckled, and the sound burrowed into my chest. "My stubborn girl."

"But you're the first one I *heard*," I said, my smile faltering as I swallowed thickly. "You're the first one who made me realize what I was missing." A breath left me in a rush, and the words spilled out. "Fates, I wanted you too. I think I wanted you more than I've ever wanted anything. And knowing I couldn't have you, the *one* selfish thing I'd finally allowed myself, was just another part of my duty to accept. Things have changed, but our lives…they're just too different. *That* hasn't changed." My eyes darted around him. "We live an ocean apart. I—I don't know where to go from here. After everything that's happened, I just—"

Thorne dug his thumb into the back of my neck to cut me off, making me look up at him. I stared into those eyes that had become both my sanctuary and my downfall.

"I've never been in love, Thorne," I whispered. "I don't know what we're supposed to do."

He leaned in to brush his lips over my cheek, then slowly captured my mouth with his. I instantly felt a weight lifting from my shoulders as I rose onto my knees to deepen the kiss. I'd kissed him before, but this time felt…freer. Like it was something beautiful given to us, instead of a moment we had to steal.

"Do you love me?" he breathed into me.

"Yes," I said without hesitation.

"Then we'll figure it out. Together."

I wrapped my arms around his neck, angling my body to press further into him, molding my curves to his hard planes. His hands grasped my waist and pulled me closer. Warm fingers lifted the edges of my shirt and traveled over my skin, making my stomach tighten with every passing second.

In that moment, I saw my future laid out before me.

It was the future I'd always planned for, yes. Meetings with my council, drinks at the Drakin's Lair with Chaz and Lark, arguments with Lord Stryker over taxes and land permits, signing decrees at my father's old desk. But for the first time…it was more than that.

It was early mornings with Thorne's skin pressed into mine. Late nights and a little girl tucked between our arms. Deep laughter that made my toes curl, grinning faces peering at me over stacks of paperwork. Smirks and bright eyes and warm, rough hands. Dancing in the kitchen with nobody around, like my parents used to do in our cottage. Those little stolen glances in a crowded room that say *"you're mine."*

I wanted that. I wanted all of it. My empire *and* my happily ever after.

"Come with me," I said.

His hands paused on my abdomen. "What?"

"You and Marigold. Come with me." I kissed him again. "Back to the empire."

He jerked backward onto his heels, then rose to his feet, his lips parting. "Are you serious?"

Heat flooded my cheeks as I stood and dusted off my leggings. "Well, I mean—only if you want to. You can say no." I never made these rash decisions. Embarrassment made my words stammer, tumbling over one another. "I know that's a lot to ask. We can talk about it first, how everything would work, but I—"

Seizing my waist, he lifted me in the air and spun me in his arms. "Tell me to run, and I'll run. Tell me to stand at your side, and I'll stand. Wherever, *whenever* you want me. Haven't you figured that out by now?" He stopped moving and tilted his head to the side, his nose grazing mine. "I've been yours since the day you stepped off that ship, Clarissa."

A beam broke out across my face. We were both breathless, our chests heaving against one another as my hair flowed down his cheek and neck, cocooning us in our own little world.

"So, is that yes?" I asked.

His answering smile rivaled the setting sun. "That's a yes for me, Empress. But there's someone I need to talk to first."

67

THORNE

The next few days passed in a whirlwind.

Clarissa immediately chartered a ship to take her mother, Rose, Leo, Nox, and Devora back to the Veridian Empire, with a letter to her council explaining what occurred during her time here and a list of necessary actions for them to consider for when she returned. I knew she was still partially tied down by their approval until the one-year mark was up on her provisional status as empress-elect, but I could see how much she hated having to give them an ounce of consideration.

Isabella Grimaldi was the acting Queen of Mysthelm in the wake of Galen's death. I did not envy her position. I remembered how she'd been somewhat absent as a mother to Galen, but she'd always been respected by our kingdom. She was the only choice to help our people get back on their feet after the shocking blow Galen's death dealt us.

But no parent should outlive their child. My mother's poison had done its job ravaging her body, and now her mind was shadowed in grief as well. Rose had left us with the rest of the tonic she gave Isabella to help briefly clear the effects of the foxglove and hellebore, but she told us it wasn't a permanent solution. Just enough to give Isabella time to get her affairs in order.

The Grimaldi line was dying. Soon, it would be gone.

And it was my mother's fault.

As much as Clarissa tried to convince me my guilt was misplaced, it didn't erase the pit in my stomach. It didn't erase the mounting pile of "what-ifs" and all the things I should have done, or the rose-colored glasses that blinded me to my mother's machinations for so long.

I should have trusted my instincts. I should have seen through her condescension masked as motherly affection and known she was up to something more. But nobody wanted to believe someone they'd known their entire lives—someone they *loved*—was capable of such terrible things.

I kept my promise. I refused to let her see Marigold. And, Fates, if that wasn't the hardest part of it all.

How was I supposed to explain to my seven-year-old daughter that she couldn't see her grandmother anymore, the only other person besides me she called family? The woman who'd read her nearly as many bedtime stories as I had, who watched her play dress-up and fixed her skinned knees and wiped the tears from her little cheeks. Those big brown eyes, wide with confusion, were nearly my undoing.

"Your grandmother has done some very bad things, sweetheart. Things that have hurt people. I know it makes you sad, but our actions have consequences," I told her that first night, while we were squeezed under the covers of her bed back in our house, shadows dancing on the walls from the fading candlelight. Mia nestled into Marigold's back—the two of them had been bound at the hip since we got back to the North Territory. I thought Clarissa knew it brought Marigold comfort to have the pup nearby.

"But...why?" She buried her face in the crook of my elbow as Mia's soft snores vibrated in the air. "Why would she hurt someone?"

"I don't know," I answered honestly. "Do you remember the story of the lost princess? Where the golden-haired woman takes her away to the enchanted garden, but when she doesn't get what she wants, she becomes cruel? I think sometimes people get so angry that they take it out on others who don't deserve it."

"If Grandma was angry...was she angry at me? Is that why I can't see her?" Marigold asked, her voice so muffled, I could barely hear it.

My heart clenched. I forgot how small the world seemed to a child, how deeply sensitive she was toward those around her. I gathered her in my arms and kissed the top of her head as a sting formed behind my eyes.

"Of *course* not, Marigold. She was never angry with you. She knows you love her so much, and she loves you too. But there are some things that love can't fix in a person if they let all the bad things control them instead. Things like anger or fear or hatred." I nudged her chin to look up at me, and her bottom lip trembled. "You are none of those things, sweetheart. And absolutely none of this is your fault."

I rocked her to sleep as she sniffled against me, then fell into a restless sleep of my own. This little girl and I had already been through so much together in her short life. I knew we'd get through this, too, but I would never stop wishing I could shield her from things.

Which was why I didn't immediately tell her of Clarissa's invitation to join her in the Veridian Empire. There was so much change going on, I needed a moment of reprieve. I didn't want to be selfish with my daughter's life. I had to make the best decision for both of us, not just my heart. Would moving our family give her the best chance for happiness? Or would it simply cause more pain? Would their people even accept us?

There were so many unanswered questions, one of which being the idea of my father still being alive all the way across the waters. Clarissa had gently broached the subject during one of our evenings together—was that something I wanted to pursue? If we moved to the empire, would I want to find him?

I simply didn't know.

And there was too much commotion in the palace in those first few days after Galen's death for me to dwell on it for long. The regent families arrived as quickly as they could, and we got to work. Statements had to be written and rewritten to inform the kingdom of his passing, his disorganized office with countless records and requests had to be filtered through, and most importantly, we had to figure out where the monarchy went from here once the Grimaldi line ceased to exist.

We all met with Isabella day in and day out. One thing had become clear over the past months with Galen on the throne: the regents did more work in their respective territories than we'd ever been given credit for. *We* were the ones the people turned to in times of need. Disasters, crimes, financial struggles. We knew what our territories required better than anyone. I'd seen that for myself as we spent time with them on the tour—even the self-righteous Rhys Penworth ultimately wanted to do right by his people.

Perhaps the answer truly was that simple.

Dion Silenus was the first one to suggest it. Some sort of ruling body made up of the regent families, built to keep each other in line but with enough power to take care of their territories. No more requesting permission from the crown to rebuild the ports when storms came through, no more waiting for funds when entire fields of crops were burned in wildfires.

I was inclined to agree with his ideas. Maybe it was time for Mysthelm to make a change. We knew it wouldn't happen within a few panic-induced meetings, but it was a starting point.

I spent my days in close quarters with the other regents, poring over notes and settling disagreements. Breaking up a fight or two. Nothing that wasn't expected when this many big personalities shared a space. It left me exhausted, both physically and mentally, and getting to go home to Clarissa was like peeling back the curtains of a dark room and letting the sunshine in.

She'd told her family when they set sail to the empire that she would follow them in a week's time. She felt a personal obligation to help Isabella get things settled before taking off—her heart was so big, her concern for others so all-encompassing. And I knew a bit of guilt would always linger over the part she believed she played in Galen's death. This was her way of making up for it.

So, while my days were consumed by meetings, my nights were consumed by her.

I'd forgotten what it was like to love so freely. Before, she had been like a story in one of Marigold's books—beautiful and enrapturing, but when you got to the end, the last page was ripped out. She was a tale I was never meant to know the ending of. Never meant to be part of.

Now...she *was* the end. She and Marigold were all I saw when I looked at my future. And it was the most beautiful future I could never deserve.

But there were still so many unknowns. This wasn't a fairytale —as much as I wanted to throw her over my shoulder and ride off into the sunset. I had no idea what our lives would look like if I uprooted everything Marigold and I had built here.

I had told Clarissa yes. There was just one last piece of the puzzle.

I knocked on Marigold's door, which was already cracked. I could see the corner of her arm and her dolls moving up and down on the opposite side of the room. "It's me," I called.

"Daddy, you're home!" she squealed.

I pushed the door open wider as she and Mia both ran up to me, one wrapping her arms around my waist and the other circling my feet.

I smiled when I saw Clarissa sitting on the floor, a female doll in her grip and a male one lying on its back, its legs bent at an odd angle.

I raised an eyebrow. "Are you girls having...fun?"

"Rissa's showing me and my dolls how to fight!" Without warning, Marigold jumped back and kicked at my waist. I quickly grabbed her ankle before she could make contact and shot Clarissa a bemused look.

"Good form, but what did we talk about?" Clarissa asked.

Marigold giggled when I tickled her calf. "Only when I feel unsafe."

"There you go." Clarissa winked at me. "What? Is this not what they're teaching little girls nowadays?"

I chuckled and shook my head, releasing Marigold's leg and ruffling her hair. "You'll have to show me what else Rissa is teaching you after dinner, yes?"

She nodded eagerly. "Is she staying the night again?"

I glanced over her head toward Clarissa. She'd been sleeping at the mansion ever since her family left four nights ago. "Yes, she is."

Marigold bounced over to the rest of her discarded toys and began picking them up one by one. She could never stand still for too long. "Okay! And that means Mia gets to stay too." Mia stopped sniffing at my ankles at the sound of her name. Her ears perked up, and she trotted over to Clarissa and Marigold.

I licked my lips, sharing another look with Clarissa. We'd spent the last few evenings alone together dreaming of the future. I listened to her talk about her empire, of all the provinces and their magic and the sights she wanted to show us. I hung onto her every word, to the way her voice sped up in excitement when she mentioned her friends or the little cottage she grew up in, how a smile peeked at the corners of her lips when she spoke of the south sector that was so close to her heart. The schools, the food, the colors and sounds of Veridia City. She made it come alive. She made what our life could be like feel real.

I'd been avoiding the subject with Marigold all week, but I supposed there would never be a perfect time.

Clarissa seemed to understand, for she eased up onto her feet and stretched. "I'm going to go get ready for dinner," she said. "Mia, let's go, girl!" Mia bounded to her, her tail wagging back and forth across the floor.

When they crossed the room, Clarissa brushed the side of her hand against me and wrapped her pinky around mine for a split second—what had become our way of silently giving strength. Of saying "*I'm here*," even when we couldn't always be.

"Marigold, sweetheart, why don't you come here for a second?" I asked once the door shut behind them, taking a seat at the foot of Marigold's bed.

With a little dance, she plopped next to me, scooting closer with her doll in hand.

I'd been thinking about this conversation for a while, but sitting here with her made the words a thousand times harder. "Do you remember how sometimes we talk about your mommy?" I began, my voice hoarse.

She nodded as she patted the doll's hands together. "Yes. And we talk about magic and how she watches us from the stars and loves us very much," she said all in one breath.

"That's right. I know you don't remember much about her, but she took such good care of us. And I will always have love for your mommy. I think about her every day, and how much you look like her. Did you know that?"

Her eyes grew wide. "I do?"

An ache formed in my chest. I brushed back a piece of her hair and curled it around my finger. "You do. She had this same brown hair, and those same big brown eyes. Darker than mine, see?" I leaned down, and she lifted a finger to poke my cheek. "I miss her, just like I'm sure you do. But our hearts are so big that it's possible to have that much love for someone else too."

"You mean Rissa?"

I cocked my head. *Perceptive little girl.* "Yes, I mean Rissa." I paused, waiting to see if she would say more. "I love her very much, Marigold. And she loves you and me both. She wants to be in our lives for longer than just this tour. That's why she's asked if we would come live with her in the Veridian Empire."

She drank in my words, a small crease appearing between her eyes as she mulled the idea over. "So we'd be...leaving our home? We wouldn't be here anymore?"

I nodded, moving to kneel in front of her so I could see her face. "That's right. But there's so much to see in the empire. You'd get to live in a palace, since Rissa is Empress. We can decorate your new room however you like, and you'd see Mia every day. You'll make so many new friends, and Rissa even said there's a school nearby in Veridia City you could go to soon."

My usual exuberant, wears-her-heart-on-her-sleeve daughter was now expressionless. Her head tilted to the side as she peered down at me. She looked far beyond her seven years of life.

I grabbed her little hands. "Look, sweetheart, I know there have been a lot of changes lately. I know change can be scary. *I'm* a little scared too. But we've always gotten through it, haven't we? We're a team, you and I. We always will be. And we can do scary things together."

"I don't think I'm scared, Daddy. It's just...I'm kind of sad." She rubbed her chest with the heel of her hand. "I'll miss my room. And my friends. And Grandma." Her bottom lip puckered in a small pout.

"I know you will." I pulled her off the bed and set her on my knee as I crouched on the ground. "It's okay to be sad."

Resting her head on my shoulder, she twined a lock of my hair around her finger. "But I think I love Rissa too. She's nice. And pretty. And she makes you smile."

I struggled to take in a breath through the emotion clogging my throat. "Yes. Yes, she does."

She looked up at me, and while I could still see the hesitancy there, could still see sadness swirling at the surface, she managed to bring a gap-toothed grin to her face. "She makes me smile too."

68

CLARISSA

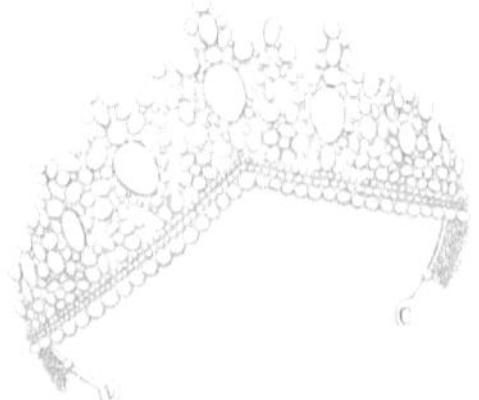

My fingers trailed the side of Thorne's face and down to his jaw as I took him in. The rising sunlight spilled from the porthole and across the floor of my cabin.

Most of my life was spent on the move, my mind constantly working through problems and my attention often pulled in multiple directions. But right now...I wished I could freeze time. Catch us in this single breath, this perfect moment where his chest rose with mine and his eyes danced like the waves of the ocean rocking beneath us.

"We'll be there soon," I whispered, softly scraping my fingernail against his bottom lip. "How do you feel?"

He kissed my finger and put an arm around my waist to pull me closer. "I'm not having second thoughts, if that's what you're thinking."

A laugh bubbled out of my throat. "Well, that's a good thing. The only way you're getting back to Mysthelm is if I toss you off this boat."

I rested my head against his heart. I'd gotten so used to these moments in the two weeks since the wedding. The quiet space between sleep and the movement of the day, where we could just... be. Together. No hiding, no curses, no manipulations and secrets.

"What are you thinking about?" I asked.

His thumb swirled around the top of my shoulder where his shirt had slipped down my arm. "I'm thinking about this freckle on your shoulder." He kissed the spot. "I'm thinking about how I can't wait to watch you squash your council like bugs." I chuckled at that. He knew my stab-like tendencies with some of them. "And... I'm thinking I'm a little anxious."

"Anxious? Why?"

He sighed. "We saw how my kingdom struggled to accept you. Part of me has been nervous about bringing my daughter into a new land with new threats I can't control. The magic you've told me about...it sounds wonderful, truly. But it's also unknown to us. And being surrounded by strangers who can wield it...it's a lot to come to terms with."

I couldn't blame him for his fears. He'd seen firsthand how difficult it was for me in Mysthelm, and I'd be lying if I said their first few weeks here would be sunshine and rainbows. But nothing worth fighting for ever was.

"I know what it's like to not be accepted," I started. "It's terrifying. But that's what I've been working toward. I want to make my empire a safe place, where people don't have to fear the kind of mistreatment I and so many others have faced before. My people are *good* people. They trust me, and most of them want the same things I do."

I put a hand on his neck. "This could be another step in our people realizing we don't have to be enemies. We don't have to live apart just because we're different or because our past dictates we must. I think...I think you and Marigold could have a good life here. There would be more than enough people to spoil her and look out for her the way she deserves. To love her the way I do," I said, my voice dropping. "Because I do, you know. I love her. And I would never let anything happen to her, Thorne."

His eyes softened. "I know you do. It's one of the reasons I fell in love with you in the first place."

"I promise you, I will protect you both with everything I have."

"Shouldn't that be my line, Empress?" he said with a smirk.

I rolled my eyes. "Please. Don't get all alpha male on me now. You're the hopeless romantic, remember?"

His fingers dug into my waist, then he leaned forward and ran his lips along the side of my neck. "I have layers, you know," his gruff voice said against my skin.

I laughed again. "Like a beautiful onion."

The humor faded from him, leaving behind a look I couldn't quite place. "You're good at this. Easing people's fears. I can see why others have always been eager to follow you."

My cheeks heated beneath his praise. "Maybe I'm just good at getting what I want. And what I *want* is for you to feel comfortable." I kissed his neck. "And safe." I moved to his cheek. "And be with me." My lips met his in a tender kiss.

"You have me, Empress." He smiled into my lips, and the thought of his joy despite his fears—joy of simply being with *me*—was almost too much to comprehend. "Now what will you do with me?"

Everything, I wanted to say. Wake up to him every morning, argue and make up and cry and laugh. Show him my world and make it ours. Watch his daughter grow up and give her the best life she could ask for.

I wanted to love him. *Both of them*. For the rest of my life.

"I want to marry you," I suddenly said, his lips on my neck and hands at my hips.

He froze. His chest moved as he breathed in deeply. "You... what?"

"I want. To marry. *You*." My lips curved into a smirk at the look on his face.

His mouth opened and closed. "Clarissa, that's—"

"If you say 'that's my line,' I might have to smother you with a pillow."

"There's that violent streak again." He shook his head with a small smile and a dazed expression.

"We're both lying if we say that isn't where this is headed," I said. "It doesn't have to be now. It doesn't have to be a *year* from now. But you and Marigold are my family, Thorne, whether you like it or not. Fates, I asked you to move across kingdoms to be with me. You're not getting rid of me anytime soon."

He stared at me, and I bit my lip, laughing at my own outburst. Raking my fingers through my hair, I said, "I can't believe I just asked you that. I've never been this...impulsive." I let out a breath. "The first time I agreed to marry anyone, it was a calculated decision based on how it would be good for my empire. And I was willing to go through with it. I was willing to spend my entire life in ignorance of what it felt like to truly *love*. Because that's my purpose. That's my duty."

I wrapped my arms around his waist and looked at him. "You know what? *Screw* my duty. I can lead my people and still have the love I deserve. And that's with *you*. So, yes. I want to marry you. I want to spend the rest of my life with you and Marigold."

A slow smile grew on his face, and he raised a hand to cup my neck. "Just when I think you can't surprise me anymore," he murmured. "I suppose you do always get what you want."

I eyed him hesitantly. "Does that mean..."

"Thorne Aris has a nice ring to it, doesn't it?" he said with a chuckle.

My eyes widened. I opened my mouth to respond when a jolt slammed into my body. I sucked in a breath and doubled over, my hands shaking as familiar power filled my veins.

"Clarissa? What's wrong?" he asked, his voice urgent.

"It—it's fine. It's my magic," I choked out, my body working to suppress a sudden shift. I didn't need to hurt him again.

I stumbled to the porthole and shielded my eyes against the sun. Sure enough, the dark outline of an oncoming shore appeared on the horizon.

We'd crossed the borders into the Veridian Empire, and my magic had returned. I closed my eyes and breathed it in, feeling my fox half leap inside of me as my Shifter powers flooded my senses.

It was even better than I remembered. Better than the small spurts of magic I'd gotten in Mysthelm when I siphoned the curse.

That well in my chest exploded with endless power. My skin buzzed with heightened senses—the air in the cabin swirled around me, bringing with it the distant scent of salt and brine on the sea, the drops of savory soup at the bottom of a dinner bowl Thorne and I left outside the door, and *him*. The overwhelming smell of sweet grass, like the kind I trampled beneath my paws in the field by my cottage, and of musky leather from the notebooks my father kept in his office.

Everything was brighter. Sharper. Clearer. I'd forgotten how intense it could be. I had to grip the edge of the porthole as my arms shook from the force of it, taking a breath to steady my racing pulse.

Thorne approached me carefully, placing a hand on my forearm. "Does it hurt?"

I let out a breathless laugh. "It doesn't hurt. It's just...a lot. But it's amazing." I beamed at him as my magic finally settled into place. "It feels like everything is right again." I grabbed his hand, and he wrapped both arms around my stomach, holding my back to his chest as we stared out the porthole and into the oncoming shoreline.

"It feels like home," I said quietly. "Like I'm finally going home."

69

CLARISSA

THREE MONTHS LATER

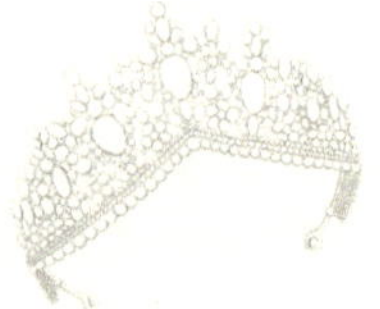

"Why am I not surprised to find you here, on today of all days?"

I looked up from my desk to see Leo leaning against the doorframe of my office, his eyebrows quirked in that semi-judgmental but always loving expression he wore so well.

I waved him off. "Just finishing the paperwork for the accords with Mysthelm. I'll be there in a second."

"Rissa, literally everyone here is waiting for you. This will still be right where you left it when it's over."

With a sigh, I set the parchment down and glanced at the gown hanging from the door that led to my bedchamber. The solid gold fabric trailed down and pooled in waves on the floor. Pleats with thousands of glittering gold beads cascaded from the fitted bodice.

"You know when it feels like every decision you've ever made all leads to this one thing? But when the time finally comes, it's like you're looking over the top of a hill," I said quietly, still staring at the dress as I ran a finger along my lip. "And the only place to go is down."

"What are you talking about?" Leo stepped into the office, flicking the door closed behind him with his tail. "Take it from someone who's known you your entire life: there's only one direction you know how to go. And that's *up*. I've never seen anything you've been unable to take on. You started an entire rebellion when you were twenty-two, for Fates' sake. And now look at you, six years later and you're about to be crowned the youngest empress in history."

He reached my desk and pulled me from the seat as my head rolled back on my shoulders in defiance. "I don't think there's a single mountain you can't climb. You don't have to be worried about looking down."

"And what makes you so confident?"

"Because," that half-smirk of his worked its way onto his face, "you're my big sister."

I rolled my eyes but couldn't help the smile that formed. "First Rose, now you. When did the two of you get so good at motivational speeches? Aren't you the grumpy one?"

"Blame it on Rose. I drew the short straw, and she made me come talk to you."

I chuckled. "Now, that sounds more likely."

"Come on," he said, heading back to the door. "Get dressed. You've been running this empire for a year—it's about time we finally got that crown on your head."

———

I HEARD trumpets echoing down the hall before I even reached the throne room. The swishing of skirts against hardwood floor, the chatter fading to a dull whisper as anticipation swept through the crowd just beyond the double doors. I couldn't see them yet, but I could smell the plethora of perfumes mingling in the air, the crisp scent of autumn leaves lingering on cloaks, the recently waxed floors and fresh coat of paint we'd added three days ago.

I made my way down the corridor, which was empty save for a handful of guards and the seven members of my council. I had to admit, they all cleaned up rather nicely in their matching emerald Veridian robes.

I caught my reflection in one of the decorative mirrors near the door. The neckline of my gown plunged low into the gold, fitted bodice. A sheer cape attached at the shoulders and flowed down to my wrists, extending whenever I moved my arms. The myriad of gold jewels caught the light and scattered across the floor as I approached the council.

"You look beautiful, Your Majesty," Lord Cabot said, bowing low. Several of the others murmured in agreement, while Lord Stryker caught my eye and inclined his head ever so slightly.

I suppressed a smirk. He likely knew today marked his final day on the council.

It had officially been a year since I became the empress-elect. A year since Gayl died and our empire was thrown into turmoil. A year that I'd had to cater to the whims of these men, ruling with what slack the law deigned to give me in our time of transition.

I'd proven myself. I'd done what was asked of me. Now, it was time to claim what was mine. To rebuild the legacy that was stolen from my father and bring peace back to a land drenched in decades of division. There was a long road ahead of me and more questions than answers. But I was ready.

Leo was right. It was finally time.

"On your word, Your Majesty," Lord Temvaren said.

I nodded. "Open the doors."

Two guards pulled the handles of the double doors, revealing the throne room packed with guests. The governors from every province and their families had been invited—although Kane Scarven declined, as expected. Everything had been silent on that front for three months now. No more suspicious notes, no threats, no assassination attempts. I supposed Nox was keeping him busy.

It seemed like the entirety of Veridia City was in attendance. Members of nobility gazed back at me from both sides of a long aisle, their hair perfectly curled and styled, their gowns and cloaks made of the finest silks.

But what held my attention were the rows and rows of towns-people from the south sector. The sight of worn linen shirts and pressed cotton dresses, hair pulled back from tan and wrinkled faces, hands callused from years of hard work as they carefully took off their caps in respect. I saw Dippy, our favorite old bartender from the Drakin's Lair, and his wife and five children. Mali, the shopkeeper of the dress salon we frequented, with Angeline, the baker from down the street who made the best cream dumplings. The butcher and the team of Veridia City reporters next to Rothy from Rose's favorite tea house.

A lump formed in my throat as I took in their familiar, comforting faces. The faces of the people I was pledging my life to serve. The faces of the people who'd watched me grow up, from an uncontrollable little Shifter to the leader of their rebellion.

The trumpets on the outer edges of the room blared again. One by one, the members of my council descended the green-draped aisle. Only when they were all standing in a line at the opposite end of the throne room did I step onto the carpet.

All eyes fell on me.

Their weight sank into my skin as I walked. The weight of their expectations, of their needs and desires and concerns. But it wasn't a burden. It was a *privilege*. An honor I'd spend my life making sure I lived up to.

As I passed the middle of the aisle, the faces became more and more familiar.

My old Sentinels. Ones who followed me into hell itself in order to fight for those who couldn't defend themselves.

Chaz and Lark—my closest confidants and dearest friends. Chaz beamed at me as he crossed his arms, his chest puffed out with pride. Lark sat in her wheelchair at his side. Her black hair was in a long braid down her back, and she clutched a handkerchief that was already streaked with dark makeup. In over a decade, I didn't think I'd ever seen the woman cry.

The only one missing was Nox—but he had his hands full in Drakorum. And with a certain Shadow Wielder.

A row ahead of them stood Rose, Leo, and my mother. A burning sensation pinched the bridge of my nose and my eyes. I never expected Mother to be here for this. For so long, we'd given up hope that she'd return to us after her mind faded beyond repair. I'd come to terms with the fact that it would just be Leo and me for the rest of our lives. But here she was. A miracle. The wrinkles around her eyes deepened with a smile as I passed, and the look of pride shining back at me was almost enough to make me stop in my tracks.

And when I saw her holding Marigold's hand, the lump in my throat grew bigger.

Marigold waved and pointed excitedly to the flower crown on top of her head. I grinned back at her. She had blossomed since they moved here. The first couple of weeks were an adjustment, but the palace staff worshipped her. Within the month, she was bounding through the kitchens with the other children, traipsing in the gardens and giving her father heart attacks by climbing the tall forest trees. Rose and Leo were already Aunt Rose and Uncle Monkey—Rose's highest accomplishment to date—and she'd even called my mother Grandma Eva a couple of times.

She'd been scared about losing her family, but she'd gained a bigger one than she'd ever imagined.

My eyes met ones of icy blue right as the music of the trumpets swelled and I neared the end of the aisle.

When Thorne gazed back at me, the world disappeared. A slow smile curved beneath his beard, and I felt the roughness of it like a ghost on my skin. Just three months ago, I'd been walking down a very different aisle to a very different man, wishing it were him. And one day it would be. But today, I was walking to my destiny— and he was at my side, as he always was. My steady, immovable rock. My anchor when the storms breached.

I took a step up the raised dais. The hall was silent, save for the rustle of the priest's cloak in front of me as he walked forward holding a golden scepter and sword.

I took a deep breath.

The priest placed the scepter and sword in my outstretched hands, then raised his voice. "Clarissa Valienne Aris, daughter of Emperor Branock Aris, the nineteenth Emperor of the Veridian Empire, chosen by the Fates and leader of our people. Do you swear by the Fates to rule with justice, wisdom, and strength?"

"I do," I answered.

"Do you swear to uphold the laws and ideals of the Veridian Empire, to lead our people with mercy and truth, and to protect this land from those who seek us harm?"

"I do."

He took the emblems from me and set them to the side, then turned to the pillar behind him. On top of it rested a green cushion with a delicate gold crown inlaid with a dozen sparkling emeralds. He carefully lifted the crown and faced me once more.

"Look upon your people, Your Majesty," he said, in a whisper this time. A tingling sensation prickled down my spine, goosebumps rising on my skin. Slowly, I turned on my heel.

"Then, by the will and power of the Fates, I anoint you, Clarissa Valienne Aris, the twenty-first Empress of the Veridian Empire."

The crown settled atop my head.

I looked out into the crowd—my family, my people, my empire. And I smiled.

EPILOGUE
NOX

The cold, rocky coastline of Drakorum came into view beyond choppy waves. Moonlight glistened off the dark water, making the reflection of the oncoming cliffs shimmer.

Home sweet home.

I let out a snort. More like *hell fresh hell.*

I couldn't remember the last time those shores felt like home. I couldn't remember the last time *anywhere* felt like home.

My dragon stretched under my skin, tired of being dormant for the near-week journey back to the empire.

"Is this it?" a husky voice asked at my back.

Something else moved inside me. Something sharp and heated with anger. My *other* reason for being tired of this long trip.

I ignored her. As I had for six days.

I sauntered back to my cabin to grab my bags, leaving them by the railings of the quarterdeck. Then I checked in on the crew members to make sure they didn't need any help before we made port. Anything to keep my feet moving. Anything to keep my mind occupied and off the tall silhouette that grew larger and larger as we pulled into the dock.

"You can't ignore me forever, Nox."

And anything to keep her out of my head.

"You promised you would help me find my family."

Sharp claws extended from my hand. A growl built in the back of my throat, and I almost shredded a net when I reached for the railing next to the gangplank.

"Nox, *look at me.*"

I whipped around to find her glaring at me, her red hair like a blazing fire in the night air.

"You do not command me, *Shadow Wielder*," I snarled. My primal territorialism raged to the surface. "I promised you nothing. I said *if* you earned it, I would help you. What have you done to earn it, hmm? You betrayed my best friend, then sat on this ship for six days. You'll have to try harder than that."

She crossed her arms, drawing my attention to her full chest. My eyes turned to slits as they raked up her form. My outburst hadn't fazed her. That made me even angrier.

"You're upset," she said. "You've been getting more agitated every day. Why?"

My mouth fell open. She was unbelievable. After what she'd just done to Clarissa, she had the nerve to ask *why* I was upset.

What I hated most was that she was right.

Every mile, every hour, every breath closer to this place made my dragon writhe with anxiety.

It was my prison. A prison I couldn't escape yet even if I wanted to. Because Vera was still there. My *sister* was still there.

"Get back to your cabin, Devora," I warned, pulling the hood of my cloak over my head. "This is Shifter territory. You don't want to be seen."

She ran her tongue along her teeth as if she wanted to argue, but with one glance to the foggy, menacing dock ahead, she seemed to realize the danger. The wood creaked under her boots as she slunk back into the relative safety of her cabin. I looked out at the deck to my right, the ship rocking beneath me as the crew members anchored us and secured us to the port.

Someone lowered the gangway, and that silhouette moved closer.

Dark boots thudded against the wet wood. Black pants were tucked inside of them, with a gray cloak sweeping at his ankles with each step. Several weapons hung from a belt, but anyone with half a brain could tell he had no use for sharp blades. Not when he was a weapon himself.

A chiseled jaw flexed, a trimmed, sharp beard twitching with a smirk as my gaze trailed up to his face.

"Scarven," I said, voice tight. I gave him a curt nod of greeting.

"Nox." He tipped his head slightly, then his black eyes landed back on mine. "Welcome home, brother."

To be continued in book 3...

ALSO BY V.B. LACEY

The Elementals of Iona:

Long Live

Forever Reign

Wildfire

The Veridian Empire

In the Wake of the Wicked

Of the Curse or the Crown

From the Silence of the Shadows

By the Flames of Her Fury

Acknowledgments

Here we are, at the end of another book! My fourth novel. It's hard to believe I started this journey over three years ago when I began writing my debut. It feels both new every time and like I've been doing it my entire life.

I always want to give the glory to God for the blessings this life has brought me and for the ability to keep doing what I love with the support of those closest to me.

To Taylor—my real-life book boyfriend. Thanks for walking by my side and never blinking twice at what this job requires of me, from housing boxes and boxes of inventory, to helping package orders, to late nights writing and trips across the country. I love our life and I'm so lucky you're the one I get to share it with. So, when are we going to Hawaii?

To my family and friends—not many people pursuing their dreams have the full support of those in their life, but I know that every one of you will always be there. You show up release after release with your excitement and pride, even if what I write isn't necessarily "your thing." I love you all so much.

To my editor, Krista—thank you for taking a chance on this book and helping craft it into its best version!

To my beta readers—I have such a good feeling about this book, and it's largely thanks to you. You helped me perfect their story and gave me the strength I needed during a rough time in my life, and I'm forever grateful for you.

To my street team—you have my back every step of the way, and I'm so lucky to have a team like you. I can always count on you to share your love for these books and indie authors in general, which is something this world needs more of! Thank you for your excitement, your willingness to rally, and your constant encouragement. Oh—and all the Rissa emojis. Are you ready to add some dragon ones?

Something I absolutely couldn't do any of this without is my fellow authors. I've been fortunate to have made incredible friendships with some talented, compassionate, hardworking, loyal, ambitious writers who give me the will to keep going every day. This job can be very isolating, but having them by my side makes it easier. Thank you for everything you do for me, whether or not you know how impactful it is.

Lastly, to my readers—I know authors say this all the time, but we're truly so, so thankful for you. *I* am thankful for you. I wouldn't have been able to turn a lifelong passion into a reality if it weren't for you and your love for epic worlds, swoon worthy romance, and broken characters finding their strength. Never stop escaping—this world can be dark, and my highest hope is that you find a spark of light when it becomes too heavy to bear.

cue This Is My Time by Raven Symoné

Till next time, darling...

ABOUT THE AUTHOR

V.B. Lacey is an office manager by day and an avid reader-turned-writer by night. She grew up on stories of magic, love, and sarcasm, and equips her writing with all three. She lives in Texas with her supportive husband and two rambunctious dogs. When she's not writing about morally grey characters and far-off kingdoms, you can find her reading (mostly fantasy and contemporary romance), playing board games, or spending time with friends.

Visit her online at www.vblaceybooks.com, or follow her on Instagram and TikTok: @vblacey.books.